The
Fourth Monkey

The
Fourth Monkey

J. D. Barker

Houghton Mifflin Harcourt
Boston • New York
2017

www.hmhco.com

Library of Congress Cataloging-in-Publication Data
Names: Barker, J. D. (Jonathan Dylan), date, author.
Title: The fourth monkey / J. D. Barker.
Description: Boston : Houghton Mifflin Harcourt, 2017.
Identifiers: LCCN 2016050862 (print) | LCCN 2017007798 (ebook) |
ISBN 9780544968844 (hardback) | ISBN 9780544969940 (ebook)
Subjects: LCSH: Detectives—Illinois—Chicago—Fiction. | Serial
murderers—Fiction. | BISAC: FICTION / Mystery & Detective / Hard-Boiled. |
FICTION / Mystery & Detective / Police Procedural. | GSAFD: Mystery fiction.
Classification: LCC PS3602.A775525 F68 2017 (print) |
LCC PS3602.A775525 (ebook) |
DDC 813/.6—dc23
LC record available at https://lccn.loc.gov/2016050862

Book design by Chrissy Kurpeski

Printed in the United States of America
DOC 10 9 8 7 6 5 4 3 2 1

For Mother

Don't stop reading. I need you to understand what I have done.

— DIARY

The
Fourth Monkey

1

Porter

Day 1 • 6:14 a.m.

There it was again, that incessant ping.

I turned the ringer off. Why am I hearing text notifications? Why am I hearing anything?

Apple's gone to shit without Steve Jobs.

Sam Porter rolled to his right, his hand blindly groping for the phone on the nightstand.

His alarm clock crashed to the floor with a thunk unique to cheap electronics from China.

"Fuck me."

When his fingers found the phone, he wrestled the device from the charging cable and brought it to his face, squinting at the small, bright screen.

CALL ME — 911.

A text from Nash.

Porter looked over at his wife's side of the bed, empty except for a note —

Went to get milk, be back soon.
xoxo,
Heather

He grunted and again glanced at his phone.

6:15 a.m.

So much for a quiet morning.

Porter sat up and dialed his partner. He answered on the second ring.

"Sam?"

"Hey, Nash."

The other man fell silent for a moment. "I'm sorry, Porter. I debated whether or not to contact you. Must have dialed your number a dozen times and couldn't bring myself to actually place the call. I finally decided it would be best just to text you. Give you a chance to ignore me, you know?"

"It's fine, Nash. What have you got?"

Another pause. "You'll want to see for yourself."

"See what?"

"There's been an accident."

Porter rubbed his temple. "An accident? We're Homicide. Why would we respond to an accident?"

"You've gotta trust me on this. You'll want to see it," Nash told him again. There was an edge to his voice.

Porter sighed. "Where?"

"Near Hyde Park, off Fifty-Fifth. I just texted you the address."

His phone pinged loudly in his ear, and he jerked it away from his head.

Fucking iPhone.

He looked down at the screen, noted the address, and went back to the call.

"I can be there in about thirty minutes. Will that work?"

"Yeah," Nash replied. "We're not going anywhere soon."

Porter disconnected the call and eased his legs off the side of the bed, listening to the various pops and creaks his tired fifty-two-year-old body made in protest.

The sun had begun its ascent, and light peeked in from between the closed blinds of the bedroom window. Funny how quiet and gloomy the apartment felt without Heather around.

Went to get milk.

From the hardwood floor his alarm clock blinked up at him with a cracked face displaying characters no longer resembling numbers.

Today was going to be one of those days.

There had been a lot of those days lately.

Porter emerged from the apartment ten minutes later dressed in his Sunday best—a rumpled navy suit he'd bought off the rack at Men's Wearhouse nearly a decade earlier—and made his way down the four flights of stairs to the cramped lobby of his building. He stopped at the mailboxes, pulled out his cell phone, and punched in his wife's phone number.

You've reached the phone of Heather Porter. Since this is voice mail, I most likely saw your name on caller ID and decided I most certainly did not wish to speak to you. If you're willing to pay tribute in the form of chocolate cake or other assorted offerings of dietary delight, text me the details and I'll reconsider your position in my social roster and possibly get back to you later. If you're a salesperson trying to get me to switch carriers, you might as well hang up now. AT&T owns me for at least another year. All others, please leave a message. Keep in mind my loving husband is a cop with anger issues, and he carries a large gun.

Porter smiled. Her voice always made him smile. "Hey, Button. It's just me. Nash called. There's something going on near Hyde Park; I'm meeting him down there. I'll give you a call later when I know what time I'll be home." He added, "Oh, and I think there's something wrong with our alarm clock."

He dropped the phone into his pocket and pushed through the door, the brisk Chicago air reminding him that fall was preparing to step aside for winter.

2

Porter

Day I • 6:45 a.m.

Porter took Lake Park Avenue and made good time, arriving at about a quarter to seven. Chicago Metro had Woodlawn at Fifty-Fifth completely barricaded. He could make out the lights from blocks away—at least a dozen units, an ambulance, two fire trucks. Twenty officers, possibly more. Press too.

He slowed his late-model Dodge Charger as he approached the chaos, and held his badge out the window. A young officer, no more than a kid, ducked under the yellow crime-scene tape and ran over. "Detective Porter? Nash told me to wait for you. Park anywhere—we've cordoned off the entire block."

Porter nodded, then pulled up beside one of the fire trucks and climbed out. "Where's Nash?"

The kid handed him a cup of coffee. "Over there, near the ambulance."

He spotted Nash's large frame speaking to Tom Eisley from the medical examiner's office. At nearly six foot three, he towered over the much smaller man. He looked like he'd put on a few pounds in the weeks since Porter had seen him, the telltale cop's belly hanging prominently over his belt.

Nash waved him over.

Eisley greeted Porter with a slight nod and pushed his glasses up the bridge of his nose. "How are you holding up, Sam?" He held a clipboard loaded with at least a ream of paper. In today's world of tablets and smartphones, the man always seemed to have a clipboard on hand; his fingers flipped nervously through the pages.

"I imagine he's getting tired of people asking him how he's holding up, how he's doing, how he's hanging, or any other variation of well-being assertion," Nash grumbled.

"It's fine. I'm fine." He forced a smile. "Thank you for asking, Tom."

"Anything you need, just ask." Eisley shot Nash a glance.

"I appreciate that." Porter turned back to Nash. "So, an accident?"

Nash nodded at a city bus parked near the curb about fifty feet away. "Man versus machine. Come on."

Porter followed him, with Eisley a few paces behind, clipboard in tow.

A CSI tech photographed the front of the bus. Dented grill. Cracked paint an inch above the right headlight. Another investigator picked at something buried in the right front tire tread.

As they neared, he spotted the black body bag among a sea of uniforms standing before a growing crowd.

"The bus was moving at a good clip; its next stop is nearly a mile down the road," Nash told them.

"I wasn't speeding, dammit! Check the GPS. Don't be throwing accusations like that out there!"

Porter turned to his left to find the bus driver. He was a big man, at least three hundred pounds. His black CTA jacket strained against the bulk it had been tasked to hold together. His wiry gray hair was matted on the left and reaching for the sky on the right. Nervous eyes stared back at them, jumping from Porter, to Nash, then Eisley, and back again. "That crazy fucker jumped right out in front of me. This ain't no accident. He offed himself."

"Nobody said you did anything wrong," Nash assured him.

Eisley's phone rang. He glanced at the display, held up a finger, and walked a few paces to the side to take the call.

The driver went on. "You start spreading around that I was speeding, and there goes my job, my pension . . . think I wanna be looking for work at my age? In this shit economy?"

Porter caught a glimpse of the man's name tag. "Mr. Nelson, how about you take a deep breath and try to calm down?"

Sweat trickled down the man's red face. "I'm gonna be pushing a broom somewhere all because that little prick picked my bus. I got thirty-one years behind me without an incident, and now this bullshit."

Porter put his hand on the man's shoulder. "Do you think you can tell me what happened?"

"I need to keep my mouth shut until my union rep gets here, that's what I need to do."

"I can't help you if you don't talk to me."

The driver frowned. "What are you gonna do for me?"

"I can put in a good word with Manny Polanski down at Transit, for starters. If you didn't do anything wrong, if you cooperate with us, there's no reason for you to get suspended."

"Shit. You think I'll get suspended over this?" He wiped the sweat from his brow. "Jesus, I can't afford that."

"I don't think they'll do that if they know you worked with us, that you tried to help. There might not even be a need for a hearing," Porter assured him.

"A hearing?"

"Why don't you tell me what happened? Then I can talk to Manny for you, maybe save you the pain of all that."

"You know Manny?"

"I worked my first two years on the job as a uniform with Transit. He'll listen to me. You help us out, and I'll put in a good word, I promise."

The driver considered this, then finally took a deep breath and nodded. "It happened just like I said to your friend here. I made the stop at Ellis right on time — picked up two, dropped off one. I ran east down Fifty-Fifth, came around the bend. The light at Woodlawn was green, so there was no need to slow down — not that I was speeding. Check the GPS."

"I'm sure you weren't."

"I wasn't, I was just moving with the traffic. I might have been a few miles over the limit, but I wasn't speeding," he said.

Porter waved his hand dismissively. "You were heading east on Fifty-Fifth . . ."

The driver nodded. "Yeah. I saw a few people at the corner, not many. Three, maybe four. Then, just as I got close, this guy jumps out in front of my bus. No warning or nothing. One second he's standing there, the next he's in the street. I hit the brakes, but this thing doesn't exactly stop on a dime. I hit him dead center. Launched him a good thirty feet."

"What color was the light?" Porter asked.

"Green."

"Not yellow?"

The driver shook his head. "No, green. I know, 'cause I watched it change. It didn't turn yellow for another twenty seconds or so. I was already out of the bus when I saw it switch." He pointed up at the signal. "Check the camera."

Porter looked up. Over the last decade, nearly every intersection in the city had been outfitted with CCTV cameras. He'd remind Nash to pull the footage when they got back to the station. Most likely, his partner had already put in the order.

"He wasn't crossing the street; that man jumped. You'll see when you watch the video."

Porter handed him a card. "Can you stick around a little bit, just in case I have more questions?"

The man shrugged. "You're going to talk to Manny, right?"

Porter nodded. "Can you excuse us for a second?" He pulled Nash aside, lowering his voice. "He didn't kill him intentionally. Even if this was a suicide, we've got no business here. Why'd you call me out?"

Nash put a hand on his partner's shoulder. "Are you sure you're okay to do this? If you need more time, I get it—"

"I'm good," Porter said. "Tell me what's going on."

"If you need to talk—"

"Nash, I'm not a fucking child. Take off the kid gloves."

"All right." He finally relented. "But if this gets to be too much too soon, you gotta promise me you'll tap out, got it? Nobody will think twice if you need to do that."

"I think working will do me some good. I've been getting stir-crazy sitting around the apartment," he admitted.

"This is big, Porter," he said in a low voice. "You deserve to be here."

"Christ, Nash. Will you spit it out?"

"It's a good bet our vic was heading to that mailbox over there." He glanced toward a blue postal box in front of a brick apartment building.

"How do you know?"

A grin spread across his partner's face. "He was carrying a small white box tied up with black string."

Porter's eyes went wide. "Nooo."

"Uh-huh."

3

Porter

Day I • 6:53 a.m.

Porter found himself staring down at the body, at the lumpy form under the black plastic shroud.

Words escaped him.

Nash asked the other officers and CSI techs to step back and give Porter space, to give him time alone with the victim. They shuffled back behind the yellow crime-scene tape, their voices low as they watched. To Porter, they were invisible. He only saw the black body bag and the small package lying beside it. It had been tagged with NUMBER 1 by CSI, no doubt photographed dozens of times from every possible angle. They knew better than to open it, though. They left that for him.

How many boxes just like it had there been now?

A dozen? No. Closer to two dozen.

He did the math.

Seven victims. Three boxes each.

Twenty-one.

Twenty-one boxes over nearly five years.

He had toyed with them. Never left a clue behind. Only the boxes. A ghost.

Porter had seen so many officers come and go from the task force. With each new victim, the team would expand. The press would get wind of a new box, and they'd swarm like vultures. The entire city would come together on a massive manhunt. But then the third box would eventually arrive, the body would be found, and he'd disappear again. Lost among the shadows of obscurity. Months would pass; he'd fall out of the papers. The task force dwindled as the team got pulled apart for more pressing matters.

Porter was the only one who had seen it through from the beginning. He had been there for the first box, recognizing it immediately for what it was—the start of a serial killer's deranged spree. When the second box arrived, then the third, and finally the body, others saw too.

It was the start of something horrible. Something planned. Something evil.

He had been there at the beginning. Was he now witnessing the end?

"What's in the box?"

"We haven't opened it yet," Nash replied. "But I think you know."

The package was small. Approximately four inches square and three inches high.

Like the others.

Wrapped in white paper and secured with black string. The address label was handwritten in careful script. There wouldn't be any prints, never were. The stamps were self-adhesive—they wouldn't find saliva.

He glanced back at the body bag. "Do you really think it's him? Do you have a name?"

Nash shook his head. "No wallet or ID on him. He left his face on the pavement and in the bus's grill. We ran his prints but couldn't find a match. He's a nobody."

"Oh, he's somebody," Porter said. "Do you have any gloves?"

Nash pulled a pair of latex gloves from his pocket and handed them to Porter. Porter slipped them on and nodded toward the box. "Do you mind?"

"We waited for you," Nash said. "This is your case, Sam. Always was."

When Porter crouched and reached for the box, one of the crime-scene techs rushed over, fumbling with a small video camera. "I'm sorry, sir, but I have orders to document this."

"It's fine, son. Only you, though. Are you ready?"

A red light on the front of the camera blinked to life, and the tech nodded. "Go ahead, sir."

Porter turned the box so he could read the address label, carefully avoiding the droplets of crimson. "Arthur Talbot, 1547 Dearborn Parkway."

Nash whistled. "Ritzy neighborhood. Old money. I don't recognize the name, though."

"Talbot's an investment banker," the CSI tech replied. "Heavy into real estate too. Lately he's been converting warehouses near the lakefront into lofts—doing his part to force out low-income families and replace them with people who can afford the high rent and Starbucks grandes on the regular."

Porter knew exactly who Arthur Talbot was. He looked up at the tech. "What's your name, kid?"

"Paul Watson, sir."

Porter couldn't help but grin. "You'll make an excellent detective one day, Dr. Watson."

"I'm not a doctor, sir. I'm working on my thesis, but I've got at least two more years to go."

Porter chuckled. "Doesn't anyone read anymore?"

"Sam, the box?"

"Right. The box."

He tugged at the string and watched as the knot unraveled and came apart. The white paper beneath had been neatly folded over the corners, ending in perfect little triangles.

Like a gift. He wrapped it like a gift.

The paper came away easily, revealing a black box. Porter set the paper and string aside, glanced at Nash and Watson, then slowly lifted the lid.

The ear had been washed clean of blood and rested on a blanket of cotton.

Just like the others.

4

Porter

Day 1 • 7:05 a.m.

"I need to see his body."

Nash glanced nervously at the growing crowd. "Are you sure you want to do that here? There are a lot of eyes on you right now."

"Let's get a tent up."

Nash signaled to one of the officers.

Fifteen minutes later, much to the dismay of oncoming traffic, a twelve-by-twelve tent stood on Fifty-Fifth Street, blocking one of the two eastbound lanes. Nash and Porter slipped through the flap, followed closely by Eisley and Watson. A uniformed guard took up position at the door in case someone snuck past the barricades at the scene perimeter and tried to get in.

Six 1,200-watt halogen floodlights stood on yellow metal tripods in a semicircle around the body, filling the small space with sharp, bright light.

Eisley reached down and peeled back the top flap of the bag.

Porter knelt. "Has he been moved at all?"

Eisley shook his head. "We photographed him, and then I got him covered as quickly as I could. That's how he landed."

He was facedown on the blacktop. There was a small pool of blood near his head with a streak leading toward the edge of the tent. His dark hair was close-cropped, sprinkled with gray.

Porter donned another pair of latex gloves from a box at his left and gently lifted the man's head. It pulled away from the cold asphalt with a slurp not unlike Fruit Roll-Ups as they're peeled from the plastic. His stomach grumbled, and he realized he hadn't eaten yet. Probably a good thing. "Can you help me turn him over?"

Eisley took the man's shoulder, and Nash positioned himself at his feet.

"On three. One, two . . ."

It was too soon for rigor to set in; the body was loose. It looked like the right leg was broken in at least three spots; the left arm too, probably more.

"Oh, God. That's nasty." Nash's eyes were fixed on the man's face. More accurately, where his face should have been. His cheeks were gone, only torn flaps remaining. His jawbone was clearly visible but broken—his mouth gaped open as if someone had gripped both halves of his jaw and pulled them apart like a bear trap. One eye was ruptured, oozing vitreous fluid. The other stared blindly up at them, green in the bright light.

Porter leaned in closer. "Do you think you can reconstruct this?"

Eisley nodded. "I'll get somebody on it as soon as we get him back to my lab."

"Tough to say, but based on his build and the slight graying in the hair, I'd guess he's late forties, early fifties, at the most."

"I should be able to get you a more precise age too," Eisley said. He was examining the man's eyes with a penlight. "The cornea is still intact."

Porter knew they were able to able to estimate age through the carbon dating of material in the eyes; it was called the Lynnerup method. The process could narrow the age down to within a year or two.

The man wore a navy pinstripe suit. The left sleeve was shredded; a jagged bone poked out near the elbow.

"Did someone find his other shoe?" The right was missing. His dark sock was damp with blood.

"A uniform picked it up. It's on that table over there." Nash pointed to the far right. "He was wearing a fedora too."

"A fedora? Are those making a comeback?"

"Only in the movies."

"There's something in this pocket." Watson was pointing at the right breast pocket of the man's jacket. "It's square. Another box?"

"No, too thin." Porter carefully unbuttoned the jacket and reached inside, retrieving a small Tops composition book, like the ones students carried prior to tablets and smartphones: 4½" x 3¼" with a black and white cover and college-ruled pages. It was nearly full, each page covered in handwriting so small and precise that two lines of text filled the space normally occupied by one. "This could be something. Looks like some kind of diary. Good catch, Doc."

"I'm not a—"

Porter waved a hand at him. "Yeah, yeah." He turned back to Nash. "I thought you said you checked his pockets?"

"We only searched the pants for a wallet. I wanted to wait for you to process the body."

"We should check the rest, then."

He began with the right front pants pocket, checking them again in case something was missed, then worked his way around the body. As items were discovered, he gently set them down at his side. Nash tagged them and Watson photographed.

"That's it. Not much to go on."

Porter examined the items:

Dry cleaner's receipt
Pocket watch
Seventy-five cents in assorted change

The receipt was generic. Aside from number 54873, it didn't contain any identifying information, not even the name or address of the cleaners.

"Run everything for prints," Porter instructed.

Nash frowned. "What for? We have him, and his prints came back negative."

"Guess I'm hoping for a Hail Mary. Maybe we'll find a match and it will lead to someone who can identify him. What do you make of the watch?"

Nash held the timepiece up to the light. "I don't know anyone who carries a pocket watch anymore. Think maybe this guy's older than you thought?"

"The fedora would suggest that too."

"Unless he's just into vintage," Watson pointed out. "I know a lot of guys like that."

Nash pushed the crown, and the watch's face snapped open. "Huh."

"What?"

"It stopped at fourteen past three. That's not when this guy got hit."

"Maybe the impact jarred it?" Porter thought aloud.

"There's not a scratch on it, though, no sign of damage."

"Probably something internal, or maybe it wasn't wound. Can I take a look?"

Nash handed the pocket watch to Porter.

Porter twisted the crown. "It's loose. The spring's not grabbing. Amazing craftsmanship though. I think it's handmade. Collectible for sure."

"I've got an uncle," Watson announced.

"Well, congrats on that, kid," Porter replied.

"He owns an antique shop downtown. I bet he could give us some color on this."

"You're really trying to earn a gold star today, aren't you? Okay, you're on watch duty. Once these things are logged into inventory, take it down there and see what you can find out."

Watson nodded, his face beaming.

"Anybody notice anything odd about what he's wearing?"

Nash examined the body once more, then shook his head.

"The shoes are nice," Eisley said.

Porter smiled. "They are, aren't they? Those are John Lobbs. They go for about fifteen hundred a pair. The suit is cheap, though, possibly from a box store or the mall. Probably no more than a few hundred at best."

"So, what are you thinking?" Nash asked. "He works in shoes?"

"Not sure. I don't want to jump to conclusions. Just seems odd a man would spend so much on shoes without a comparable spend on his suit."

"Unless he works in shoe sales and got some kind of deal? That *does* makes sense," Watson said.

"I'm glad you concur. Silly comments will get your gold star revoked."

"Sorry."

"No worries, Doc. I'm just busting your balls. I'd pick on Nash, but he's too used to my shit at this point. It's no fun anymore." Porter's attention drifted back to the small composition book. "Can you hand me that?"

Watson passed it to him, and he turned to the first page. Porter's eyes narrowed as he scanned the text.

Hello, my friend.

I am a thief, a murderer, a kidnapper. I've killed for fun. I've killed out of necessity. I have killed for hate. I have killed simply to satisfy the need that tends to grow in me with the passage of time. A need much like a hunger that can only be quenched by the draw of blood or the song found in a tortured scream.

I tell you this not to frighten you or impress you but simply to state the facts, to put my cards on the table.

My IQ is 156, a genius level by all accounts.

A wise man once said, "To measure your own IQ, to attempt to label your intelligence, is a sign of your own ignorance." I did not ask to take an IQ test; it was administered upon me—take from that what you will.

None of this defines who I am, only what I am. That is why I've chosen to put pen to paper, to share that which I am about to share. Without the sharing of knowledge, there can be no growth. You (as a society) will not learn from your many mistakes. And you have so much to learn.

Who am I?

To share my name would simply take the fun out of this, don't you think?

You most likely know me as the Four Monkey Killer. Why don't we leave it at that? Perhaps 4MK, for those of you prone to abbreviate? The simpler of the lot. No need to exclude anyone.

We are going to have such fun, you and I.

"Holy fuck," Porter muttered.

5

Diary

I'd like to set the record straight from the very beginning.

This is not my parents' fault.

I grew up in a loving home that would have made Norman Rockwell take note.

My mother, God bless her soul, gave up a promising career in publishing to stay home after my birth, and I don't believe she ever longed to return. She had breakfast on the table every morning for my father and me, and supper was held promptly at six. We cherished such family time, and it was spent in the most jovial of ways.

Mother would recount her exploits of the day with Father and me listening attentively. The sound of her voice was that of angels, and to this day I long for more.

Father worked in finance. I am most certain he was held in high regard by his peers, although he didn't discuss his work at home. He firmly believed that the day-to-day happenings of one's employ should remain at the place of business, not brought home and spilled within the sanctuary of the residence as one might dump out a bucket of slop for the pigs to feast on. He left work at work, where it belonged.

He carried a shiny black briefcase, but I never once saw him open it. He set it beside the front door each night, and there it remained until he left for the office on the next business day. He would scoop the briefcase up on his way out, only after a loving kiss for Mother and a pat on the head for me.

"Take care of your mother, my boy!" he would say. "You are the man of the house until I return. Should the bill man come knocking, send him next door to collect. Do not pay him any mind. He is of no consequence in the large scheme of things. Better you learn this now than fret about such things when you have a family of your own."

Fedora upon his head and briefcase in hand, he would slip out the door with a smile and a wave. I would go to the picture window and watch him as he made his way down the walk (careful of the ice during the cold winters) and climbed into his little black convertible. Father drove a 1969 Porsche. It was a marvelous machine. A work of art with a throaty growl that rumbled forth with the turn of the key and grew louder still as it eased out onto the road and lapped up the pavement with hungry delight.

Oh, how Father loved that car.

Every Sunday we'd take a large blue bucket from the garage along with a handful of rags and wash it from top to bottom. He would spend hours conditioning the soft black top and applying wax to its metal curves, not once but twice. I was tasked with cleaning the spokes on the wheels, a job I took very seriously. When finished, the car shone as if the showroom was a recent memory. Then he would put the top down and take Mother and me on a Sunday drive. Although the Porsche was only a two-seater, I was a tiny lad and fit snugly in the space behind the seats. We would stop at the local Dairy Freeze for ice cream and soda, then head to the park for an afternoon stroll among the large oaks and grassy fields.

I would play with the other children as Mother and Father watched from the shade of an old tree, their hands entwined and love in their eyes. They would joke and laugh, and I could hear them as I ran after a ball or chased a Frisbee. "Watch me! Watch me!" I would shout. And they would. They watched me as parents should. They watched me with pride. Their son, their joy. I'd look back at the myself at that tender age. I'd look back at them under that tree, all in smiles. I'd look back and picture their necks sliced from ear to ear, blood pouring from the wounds and pooling in the grass beneath them. And I would laugh, my heart fluttering, I would laugh so.

Of course, that was years ago, but that is surely when it began.

6

Porter

Day I • 7:3I a.m.

Porter parked his Charger at the curb in front of 1547 Dearborn Parkway and stared up at the large stone mansion. Beside him, Nash ended the call on his phone. "That was the captain. He wants us to come in."

"We will."

"He was pretty insistent."

"4MK was about to mail the box here. The clock is ticking. We don't have time to run back to headquarters right now," Porter said. "We won't be long. It's important we stay ahead of this."

"4MK? You're really going to run with that?"

"4MK, Monkey Man, Four Monkey Killer. I don't care what we call the crazy fuck."

Nash was looking out the window. "This is one hell of a house. One family lives here?"

Porter nodded. "Arthur Talbot, his wife, a teenage daughter from his first marriage, probably one or two little yapping dogs, and a housekeeper or five."

"I checked with Missing Persons, and Talbot hasn't phoned anyone in," Nash said. They exited the car and started up the stone steps. "How do you want to play this?"

"Quickly," said Porter as he pressed the doorbell.

Nash lowered his voice. "Wife or daughter?"

"What?"

"The ear. Do you think it's the wife or daughter?"

Porter was about to answer when the door inched open, held by a security chain. A Hispanic woman, no taller than five feet, glared at them with cold brown eyes. "Help you?"

"Is Mr. or Mrs. Talbot available?"

Her eyes shifted from Porter to Nash, then back again. "*Momento.*"

She closed the door.

"My money's on the daughter," Nash said.

Porter glanced down at his phone. "Her name is Carnegie."

"Carnegie? Are you kidding me?"

"I'll never understand rich people."

When the door opened again, a blond woman in her early forties was standing at the threshold. She wore a beige sweater and tight black slacks. Her hair was pulled back in a loose ponytail. *Attractive,* Porter thought. "Mrs. Talbot?"

She smiled politely. "Yes. What can I do for you?"

The Hispanic woman appeared behind her, watching from the other side of the foyer.

"I'm Detective Porter and this is Detective Nash. We're with Chicago Metro. Is there someplace we can talk?"

Her smile disappeared. "What did she do?"

"Excuse me?"

"My husband's little shit of a daughter. I'd love to get through one week without the drama of her shoplifting or joyriding or drinking in the park with her equally little shit-whore friends. I might as well offer free coffee to any law enforcement officers who want to stop by, since half of you show up on a regular basis anyway." She stepped back from the door; it swung open behind her, revealing the sparsely furnished entry. "Come on in."

Porter and Nash followed her inside. The vaulted ceilings loomed above, centered by a chandelier glistening with crystal. He fought the urge to take his shoes off before walking on the white polished marble.

Mrs. Talbot turned to the housekeeper. "Miranda, please be a dear and fetch us some tea and bagels—unless the officers would prefer donuts?" She said the last with the hint of a smile.

Ah, rich-person humor, Porter thought. "We're fine, ma'am."

There was nothing rich white women hated more than being called—

"Please, call me Patricia."

They followed her through the foyer, down the hall, and into a large library. The polished wood floors glistened in the early-morning light, covered in specks of sun cast by the crystal chandelier hanging above a large stone fireplace. She gestured to a couch at the center of the room. Porter and Nash took a seat. She settled into a comfortable-looking overstuffed chair and ottoman across from them and reached for a cup of tea from the small table at her side. The morning *Tribune* lay untouched. "Just last week she OD'ed on some nonsense, and I had to pick her up downtown at the ER in the middle of the night. Her caring little friends dropped her there when she passed out at some club. Left her on a bench in front of the hospital. Imagine that? Arty was off on business, and I had to get her back here before he got home because nobody wants to ruffle his feathers. Best for Stepmommy to clean it up and make like it didn't happen."

The housekeeper returned with a large silver tray. She set it on the table in front of them, poured two cups of tea from a carafe, handed one to Nash and the other to Porter. There were two plates. One contained a toasted plain bagel, the other a chocolate donut.

"I'm not above stereotypes," Nash said, reaching for the donut.

"This isn't necessary," Porter said.

"Nonsense; enjoy," Patricia replied.

"Where is your husband now, Mrs. Talbot? Is he home?"

"He left early this morning to play a round of golf out at Wheaton."

Nash leaned over. "That's about an hour away."

Porter reached for a cup of tea and took a slow sip, then returned it to the tray. "And your daughter?"

"Stepdaughter."

"Stepdaughter," Porter corrected.

Mrs. Talbot frowned. "How about you tell me what kind of trouble she's in? Then I can decide if I should let you speak to her directly or ring one of our attorneys."

"So she's here?"

Her eyes widened for a moment. She refilled her cup, reached for two sugar cubes and dropped them into her tea, stirred, and drank. Her fingers twisted around the warm mug. "She's sound asleep in her room. Has been all night. I saw her a few minutes ago preparing for school."

Porter and Nash exchanged a glance. "May we see her?"

"What has she done?"

"We're following a lead, Mrs. Talbot. If she's here right now, there is nothing to worry about. We'll be on our way. If she's not"—Porter didn't want to frighten her unnecessarily—"if she's not, there may be cause for concern."

"There's no need to cover for her," Nash explained. "We just need to know she is safe."

She turned the mug in her hand. "Miranda? Could you fetch Carnegie, please?"

The housekeeper opened her mouth, considered what she was about to say, then thought better of it. Porter watched as she turned and left the library, crossing the hallway and ascending the staircase that wound up the opposite wall.

Nash elbowed him, and he turned. Porter followed his eyes to a framed picture on the fireplace mantel. A young blond girl dressed in riding gear beside a chestnut horse. He stood and walked over to it. "Is this your stepdaughter?"

Mrs. Talbot nodded. "Four years ago. She turned twelve a month before that photo. Came in first place."

Porter was looking at her hair. The Four Monkey Killer had only taken one blonde before today; all the others had been brunette.

"Patricia? What's going on?"

They turned.

Standing at the doorway was a teenager dressed in a Mötley Crüe T-shirt, white robe, and slippers. Her blond hair was frazzled.

"Please don't call me Patricia," Mrs. Talbot snapped.

"Sorry, *Mother*."

"Carnegie, these gentlemen are from Chicago Metro."

The girl's face went pale. "Why are the police here, Patricia?"

Porter and Nash were staring at her ears. *Both* her ears. Right where they should be.

7

Porter

Day 1 • 7:48 a.m.

A drizzle had begun to fall. The flagstone steps were wet and slippery as Porter and Nash rushed from the Talbot residence back to their car at the curb. Both jumped inside and pulled the doors shut behind them, eyeing the foreboding sky. "We don't need this shit, not today," Porter complained. "If it starts to rain, Talbot may call his game off and we lose him."

"We have a bigger problem." Nash was tapping at his iPhone.

"Captain Dalton again?"

"No, worse. Somebody tweeted."

"Somebody what?"

"Tweeted."

"What the hell is a *tweet?*"

Nash handed him the phone.

Porter read the tiny print.

@4MK4EVER IS THIS THE FOUR MONKEY KILLER?

It was followed by a photograph of their bus victim from this morning, facedown against the asphalt. The edge of the city bus was barely visible at the corner.

Porter frowned. "Who released a photo to the press?"

"Shit, Sam. You really need to get with the times. Nobody released anything. Somebody snapped a picture with their phone and put it out there for everyone to see," Nash explained. "That's how Twitter works."

"Everyone? How many people is *everyone?*"

Nash was tapping again. "They posted it twenty minutes ago, and it's been favorited 3,212 times. Retweeted more than five hundred."

"Favorited? Retweeted? What the fuck, Nash. Speak English."

"It means it's out there, Porter. Viral. The world knows he's dead."

Nash's phone rang. "Now that's the captain. What should I tell him?"

Porter started the car, threw it into gear, and sped down West North Street toward 294. "Tell him we're chasing a lead."

"What lead?"

"The Talbots."

Nash looked puzzled. "But it's not the Talbots—they're home."

"It's not those Talbots. We're going to chat with Arthur. I'm willing to bet the wife and daughter aren't the only women in his life," Porter said.

Nash nodded and answered the call. Porter heard the captain screaming from the tiny speaker. After about a minute of repeating "Yes, sir," Nash cupped his hand over the phone. "He wants to talk to you."

"Tell him I'm driving. It's not safe to talk on the phone while driving." He tugged the wheel hard to the left, circling around a minivan traveling much slower than their current speed of eighty-seven.

"Yes, Captain," Nash said. "I'm putting you on speaker. Hold on—"

The captain's voice went from tiny and tinny to loud and booming as the iPhone switched to the Bluetooth speaker system in the car. ". . . back at the station in ten minutes so we can get a team together and get in front of this. I've got every television and print reporter clawing at me."

"Captain, this is Porter. You know his timeline as well as I do. He was about to mail the ear this morning. That means he grabbed her a day or two ago. The good news is he never kills them right away, so we can be sure she's still alive . . . somewhere. We don't know how much time she's got. If he just planned to run out and mail the package, chances are he didn't leave her with food or water. The average person can live three days without water, three weeks without food. Her clock is ticking, Captain. At best, I think we've got three days to find her, maybe less."

"That's why I need you back here."

"We need to chase this down first. Until we figure out who he's got, we're spinning wheels. You want something—give me an hour, and hopefully I can give you a name for the press. You put a picture of the missing girl out to them, and they'll back down," Porter said.

The captain fell silent for a moment. "One hour. No more."

"That's all we need."

"Tread gently around Talbot. He rubs elbows with the mayor," the captain replied.

"Kid gloves, got it."

"Call me back after you speak with him." The captain disconnected the call.

Porter raced up the ramp onto 294. Nash plugged Wheaton into the GPS. "We're twenty-eight miles out."

The car picked up speed as Porter forced the accelerator down just a little more.

Nash flipped on the radio.

. . . Although Chicago Metro has yet to make an announcement, speculation is that the pedestrian killed early this morning by a city transit bus in Hyde Park is, in fact, the Four Monkey Killer. A box photographed at the scene matches those sent by the killer in the past. He was dubbed the Four Monkey Killer by Samuel Porter, a detective with Chicago Metro, and one of the first to recognize his behavior, or signature.

"That's not true; I didn't come up with that—"

"Shh!" Nash interrupted.

The four monkeys comes from the Tosho-gu Shrine in Nikko, Japan, where a carving of three apes resides above the entrance. The first covering his ears, the second covering his eyes, and the third covering his mouth, they depict the proverb "Hear no evil, see no evil, speak no evil." The fourth monkey represents "Do no evil." The killer's pattern has remained consistent since his first victim, Calli Tremell, five and a half years ago. Two days after her kidnapping, the Tremell family received her ear in the mail. Two days after that, they received her eyes. Two days later, her tongue arrived. Her body was found in Bedford Park two days following the postmark on the last package, a note clenched in her hand that simply read, DO NO EVIL. *Later it was discovered that Michael Tremell, the victim's father, had been involved in an underground gambling scheme funneling millions of dollars into offshore accounts . . .*

Nash clicked off the radio. "He always takes a child or sibling to punish the father for some kind of crime. Why not this time? Why didn't he take Carnegie?"

"I don't know."

"We should get someone to check out Talbot's finances," Nash suggested.

"Good idea. Who do we have?"

"Matt Hosman?"

Porter nodded. "Make the call." He reached into his breast pocket, pulled out the diary, and tossed it into Nash's lap. "Then read this aloud."

8

Diary

Mother and Father were rather close to our neighbors, Simon and Lisa Carter. As just a boy of eleven the summer when they first joined our wonderful neighborhood, I considered them all to be old in the limited pages of my book. Looking back, though, I realize that Mother and Father were in their mid-thirties, and I can't imagine the Carters were more than one or two years younger than my parents. Three, at most. Maybe four, but I doubt more than five. They moved into the house next door, the only other house at our end of the quiet lane.

Have I mentioned how incredibly beautiful my mother was?

How rude of me to leave out such a detail. Blubbering on about such minute matters and neglecting to paint a picture that properly illustrates the narrative you so graciously agreed to follow along with me.

If you could reach into this tome and slap me silly, I would encourage you to do so. Sometimes I ramble, and a firm swat is necessary to put my little train back on the rails.

Where was I?

Mother.

Mother was beautiful.

Her hair was silk. Blond, full of body, and shimmering with just the right amount of healthy glimmer. It fell halfway down her slender back in luxurious waves. Oh, and her eyes! They were the brightest of green, emeralds set in her perfect porcelain skin.

I am not ashamed to admit that her figure caught many an eye as well. She ran daily, and I would venture to say she didn't carry an ounce of fat. She probably weighed no more than 110 soaking wet, and she came to my father's shoulders, which would make her about five foot four or so.

She had a fondness for sundresses.

Mother would wear a sundress on the hottest of days or in the dead of winter. She paid no mind to the cold. I recall one winter with snowdrifts nearly to the windowsill, and I found her humming happily in the kitchen, a short, white, flowered sundress fluttering about her frame. Mrs. Carter sat at the kitchen table with a steaming cup of happiness in her hands, and Mother told her she wore such dresses because they made her feel free. And she favored short dresses because her legs, she felt, were her best asset. She went on to say how Father was so fond of them. How he would caress them. How he enjoyed them on his shoulders, or wrapped around—

Mother spotted me at that point, and I took leave.

9

Porter

Day I • 8:49 a.m.

Porter knew little about golf. The idea of hitting a little white ball, then chasing after it for hours on end, did not appeal to him. While he understood it was challenging, he did not consider it a sport. Baseball was a sport. Football was a sport. Anything you could play at eighty years old while toting your oxygen tank and wearing pastel slacks would never be a sport in his book.

The restaurant was nice, though. He had taken Heather to the Chicago Golf Club two years ago for their anniversary and purchased the most expensive steak he had ever eaten. Heather had ordered the lobster and raved about it for weeks. A cop's salary didn't allow for much, but anything that made her happy was a worthwhile spend.

He pulled up to the large clubhouse and handed his keys to the valet. "Keep it close. We won't be long."

They had beaten the weather. While the sky appeared hazy, the dark storm clouds had paused over the city.

The lobby was large and well-appointed. Several members were gathered around a fireplace in the far corner overlooking the lush course just beyond french doors. Their voices echoed off the marble floor and mahogany wainscoting.

Nash whistled softly.

"If I catch you panhandling, I'll make you wait in the car."

"As this day progresses, I find myself regretting I didn't wear a nicer suit," Nash admitted. "This is a very different world than the one we putt around in, Sam."

"Do you play?"

"The last time I held a golf club, I couldn't get past the windmill. This here is big-boy golf. I don't have the patience for it," Nash replied.

A young woman sat at a desk near the center of the lobby. As they approached, she glanced up from her laptop and smiled. "Good morning, gentlemen. Welcome to the Chicago Golf Club. How may I help you?"

Behind her gleaming white smile, Porter could sense her sizing them up. She hadn't asked if they had a reservation, and he doubted that was an oversight. He pulled out his badge and held it up to her. "We're looking for Arthur Talbot. His wife said he was playing today."

Her smile faded as her eyes darted from the badge to Porter, then Nash. She picked up the receiver on her desk and dialed an extension, spoke softly, then disconnected. "Please take a seat. Someone will be with you in a moment." She gestured toward a couch in the far corner.

"We're fine, thank you," Porter told her.

The smile again. She returned to her computer, slim, manicured fingers bouncing across the keys.

Porter checked his watch. Nearly 9:00 a.m.

A man in his mid-fifties entered the lobby from a door to their left. His salt-and-pepper hair was combed neatly back, his dark-blue suit pressed to perfection. As he approached, he extended his hand to Porter. "Detective. I've been told you're here to see Mr. Talbot?" His grip was soft. Porter's father had called it a *dead fish shake*. "I'm Douglas Prescott, senior manager."

Porter flashed his badge. "I'm Detective Porter, and this is Detective Nash with Chicago Metro. This is extremely urgent. Do you know where we can find Mr. Talbot?"

The blond woman was watching them. When Prescott glanced at her, she turned back to her laptop. His gaze returned to Porter. "I believe Mr. Talbot's party had a seven-thirty tee time, so they're out on the course. You're more than welcome to wait for him. You'll find a fine complimentary breakfast in the dining room. If you like cigars, our humidor is top-notch."

"This can't wait."

Prescott frowned. "We don't disturb our guests during play, gentlemen."

"We don't?" Nash said.

"We do not," Prescott insisted.

Porter rolled his eyes. Why did everyone seem to go out of their way to make things difficult? "Mr. Prescott, we don't have the time or patience for this. The way I see it, you've got two choices. You can take us to Mr. Talbot, or my partner here will arrest you for obstruction, handcuff you to that desk, and start shouting Talbot's name until he comes to us. I've seen him do it—the man is loud. It's your choice, but I honestly think option A will prove least disruptive to your business."

The receptionist stifled a chuckle.

Prescott shot her an angry glance, then stepped closer, lowering his voice. "Mr. Talbot is a substantial contributor and personal friends with your boss, the mayor. They played together just two weeks ago. I don't think either would be happy to learn two officers were willing to blemish the record of Chicago Metro by threatening civilians simply for doing their job. If I were to call him right now and tell him you were here, preparing to make a scene, he would no doubt refer you to his attorney before he would consider taking the time to speak with you."

Nash pulled the handcuffs from his belt. "I'm arresting this little shit, Sam. I want to see how well he holds up in the tank surrounded by crackheads and bangers. I'm sure Ms."—he glanced down at the blond woman's name tag—"Piper will be more than willing to help us out."

Prescott's face grew red.

"Take a deep breath and think carefully about the next thing you say, Mr. Prescott," Porter warned.

Prescott rolled his eyes, then turned to Ms. Piper. "Where is Mr. Talbot's party now?"

She pointed a pink-shellacked finger at her monitor. "They just pulled up to the sixth hole."

"You have video?" Nash asked.

She shook her head. "Our golf carts are equipped with GPS trackers. It allows us to watch for bottlenecks and keep everyone's game moving efficiently."

"So if someone is playing slow, you pluck them off the course and take them to the kiddy range?"

"Nothing that drastic. We may send a pro out to give them a few tips. Help them move along," she explained.

"Can you give us a ride out there?"

She eyed Prescott. He raised both hands in defeat. "Just go."

Ms. Piper plucked her purse from beneath her desk and gestured toward a hallway at the west end of the building. "This way, gentlemen."

A moment later they were in a golf cart heading down a cobblestone path. Ms. Piper was driving, with Porter beside her and Nash on a small bench behind them. He cursed as they hit a bump, bouncing him in the seat.

Porter shoved his hands into his pockets. It was cold out here in the open.

"I apologize for my boss. He can be a little . . ." She paused, searching for the right word. "A bit of a mucker sometimes."

"What the hell is a mucker?" Nash asked.

"Someone you wouldn't want at your bachelor party," Porter said.

Nash snickered. "I'm not walking down the aisle anytime soon, unless Ms. Piper has a friend in search of a civil servant who makes a low wage for getting shot at on a fairly regular basis. I also tend to work long hours and hit the bottle far more often than I'm willing to admit to someone I just met."

Porter turned back to Ms. Piper. "Ignore him, miss. You're under no legal obligation to set up members of law enforcement with attractive friends."

She glanced up at the rearview mirror. "You sound like quite the catch, Detective. I'll reach out to my sorority sisters the moment I get back to my desk."

"That would be much appreciated," Nash said.

Porter couldn't help but marvel at the landscaping. The grass was short and lush, not a single weed or blade out of place. Tiny ponds dotted the course on either side of the cart path. Large oaks loomed over the sides of the fairway, their branches shielding the players from the sun and wind.

"There they are." Ms. Piper nodded toward a group of four men standing around something that resembled a tall, skinny water fountain.

"What is that thing?" Nash asked.

"What thing?"

Ms. Piper smiled. "That, gentlemen, is a ball washer."

Nash massaged his temple and closed his eyes. "So many jokes just popped into my head, it actually hurts."

Ms. Piper pulled to a stop behind Talbot's cart and locked the brake. "Would you like me to wait for you?"

Porter smiled. "That would be nice, thank you."

Nash jumped off the back. "I'm calling shotgun for the ride back. The rumble seat is all yours."

Porter walked over to the four men preparing to tee off and showed his badge. "Morning, gentlemen. I'm Detective Sam Porter with Chicago Metro. This is my partner, Detective Nash. I'm sorry to interrupt your game, but we have a situation that simply couldn't wait. Which one of you is Arthur Talbot?"

A tall man in his early fifties with short-cropped salt-and-pepper hair cocked his head slightly and offered what Nash liked to call a politician's grin. "I'm Arthur Talbot."

Porter lowered his voice. "Could we speak to you alone for a moment?"

Talbot was dressed in a brown windbreaker over a white golf shirt, brown belt, and khakis. He shook his head. "No need, Detective. These guys are my business partners. I don't keep secrets from these men."

The older man to his left pushed his wireframe glasses up the bridge of his nose and flattened what was a promising start to a comb-over against the thin breeze. Anxious eyes locked on Porter. "We can play on, Arty. You can catch up if you need a minute."

Talbot raised a hand, silencing him. "What can I do for you, Detective?"

"You seem very familiar," Nash said to the man on Talbot's right.

Porter thought so too but couldn't place him. About six feet tall. Thick, dark hair. Fit. Mid-forties.

"Louis Fischman. We met a few years ago. You were working the Elle Borton case, and I was with the district attorney's office. I'm in the private sector now."

Talbot frowned. "Elle Borton. Why do I recognize that name?"

"She was one of the Monkey Killer's victims, wasn't she?" the third man chimed in. He had begun fiddling with the ball washer.

Porter nodded. "His second."

"Right."

"Fucking crazy bastard," the man with glasses muttered. "Any leads?"

"City transit may have clipped him this morning," Nash said.

"City transit? A cabdriver turned him in?" Fischman asked.

Porter shook his head and explained.

"And you believe it's the Monkey Killer?"

"Looks like it."

Arthur Talbot frowned. "Why are you here to see me?"

Porter took a deep breath. He hated this part of his job. "The man who was killed, we believe he was trying to cross the street to get to a mailbox."

"Oh?"

"The package had your home address on it, Mr. Talbot."

His face went pale. Like most of Chicago, he was familiar with the Monkey Killer's MO.

Fischman put his hand on Talbot's shoulder. "What was in the package, Detective?"

"An ear."

"Oh no. Carnegie—"

"It's not Carnegie, Mr. Talbot. It's not Patricia, either. They're both safe. We stopped at your residence before driving out here. Your wife told us where to find you," Porter said as quickly as he could, then lowered his voice in an attempt to calm the man down. "We need your help, Mr. Talbot. We need you to help us determine who he took."

"I've got to sit down," Talbot said. "I feel like I'm going to throw up."

Fischman glanced at Porter, then tightened his grip on the man's shoulder. "Arty, let's get you back to the cart." Moving away from the tee box, he guided a white-faced Talbot to the golf cart and lowered him into the seat.

Porter motioned for Nash to stay put and followed the other two men back to the vehicle. He sat beside Talbot so he could speak quietly. "You know how he operates, don't you? His pattern?"

Talbot nodded. "Do no evil," he whispered.

"That's right. He finds someone who has done something wrong, something *he* feels is wrong, and he takes someone close to them. Someone they care about."

"I di-didn't . . ." Talbot stammered.

Fischman dropped into lawyer mode. "Arty, I don't think you should say another word until we have a moment to talk."

Talbot's breathing was heavy. "My address? You're sure?"

"It's 1547 Dearborn Parkway," Porter told him. "We're sure."

"Arty . . ." Fischman muttered under his breath.

"We need to figure out who it is, who he took." Porter hesitated for a moment before continuing. "Do you have a mistress, Mr. Talbot?" He leaned in close. "If it's another woman, you can tell us. We'll be discreet. You've got my word. We only want to find whomever he has taken."

"It's not like that," said Talbot.

Porter put a hand on Talbot's shoulder. "Do you know who he has?"

Talbot shook him off and stood. He reached into his pocket and pulled out a cell phone, crossed to the other side of the cart path, and hammered in a number. "Come on, answer. Please pick up . . ."

Porter stood and slowly approached him. "Who are you calling, Mr. Talbot?"

Arthur Talbot swore and disconnected the call.

Fischman walked over to him. "If you tell them, you can't *untell* them. You understand? Once it's out there, the press could get wind. Your wife. Your shareholders. You have obligations. This is bigger than you. You need to think this through. Maybe talk to one of your other attorneys, if you're not comfortable discussing this matter with me."

Talbot shot him an angry glance. "I'm not going to wait for a stock analysis while some psycho has—"

"Arty!" Fischman interjected. "Let's at least confirm it on our own first. Let's be sure."

"That sounds like a great way to get this person killed," Porter said.

Arthur Talbot waved a frustrated hand at him and hit Redial on his phone, the anxiety growing on his face. When he disconnected the call, he tapped the screen so hard that Porter wondered if he had broken it.

Porter signaled Nash to approach, then: "You have another daughter, don't you, Mr. Talbot? A daughter outside your marriage?" As Porter said the words, Talbot looked away. Fischman seemed to deflate, letting out a deep breath.

Talbot glanced at Porter, then Fischman, then back to Porter again. He ran his hand through his hair. "Patricia and Carnegie know nothing about her."

Porter stepped closer to the man. "Is she here in Chicago?"

Talbot was shaking, flustered. Again, he nodded. "Flair Tower. She has penthouse 2704 with her caregiver. I'll call and let them know you're coming so you're able to get in."

"Where's her mother?"

"Dead. Going on twelve years now. God, she's only fifteen . . ."

Nash turned his back and made a phone call to Dispatch. They could have someone at Flair Tower in a few minutes.

Porter followed Talbot back to the golf cart and sat beside him. "Who takes care of her?"

"She had cancer, her mother. I promised her I would take care of our daughter when she was gone. The tumor grew so fast; it was over in just about a month." He tapped the side of his head. "It was right here. They couldn't operate, though; it was too deep. I would have paid anything. I tried. But they wouldn't operate. We must have talked to three dozen doctors. I loved her more than anything. I had to marry Patricia, I had . . . commitments. There were reasons beyond my control. But I wanted to marry Catrina. Sometimes life gets in the way, you know? Sometimes you have to do things for the greater good."

Porter didn't know. In fact, he didn't understand. Was this the 1400s? Forced marriages were long gone. This guy needed to grow a spine. Aloud, he said, "We're not here to judge you, Mr. Talbot. What's her name?"

"Emory," he said. "Emory Conners."

"Do you have a photo?"

Talbot hesitated for a moment, then shook his head. "Not on me. I couldn't risk Patricia finding it."

10

Porter

Day 1 • 9:23 a.m.

"Carnegie and Emory? I'm buying this family a baby-name book for Christmas," Nash said. "And how the hell do you hide a daughter and your girlfriend in one of the most expensive penthouses in the city without your current wife catching on?"

Porter tossed him the keys and rounded his Charger to the passenger door. "You drive; I need to keep reading this diary. There might be something helpful in it."

"Lazy bastard, you just like to be chauffeured around. Driving Ms. Porter . . ."

"Fuck you."

"I'm lighting the apple; we need to make good time." Nash flicked a switch on the dashboard.

Porter hadn't heard that term since he was a rookie. They used to call the magnetic police light on undercover cars *apples*. In today's world they were long gone, replaced with LED light bars so slim along the window's edge, you couldn't see them from the inside.

Nash dropped the car into third without letting up on the gas and steered for the exit gate. The car jerked and the tires squealed with delight as power surged through them.

"I said you could drive, not play Grand Theft Auto with my wheels." Porter frowned.

"I drive a 1988 Ford Fiesta. Do you have any idea what that's like? The humiliation I suffer every time I climb inside and pull that squeaky door shut and fire up that monster of a four-cylinder engine? It sounds like an electric pencil sharpener. I'm a man; I need this every once in a while. Humor me."

Porter waved him off. "We told the captain we'd call him back after we spoke to Talbot."

Nash tugged the wheel hard to the left and raced past a minivan dutifully driving the speed limit. They drew so close, Porter spotted Angry Birds on the iPad screen of a little girl secured in the back seat. She looked up and grinned at the flashing lights, then went back to her game.

"I shot him a text back at Wheaton. He knows we're going to Flair Tower," Nash said.

Porter thought about the little girl with the iPad. "How *do* you hide a daughter for fifteen years in today's world? It can't be easy, right? Birth records aside, how do you keep that secret online? All the social networks? Press? Talbot's on the news all the time, particularly since he started that new waterfront project. Cameras follow him around just waiting for him to fuck up. You'd think someone would have caught a picture or something."

"Money can hide a lot of things," Nash pointed out, squealing around a hard left back onto the highway.

Porter sighed and returned to the diary.

II

Diary

The summers on our little piece of earth could be quite warm. By June I would find myself spending most of my time outside. Behind our house there were woods, and deep within the woods was a small lake. It froze during the winter, but during the summer its water would be the clearest blue and the most soothing temperature.

I liked to visit the lake.

I would tell Mother I was going fishing, but truth be told, I wasn't one to fish. The idea of piercing a worm with a hook and tossing the creature into the water only to wait for something to come along and nibble at the creepy-crawly did not appeal to me. Did fish eat worms in the wild? I had my doubts. I had yet to see a worm enter the lake of its own accord. As I understood it, fish ate smaller fish, not worms. Perhaps if one were to fish with smaller fish in hopes of catching a larger one, one would be more successful? Regardless, I never had the patience for such silliness.

I did enjoy the lake, though.

So did Mrs. Carter.

I remember the first time I saw her there.

It was June 20. School had been out for seven glorious days and the sun was high in the sky, smiling down upon our little patch of earth with bright yellow love. I walked to the lake with my fishing pole in hand and the whistle of a smart tune on my lips. I was always such a happy child. Right as rain, I was.

I plopped down at my favorite tree, a large oak looming with the kind of size that can only come with age. I imagined if I sliced the tree's belly and counted the rings, there would have been many, perhaps a hundred or more. Years came and went as the oak stood its ground and looked down upon the rest of the forest. It was a fine tree indeed.

As the summer progressed, I wore a nice little spot at the base of that tree. I always placed my fishing pole to my left and my lunch bag (containing a peanut butter and grape jam sandwich, of course) to my right. Then I would pull my latest read from my pocket and get lost within the book's pages.

On this day, I was researching a theory. The month before in science class, we had learned that Earth was 4.5 billion years old. We'd previously learned the human race was only 200,000 years old. After I'd heard these factoids, a thought raised its hand at the back of my mind. Hence the reason I had picked up this particular book from the library the day before — a book about fossils.

You see, objects embedded in rocks are "fossilized" and stay that way for . . . for — I don't know, but it's a very long time, millions of years, in the case of dinosaurs. And most animals don't even become fossils at all. After all, an animal would first have to get trapped in the rock to become fossilized. If the elements destroyed it before that could happen, the evidence would disappear without a trace.

The month before, I had killed a cat and laid the stiff body out at the edge of the lake to see what would happen.

Don't worry, it wasn't someone's pet, only a stray cat. A little tabby that lived in the forest. At least, that is where I found it. If the animal did, in fact, belong to someone, it did not wear a tag. If it was a pet and they allowed it to roam free without a tag, any blame for the creature's demise should fall upon the careless owners.

The cat did not look well. It hadn't for some time.

The remains smelled something awful the first few days, but that quickly passed. First the flies came, then the maggots. Something larger may have picked at it some night during those early days. Now, though, after only a month, nothing remained but bones. Wind and rain would surely take those. Then it would be gone.

I imagine a person would disappear just as quickly.

At first the noise startled me. In all the time I had been coming to the lake, I had yet to spot another person. Nothing is forever, though, and here one stood less than a hundred feet away at the lake's edge, gazing out over the water.

I shuffled around to the side of my tree so as not to be spotted.

Although her angle prevented me from seeing her face, I immediately recognized her hair, those long chocolate curls at her back.

She glanced in my direction and I ducked back. Then she turned to her right, surveying her surroundings. Finally content she was alone, she reached into a large bag, pulled out a towel, and spread it on the shore.

After she looked one more time in all directions, her hand went to the back of her dress and untied it at the neck. It fell from her body and pooled at her feet in a puddle of white, flowered cloth.

My mouth dropped open.

She wore nothing else.

I had never seen a naked woman before.

She closed her eyes and turned her head up to the sun and smiled.

Her legs were so long.

And breasts!

Oh my. I felt my face blush. It blushes to this day.

I saw a tiny tuft of hair at that spot, that special little spot.

Mrs. Carter walked to the water and stepped in, hesitant at first. No doubt it was cold.

She went farther still, slowly disappearing with the increasing depth.

When the water climbed above her knees, she bent down, took a handful, and splashed it over her chest. She dove in a moment later and swam toward the center of the lake.

From the safety of my tree, I watched.

• • •

The night came and went and proved to be quite restless.

With summer also came the heat, and my room became rather toasty once spring shrugged off its coat.

It wasn't the heat that had kept me up, though; it was thoughts of Mrs. Carter. I dare to say, they were most unpure and very new to me. When I closed my eyes I still saw her standing in the lake, the water glistening on her damp flesh in the bright light. Her long legs . . . so long and tender. It made blood rush to a place it never had before, made me feel—

Let us say for a young boy, I was smitten.

I woke the next morning to the sound of her voice.

At first I thought it was only another dream, and I welcomed it, wishing to watch her remove her dress and walk into the lake again and again in the theater of my mind. Her voice drifted through the air on a whisper, followed by Mother's chuckle. My eyes snapped open.

"It was kinky," she said. "I had never been tied up before."

"Never?" Mother replied.

Mrs. Carter giggled. "Does that make me a prude?"

"It just makes you inexperienced. In time, you'll be surprised by what your husband can come up with to get his rocks off."

"Really?"

"Oh yes. Just last week . . ." Mother's voice dropped to a whisper.

I sat up in bed. Now the voices were faint, somewhere else in the house.

I hastily dressed and pressed my ear to my door, but still I couldn't make out the words.

With a gentle twist of the knob, I opened the door and made my way down the hallway, my stockinged feet noiseless on the hardwood floor.

The hallway ended at the living room, which in turn faced the kitchen. I smelled something baking: the lofty aroma of apples and bread. Pie, perhaps? I love a good pie.

Mother and Mrs. Carter burst out laughing simultaneously.

I crouched low against the wall near the end of the hallway. I was still unable to hear well but dared not enter the living room. This position would have to do.

"My Simon is not that adventurous," Mrs. Carter said. "I'm afraid to say his bag of tricks is rather light. More of a satchel than a bag, really. Or perhaps one of those little paper lunch sacks."

The refrigerator door opened with the jingle of bottles.

"Not my husband," Mother replied. "Sometimes I'll put on the game just to get his mind out of the bedroom. Or the laundry room. Or the kitchen table."

"No!" Mrs. Carter cried out with a laugh.

"Oh yes," said Mother. "The man is like an animal in heat. Sometimes there is no stopping him."

"But you have a kid."

"Oh, that boy is always off doing something. When he's not, he's in bed sleeping like a bear in the dead of winter. The earth could open up beneath him, and he'd sleep through the carnage."

I eased my head around the corner without so much as a sound, immediately drawing it back so as not to be seen.

Mother was mixing something at the counter. Mrs. Carter sat at the kitchen table, coffee mug at hand.

"Maybe you should try something to spice things up," Mother continued. "Missionary is for missionaries, I always say. Introduce a toy or bring some food into the bedroom. All men like whipped cream."

I was not permitted to bring food into my room. Not since Mother had found a half-eaten tin of cookies under my bed.

Mrs. Carter giggled again. "I could never."

"You should."

"But what if he doesn't like it, or thinks I'm some kind of freak? How would I survive the embarrassment?"

"Oh, he'll like it. They always do."

"You think so?"

"I know so."

The women fell silent for a moment, then Mrs. Carter spoke. "Has your husband ever, you know, not been able to, well, you know . . ."

"My husband?" Mother shrieked with amusement. "My Lord, no. His plumbing is in top order."

"Even when he drinks?"

"Especially when he drinks."

One of our wooden chairs scraped against the floor.

I peeked around the corner for just an instant. Mother had sat beside Mrs. Carter and put a hand on her shoulder. "Does it happen a lot?"

"Only when he drinks."

"Does he drink a lot?"

Mrs. Carter paused, searching for the right words. "Not every night."

Mother squeezed her shoulder. "Well, men will be men. He still has some growing up to do."

"You think?"

"Sure. When starting out in life, there are so many pressures on a man, on both of you, but especially on him. He bought you that lovely home. I imagine you've talked of children?"

Mrs. Carter nodded.

"All those things, they add up like big, heavy weights on his shoulders. Each one adding another pound or two until he can barely walk, barely stand. He drinks to help deal with that, that's all. I find nothing wrong with a little sauce to calm an edgy nerve. Don't you fret. When things improve, when the pressure lifts, things will get better. Just you wait and see."

"You don't think it's me?" Mrs. Carter said, her voice almost childlike.

"A pretty thing like you? Of course not," Mother told her.

"You think I'm pretty?"

Mother snorted. "I can't believe you'd even have to ask. You are gorgeous. One of the most beautiful women I've ever laid eyes on."

"That is so sweet of you to say," Mrs. Carter said.

"It's the truth. Any man would be lucky to have you," Mother told her.

The women fell silent again, and I stole another glance, crawling around the corner as quiet as a mouse.

Mother and Mrs. Carter were kissing.

12

Emory

Day 1 • 9:29 a.m.

Darkness.

It swirled around her like the current of the deepest sea. Cold and silent, crawling across her body with the touch of a stranger.

"Em," her mother whispered. "You gotta get up. You're going to be late for school."

"*No,*" she groaned. "A few more minutes . . ."

"Now, baby, I'm not going to tell you again."

"I've got a bad headache. Can I stay home?" Her voice was soft and distant, soaked and heavy with sleep.

"I'm not going to make up another excuse for you with the principal. Why do we have to go through this every day?"

But this wasn't right. Her mother had died long ago, when she was only three. Her mother had not been there on her first day of school. She had never sent her off to school. She had been homeschooled most of her life.

"Momma?" she said softly.

Silence.

Her head hurt so bad.

She tried to force her eyelids open, but they fought her.

Her head ached, throbbed. She heard the pounding of her own heartbeat, the rhythm fast and strong behind her eyes.

"Are you there, Momma?"

She peered through the darkness at her left, searching for the illuminated red numbers of her alarm clock. The clock wasn't there, though; her room was pitch-dark.

The city lights normally cast a glow on her ceiling, but they too were dark.

She couldn't see anything.

It's not your room.

The thought came swiftly, an unknown voice.

Where?

Emory Connors tried to sit up, but a hammer of pain pulsed on the left side of her head, forcing her to lie back down. Her hand went to her ear and found a thick bandage. Wetness.

Blood?

Then she remembered the shot.

He had given her a shot.

Who was he?

Emory didn't know. She couldn't remember. She remembered the shot, though. His arm had reached around from behind and plunged the needle into her neck. Cold liquid rushed out under her skin.

She had tried to turn.

She had wanted to hurt him. That was what she had been taught to do, all those self-defense classes her father insisted she take. *Punish and maim. Crack him in the nuts, honey. That's my girl.*

She had wanted to spin around with a well-placed kick and a punch to his nose or his windpipe, or maybe his eyes. She had wanted to hurt him before he could hurt her, she had wanted to . . .

She didn't turn.

Instead, her world had gone dark, and sleep engulfed her.

He'll rape and kill me, she had thought as consciousness slipped away. *Help me, Momma,* she had thought as the world faded to black.

Her mom was gone. Dead. And she was about to join her.

That was okay, that was good. She would like to see her mom again.

He hadn't killed her, though. *Had he?*

No. The dead do not feel pain, and her ear throbbed.

She forced herself to sit up.

The blood rushed from her head, and she almost passed out again. The room spun for a second before settling.

What had he given her?

She had heard of girls getting roofied at parties and clubs, waking up in strange places with their clothes askew and no memory of what had happened. She hadn't been at a party; she had been running in the park. He had lost his dog. He looked so sad standing there with the leash, calling out her name.

Bella? Stella? What was the dog's name?

She couldn't remember. Her mind was foggy, thick with smoke, choking her thoughts.

"Which way did it go?" she had asked him.

He frowned, near tears. "She saw a squirrel and took off after it, that way." He pointed to the east. "She's never run away before. I don't get it." Emory had turned, her gaze following his.

Then the arm around her neck.

The shot.

"Sleepy time, beautiful," he whispered at her ear.

There had been no dog. How could she have been so stupid?

She was cold.

Something held her right wrist down. Emory tugged and heard the clank of metal on metal. Reaching over with her left hand, she explored the smooth steel around her wrist, the thin chain.

Handcuffs.

Fastened to whatever she was lying on.

Her right wrist was handcuffed to something; her left was free.

She took a deep breath. The air was stale, damp.

Don't panic, Em. Don't let yourself give in to the panic.

Her eyes tried to adjust to the darkness, but it was so black, absolute. Her fingertips brushed the surface of the bed.

No, not a bed. Something else.

It was steel.

Hospital gurney.

Emory wasn't sure how she knew, but she did, she just knew.

Oh God, where was she?

She shivered, realizing for the first time that she was naked.

She hesitated for a moment, then reached down and felt between her legs. She wasn't sore.

If he had raped her, she would know, wouldn't she?

She wasn't sure.

She had only had sex once before, and it had hurt. Not painful, just uncomfortable, and only at first. Her boyfriend, Tyler, had promised to be gentle, and he had. It was over fast, his first time too. That was only a few weeks ago. Her father had let her go to Tyler's homecoming dance at Whatney Vale High. Tyler had rented a room at the Union, and even managed to score a bottle of champagne from somewhere.

God, her head.

She reached back up and tentatively touched the bandages. Her ear was completely wrapped up. Some kind of tape held the dressing in place. Gently, she peeled back the bandage. "Fuck!"

The cool air felt like the blade of a knife.

She pulled at the bandage anyway, tugging until she could get her hand under the cloth.

Tears welled in her eyes as her fingertips brushed over what remained of her ear, a ragged wound at best, stitched and tender. "No . . . no . . . no," she cried.

Her voice bounced off the walls and echoed back at her mockingly.

13

Porter

Day 1 • 10:04 a.m.

Nash pulled the Charger into a handicapped spot at the front of Flair Tower and killed the engine.

"You're really going to park here?" Porter frowned.

Nash shrugged. "We're the po-po; we get to do things like that."

"Remind me to put in for a new partner when this is all over."

"That sounds like an excellent plan. Then maybe I'll get saddled with some hot female rookie fresh out of the academy." Nash grinned.

"Maybe you can requisition one with daddy issues."

"I don't recall that question on the form, but I may have missed it."

The doorman propped open the large glass doors for them, and they moved past him to the front desk. Porter flashed his badge. "Penthouse twenty-seven?"

A young woman with close-cropped brown hair and blue eyes smiled back at him. "Your colleagues arrived about twenty-five minutes ago. Take elevator number six to the twenty-seventh floor. The penthouse will be on your right as you exit." She handed him a keycard. "You'll need this."

They boarded elevator number six, and the door closed behind them with a quick swoosh of air. Porter pressed the button for the twenty-seventh floor, but nothing happened.

"You need to slide the card through the thingy," Nash instructed.

"The thingy? How the fuck did you become a detective?"

"Forgive me for not consulting my word-a-day calendar this morning," he retorted. "The card reader over there. Looks like a credit card machine."

"Got it, Einstein." Porter slid the plastic access card through the reader and pushed the button again. This time the panel lit up in bright blue, and they began to ascend.

The elevator door opened onto a hallway that extended in both directions. Large railed openings offered views of a massive atrium on the floor below. Near the end of the hallway to the right a door was open, a uniformed officer standing guard.

Porter and Nash approached, showed their badges, and stepped inside.

The view was breathtaking.

The penthouse occupied the entire northeast corner of the building. The outer walls consisted of floor-to-ceiling windows with a balcony. The city sprawled out around them, with Lake Michigan visible in the distance. "When I was fifteen," Porter said, "my room was nothing like this."

"My apartment could fit in this living room," Nash said. "After today, I may have to trade in my badge and become a real estate mogul."

"I don't think you can jump right into something like that," said Porter. "You probably need to take some kind of course on the Internet."

Nash pulled two pairs of latex gloves from his pocket, handed one set to Porter, and put on the other.

A number of CSI techs were already hard at work inside. Paul Watson spotted them and came over from the floor-to-ceiling bookcase on the far wall. "If there was a struggle, there's no sign. This is the cleanest apartment I've ever seen. The fridge is fully stocked. I found a receipt in the trash from two days ago. We're pulling the phone records, but I don't think we'll find anything there, either. I was able to scroll back through the last ten incoming numbers, and they all belonged to her father."

"She has a landline? Really?"

Watson shrugged. "Maybe it came with the apartment."

"Daddy probably put it in. Can't claim no signal or missed calls with a landline," Nash pointed out.

Porter asked, "What about outgoing?"

"Three numbers. We're running them now," said Watson.

Porter began walking around the apartment, his shoes squeaking on the hardwood floors.

The kitchen had cherry cabinets and dark granite countertops. All stainless steel appliances—Viking stove and Sub-Zero refrigerator. The living room held a large sectional beige leather couch. It appeared so comfortable, Porter got tired just glancing at the plush cushions. The television was at least eighty inches. "That's a 4K display," Watson told him.

"4K?"

"Four times more pixels than your standard 1080p HD television."

Porter only nodded. He still had a nineteen-inch tube television at home. He refused to replace the ancient unit with a flat panel while it was working, and the damn thing wouldn't die.

There was a den with a large oak desk. A tech was copying the files from a twenty-seven-inch iMac.

"Anything useful?" he asked.

The tech shook his head. "Nothing stands out. We'll analyze her files and social network activity back at the station."

Porter continued on into the master bedroom. The bed was neatly made. No posters were on the walls, only a few paintings. "This doesn't feel right."

Nash pulled a few of the drawers; each was lined with perfectly folded clothes. "Yeah. Seems more like a model home, almost staged. If a fifteen-year-old girl lives here, she's the neatest teenager I've ever come across," Nash said.

There was a single framed picture on her nightstand of a woman in her mid- to late twenties. Flowing brown hair, the greenest eyes Porter had ever seen. "Her mother?" he asked nobody in particular.

"I believe so," Watson replied.

"Talbot said she died of cancer when Emory was only three," Porter said, studying the photograph. "A brain tumor, of all things."

"I can research that if you'd like," Watson proposed eagerly.

Porter nodded and replaced the picture. "That would be helpful."

"You could bounce a quarter on this bed," said Nash. "I don't think a kid made it."

"I'm still not convinced a kid lives here."

The master bathroom was amazing—all granite and porcelain tile. Two sinks. You could throw a party in the shower. Porter counted no fewer than six showerheads with additional jets built into the walls.

He walked over to the sink and touched the tip of her toothbrush. "Still damp," he said.

"I'll get someone to bag that," Watson told him. "In case we need the DNA. Hand me that hairbrush too."

There was a sitting room attached to the master. The walls were lined with shelves teeming with books, a few hundred or more. Porter spotted everything from Charles Dickens to J. K. Rowling. A Thad McAlister novel was lying open on a large, fluffy recliner at the center of the room. "Maybe she does live here after all," Porter said, picking up the book. "This came out a few weeks ago."

"And you know this how?" Nash asked.

"Heather picked it up. She's a big fan of this guy."

"Ah."

"Look at this," Watson said. He was holding up an English literature textbook. "I remember spotting a calculus book on the desk in the den. This particular brand, Worthington Studies, is popular with homeschoolers. Did Mr. Talbot say where she went to school?"

Porter and Nash glanced at each other. "We didn't ask."

Watson was flipping through the pages. "If she was enrolled somewhere, we can track down some of her friends." His face grew red. "I'm sorry, sir. I mean, *you* can track down some of her friends. If you think that might be useful."

Talbot had given Porter a business card with his cell phone number. He tapped his pocket, confirming it was still there. "I'll check with her father when we're done here."

They left the master and continued down the hall. "How many bedrooms in this place?"

"Three," Watson replied. "Take a look at this one." He gestured to a room on their right.

Porter stepped inside. A basket of laundry sat atop a queen-size bed. A large Catholic cross hung over the headboard. The dresser was covered in framed photographs, two rows deep.

Nash picked one up. "Is that her? Emory?"

"Must be."

They ranged in age from a toddler to a picture of a stunning young girl in a dark-blue dress next to a boy of about sixteen with long, wavy dark hair. A small caption in the corner read WHATNEY VALE HIGH HOMECOMING, 2014.

"Is she enrolled there?" Porter asked.

"I'll find out." Watson pointed at the young man standing next to her. "Think that's her boyfriend?"

"Might be."

"Can I see that?" Watson asked.

Porter handed him the frame.

Watson flipped it over and slid the tiny tabs aside, then removed the backing board. He carefully extracted the photo. "Em and Ty." He showed them the back. The names were in small print on the bottom right.

"Elementary, my dear Watson," Porter said.

"No, Whatney Vale is a high school."

Nash chuckled. "I love this guy. Can we keep him?"

"The captain will kill me if I bring home another stray," Porter said.

"I'm serious, Sam. We're going to need the manpower. We've got two, possibly three days on the outside to find this girl. He's got a good head on his shoulders," Nash said. "If you don't fill the task force bench, the captain will. Better you do it, or we'll get stuck with someone like Murray." He nodded toward a detective standing in the hallway, who was staring at the tip of his ballpoint pen. "I'm thinking we bring the kid in as a CSI liaison."

Porter thought about this for a moment, then turned back to Watson. "Any interest in working this case?"

"I'm a private contractor with CSI. Can I work as law enforcement?"

"As long as you don't shoot anyone," Nash said.

"I don't carry a weapon," he replied. "I never felt the need to take the exam. I'm more of a bookworm."

"Chicago Metro has an agreement with the crime lab. Officially, you'd be a consult on loan," Porter explained. "Think you can clear it with your supervisor?"

Watson set the photo down on the dresser and pulled out his cell phone. "Give me a minute—I'll call him." He walked to the far corner of the room and punched in the number.

"Sharp kid," Nash said.

"It will be good to have some fresh eyes on this," Porter agreed. "God knows you're not much help."

"Fuck you too, buddy." Nash stuffed the photo into an evidence bag. "I'll take this back to the war room."

Porter ran his hand through his hair and glanced around the room. "You know what I haven't seen yet?"

"What?"

"A single photo of the father," he replied. "There's not a damn thing in this place to indicate they're related. I bet if we check the records, we won't find anything to link him back here. The apartment is probably owned by a company that's owned by a company that's owned by a shell out of an island so remote, Gilligan's bones are probably buried on the beach."

Nash shrugged. "That surprise you? He's got a family, a life. He's the kind of guy who has political office on the brain. Illegitimate children don't bode well in a campaign unless they belong to your opponent—same with mistresses. Let's face it: even though he said he cared for this woman, that's all she was to him, or he would have left the wife and married her rather than hide her in this tower, away from prying eyes. Kid or no kid."

Watson returned, pocketing his cell phone. "He said as long as I stay on top of my current caseload, he's okay with it."

"Will that be a problem?"

He shook his head. "I can handle it. Frankly, I think I'll enjoy the change of pace. It'll be nice to get out of the lab for a little while."

"Okay, then. Welcome to the Four Monkey Killer task force. We'll take care of the paperwork back at the station."

"Not very ceremonious, Sam. You'll need to work on that," Nash said.

Watson pointed at the photo. "Do you want me to try and track down Ty?"

"Yeah," Porter replied. "See what you can dig up."

He dropped the photograph into an evidence bag.

Nash pulled open the top left dresser drawer. Women's underwear. He stretched them out between his hands and whistled. "Those are some big 'uns."

"I'm thinking some kind of nanny or housekeeper lives in this room," Porter said. "Emory's only fifteen. There is no way she lives here by herself."

"Okay, but then where is she now? Why hasn't she reported the girl missing?" Nash asked. "It's been at least a day, possibly longer."

"She didn't report anything to the police. Maybe she called somebody else," Porter suggested.

"You mean Talbot?" Nash shook his head. "I don't think so. He seemed genuinely surprised and upset when you told him."

"If she's illegal, she wouldn't call the police," Watson said. "Makes sense she would reach out to him."

"Or someone who works for him."

"Okay, assuming that's the case, then why would Talbot pretend to be in the dark? Wouldn't he want to find her?"

Porter shrugged. "His lawyer was pretty insistent about keeping all this quiet. Maybe that's the Talbot stance. They've kept this girl a secret for fifteen years. Why stop now? He's got resources, he's probably got his own people out looking for her; no need for us."

"Then why tell us about her at all? If his primary concern is hiding her from the world, wouldn't he point us in another direction?"

Porter walked over to the laundry basket and felt a towel near the center. "Still warm."

Nash nodded slowly. "So somebody phoned her, told her we were coming . . ."

"That would be my guess. She probably cleared out right after getting the call."

"That doesn't mean there's some big conspiracy. She might just be an illegal like Dr. Watson over there suggested, and he didn't want to see her get deported," Nash said.

"I'm not a—"

Nash cut him off with a wave of his hand. "I bet she's still close, then. We should post someone to keep an eye on the place."

Nash's phone rang, and he glanced at the display. "It's Eisley." He tapped the Answer button. "This is Nash."

Porter took the opportunity to dial his wife. When he got voice mail, he disconnected without leaving a message.

Nash hung up and dropped his phone into his front pants pocket. "He wants us down at the morgue."

"What did he find?"

"Said we needed to see for ourselves."

14

Diary

"Would you like honey in your oatmeal, dear?"

Mother made wonderful oatmeal. Not the prepackaged kind, no sir. She purchased raw oats and cooked them to a magical deliciousness and served them with toast and juice at the little breakfast nook in our kitchen.

"Yes, Mother," I replied. "More juice too, please?"

It was a little past eight in the morning on a sunny summer Thursday.

I heard a gentle knock at our screen door, and we both turned to find Mrs. Carter standing on the stoop.

Mother grinned. "Hey, you. Come on in."

Mrs. Carter smiled back and pulled open the door. Thanks to the bright sun, I saw the outline of her legs through her dress as she stepped over the threshold. She gave my shoulder a squeeze and smiled before walking over to my mother and giving her a light peck on the cheek.

I have to say, after yesterday, it was fairly tame. However, I did catch a glance as it passed between them.

Mother stroked the other woman's hair. "Your hair looks absolutely stunning today. I'd kill for hair like that. I'm having an Irish coffee. Would you care for one?"

"What is Irish coffee?"

"My, my, you are young in the ways of the world, aren't you? Irish coffee is coffee with a splash of Jameson whiskey. I find it's the perfect pick-me-up on a warm summer morning," Mother told her.

"Whiskey in the morning? How devilish! Yes, please."

Mother poured her a steaming cup of coffee, then took down a little green bottle with a yellow label from the cabinet I was not permitted to open. She removed the cap and topped off the mug before passing it to Mrs. Carter. I couldn't help but notice that their hands lingered together a moment longer than one would think necessary.

Mrs. Carter took a sip and smiled. "This is to die for. It must do wonders during the winter."

Mother looked at the woman and tilted her head. "Isn't that the same dress you were wearing yesterday?"

Mrs. Carter blushed. "I'm afraid so. I desperately need to do laundry today."

"I can't let you go through the day in yesterday's clothes. Follow me." She stood and started for her bedroom, taking the bottle with her. "I have a few dresses I don't wear anymore. I bet they would fit you perfectly."

Mrs. Carter smiled at me and chased after Mother, her Irish coffee in hand. I watched them disappear down the hall, Mother's door closing as they stepped inside.

For the briefest of moments, I considered staying there at the table and finishing my breakfast. After all, it is the most important meal of the day. As a growing boy, I understood the importance of nourishment. I didn't do it, though. Instead, I tiptoed down the hallway and put my ear to her door.

Nothing but silence came from the other side.

I went outside and circled the house.

Mother's window was on the east side, above a large rosebush shaded by an old cottonwood. Careful to ensure I could not be seen from the street, I positioned myself to the side of the tree and turned to the window. Unfortunately I was still rather short, my thin body that of a boy, and only the ceiling of the room was visible from that angle.

I quickly ran to the back of the house and returned with a five-gallon plastic bucket. Placing it upside down beside the tree, I climbed atop and again turned to the window.

Mrs. Carter's back was to me, watching Mother as she dug through her closet with the ferocity of a dog creating a hole for its favorite bone. When Mother emerged, she held three dresses. Words were exchanged, but I was unable to make them out, as Mother's window was closed. She wasn't one to open her bedroom window, even at the peak of summer heat.

Mrs. Carter reached behind her head and untied the bow that held the back of her dress together. My breath caught in my throat as the thin material fell away. Aside from thin white cotton panties, she was naked. Mother handed her one of the dresses, and she slipped it over her head. Mother then stepped back and appraised the other woman. She produced the small green bottle with the yellow label and drank directly from it. She shivered, grinned, and handed the bottle to Mrs. Carter, who hesitated only for a moment before bringing the bottle to her own lips and taking a drink.

I knew what alcohol was, but I couldn't recall ever seeing Mother drink, only Father. It was commonplace for him to pour a drink or two after a long day at work, but not Mother. This was new. This was different.

Our neighbor handed the bottle back to Mother, who drank again, then passed it back, the two of them laughing silently behind the glass.

Mother held up one of the other dresses, and Mrs. Carter nodded with enthusiasm. She removed her dress and walked over to Mother's large mirror, holding the second dress against her chest.

My heart quickened.

Mother stepped up behind her and brushed her hair to the side, revealing the curve of her neck. I peered in as Mother kissed her ever so tenderly on that spot where neck meets shoulder. Mrs. Carter closed her eyes and leaned back slightly, pressing against her. She dropped the dress to the floor. In the mirror's reflection, I watched as Mother's hand inched up the other woman's stomach and found her right breast.

Unlike Mrs. Carter's, Mother's eyes were open. I know this because I could see them. I could see them staring back at me in the mirror's reflection as her hands drifted down the length of the other woman's body and disappeared within her panties.

15

Porter

Day 1 • 10:31 a.m.

The Cook County Medical Examiner's Office was on West Harrison Street in downtown Chicago. Porter and Nash made good time from Flair Tower and parked in one of the spaces out front reserved for law enforcement. Eisley had instructed them to meet him in the morgue.

Porter had never been a fan of the morgue. Formaldehyde and bleach seemed to be the air freshener of choice, but there was no disguising the fact that the morgue smelled like feet, stale cheese, and cheap perfume. Whenever he stepped through the doorway, he was reminded of the fetal pig Mr. Scarletto had forced him to dissect in high school. He just wanted to get out as quickly as possible. The walls were painted a cheerful light blue, which did little to help one forget one was surrounded by dead people. The employees all seemed to wear the same nonchalant expression, one that made Porter wonder what he'd find if he took a gander inside their home refrigerators. Nash didn't seem to mind, though. He had stopped halfway down the hallway and was peering into a vending machine.

"How could they run out of Snickers bars? Who's in charge of this shit show?" he grumbled to nobody in particular. "Hey, Sam, can I borrow a quarter?"

Porter ignored him and pushed through the double swinging stainless steel doors opposite a green leather sofa that might have been new around the time JFK took office.

"Come on, man. I'm hungry!" Nash shouted from behind him.

Tom Eisley sat at a metal desk in the far corner of the room, typing feverishly at a computer. He glanced up and frowned. "Did you walk here?"

Porter considered telling him that they did, in fact, drive quite fast, lights and all, but thought better of it. "We were over at Flair Tower. We tracked down the victim's apartment."

Most people would have asked him what they found, but not Eisley; his interest in people started when their pulse stopped.

Nash came through the double doors, the remnants of a Kit Kat on his fingers.

"Feel better?" Porter asked him.

"Cut me some slack. I'm running on fumes."

Eisley stood from the desk. "Put on gloves, both of you. Follow me."

He led them past the desk and through another set of double doors at the back of the space into a large examination room. As they stepped inside, the temperature felt as if it dropped twenty degrees. Low enough for Porter to see his breath. Goose flesh crawled across his arms.

A large round surgical light with handles on either side swung over the exam table at the center of the room, a naked male body lying atop. The face had been covered with a white cloth. The chest had been splayed open with a large Y incision that started at his navel and branched at the pectoral muscles.

He should have brought gum—gum helped with the smell.

"Is that our boy?" Nash asked.

"It is," Eisley said.

The dirt and grime from the road had been washed away, but there was no cleansing the road rash, which covered his skin in patches. Porter took a closer look. "I didn't catch that this morning."

Eisley pointed at a large purple and black bruise on the right arm and leg. "The bus hit him here. See these lines? That's from the grill.

Based on the measurements we took at the scene, the impact threw him a little over twenty feet, then he slid on the pavement for another twelve. I found tremendous internal damage. More than half his ribs cracked. Four of them punctured his right lung, two punctured the left. His spleen ruptured. So did one kidney. The head trauma appears to be the actual cause of death, although any one of the other injuries would have proved fatal. His death was near instantaneous. Nothing to be done."

"That's your big news?" Nash balked. "I thought you found something."

Eisley's brow creased. "Oh, there's something."

"I'm not big on suspense, Tom. What'd you find?" Porter said.

Eisley walked over to a stainless steel table and pointed at what appeared to be a brown ziplock bag filled with—

"Is that his stomach?" Nash asked.

Eisley nodded. "Notice anything odd?"

"Yeah. It's not in him anymore," said Porter.

"Anything else?"

"No time for this, Doc."

Eisley let out a sigh. "See these spots? Here and here?"

Porter leaned in a little closer. "What are they?"

"Stomach cancer," Eisley told them.

"He was dying? Did he know?"

"This is advanced. There's no corrective treatment when the disease gets to this point. It would have been very painful. I'm sure he was well aware. I found a few interesting things in the tox screen. He was on a high dose of octreotide, which is typically used to control nausea and diarrhea. There was also a concentration of trastuzumab. It's an interesting drug. They first used it to treat breast cancer, then discovered it helped with other types of cancer too."

"You think we can track him down with the drugs?"

Eisley nodded slowly. "Probably. Trastuzumab in particular is administered intravenously for an hour, no less than once a week, possibly more often at this stage. I'm not aware of anyone offering this particular medication in private practice, which means he probably went to a hospital or a high-end cancer treatment center. There are only a handful of options in the city. It can cause heart complications, so they monitor patients closely."

Nash turned to Porter. "If he was dying, do you think he stepped out in front of that bus intentionally?"

"I doubt it. Then why kidnap another girl? I think he'd want to see it through." He turned back to Eisley. "How much time do you think he had left?"

Eisley shrugged. "Hard to say. Not much, though—a few weeks. A month on the outside."

"Was he on something for the pain?" Porter asked.

"I found a partially digested oxycodone tablet in his stomach. We're testing his hair for older medications, things that left his system. I imagine we'll turn up morphine," said Eisley.

Porter glanced at the man's dark hair. Hair retained trace evidence of medication and diet. 4MK cut it short, no more than an inch long. The average person's hair grows half an inch per month, meaning they should be able to get a history dating back at least a couple of months. Drug testing of hair was nearly five times more accurate than a urine sample. Over the years, he had seen suspects flush drugs out of their system with everything from cranberry juice to consumption of actual urine. There was no flushing out your hair, though. This was the reason many drug addicts on probation shaved their heads.

"He has hair," Porter said quietly.

Eisley furrowed his brow for a moment, then realized Porter's point. "I didn't find any sign of chemotherapy, not even a single cycle. It's possible they discovered the cancer too late and traditional treatment wasn't an option." Eisley walked over to another table. The man's personal effects were neatly laid out. "That little metal tin right there"—he pointed to a small silver box—"is full of lorazepam."

"That's for anxiety, right?"

Nash smirked. "Being a serial killer is an odd choice of pastime for someone with anxiety issues."

"Generic Ativan. With stomach cancer, doctors sometimes prescribe it to help manage acids. Anxiety leads to increased production, lorazepam cuts it back," Eisley said. "Chances are, he was calmer than any of us."

Porter glanced down at the pocket watch, now tagged and sealed in a plastic evidence bag. The cover was intricately carved, the hands visible beneath. "Were you able to get prints from this?"

Eisley nodded. "He got a few abrasions on the hands, but the fingertips weren't damaged. I pulled a full set and sent them to the lab. Haven't heard back yet."

Porter's eyes landed on the shoes.

Eisley followed his gaze. "Oh, I almost forgot about those. Check this out, very odd." He picked up one of the shoes and returned to the body, then placed the heel of the shoe against the man's bare foot. "They're nearly two sizes too big for this guy. He had tissue paper stuffed in at the toes."

"Who wears shoes two sizes too big?" Nash asked. "Didn't you say those go for around fifteen hundred?"

Porter nodded. "Maybe they're not his. We should dust them for prints."

Nash glanced at Eisley, then around the room. "Do you have a . . . never mind—I got it." He hurried over to another counter and returned with a fingerprint kit. With expert precision, he powdered the shoes. "Bingo."

"Lift them and send them to the lab. Make sure they understand how urgent this is," Porter said.

"On it."

Porter turned back to Eisley. "Anything else?"

Eisley frowned. "What? The drug evidence isn't enough for you?"

"That's not—"

"There is one other thing."

He led Porter to the other side of the body and picked up the man's right hand. Porter tried not to look into the gaping hole in his chest.

"I found a small tattoo," Eisley told him. He pointed at a small black spot on the man's inner wrist. "I think it's the number eight."

Porter leaned in. "Or an infinity symbol." He pulled out his phone and snapped a picture.

"It's fresh. See the redness? He got it less than a week ago."

Porter tried to make sense of it all. "Could be some kind of religious thing. He was dying."

"I'll leave the detecting to you detectives," Eisley said.

Porter lifted the edge of the white cloth covering the head. The material peeled away with a sound not unlike Velcro.

"I'm going to try and reconstruct his face."

"Yeah? You think you can do that?" Porter asked.

"Well, not me," Eisley confessed. "I've got a friend who works at the Museum of Science and Industry. She specializes in this sort of thing—old remains and such. She spent the last six years restoring the remains of an Illiniwek tribe discovered downstate near McHenry County. She normally works with skull and bone fragments, nothing this . . . fresh. But I think she can do it. I put in a call."

"She, huh?" Nash chimed in. "Did you make a lady friend?" He finished with the shoes and packed up the fingerprint kit. "I've got six partials and at least three full thumbs. Three thumbprints, I should say. I don't mean to imply our unsub has three thumbs, although that would make him a lot easier to identify. I'm going to walk these down. Do you want to regroup in the war room? Maybe an hour? I'll check in with the captain too."

Porter thought of the diary in his pocket. An hour sounded good.

16

Diary

Mother saw me, but I did not run away. I knew I should go. I knew this was a private moment, something not meant for my eyes, but I kept watching anyway. I don't think I could have stopped even if I wanted to. I stayed next to that tree until Mother and Mrs. Carter disappeared from view. More accurately, they sank from view, whether to the bed or the floor, I was not sure.

Beneath me, my bucket wobbled. I wobbled. My legs felt like Jell-O. Wiggle waggle! My heart thudded with a parade cadence. I'll tell you, it was exhilarating to say the least!

I found myself so ensconced in this activity, I didn't hear Mr. Carter's car drive past our house. It wasn't until it crunched down the gravel driveway next door that I took notice. Mrs. Carter must have heard the car then too. Like a groundhog on the last day of winter, her head popped up in the window frame, her breasts bouncing, her mouth open in a gasp. She spotted me the same moment I saw her. There was nothing to do, I froze looking back at her. She turned and shouted something, and then my mother appeared. She did not look out at me.

Both disappeared from the window.

Mr. Carter's car door slammed. He was never home at such an hour. Normally he did not return from work until after five, about the same time as my father. He saw me standing next to the tree, perched high on my bucket, and gave me a puzzled glance. I waved. He did not wave back. Instead, he bounded up his front walk and disappeared into his house.

A moment later Mrs. Carter walked briskly out our front door and crossed the lawn, her hands smoothing her dress as she went. She gave me a quick glance as she passed. I offered her a howdy-do, but she did not reciprocate. When she entered her own house, she did so with caution, closing the front door ever so softly behind her.

I jumped down off my bucket and followed her.

I wouldn't call myself a nosy child. I was curious, that's all. So I crossed over to the Carters' lawn without a second thought. I was halfway to their driveway when I heard the slap.

There was no mistaking that particular sound. My father was a firm believer in discipline, and he had brought his hand to my backside on more than one occasion. Without going into detail, I am willing to admit I deserved a good whack or two on each and every one of those occasions, and I hold no ill will toward him for doing so. That sound was well-known to me, and after being on the receiving end (no pun intended) I also recognized the quick scream that followed such pain.

When Mrs. Carter cried out immediately following the slap, I realized that Mr. Carter had hit her. Another slap quickly followed, then another sharp yelp.

I reached Mr. Carter's car. The engine still made a steady tick, tick, tick. Heat floated above the hood, and exhaust filled the air.

Mr. Carter crashed through the front door as I stood beside his car. "What the fuck are you doing out here?" he growled, before pushing past me and walking across the lawn toward my house.

Mrs. Carter appeared in the doorway but stopped at the threshold. She held a damp towel to the side of her face. Her right eye was puffy, pink, and teary. When she noticed me, her lips trembled. "Don't let him hurt your mother," she whispered.

Mr. Carter reached our kitchen door and pounded the frame with his fist. I found it odd that it was closed. Nearly every summer day, the door was opened in the morning and remained that way until late into the night, with only the screen door to keep Mother Nature's creatures out of the house. Mother must have—

I spotted Mother standing in a side window. She glared at Mr. Carter on our back stoop.

"Open the door, you fucking cunt!" he shouted. "Open the goddamn door!"

Mother watched him but remained still.

I started back toward the house, and her hand shot up, motioning for me to stay put. I stopped in my tracks, unsure of what I should do. Looking back, I see it was naive of me to believe I could do much of anything. Mr. Carter was a large man, maybe even bigger than Father. If I attempted to stop him in any way, he would swat me as if I were an annoying fly buzzing around his head.

"You think you can turn my wife into your own personal rug cleaner?" He banged at the door. "I knew it, I fucking knew it, you insatiable little cunt. I knew something was going on. Always over at your house. Smelling of your stink. I tasted you on her, you know that? Believe it. I sure as shit could. Now I think you owe me. A tit for tat. Or how about a tit for a twat—if I dumb it down, does it make more sense to you? There's consequences, you little bitch. There's payment due. Nothing in this world is free!"

Mother disappeared from the window.

Mrs. Carter began to sob behind me.

Mr. Carter turned and shook an angry finger at her. "Shut the fuck up!" His face burned bright red. Sweat glistened on his brow. "Don't think I'm done with you. When I finish up over here, you and I are going to have a long, hard talk. Believe that. When I'm done collecting from this hussy, it's your turn. You think that little scratch hurts? Wait until I come home for dessert!"

It was then our back door opened. Mother stepped out into the light and beckoned him inside.

Mr. Carter stood there for a moment, glaring at Mother. His face as red as a stop sign, his brow all crunched up and sweaty. His hands were balled in tight fists. At first I thought he would hit her, but he didn't.

Mother peered over his shoulder, her eyes locking with mine for a moment before turning back to him. "It's a one-time offer. Now or never." She twirled a finger around a lock of blond hair, then slid it down the side of her neck, a grin playing at her lips.

"Are you kidding me?"

Mother turned back into the kitchen and nodded. "Come on."

He watched her disappear through the doorway, then turned back to his wife. "Consider this part one of the lesson. When I'm done here, I'll be home to teach you part two." He snorted as if he had made the joke of all jokes, then walked into our house, slamming the door behind him.

Mrs. Carter sobbed.

I was but a boy, and I had no idea how to comfort a crying woman, nor did I have any desire to. Instead, I raced back around the house to Mother's window and hopped back up on my bucket. I found the room empty.

From somewhere within the house, I heard a horrible scream. It had not come from Mother.

17

Emory

Emory was going to throw up.

The vomit crept up the back of her throat, thick and vile. She choked it down, cringing at the foul aftertaste.

She took a deep breath, the air catching between sobs.

He had cut off her ear! What the fuck? Why—

The answer came to her in an instant, and she drew in another breath so hard and fast that she whistled before coughing out another sob. The tears welled in her eyes and dripped on her knees. She tried to wipe them from her cheeks, but more came, salty and sharp.

She hiccupped between ragged breaths.

Her body shook with violent spasms. Snot dripped from her nose and mixed with her tears. Just when she thought it was over, her mind would flood with a mix of fear, pain, and anger, and the pattern would start again, lessening only a little each time.

When the fit finally ended, when she was able to reel in a breath and keep it, she found herself sitting in utter silence. Her mind was painfully hollow and quiet, her body sore, muscles aching, her face puffy and red. Her fingers brushed over the handcuffs, searching for some kind of release, hoping they weren't real handcuffs but the kind you buy in a sex shop or a toy store—her friend Laurie had told her about those, how her boyfriend wanted to use them and she said no way, nohow.

There was no release switch, and the band around her wrist was tight; they weren't coming off without a key. She could try to pick them, but that would mean finding something to pick them with, and that would mean exploring.

Who was she kidding? She had no clue how to pick a lock.

The handcuffs had an abnormally long chain on them too, at least two feet, the kind you find in prison movies where the bad guy's hands are shackled to his feet and he's forced to shuffle down some dark hallway. The cuffs were designed to allow some movement but not much.

She knew of the Four Monkey Killer. Everyone in Chicago did, possibly everyone in the entire world. Not just that he was a serial killer, but the way he first tortured his victims before killing them, mailing body parts back to their families. First an ear, then—

Emory's free hand went to her eyes. The room was dark, but she could still make out faint outlines. He hadn't touched her eyes.

Not yet. Maybe he'll have time when he gets back.

Her heart pounded within her chest.

How long before . . .

She couldn't think about it. She just couldn't.

The idea of someone taking out her eyes, taking them out when she was alive.

Your tongue too, dear. Don't forget about the tongue. He likes to take that third and mail the little stump of flesh back to Mommy and Daddy. You know, right before he finally—

The voice in her head seemed oddly familiar.

You don't remember me, dear?

Then she knew, just like that, she knew, and anger swirled.

"You're not my mother," Emory said, seething. "My mother is dead."

Christ. She was going crazy. Talking to herself. Was it the shot? What had he given her? Was she hallucinating? Maybe all of this was just some kind of nasty dream, a bad trip. She might be—

You should try to figure the rough patches all out later, dear. When you have more time? Right now I think you should focus on finding a way out of this place. You know, before he gets back. Don't you agree?

Emory caught herself nodding.

I only want what's best for you.

"Stop."

When you're safe. Until then . . . this is a tough spot, Em. I can't write you a note and get you out of this one. This is way worse than the principal.

"Quiet!"

Silence.

The only sound was that of her own breath and the blood pumping at her ear, warm and throbbing under the bandage.

Where your ear used to be, dear.

"Please don't. Please be quiet—"

Better that you accept it now. Accept it and move on.

Emory lowered her legs over the side of her makeshift bed. The wheels squeaked as the gurney rolled a few inches before scraping against a wall and stopped. When her feet touched the cold concrete, she almost pulled them back up. Not knowing what was beneath her creeped her out, but remaining still while waiting for her captor to return was not an option she was willing to consider. She had to find a way out.

Her eyes fought the darkness, trying to adjust and pull in the smallest bit of light, but there simply wasn't enough. She raised her hand to her face, and it was barely visible unless she practically touched her nose.

Emory forced herself to stand, ignoring the dizziness swooning through her head and the pain at her ear. She took a deep breath and held the edge of the gurney for balance just below where her handcuffs were attached, standing still until the nausea left her.

It was so dark. Too dark.

What if you fall, dear? What if you try to walk, trip over something, and fall? Are you sure this is wise? Why don't you sit back down and figure things out. How would that be?

Emory ignored the voice and tentatively reached out, her left hand stretching into the blackness, her fingers groping. When they found nothing, she took a step toward the top of the gurney, toward the wall it rested against. Right hand on the gurney, left hand reaching. One step, then another, then a—

Her fingers found the wall, and she nearly jumped back. The rough surface felt damp and grimy. Cautiously running her hand across the wall, she found a groove and traced the edge with the tip of her finger, following horizontally until she found another groove, this one vertical. The pattern repeated about a foot down. Rectangles.

Cinder blocks.

You know, where there's one wall, there's usually another. Sometimes there's a door or a window or two. Perhaps a walk of the perimeter is in order? Figure out just what kind of mess you've gotten yourself into? You're tied to that pesky gurney, though—not really fit for travel.

Emory tugged on the gurney until the frame moved, rolling an inch or so on squeaky wheels. She squeezed the rail. Just holding the metal frame, holding on to something, made her feel a little safer. It was silly, she knew that, but—

It's a crutch. Isn't that the word?

"Fuck you," she muttered.

With her left hand on the wall and her right dragging the gurney, she inched along, her feet shuffling. She counted as she went, attempting to map out the space in her mind's eye. She took twelve steps before finding the first corner. Emory estimated the first wall to be about ten feet long.

She continued along the second wall. More cinder block. She ran her fingers up and down the wall in search of a light switch, a door, anything, but she found none; only more block.

Emory stopped for a second, her head turning up. She couldn't help but wonder—how high could this room be? Was there a ceiling?

Of course there's a ceiling, dear. Serial killers are smart; you're not the first girl to attend his rodeo. He's taken how many girls? Five? Six? He's probably got the routine down to a science at this point. I'm sure this room is sealed up tight. You should keep exploring, though. I like this. Much better than sitting around waiting for him to come back. That's a fool's game. This has purpose. This shows initiative.

She continued around the room. The gurney fought again as she turned the corner, and she pulled the frame toward her with an angry yank.

Hey. I just thought of something. What if he's watching you? What if he's got cameras?

"It's too dark."

Infrared cameras can see in the dark plain as day. He's probably got his feet up on a desk somewhere, watching Emory TV, *a big, fat grin on his face. Naked girl in box. Naked girl trying to get out of box. The last girl took thirty minutes to venture this far around the room. This one is on a tear—she got there in twenty. How exciting. How entertaining.*

Emory stopped moving and stared into the blackness. "Are you there? Are you . . . watching me?"

Silence.

"Hello?"

Perhaps he's shy?

"Shut up."

I bet he's got his pants around his ankles and his pecker out with a DO NOT DISTURB *sign on the door.* Emory TV After Dark *is on, and the party is just getting started. This one's a keeper. Did you see how high she jumped?*

"Now I know you're not my mother; she would never say that," Emory said.

Well, I think he's watching. Why else would he take your clothes? Men are perverts, dear. The whole lot of them. The earlier you realize that, the better.

Emory turned in a slow circle and peered into the darkness, her head tilted up. "There's no camera in here. I'd see the little red light."

Right. Because all cameras have little red lights. Flashing little red lights you can spot from a mile away. I know if I were a camera manufacturer, I'd never consider building one without the little red flashing light. I'm sure there's an oversight committee that checks each of them to be sure—

"Will you shut the fuck up?" Emory shouted. Then her face flushed. She was fucking arguing with herself.

All I'm saying is not all cameras have little red lights, that's all. No need to get huffy.

Emory let out a frustrated breath and reached back for the wall. In her mind's eye, she pictured the room as a giant square. She had checked two walls without finding the door. That left two more.

She began to inch across the third wall with the gurney in tow, her fingers following the now familiar cinder block pattern, drawing a path through the thick dust. No door.

One wall left.

She pulled at the gurney, more angry now than scared, counting off the steps. When she reached twelve and her fingers found the corner, she stopped. Where was the door? Had she missed it? Four corners, four left turns. She knew she had traveled full circle. She had traveled full circle, right?

Was it possible the room didn't have a door?

Well, that seems like a horrible design. Who builds a room without a door? I bet you skipped right past the opening.

"I didn't miss it. There's no door."

Then how did you get in?

High above her, a click echoed over the walls. Music screeched down at her so loud, it felt as if someone had jammed knives into her ears. She slammed her hands against the sides of her head, and a lightning bolt of pain shot through her as her left hand impacted the tender flesh where her ear had been. The handcuff cut into her other wrist. She bent forward and cried out in pain. She couldn't block out the music, though—a song she had heard before. Mick Jagger howling about the devil.

18

Porter

Day I • II:30 a.m.

Although only two weeks had passed since the last time Porter stepped into room 1523, deep within the basement of Chicago Metro headquarters on Michigan Avenue, the space seemed dormant, lifeless.

Sleeping.

Waiting.

He flicked on the light switch and listened as the fluorescent bulbs hummed to life, sending a charge through the stale air. He walked over to his desk and shuffled through the various papers and files scattered across the surface. Everything was just as he had left it.

His wife watched him from a silver frame at the far right corner. He couldn't help but smile at the sight of her.

Sitting on the edge of the desk, he pulled the phone over and punched in her cell number. Three rings, followed by her familiar voice mail message:

You've reached the phone of Heather Porter. Since this is voice mail, I most likely saw your name on caller ID and decided I most certainly did not wish to speak to you. If you're willing to pay tribute in the form of chocolate cake or other assorted offerings of dietary delight, text me the details and I'll reconsider your position in my social roster and possibly—

Porter disconnected and thumbed through a folder labeled *Four Monkey Killer*. Everything they had learned about him fit in this single folder, at least until today.

He had chased the Four Monkey Killer for half a decade. Seven dead girls.

Twenty-one boxes. You can't forget about the boxes.

He'd never forget the boxes. They haunted him every time he closed his eyes.

The room wasn't very large, thirty by twenty-five or so. Aside from Porter's, there were five metal desks older than most of the Metro staff arranged haphazardly around the space. In the far corner stood an old wooden conference table Porter had found in a storage room down the hall. The surface was scratched and nicked; the dull maple finish was covered with tiny rings from the hundreds of glasses, mugs, and cans that had sat upon it over the years. There was a large brown stain on it that Nash swore resembled Jesus (Porter thought it only looked like coffee). They had given up trying to scrub the discoloration away a long time ago.

Behind the conference table stood three whiteboards. The first two held pictures of 4MK's victims and the various crime scenes; the third was currently blank. The group tended to use the last one primarily for brainstorming sessions.

Nash walked in and handed him a cup of coffee. "Watson hit Starbucks. I told him to meet us down here after he checks in with the lieutenant upstairs. The others are on their way too. What's going through that head of yours? I smell smoke."

"Five years, Nash. I was beginning to think we'd never see an end to this."

"There's at least one more out there. We need to find her."

Porter nodded. "Yeah, I know. And we will. We'll bring her home." He had said the same thing with Jodi Blumington just six months earlier, and they didn't find her in time. He couldn't face another family, not again, not ever.

"Well, there you are!" Clair Norton hollered from the doorway.

Porter and Nash turned from the whiteboards.

"This place has been like a morgue without you, Sammy. Give me some sugar!" She crossed the room and wrapped her arms around him. "If you need anything at all, you call me, okay? I want you to promise me," she whispered at his ear. "I'm there for you, twenty-four/seven."

Any attempt at affection made Porter nervous. He patted her on the back and drew away. He imagined he appeared as uncomfortable as a priest returning the hug of an altar boy with the eyes of the congregation upon him. "I appreciate that, Clair. Thanks for holding down the fort."

Clair Norton had been on the force for nearly fifteen years. She became Chicago Metro's youngest black female detective after only three years on patrol, when she helped break up one of the largest narcotics rings in the city's history—every person involved was under eighteen. Twenty-four students in total, primarily from Cooley High, although the crimes spread across six high schools. They operated completely on school property, which made things difficult, and meant the young-looking Clair had to go undercover as a student.

The event had earned her the nickname Jump Street, after the old Fox TV show—nobody on the task force dared call her that to her face.

Clair shook her head. "Hell, you should be thanking me for babysitting your partner over there. He's as dumb as a box of rocks. I bet if you locked him in a room, you'd come back an hour later to find him dead on the floor with his tongue stuck in an electrical outlet."

"I'm standing right here," Nash said. "I can hear you."

"I know." She turned and plucked the coffee from his hand. "Thank you, baby doll."

Edwin Klozowski, "Kloz" to most, strolled in behind her, an overflowing briefcase in one hand and the remains of a Little Debbie chocolate cupcake in the other. "So, we're finally getting the band back together? It's about time. If I had to spend one more minute down in Central IT dissecting the hard drive of another porn lover gone rogue, I might have considered going back to video game design. How you doing, Sammy?" He reached out and smacked Porter's shoulder.

"Hey, Kloz."

"Good to see you back." He dropped his briefcase on one of the empty desks and shoved the rest of the cupcake into his mouth.

Porter spied Watson standing at the door and motioned for him to come inside. "Kloz, Clair, this is Paul Watson. He's on loan from CSI. He's going to be helping us out. Has anyone seen Hosman?"

Clair nodded. "I talked to him about twenty minutes ago. He's running Talbot's finances but hasn't come up with anything yet. Said he'll get in touch with you as soon as he finds something."

Porter nodded. "All right, let's get started."

They crossed the room and settled at the conference table. The Four Monkey Killer's victims stared down at them from the whiteboards. "Nash, where's that picture of Emory?"

Nash dug the photo out of his pocket and handed it to him. Porter taped it onto the board at the far right. "I'm going to run through this from the beginning. It's old news for most of you, but Watson hasn't heard it before and maybe we'll pick something up from the refresher." He pointed to the picture in the top left corner. "Calli Tremell. Twenty years old, taken March 15, 2009. This was his first victim—"

"That we know of," Clair interjected.

"She's the first victim in his pattern as 4MK, but the evidence suggests he's sophisticated and had most likely killed before," Klozowski said. "Nobody comes out of the box killing like him. They build up, developing methods and technique over time."

Porter went on. "Her parents reported her missing that Tuesday, and they received her ear in the mail on Thursday. Her eyes followed on Saturday, and her tongue arrived on Tuesday. All were packaged in small white boxes tied with black strings, handwritten shipping labels, and zero prints. He's always been careful."

"Suggesting she wasn't really his first," Klozowski reiterated.

"Three days after the last box arrived, a jogger found her body in Almond Park. She had been propped up on a bench with a cardboard sign glued to her hands, which read DO NO EVIL. We had picked up on his MO when her eyes arrived, but that sign confirmed our theory."

Watson raised his hand.

Nash rolled his eyes. "This isn't third grade, Doc. Feel free to speak up."

"Doc?" Klozowski repeated. "Oh, I get it."

"Didn't I read somewhere that was how he picked his victims? 'Do no evil'?" Watson asked.

Porter nodded. "With his second victim, Elle Borton, we caught that. Initially we thought the victims themselves had done something 4MK deemed wrong, and that was why he went after them, but with Elle we learned his focus wasn't on the victims at all but on their families. Elle Borton disappeared on April 2, 2010, nearly a year after his first victim. She was twenty-three. Her case was handed to us when her parents received her ear in the mail two days later. When her body was found a little over a week after that, she was holding a tax return in her grandmother's name covering tax year 2008. We dug a little bit and discovered that she actually died in 2005. Her father had been filing false returns for the past three years. We brought Matt Hosman in from Financial Crimes at that point, and he discovered that the scam went much deeper. Elle's father had filed returns on more than a dozen people, all deceased. They were residents of the nursing home he managed."

"How could 4MK possibly know that?" Watson asked.

Porter shrugged. "Not sure. But the new evidence prompted us to go back and look at Calli Tremell's family."

"The first victim."

"Turns out her mother was laundering money from the bank where she worked, upward of three million dollars over the previous ten years," Porter said.

Watson frowned. "Again, how could 4MK know what she was doing? Maybe that's the link. Figure out who has access to this information, and you find 4MK's identity."

Klozowski snorted. "Yeah, 'cause it's that easy." He stood up and walked to the board. "Melissa Lumax, victim number three. Her father was selling kiddie porn. Susan Devoro's father swapped fake diamonds for the real ones at his own jewelry store. Barbara McInley's sister hit and killed a pedestrian six years before Barbara went missing. Nobody connected the sister to the crime until 4MK. Allison Crammer's brother ran a sweatshop full of illegals down in Florida. Then there's Jodi Blumington, his most recent victim—"

"Prior to Emory Connors," Nash chimed in.

"Sorry, his most recent victim prior to Ms. Connors. Her father was importing coke for the Carlito Cartel." He tapped each of the photos. "All of these girls are related to someone who did something bad, but there is no connection between them. The crimes are across the board, no common thread."

"He's like a vigilante," Watson muttered.

"Yeah, with better intel than law enforcement. None of these crimes were on our radar; we found them while investigating the murders," Porter told him. "Without 4MK, these people would still be on the streets."

Watson stood and walked over to the board, his eyes narrowing as he reviewed the photographs one by one.

"What's up, Doc?" Kloz said, before bursting into laughter.

Everyone stared at him.

Kloz frowned. "Oh, so it's funny when Nash does it, but not the IT guy? I see how things work down here in the basement."

Watson tapped the board. "He's escalating. Look at the dates."

"Escalated," Nash said. "His killing days are behind him."

"Right, escalated. About one per year until after his fifth victim, Barbara McInley, then about every six or seven months. There's this too." He pointed at the photo of Barbara McInley. "She's the only blonde. All the others are brunettes. Is there any significance to that?"

Porter ran his hand through his hair. "I don't think so. With these kills, he's really punishing the families for their crimes. I don't think it was ever about the victims for him."

"All these other girls are similar in appearance. Pretty, long brown hair, close in age. For someone without a type, he sure seems to have a type. All but Barbara, the only blonde. She's an anomaly." Watson paused for a second before asking, "Were any of the girls sexually assaulted?"

Clair shook her head. "Not one."

"Did any of the girls have a brother?"

"Melissa Lumax, Susan Devoro, and Calli Tremell each had brothers; Allison Crammer had two," Clair said. "I spoke to them when I interviewed the families."

Watson nodded, the gears churning in his head. "If we assume half these families had at least one son and he grabbed their children at random, one or two male victims should have presented. That didn't happen, so there was a reason he took the daughters over the sons—we just don't know why."

Porter cleared his throat. "Honestly, I'm not sure that matters anymore. We don't need to worry about his future victims. Like Nash said, he's done killing. We need to focus on his last one."

Watson returned to his chair. "I'm sorry. Sometimes my mind starts going down all these paths and I lose focus."

"Not at all. This is why we asked you to join us. You're a fresh pair of eyes on some old evidence and information."

"Fair enough," Watson said.

Porter picked up a blue marker and wrote EMORY CONNORS in large letters at the top of the third board. "Okay, what do we know about our victim?"

"According to the front desk at her building, she left for a jog yesterday at a little after six in the evening," Clair said. "They said that was the norm for her. She ran nearly every day, usually in the evenings. Nobody saw her come back."

"Did anyone know where she liked to run?" Nash asked.

Clair shook her head. "They only saw her come and go."

"I might be able to answer that," Kloz said. He was pecking away at a MacBook Air. "She wore a Fitbit Surge."

"A what?"

"It's a watch that monitors your heart rate, calories burned, distance traveled. It also has a built-in GPS. I found a program installed on her computer that recorded all the data. I'm accessing the information now."

"Any chance the GPS is still active?"

Kloz shook his head. "Doesn't work that way. The watch records the GPS data as you wear it, then syncs to the cloud with a phone app or by interfacing with a computer. She paired with her phone—that's dead too, but I think I know where she went." He flipped his Mac around so the others could view his screen. A map filled the display. There was a dotted blue line beginning at Flair Tower, which followed West Erie Street toward the river. At the water's edge, the trail circled a large green space. "I found the same pattern nearly every day." He tapped the screen. "This is A. Montgomery Ward Park."

Porter leaned in close. His eyesight was going to shit. "Clair, you want to check it out when we finish up here?"

"Will do, boss."

He turned back to Kloz. "Did you find anything else on her computer?"

Kloz flipped the Mac back around and pecked at the keys. "You gave me the opportunity to legally search the hard drive of a hot teenage girl. Needless to say, I was thorough."

Clair wrinkled her nose. "Fucking sicko."

Kloz smirked. "I pride myself on my sicko-ness, my dear. One day you will thank me." He studied the screen for a moment. "Emory's boyfriend's name is Tyler Mathers. He's a junior at Whatney Vale High. And"—all the cell phones in the room beeped simultaneously—"I shot you a recent photo, his cell phone number, and home address," Kloz said. "They've been beau and boo for about a month. She thinks they're exclusive."

"And they're not?" Porter asked.

Kloz grinned mischievously. "I may have taken a peek at his private Facebook messages, and our boy is a bit of a player."

The group stared at him.

"Oh, come on! If you use your wife's or girlfriend's name as your password, you deserve to get hacked."

Porter made a mental note to change his e-mail password. "Next time, wait for the warrant. We don't need you mucking up the case."

Kloz saluted him. "Yes, my cap-i-tan."

Porter wrote TYLER MATHERS on the whiteboard and drew an arrow to the boy in the homecoming picture with Emory. "Nash and I will pay Tyler a visit this afternoon. Anything else on her PC?"

"Emory has a Mac, a very nice one at that. Please don't insult such a fine piece of engineering by calling it a PC. Such insults are beneath you," Kloz said.

"Forgive me. Anything else on her Mac?"

Kloz shook his head. "No, sir."

"What about the three outgoing numbers on the landline?"

Kloz held up his hand and ticked off three fingers. "A pizza place, a Chinese place, and Italian takeout. This girl knows how to eat."

Clair cleared her throat. "There's a T. Mathers on the permanent guest list. The only other person listed is A. Talbot."

Porter wrote ARTHUR TALBOT on the whiteboard with the word FINANCES? directly beneath. "I'm really curious to see what Hosman turns up on this guy. 4MK took this girl for a reason; I'm willing to bet the guy's crooked."

"Why not bring him in?" Clair asked.

"We bring him in and he'll just lawyer up—we won't get a thing out of him. If we need to talk to him again, I think it's best to keep it an informal setting, try and catch him off-guard someplace he feels comfortable. He's more likely to slip," Porter told her. "He's also a bigwig around town, buddies with the mayor and who knows who else. If we bring him in early, we may get nothing, then if we try to bring him back, he may call one of his buddies to run interference. Best to wait until we have something concrete."

"This is interesting," Kloz said. His eyes were fixed on his Mac-Book again. "The fancy elevators in that building record all the card traffic in and out."

Porter groaned. "Are you operating under the same warrant you used to hack the boyfriend's Facebook page right now? 'Cause if you are—"

Kloz raised both hands. "Come on now, do I look like a repeat offender?"

"Oh, hell yeah," Clair said under her breath.

"Fuck you too, Ms. Norton."

She smirked and stuck out her tongue.

"The building manager was kind enough to provide access to us," Kloz said.

"What do you see?" Porter asked.

He pursed his lips and squinted as he scrolled through a text file. "We've got Emory going down at 6:03 p.m. yesterday; she never comes back. All is quiet until 9:23 p.m.; then an N. Burrow goes up. She came back down at 9:06 this morning."

"That's only a few minutes before Metro arrived," Clair said.

"I'm willing to bet that's our missing housekeeper," Porter said. "Can you run that by the front desk at Flair Tower? Ask if they can provide a full name?"

"Will do," Kloz said, making a note.

Porter drew in a breath. "All right, that brings us to the man of the hour, our victim from this morning." He told the group what they had learned from Eisley.

"Shit, he was dying?" Kloz said.

"Less than a month left."

"Do you think he stepped in front of that bus intentionally?"

"I think we need to consider that a possibility," Porter replied. He wrote 4MK on the board and listed the following:

Dry cleaner receipt
Expensive shoes—two sizes too big
Cheap suit
Fedora
.75 in change (two quarters, two dimes, and a nickel)
Pocket watch
Dying of stomach cancer

"I can't believe the fucker was dying," Kloz muttered, picking at something on his arm.

Porter tapped on the whiteboard. "What do the personal items tell us?"

"The dry cleaner receipt is a bust," Clair said. "Aside from the number, there's no identifying information, not even the name or address of the cleaners. It's from a generic receipt book that can be ordered from hundreds of shops online. Half the cleaners in the city use the same one."

"Kloz, I want you on that. Create a list of all cleaners within five miles of the accident this morning, and contact each one. Find out if they use this particular type of receipt. If they do, ask if number 54873 is active. Obviously, 4MK won't be picking it up. Even if you find more than one, we'll be able to narrow down the list as the other tickets get closed out. If you don't find anything, expand your search grid. He was walking, though—I think the cleaners will be close."

Kloz waved at him. "I accept your challenge."

Nash scanned the board. "What do we do about the suit and shoes?"

"Kloz can check all the shoe stores while he's running the dry cleaners," Clair said.

Kloz raised his middle finger and stuck his tongue out at her.

Porter stared at the board a moment. "I'd rather Kloz focused on the cleaners. The size mismatch definitely bugs me too, but it's just noise right now. We'll keep the info on the board in case it comes into play later."

"Coins aren't much of a clue, either," Nash pointed out. "Everyone in this room probably has a pocket of change right now."

Porter considered erasing the seventy-five cents, then changed his mind. "We'll leave that up there too." He turned to Watson. "Any luck on the pocket watch?"

"I'll head over to my uncle's shop once we finish up here," he replied.

Porter turned back to the board. "I think we'll find him with this," he said as he drew a line under DYING OF CANCER. "Eisley said he found octreotide, trastuzumab, oxycodone, and lorazepam in his system. Trastuzumab can only be administered by a handful of centers in the city. We need to reach out to each of them with a description of 4MK and hunt for missing patients."

"I can do that," Clair said. "How many fedora-wearing, cheap suit buying, expensive shoe owning stomach cancer patients can there possibly be out there? That's where the clothing items will help us. He'd stand out walking into a treatment center dressed like that."

"Good point," Porter said. "Eisley also found a small tattoo on the man's right inner wrist." He loaded the image onto his phone's screen and passed it around the room. "It's fresh. Eisley said he probably got inked within the past week."

Kloz studied it closely. "Is that an infinity symbol? Kinda ironic for a guy on his way out the exit door."

"It obviously meant something to him," Clair said, leaning over his shoulder to get a better look. "If you're going to permanently mark your body, you put some serious thought behind your ink."

Kloz grinned up at her. "Speaking from experience? Is there something you want to show the group?"

She winked at him. "You wish, geek boy."

Porter reached into his pocket, removed the diary, and dropped it onto the table. "Then there's this." They all fell silent for a moment and stared at it.

"Shit, I thought Nash made that up," Kloz said. "The fucker really had a diary on him? Did you log that into evidence? There's no reference on the case log."

Porter shook his head. "I don't want the press to know. Not yet."

Kloz whistled. "4MK's handwritten manifesto? Hell, that's worth a fortune."

"It's not a manifesto. It reads more like an autobiography, dating back to when he was a kid."

Kloz leaned back in his chair. "What, like, 'Today Becky Smith wore that little red dress I like to school. It made me happy. I decided to follow her home and ask her if she'd go steady with me. When she said no, I gutted her in her living room. Tomorrow is pizza day in the cafeteria. I like pizza, but not as much as burgers, burgers with cheese are—'"

Clair threw a pen at him.

"Ow!"

Nash nodded at the diary. "Okay, I'm going to ask about the elephant in the room. Have you flipped to the end? What's on the last page?"

Porter reached out and gave it a little push. The book slid across the table, stopping in front of his partner. "Go ahead, take a peek."

Nash's eyes narrowed as he reached for the diary. The room had gotten very still. He turned the book over and opened to the last page, reading aloud.

Ah, good sir. Didn't your mother ever tell you sneaking a look-see at the end of a good book before you've earned the right is a mortal sin? Authors around this great planet of ours are spinning in their graves, rolling their eyes in disgust, or flat out wishing ill will on you and yours. I would like to say I am truly disappointed in you, but that would be a lie. If circumstances were reversed and I were standing in your shiny loafers, I no doubt would have done the same. But alas, the answers that you seek are not to be found here at the end. I suggest you pour yourself a nice cup of joe, plant your posterior in your favorite chair, and turn back to the beginning. You really should start there, don't you think? How could you understand how our story will end without knowing how I began? To know me is to know my reasons, and there are reasons. You only need to know where to take a gander. You need to understand how to read between the silly little lines. That's half the fun, isn't it? Learning how to play the game? Good luck, my friend. I'm rooting for you, I really am. This is all such fun, don't you think?

Nash flipped through a few more pages before tossing the diary back onto the table. "Motherfucker."

Porter shrugged. "Told you."

Porter picked up the diary. "I've been reading this thing, and I'm still not sure what to make of it. It's an autobiographical account of 4MK's life, but so far I haven't come across anything that will help us find Emory. All I've found are the ramblings of a very disturbed individual."

"The fucker is dead and he's still taunting us."

"Maybe you should make some copies; if we all read it, we'll get through it faster," Clair said.

Porter shook his head. "We don't have time to turn this into a book club, and I want all of you focusing on your assignments. I don't trust anyone outside this room with it, so that leaves me. I'm a quick read—I find anything, I'll get it out to you."

"What about the camera at the scene?" Watson asked. "Has anyone reviewed the footage yet?"

"I put in a requisition, but Central hasn't provided an analysis yet," Kloz said. "I'll chase it down."

"At the very least, the video will tell us if he jumped in front of that bus on purpose, or if it was really an accident," Porter replied. "If we're lucky, we may get a good shot of his face."

Nash shrugged. "My money is on suicide. Why else would he be carrying that book? He knew somebody was going to read it soon, or he wouldn't have written that last page. He wanted to check out on his own terms rather than let the cancer eat him up. I'd be willing to bet he wanted us to find that book as a final fuck-you."

"If he planned to kill himself, why do it before he even mailed the ear?" Watson asked. "Wouldn't it make more sense to finish with the last victim first?"

"Serial killers aren't the most rational members of the tribe," Nash told him. "He may have held on to the ear, knowing it would help us ID him as 4MK." He turned back to Porter. "Don't forget to tell them about Eisley's girlfriend."

Porter nodded. "Yeah, almost forgot. Eisley's got a friend at the museum who may be able to reconstruct his face from his skull. A *female* friend. If that pans out, we may get a usable photo."

"Eisley has a girlfriend? Who dates a guy who works in the morgue?" Kloz wondered aloud.

"Sounds like she volunteered. I'm not going to turn down the help," Porter said.

Watson was staring at the image of the tattoo again. "You know, this could all be about legacy."

"What do you mean?"

He set the phone back down. "He was dying, so he writes the journal, then he kidnaps his last victim and steps in front of that bus, knowing we'd identify him as 4MK because of the ear in the box. The infinity tattoo might mean just that—he plans to live on forever."

"A tidy bow on a serial killer's life," Porter said softly.

"The really smart ones, the ones who skirt law enforcement for so long, eventually they want people to know. They want credit for their work. If you're 4MK, would you want to die knowing the world would never know who you really are?" Watson shook his head. "Of course not; when you've eluded capture for as long as he has, you'd want to shout from a rooftop. We can't touch him now, and he gets to go down in the history books."

Porter knew the kid was right. "What does that mean for Emory?"

The room fell silent. Nobody had an answer.

Evidence Board

Victims

1. Calli Tremell, 20, March 15, 2009
2. Elle Borton, 23, April 2, 2010
3. Missy Lumax, 18, June 24, 2011
4. Susan Devoro, 26, May 3, 2012
5. Barbara McInley, 17, April 18, 2013 (only blonde)
6. Allison Crammer, 19, November 9, 2013
7. Jodi Blumington, 22, May 13, 2014

Emory Connors, 15, November 3, 2014
Left for a jog, 6:03 p.m. yesterday

TYLER MATHERS
Emory's boyfriend

ARTHUR TALBOT
Finances?

N. BURROW
Housekeeper? Nanny?

ITEMS FOUND ON 4MK
Expensive shoes — John Lobb/$1500 pair — size 11/UNSUB
    wears size 9
Cheap suit
Fedora
.75 in change (two quarters, two dimes, and a nickel)
Pocket watch
Dry cleaner receipt (ticket 54873) — Kloz is narrowing down
    stores
Dying of stomach cancer — meds: octreotide, trastuzumab,
    oxycodone, lorazepam
Tattoo, right inner wrist, fresh — figure eight, infinity?

Info needed:

- Was Emory enrolled in school? If yes, where?
- Emory and Tyler relationship
- Facial reconstruction

Assignments:

- Clair — A. Montgomery Ward Park, check cancer centers
- Nash and Porter go to see Tyler
- Kloz, research the dry cleaner ticket, get security camera footage — can we see his face?
- Watson, visit uncle regarding the watch. Background on Emory's mother

19

Diary

Father arrived home from work promptly at 5:43 p.m. His black Porsche crawled up the driveway like a jungle cat hunting its evening prey, the engine purring with excitement. He hopped out of the driver's seat and set his briefcase on top of the car. "Whatcha doing, champ?"

The top must have been down at some point, because his hair was askew. Father's well-groomed pompadour was never askew. He ran his hand through his thick mane, and all was right again.

I glanced nervously at our house. Hours had passed, but Mr. Carter had not come out. Mrs. Carter had vanished too, though for that I was grateful. Crying on one's front porch is unbecoming a lady, even one as pretty as Mrs. Carter.

"I'm hungry," Father said. "Are you hungry? I bet your mother has quite a feast waiting for us inside. What do you say we head in and get something to eat? How would that be?"

He mussed my hair with one of his burly hands. I tried to shake him off, and he did it again, this time adding a little chuckle. "Come on, champ." With one hand grabbing his briefcase and the other on my shoulder, he steered me toward the house.

My stomach twisted and I thought I might toss my cookies, but the feeling passed. I tried to walk slowly, to slow him down, but my efforts did little good. He tugged me along.

We walked up the back steps and pushed through the door into the kitchen. I felt eyes on my back. I turned for a moment and saw Mrs. Carter standing at a window, watching us. She held something against the side of her face. It looked like a bag of frozen peas.

Mother stood at the kitchen sink, drying dishes. As we entered, she smiled warmly and gave Father a little peck on the cheek. "How was your day, sweetie?"

Father returned the kiss and set his briefcase on the counter. "Oh, same old . . . something smells wonderful. What is that?" He took in a deep breath and walked over to the large pot on the stove.

Mother wrapped her arm around him. "Why, I made beef stew, your favorite! What else would it be?"

My eyes darted wildly. First the kitchen, then the living room, the hallway. The doors to both bedrooms and the bath stood open. There was no sign of Mr. Carter. I knew he hadn't left. I was certain of this. He would have had to pass me. He would have—

"Well, it smells delicious," Father crooned. "Why don't you set the table, champ? I'm going to pour myself a little something nice on the rocks."

Mother grinned at me. "Soup bowls and dinnerware, dear. Maybe those pretty red ones?"

I imagine my eyes were saucers, but Mother didn't seem to notice. She started to whistle, donned oven mitts, and carried the stew pot over to the dining table.

I stood frozen for a moment, my gaze fixed on her, then I went to the silverware drawer and pulled out three soup spoons. Although I had grown tremendously over the past year, I still couldn't reach the cabinet that housed the bowls. We kept a small stepladder in the kitchen for such moments. I climbed up, retrieved three, and proceeded to set the table.

Father returned with his drink and took a seat, tucking a napkin into his shirt. "So, what did you do today, buddy?" he asked me.

I glanced back at Mother. She was busy slicing a loaf of bread.

Mr. Carter wasn't in the kitchen, the bedrooms, or the living room. Father would have seen him. He hadn't left. I knew he hadn't.

"Just hung around. Not much," I replied.

Mother set the bread on the table and sat. She scooped a ladleful of stew and filled my bowl to the brim. "Large helpings all around!" She beamed.

I stared at the stew.

Father grinned at Mother. "What about you? How was your day?"

Mother filled his bowl with a portion equal to mine. "Oh, things were fairly quiet around here. Not much worth mentioning."

I stared at the stew.

Mr. Carter was nowhere to be seen.

She wouldn't . . . she couldn't. Right?

As I reached for my spoon, my stomach lurched. I felt as if I were about to vomit the mother of all vomits. I tried not to breathe in the beefy aroma drifting up from my bowl, the spices and scents. The stew actually did smell wonderful, and that thought made the vomit climb a little closer to the exit door.

I watched Father take a heaping spoonful and shove it into his mouth, chewing with delight. Mother watched us both as she also ate a spoonful, much more delicately than Father. I watched her smile, then dab at the corners of her mouth with her napkin. "Do you like it?" she asked. "I tried a new recipe."

I was aghast.

Father nodded happily. "This may be the best beef stew you have ever created. You are a culinary wizard, my dear."

"May I be excused?" I said, my gut twisting.

Mother and Father both turned to me as they chewed poor Mr.—

A loud moan came from the basement.

Father and I both turned toward the sound. Mother did not. She continued eating, her eyes fixed on her bowl.

"What was—"

Then it came again, unmistakable this time—a man moaning downstairs.

Father stood. "It came from the basement."

"You should finish your dinner, sweetie," Mother said.

Father walked slowly toward the door leading downstairs. "What's going on? Who is that?"

"Your stew will get cold. Nobody likes cold stew."

I got up and stood behind Father as he reached for the doorknob and twisted the worn brass.

I didn't like to go down into the basement. The stairs were steep and creaked under the slightest weight. The walls were damp and grimy. The ceiling harbored more spiders than the forest behind our house. There was only a single fixture: a bare bulb hanging at the center of the room. I always feared it would go out while I was down there. If it did, there would be no escape. I'd be trapped down there forever, the spiders descending on me one by one by one.

Monsters lived in the basement.

Father opened the door and flicked on the light switch. The bulb came to life with a yellowish glow at the base of the long staircase.

Another moan. This one louder, more urgent.

"Stay here, champ."

I wrapped my arms around him and shook my head. "Don't go down there, Father."

He pulled my arms off. "Stay up here with your mother."

Mother was still sitting at the dining table, humming a little ditty to herself. I think it was a Ritchie Valens song.

Father started down the steps. He was halfway down before I decided to go after him.

20

Clair

Day I • 1:17 p.m.

Clair stood beside a large stainless steel sculpture in A. Montgomery Ward Park. According to the plaque, it was called COMMEMORATIVE GROUND RING. She had seen it a number of times from a distance as she drove across Erie, but now, standing so close, she had to admit she had no fucking idea what the pile of metal was supposed to be. To Clair, it looked like Godzilla had eaten the inventory of a stainless steel appliance shop before taking a shit in the middle of this pristine park.

Clair shielded her eyes from the sun and surveyed her surroundings.

The park wasn't large, but Clair understood the appeal, particularly for a runner like Emory. A trail followed the perimeter, skirting along the river's edge on the west side. She spotted a playground to her left and a large fenced-in area to her right. Inside, at least ten dogs ran around with their owners chasing balls, Frisbees, and the occasional small child.

She counted twelve people in with the dogs. At the other end of the park, six adults were positioned around the playground in various states of child monitoring. Clair flipped a mental quarter, decided it landed on heads, and started toward the swing sets.

As she approached, the various mothers and two men eyed her warily.

"Hello, there!" she said in her most disarming tone. Not disarming enough—the two men forced smiles while nervously glancing around the group. Three of the mothers took their children by the hand. One even positioned her daughter behind her. You clearly needed a kid to get invited to this party—strange adults wandering the park alone were not welcome. Clair was beginning to reconsider her decision. These people seemed as if they might bite far worse than the dogs at the other end of the park. She held up her ID. "My name is Detective Norton; I'm with Chicago Metro. I'm going to need your cooperation."

Behind her, three patrol cars and a CSI van screeched to a halt, lights flashing but no sirens. A dozen officers piled out of them. The back of the van opened up, and three techs joined the group.

A woman dressed in black slacks and a gray sweater pulled her daughter from a swing and walked over. "What's going on?"

Clair knew if she mentioned 4MK, this group would grab their children and disappear into the bustling afternoon streets before she'd get the chance to ask a single question. *Vague is not lying,* she told herself. *I can be vague.* "We believe a girl disappeared from this park yesterday. If you can give us a few minutes, we'd like to ask you some questions."

A heartbeat ticked by, and they all started speaking at once—first to one another, then at her. She couldn't make out a single word. Three of the children started crying for no reason other than to be heard over the adults. Clair raised her hands above her head. "I need everyone to be quiet, please!" A fourth child started to scream. At the other side of the park a dog barked, followed by another and two more after that. Within moments, they had joined the voices in an ear-splitting mess of noise. "Enough!" she shouted in a tone she typically reserved for boyfriends just before she ended the relationship and sent them on their merry way.

The adults fell silent, with the children quickly following suit. All but one little chubby boy who stood near the teeter-totter. He continued to cry in big lumbering sobs, his face bright red and covered in a mix of snot and tears.

Gray Sweater Woman picked up her daughter and bounced her gently in her arms. "Did someone take her from here? We do our best to keep an eye on the kids, as a group. This is a nice neighborhood, but you never know who you're dealing with anymore; so many crazies out there." She paused for a second, then her mouth went wide. "Oh God, did somebody take the Andersons' little girl? I haven't seen Julie and her mother at all today. She's such a sweet baby. I hope nothing—"

Clair raised her hand. "It's not a child."

Hushed murmurs of relief swept the crowd. Gray Sweater gave the others an *I got this* look and turned back to Clair. "Who, then?" Apparently she was Queen of the Mothers, because the group yielded to her. Even the crying of the children began to peter out.

Clair loaded the photo she had received from Kloz onto her phone's screen and held it out to the woman. "Her name is Emory Connors. She's fifteen years old. We believe she came to the park last night around six for a run and was abducted. Do you recognize her?"

The woman reached for the phone. "May I?"

Clair nodded and handed it to her.

Her forehead crinkled as she squinted at the display. Her eyes narrowed and she turned back to the crowd. "Martin?"

The two men were standing at the back of the crowd. The one on the right, wearing khaki pants and a light-blue dress shirt, pushed his thick glasses up the bridge of his nose and walked over. The woman handed him the phone. "That's her, right?"

He bobbed his head. "God, I told you something was wrong. We should have called the police."

Clair retrieved her phone and clipped it to her belt, then pulled a small notepad and pen from her back pocket. "Martin? What's your last name, Martin?"

"Ortner. Martin R. Ortner." He began to spell it, but she waved him off.

"And you?" she asked, returning her gaze to the woman.

"Tina Delaine," she said. "Most of us are here a few times a week.

This time of year, though, I try to get out daily. You know, while it's still warm. Better for these kids to burn off the energy here than at home."

Clair took inventory of the children. Aside from the few clinging to their parents, they were huddled around the swing set. All but Tee-ter-Totter Boy, who was busy wiping the snot from his face with his sweater. Where were his parents? She turned back to Tina Delaine. "What did you see?"

Tina took the lead. "She runs here almost every day. Yesterday, when she circled that back corner, I lost her in the trees. She usually pops out the other side a few seconds later, but she didn't. I told Martin, and we decided to check on her. We got about halfway there and this guy came out of the trees, cradling her in his arms. He said he saw her twist her ankle and fall, banging her head on the way down. He said he knew her and he'd take her to the hospital, said that would be faster than calling an ambulance. Before either of us could respond, he rushed away, loaded her into the passenger seat of his car, and took off."

"And you didn't call the police?" Clair asked, frowning.

"He said he knew her," Martin replied, his voice soft.

"What kind of car was he driving?"

Tina pursed her lips. "A white Toyota."

Martin shook his head. "His car wasn't white. It was beige."

"No, he had a white Toyota. I'm sure of it."

"It definitely wasn't white. It was beige, or possibly silver. He wasn't driving a Toyota, though. I think it was a Ford, a Focus or a Fiesta."

"Where was he parked?"

Martin pointed to a small row of parking spaces at the end of Erie. "Right over there, under that lamppost."

Clair glanced over; she didn't see any security cameras. "Okay, all of you stay here for a minute. I'll send one of the officers back to take your statements."

"Will we get to do one of those things with a sketch artist?" Tina asked. "I've always wanted to do that!"

"How about a lineup?" Martin chimed in.

"Please, just wait here," Clair told them, before turning and stomping toward the group of officers.

Lieutenant Belkin recognized her and waved her over. "I've got officers canvassing up and down Erie and Kingsbury. What's the story here?"

Clair tilted her head back toward the mother brigade. "Those two standing out in front said they've seen her running in the park regularly. Yesterday she followed the path back behind those trees, disappeared for far too long, and then some guy carried her out. She may have been unconscious. He told them she fell and sustained a head injury, and he was taking her to the hospital. Told them he knew her."

Belkin pulled off his hat and ran his hand through his thinning blond hair. "Christ, so he snatched her like that? Did they get a good look at him?"

"They saw him load her into a white, beige, or possibly silver Toyota or Ford," Clair said. "If their recall is that bad on the vehicle, good luck getting a physical description. I only talked to the two out in front. We need to speak to all those people over at the dog park too. Get someone over there to make sure nobody tries to sneak out of here."

He pointed to two of the officers huddled in front of the CSI van and issued instructions to his team.

Clair nodded a thanks to him, then turned away to call Porter and fill him in. It wasn't much, but it was something.

21

Diary

Father was nearly downstairs before I mustered the courage to follow him. He frowned, his eyes first telling me to retreat to the kitchen, then rolling as he realized I would do no such thing.

As Father reached the bottom of the staircase, there was another moan — this one more urgent than the others. Father froze at the base of the steps, staring at something in the far corner of the basement. "Oh my. Mother? What have you done?"

Upstairs, Mother now sang rather than hummed, dishes clattering. Was she getting a second helping of stew? She did not respond to Father, although I was sure she had heard him as clearly as I heard her.

I came down the last of the steps and followed Father's gaze to the pile of a man huddled in the corner. He was handcuffed to a thick water pipe. A cloth stuck out of the corners of his mouth from under two long pieces of duct tape, which wrapped all the way around his head.

His hair will come out with those when they're finally pulled off, I thought. Yanked from his scalp, roots and all.

Mr. Carter's eyes were pleading. His white dress shirt had been torn open, the buttons no doubt lost among the dust bunnies and dirt littering the floor. His chest was riddled with long cuts, some starting as high as his shoulder and stretching all the way to his belly button. One appeared to go much lower, and I tried not to think about that one. It hurt to think about that one.

His tattered shirt and pants were dark with blood. It pooled under him so thick, the sweet scent of copper hung in the air. Both eyes were bruised, well on their way to black, and his nose was surely broken.

Father stared down at him. "This is not how we treat our neighbors. He appears to be in quite a pickle."

I tried to respond, but my dry throat only let out a weak grunt.

Mr. Carter glared at both of us, thin whimpers behind the gag. Tears stained his cheeks and the collar of his shirt.

Mother rumbled down the stairs behind us. She glowered at Mr. Carter with a contempt and heat that broiled through the room. "That, that . . . man, and I use that term in the loosest possible sense, beat his beautiful wife earlier today, then thought it proper to come over here and wave his man-bits about while telling me how he would give me what he felt I had coming. Well, I didn't believe I had anything coming, and I wasn't about to stand for the treatment he bestowed on poor little Lisa. God knows she would never do anything to hurt anyone, not even this sorry excuse."

Father pondered this for a moment. "So you beat him and chained him up in our basement?"

"Oh, I didn't beat him. I pushed him down the stairs, chained him to the water pipe, then went to work trying to slice the evil out of him. It was messy work, and even after three hours I'm afraid I only made a dent in it. I worked up such an appetite, though. I figured I would continue after we ate dinner, a dinner that is getting cold as we speak."

Father nodded slowly. Then he walked over to Mr. Carter and knelt at his side. "Is this true, Simon? Did you beat your wife? Did you come here, to my house, and threaten the woman I love? The mother of that beautiful little boy over there? Did you do these things, Simon?"

Mr. Carter shook his head violently, his eyes jumping from Father to Mother and back again.

Mother pulled a long knife out from behind her back and charged at the man. "Liar!" she screamed. She plunged the knife into the fat of the man's abdomen, and he cried out from behind the gag. His face first flushed, then went pale, and she pulled the knife back out.

Surprisingly little blood flowed from the wound. I found it fascinating how I could now see past his pale flesh to the yellow fat and dark muscle beneath. The cut opened and closed with each breath as if drawing in air on its own. I took a step closer to get a better look.

Mother raised the knife again.

If Father wished to stop her, I had no doubt that he could. He didn't, though. He watched her calmly from where he crouched beside Mr. Carter.

Mother brought the knife down into the man's thigh with such force, the tip clunked as it passed through his leg and struck the concrete floor. He let out another shriek, then began to cry again. I found this to be a little funny. Grown men should never cry. Father told me so.

Mother twisted the knife nearly a full turn, then yanked the blade back out. This time there was blood, a lot of blood. A fresh pool began to form under his twitching leg.

I couldn't help but smile. I didn't like Mr. Carter. I didn't like him one bit. And after what he did to Mrs. Carter? It was nice to see him get what he deserved. Women are to be respected and cherished, always. He would learn.

22

Porter

Day I • 1:38 p.m.

Whatney Vale High School was a squat three-story steel and glass building located just north of the University of Illinois at Chicago. Typically ranked in the top five high schools in Illinois, Whatney was one of the most sought-after schools in the city. A school security guard led Porter and Nash through the hallways to the main office and told them to wait there while he located the principal. Less than a minute passed before a short, bald man stepped inside. He was fidgeting with an iPad. "Good morning, gentlemen. I'm Principal Kolby. What can I do for you?"

Porter shook the man's hand and showed his badge. "We need to speak with one of your students, Tyler Mathers. Is he in class today?"

Kolby glanced nervously at the two women standing behind the main counter. They were watching the men intently. Three glaring students occupied a group of chairs along the wall.

"Why don't we step into my office?" He smiled, gesturing to a small room on the left.

After entering and taking a seat behind his desk, Kolby asked, "Tyler? Is he in trouble?"

Porter and Nash settled into the two chairs facing the principal. They were small and low to the ground, uncomfortable. Porter instantly felt as if he were in trouble, transported back to his own youth.

His palms were sweaty. Although shorter by at least four inches, Principal Kolby looked down at him from his large leather seat. His gaze had an authoritative edge to it that made Porter feel like he was five minutes from detention. He shook it off and leaned forward. "Not at all. We just need to speak to him about his girlfriend."

Kolby frowned. "Girlfriend? I wasn't aware he had one."

Nash loaded an image on his cell phone and slid it across the desk. "Her name is Emory Connors. Is she a student here?"

Kolby picked up the phone and studied it for a moment before keying the name into his computer and reviewing the results. "She is not." He returned the phone to Nash, then pressed a button on his desk. "Ms. Caldwell? Can you locate Tyler Mathers and ask him to report to my office?"

"Yes, sir," a disembodied voice replied.

Porter glanced over at Nash. He was never this quiet. His hands were folded neatly in his lap, and he didn't make eye contact with the principal. Porter could only guess at the kind of trouble his partner created during his time as a student; he must have been a common fixture in the principal's office. Kolby picked up on it too, but rather than saying anything he only smiled smugly and tapped away at his iPad. "Looks like he's in calculus, on the third floor. It should only be a few minutes. Can I offer you gentlemen something to drink?"

Porter shook his head.

"No, sir," Nash replied. "No, thank you."

Five minutes later there was a knock at the door and a boy of about sixteen stepped inside. He eyed the two detectives, then nodded at Kolby. "You asked for me, sir?"

Kolby stood. "Come on in, Tyler. Close the door behind you. These two gentlemen are with Chicago Metro. They would like to speak to you for a moment."

Tyler's eyes went wide. No doubt his brain was quickly sorting through everything he had done recently, trying to find the one event that would bring the police calling.

Porter put on his most reassuring smile. "Relax, son—you haven't done anything. We just need to talk to you about Emory."

He appeared puzzled. "Em? Is she okay?"

Porter turned back to Kolby. "Would you be kind enough to give us a few minutes to speak with Mr. Mathers?"

Kolby shook his head. "I'm sorry, but he is a minor. I'm afraid without a parent present, I'll need to remain in the room."

"Fair enough," Porter replied. He rose out of the tiny chair and sat on the edge of the desk, blocking Kolby's view of the student. Nash did the same. Behind them, Kolby cleared his throat but said nothing.

"When was the last time you saw Emory?"

Tyler shuffled his feet. "Saturday, I guess. We caught a movie and ate dinner downtown. Is she okay? You're making me nervous."

Porter glanced at Nash. "We believe she's been kidnapped."

The boy's face went white. "Who would . . . why?"

"We believe she was taken from A. Montgomery Ward Park while jogging yesterday. It's about a mile—"

Tyler nodded. "I know where it is. She runs there all the time. God, I told her not to go alone, but she never listens to me." His eyes filled with tears, and he wiped them on his sleeve. "She's such a pretty girl, and she wears these little jogging outfits. I'm always telling her it isn't safe. This city is full of crazies, you know? Oh, God. I've been texting her nonstop and she hasn't replied. That's not like her. I usually hear back after a minute or two at the most. But she's been quiet since yesterday. I planned to go over to her place right after school gets out."

"Where does she go to school?"

"She doesn't. I mean, she does, but she's homeschooled. Tutors, mostly," Tyler said.

"Is that who lives there with her? A tutor?"

Tyler nodded. "Ms. Burrow."

"What's her first name?"

"I don't know, sorry. She keeps to herself mostly when I go over there. I don't talk to her that much."

"Any idea where we might be able to find her?"

Tyler shook his head again. "Do you think she's okay? Emory, I mean. I can't believe someone would do this."

Behind them, Kolby stirred. Porter had nearly forgotten he was in the room.

"Is there anything I can do to help?" Tyler asked.

Porter pulled a card from his back pocket and handed it to him. "If you hear anything, call me."

"Did you guys track her phone? You can do that, right?"

"Her phone hasn't been on the network since yesterday," Nash told him. "Most likely it's been disabled."

"Both of them?"

23

Diary

Freshly showered, all damp-haired and smelling of baby powder, I strutted out of my bedroom back to the kitchen. I'd worked up quite an appetite, and the beef stew smelled simply wonderful. Plopping down into my seat at the table, I scooped mouthful after mouthful, reminding myself to chew. The Ritchie Valens song Mother sang earlier had firmly planted itself between my ears, and I found myself humming along as I ate. I always had excellent rhythm even at such a young age.

Mother and Father were still in the basement. Their laughs climbed the steps and echoed as they reached the top. They were having such fun. I lost interest when Mr. Carter checked out for the third and final time. I think it was his ticker that gave out. He had lost a lot of blood, that was sure, but not enough to kill him. The human body can typically lose 40 percent of its total volume before shutting down. Someone the size of Mr. Carter easily carried nine or ten pints. I doubt he lost more than two or three pints in total. It can be difficult to tell sometimes, but when it puddles on concrete like it did downstairs, it's an easy measure.

No, it wasn't blood loss—the fear did him in.

I watched from the stairs as Father removed Mr. Carter's eyes with a pop. I don't think Mr. Carter realized it even happened at first, but then Father put the eyes in Mr. Carter's own hand for safekeeping. He held them far too tight. Father laughed at this while Mother kept cutting. Little cuts at first, only a few deep ones. She was a tease like that —she would cut an inch or so at his shoulder, just enough to get his attention, then plunge the knife deep into his thigh with a twist (she loved to twist the knife). Without his eyes, he didn't know where or when the next cut would come. I imagine such suspense tended to really get the old ticker pumping. When Mr. Carter started to slip into shock, Father sent me upstairs to fetch the smelling salts. Nobody wanted him passing out on us in the middle of all the excitement. What fun would that be? After a while, though, there was little we could do to keep him awake. Shock tends to be a spoiler.

In the end, he inhaled a deep gasp. His body contracted in a spasm, then went rigid, then fell limp against the concrete. I think he soiled himself again, but with such a mess already, I couldn't really tell. Mother had started this one, so I knew Father would make her clean up. That was the rule. Father loved his rules.

Another round of laughter from downstairs. What could they still be doing?

I was reaching for another helping of stew when I heard the knock at the screen door in our kitchen. I turned to see Mrs. Carter standing on the other side. Both her eyes were a horrible shade of purple. A large bruise covered her left cheek too. She cradled her left wrist with her other hand. "Is my husband here?" she said in a soft voice.

I reached for my napkin and dabbed at the corners of my mouth. There was no reason, really; I wasn't a sloppy eater, but I needed a moment to think.

"He hasn't come home. It's been hours." Her voice was low, raw. She had been crying for a long time. I wondered just why she would want him to come home. He had done a number on her. Would she really let him waltz right back in as if nothing had happened?

I got up from the table and walked toward the door. I could see the lock—it wasn't engaged. At no point did I consider inviting her in, but that didn't mean she wouldn't come in of her own accord. She wasn't a stranger to our home. Typically she'd rap a couple of times on the frame and come right in. Why not? She didn't this time, though. She stood on the back stoop, swaying. She stood watching me from battered purple eyes that really wanted to close, little more than slits.

"Let me ask Mother. Give me a minute?" I said in my grown-up matter-of-fact voice, the one that implied complete casualness and confidence, the one that said, You can trust me. I'm here to help you in the fullest, kind ma'am!

She nodded. An act that must have pained her, because her face twisted into a slight grimace with the movement.

I offered a smile before bounding down the steps to the basement.

24

Porter

Day I • 3:03 p.m.

They found Kloz huddled at his workstation at the far back corner of the IT department. His desk was a cluttered mess of manuals, loose paper, fast food wrappers, and a large collection of Batman memorabilia. Nash reached for a replica of the Batmobile, only to get smacked with a ruler before he could pick it up. "When I come to your house, I don't play with your Barbies. Don't touch my stuff," Kloz growled.

"What did you find?" Porter asked him.

"The second line's a dead end," Kloz said, "but check this out." He pointed to the center screen of his five-monitor setup. A city transit bus was frozen at the far right of the screen. Near the left side, a handful of people stood at the corner, waiting to cross the street.

Porter leaned in close. "Do you see him?"

Kloz pointed at a small space on the screen between a large man in a dark suit and a woman pushing a stroller. "See that? It's the top of his fedora."

Nash squinted. "I can't make it out."

"I'll roll the video forward." Kloz tapped a few keys, and the image advanced. The woman leaned down and whispered something to the child in her stroller. For the briefest of seconds, he was visible standing behind her. The fedora was pulled down at a slight angle, shielding his face from the camera, but it was definitely him.

"Can you get in tighter?" Porter asked.

Kloz twisted a small control next to his mouse, and the image zoomed in. "The picture gets too grainy when I get up close. Doesn't really matter, though—that hat is in the way. Check this out."

He hit the Play button again, and the scene moved forward in slow motion. Porter watched the bus crawl across the screen at a fraction of the vehicle's normal speed, inching toward the intersection. In the top right corner of the screen, a traffic light blinked green. "The driver wasn't lying. The light was green when he approached."

Kloz poked the screen with his pen. "Keep an eye on our guy."

As the bus neared, the man in the fedora stepped in front of the others. His face shielded by the hat, he glanced down the road, then down at the pavement. In one quick motion, he pushed off the curb and launched himself into the street. His feet never touched the ground —his shoulder met the grill of the bus, and the impact threw him forward. Even at reduced speed, things happened fast. His body seemed to mold with the bus's nose. Then he peeled away and sailed through the air, disappearing from the screen.

"Damn," Nash muttered.

The bus rolled past, leaving the people at the corner staring in disbelief.

"Uniforms talked to all these people, and none remember the guy," Kloz told them. "Most of them were buried in their phones, walking on autopilot. Nobody was able to provide a description. You'd think a guy in a fedora would stand out."

"He clearly jumped. That's for sure," Nash said. "He never planned to reach the mailbox. Suicide by mass transit."

"I've rolled the footage a hundred times, different speeds and zooms. There is no clear shot of his face," Kloz said. "If you ask me, he played to the camera. The crazy outfit makes him stand out, yet he positioned the hat at just the right angle to block a good shot. He knew exactly what he was doing, and I think he wanted us to see him but not his face—hence the outfit."

"So 4MK knows he's dying, and rather than let nature take its course, he snags one last victim, puts on his best suit, and sets some kind of stage to ensure his legacy?" Porter pondered aloud. "He expected us to find the ear and make the connection. He leaves the diary because it spells out his history on his own terms, details where he came from. He wrote his own story so the history books get it right. He's always been meticulous. Why leave something so important open to reporters and crazies on the web? None of this is as random as it first appeared. I'm not sure any of it is random. To me, that means the other items we found on him—the watch, the dry cleaner receipt, maybe even the change, all of it may have been intentional."

Nash frowned. "I think you're reaching, Sam."

"A cheap suit, fedora, the shoes that don't fit . . . I don't think he left anything to chance. He's still toying with us, playing some kind of game, telling a story. All of this fits together. Somehow, it all means something."

"Or it could be random shit he happened to have on his person when he kissed that bus."

Porter sighed.

"Not everything is a conspiracy, that's all I'm saying," Nash said.

"This guy operated for years without leaving a single clue. Now all this. It's something." Porter's phone rang. He snatched it from his pocket and took the call. He nodded as the caller spoke. When he hung up, he grabbed his keys from Kloz's desk. "That was Murray at Flair Tower. They picked up Burrow coming up the service elevator."

25

Diary

I found Mother and Father rolling around on the bloodstained floor, their limbs twisted in an embrace. They howled like schoolchildren at the height of recess. I held my finger up to my mouth and shushed them both.

"What is it, champ?" Father said, stopping long enough to wipe a long strand of Mother's hair from her face, leaving behind a crimson trail, perhaps a little fatty tissue. It was difficult to tell; she was a mess.

"Mrs. Carter is upstairs, at the back door," I said softly. "She's looking for Mr. Carter. She saw him come over earlier. She saw him come inside with Mother. I watched her from the yard."

Father's face was difficult to read, always had been. He turned to Mother. "Is that true? Did she see?"

Mother shrugged. "I suppose it's possible. He acted completely unreasonable, violent even. I simply defended myself. Lisa will understand. She's a very understanding woman."

Father's eyes quickly glanced around the basement, taking in the scene. Mr. Carter lay in a bloody heap, still chained to the pipe, his body ravaged far worse than when I had grown bored and returned upstairs. They'd continued after he died—slicing, cutting. What remained was no longer a man; it was a pile of meat, the discarded plaything of a predator.

"She's upstairs," I repeated. "Right now."

Mother sighed. "Well, we're in no condition to receive visitors."

Father chuckled at this. "Perhaps we should ask her to stop by later?"

"I think the back door is unlocked. She could come in," I said. "She might be inside right now."

Father detangled himself from Mother and stood. "That would be unfortunate."

I had to agree.

"Do you think you can send her away?" Father asked me.

"I — I don't know," I stammered.

"You're a big boy now, champ, practically a man of the house. You're smarter than her, I have no doubt about that. Puzzle it out, find a way."

She couldn't see Mother and Father, not like this. And they'd never sneak past her. The back door was in direct sight of the basement door.

Part of me hoped she had come in, that she stood on the steps right now, listening. I thought of her at the lake; I thought about what it would be like to have her chained in the basement.

"What do you say, champ? Think you can handle her?"

I nodded. "Yes, sir."

26

Emory

Day 1 • 3:34 p.m.

Emory huddled in the corner under the gurney with one hand pressed to her ear, the other ear against the wall. She couldn't block out the music, though. It was too loud, louder than any stereo she had ever heard. She had gone to the Imagine Dragons concert last spring at the Allstate Arena with Kirstie Donaldson, and they stood about three feet from the stage and directly in front of the largest stack of amplifiers she had ever seen. They were so powerful, the sound actually blew their hair back over their shoulders, which made for some epic selfies.

This was much louder. Not only louder, the music echoed off the walls. It reverberated. The rhythm rattled her bones.

When the music first started—hours ago, it seemed—she screamed at the top of her lungs, but the music drowned her out. Her voice had been lost behind Pink Floyd, then Janis Joplin, followed by a dozen other bands she recognized but didn't know by name. She screamed anyway, the anger, hatred, and fear burning within her and needing a way out. She screamed until her throat went raw, and she was sure her voice was gone, whether she could hear it or not. She screamed until her tongue turned into sandpaper and a migraine sliced at the back of her eyes.

Emory tried to bury her head between her knees and that helped for a little while, but now her right shoulder burned from the awkward angle. She pulled at the handcuffs in frustration, but they only cut further into her wrist. She wanted to cry but had run out of tears hours earlier.

She was so cold.

Against her naked body, every surface felt damp and chilled.

"Mom?" Although she spoke the word aloud, she didn't hear it. It vanished behind the theme song from *CSI* by the Who. Or the What . . . "Are you still there, Mom?"

She lifted her head from between her knees and looked up. The music came from somewhere far above her. Over the hours, Emory's eyes had adjusted slightly to the darkness. Although still almost absolute, she could discern subtle shapes. She saw the legs of the gurney, the ones near her anyway. She could make out her hand above her cuffed to the railing, and even a little of the railing itself. She tried sliding the cuffs from one end to the other, hoping the strand would slip off the end, but instead it just rounded a slight corner before clanking against another bar, which crisscrossed it, blocking the cuff from moving any more. Then she —

Something scurried over her foot and Emory screeched, pulling her legs in close.

What was it? A roach?

No. It was too big to be a roach. Maybe a mouse or a —

Please don't let it be a rat. She hated rats. She saw them sometimes poking out of the sewers. Beady little eyes and sharp yellow teeth clattering with hunger as they scurried out to back-alley dumpsters in search of food. They would eat anything. She'd heard they sometimes attacked the homeless people in herds or packs, only that wasn't what they were called. She knew the term; it had been on a science test a few years ago. *A mischief.* That was it. A group of rats was called a *mischief.* It sounded like a silly name to her then and seemed even more ridiculous now, but there it was. The only thing worse than one rat was more than one rat. A mischief.

"Mom?"

Something brushed against her thigh, and she jumped up, banging her head on the gurney. Please no, not rats. They could see in the dark, probably really well. She pictured the furry little creature standing in the corner of the room glaring up at her, its tiny mouth filled with drool and disease.

I don't want to be a Debbie Downer, but I have to ask. What does a rat trapped in a cement box with a naked girl tend to eat?

Emory groaned, and for a second she heard herself. Then a guitar solo started and burned away any trace of other sounds. She scrambled on top of the gurney.

I know rats are not picky eaters. They tend to be grateful for any food offered up. I imagine a nice tender young girl would be the highlight of the dinner menu, though, don't you agree? You would be like Kobe beef compared with a dried up old homeless person.

Emory peered down into the darkness around her. She felt it down there watching her, but she couldn't see it.

I wonder if they can climb.

The gurney squeaked as she shuffled on her butt to its center.

I bet if there are a lot of them, they can make a little rat pyramid and get right on up. They're resourceful little critters. I've been told they'll sometimes bite their victim in the cheek to get them to open their eyes so they can pluck one right out of the socket. A little bait and switch. Mischievous. Hey, that might be where that term comes from. Mischievous little critters are full of mischief.

"It's not a rat," Emory told herself. "How would a rat get in here?"

Ah, there's the rub. Although he did put you in here. Maybe he dropped in a rat or two or three. After all, the man cuts off body parts and mails them back to their families; his choice in entertainment is questionable at best. He may not be playing with a full deck.

Emory's heart pounded—a rhythmic *thump, thump, thump* at her damaged ear.

This time when the rat scurried past, she saw it for sure, if only for a second before the plump little rodent disappeared into the gloom.

27

Diary

I ascended the steps at a snail's pace as my brain churned away, attempting to devise a believable story. Just how to keep her from entering the house, or worse—going down into the basement?

I found her sitting at the kitchen table. She had been crying again. She dabbed at her eyes with a damp napkin while picking at a slice of bread.

As I reached the top of the steps, I pulled the door closed at my back. The frame tended to swell during the summer months, and I had to give the knob a good tug before it would shut properly.

I crossed the kitchen and sat at the table, my eyes fixed on the cold stew. "There's a problem with our water heater, and Mother is downstairs helping Father try and fix it."

I spoke the words softly, so low I barely heard them. It wasn't the most creative of lies, but it would have to do. I looked up at her, at her tired face.

Mrs. Carter returned the gaze. The bruises had grown darker in just the past few minutes; the swelling had worsened. How could a man do such a thing to someone he loved? Her knee bounced under the table. When she spoke, her voice was weak and distant. "He's dead, isn't he."

It was more of a statement than a question, spoken flatly, without even a hint of emotion.

"They're working on the water heater. That old beast can be a bear to fix," I said.

She shook her head and sighed. "You can tell me the truth. It's okay."

Father asked me to handle her. He wanted me to puzzle it out. If I told her, would they kill her too? If she had to die, would it be my fault?

She needed to know, though. She had every right to know. If I didn't tell her, what would she do? Go home and call the police? Worse still, tell them Mr. Carter had come over here and not returned home? I had to tell her. "He tried to hurt Mother. She defended herself. Nobody would blame her for doing so."

She sighed again. Her hand tightened on the crumpled napkin in her palm. "No, I suppose not."

"I should take you home," I told her.

Mrs. Carter wiped her nose with the back of her hand. "What about . . . what did they do with . . . oh, God, is he really dead?"

The tears came again. Years later I would ponder this. Women seemed to have an endless supply. They came so easily and in such force at the drop of an emotional cue. Not men, though. Men rarely cried, not from emotion, anyway. For them, pain brought on the water-works, pain turned that spigot all the way to full blast. Women were perfectly capable of handling pain but not emotion. Men handled emotion but not pain. The differences were sometimes subtle, but they were there nonetheless.

I never cried. I doubted I even could.

I stood up from my chair and offered my hand to Mrs. Carter. "Come on. Let me get you home."

28

Porter

Day I • 4:17 p.m.

Officer Thomas Murray met Porter and Nash at the front door of Emory's apartment with a cup of coffee in one hand and a ham sandwich in the other. Murray had mayonnaise on the corner of his mouth, and another blotch was slowly dripping down the front of his uniform shirt. Porter considered telling him about the errant condiment, then decided to let it go. He was curious how long it would take to slide all the way down the front and drip to the floor. Nash caught it too but said nothing. The two exchanged a knowing glance. "Making yourself at home?" Porter asked him, stepping inside.

Murray took a bite of the sandwich and wiped his mouth on his sleeve. "Beats being trapped in a patrol car for eight hours," he muttered between chews. He nodded his head back toward the living room. "That couch over there has Magic Fingers or something built in. You just sit down and the cushions give you a massage. The television somehow knows when you're there too—it snaps on when you enter the room. Not that I'm sitting down on the job or anything —not for more than a minute or two, anyway. Oh, and downstairs they've got a full restaurant and deli. That's where I got this. It may be the best sandwich I ever had." He took another bite. A chunk of ham fell from the bread and landed on his shoe.

"Where is she, Tom?" Porter asked, his patience thin.

Murray pointed down the hallway, nearly spilling his coffee. "She's in her room, left door, not the right. First name's Nancy, by the way. Nancy Burrow. She's a real firecracker."

Porter pushed past him and started down the hall. Murray followed.

As Nash walked by, he said: "I want one of those."

Murray frowned. "The sandwich or a coffee?"

"The couch," Nash replied.

"Ah yeah, me too." Murray took another bite and swore as the mayonnaise finished its trek and landed on the hardwood floor with a decisive splat.

The bedroom door was closed. Porter rapped softly. "Ms. Burrow? I'm Detective Sam Porter with Chicago Metro. May I come in?"

"It's open, Detective," a woman's voice replied from the other side. She had a slight Australian accent, which reminded him of Nicole Kidman's.

Porter twisted the knob and opened the door.

Okay. A large Nicole Kidman. At least 250, possibly more.

Nancy Burrow was sitting at the desk in the corner, with a book resting in her plump lap. She frowned as he stepped inside. "That Neanderthal out there locked me in my quarters while he pillaged the kitchen and God only knows what else. You better believe I'll be filing a complaint with your supervisor, not to mention Mr. Talbot. He will not stand for this, that is for sure. Somebody even had the nerve to go through my clothing, my personal items. What gives you the right to do such a thing?"

Porter offered his best *we come in peace* smile. "I apologize, Ms. Burrow. We're all just trying to do our best to find Emory. Mr. Talbot gave us permission to enter the premises. Nobody was here, and we went about searching for anything that could help us find his little girl. If we rifled through your personal items, we had the best intensions at heart."

Her eyes narrowed. "And you expected to find a clue or two in my underwear drawer?"

Porter had no response to that. He glanced at Nash, who only shrugged. He decided to ignore the question. "How about you tell us where you were earlier?"

"I went shopping."

"She had groceries on her when she came back," Murray said from the doorway. "But I don't get how anyone spends seven hours in the Food Mart."

She let out a deep sigh. "If you must know, today is my personal day. I had my hair done and ran a few other errands. Since when is leaving one's own apartment a crime?"

Porter shifted his weight to his other leg. "When was the last time you saw Emory, Ms. Burrow?"

"She went out for a run last night around six. Quarter after at the latest," she said. "It looked like rain, but she wanted to go anyway."

"And you weren't concerned when she didn't come back?"

Burrow shook her head. "I assumed she went to her boyfriend's house. The two of them have been spending a lot of time together of late."

"At what point did you realize something was wrong?"

Her eyes shifted to the book in her hands. "I'm not sure I did. Like I said, she sometimes visits with her boyfriend."

"She's fifteen," Nash said. "Eight o'clock? Nine o'clock? Ten? What's her curfew? I've got a daughter her age. There's no way I'd let her run around the city after dark, especially with some boy."

"I'm not her mother, Detective."

Porter gestured to the pictures on her nightstand. "You played a big part in raising her. You obviously care about her."

Burrow studied the pictures, then turned back to the detectives. "I've done my best to be there for her, and I'll be the first to admit, over the years we have grown quite close, but her father has made it clear I am simply a member of his staff, nothing more, one who could be easily replaced should I step over any particular line. My own feelings about Emory aside, I enjoy the job and harbor no desire to see my employment come to an end."

"What exactly is your job, Ms. Burrow?" Nash asked.

"Primarily, I am Emory's tutor. I've been with her since her mother passed. I oversee her studies as well as the household staff."

"Like Mrs. Doubtfire?"

She frowned. "Who?"

Porter pushed him aside. "Never mind. Emory doesn't go to school?" Porter asked.

The woman let out another long sigh. "The school system in your country leaves much to be desired, Detective. Mr. Talbot wanted Emory to receive the best possible education. Such a level can only be obtained on a one-on-one basis. I graduated at the top of my class at Oxford. I hold two doctorate degrees, one in psychology, another in literature. I also spent three years at the Center for Family Research at Cambridge. I've created an environment where Emory's intellect can flourish rather than be held back by the incompetence of your schoolteachers and the peers she would encounter in a local school. She was reading at a fifth-grade level by the age of six. Her math skills exceeded your high school levels by the time she was twelve. She'll be prepared to leave for university next year—two years earlier than most students in your country."

She stated these facts as if reading from her own résumé, Porter noted. She had most likely defended homeschooling on more than one occasion.

"Who disciplines her? Who tells her not to drink? Who screens her boyfriends? Why does she even have a boyfriend at fifteen?" Nash asked.

Ms. Burrow rolled her eyes. "If you instill the right values in a child at a young age, you'll find her maturity far exceeds most. Such a child deserves trust."

"So if she wants to run around the city at all hours of the night, it's okay to turn a blind eye?" Nash growled.

"Nash, that's enough," Porter said.

"I'm sorry, but to me it seems if this girl had a parental figure in her life, she wouldn't be out jogging alone so close to dark. Why wasn't somebody keeping better tabs on her?"

Burrow frowned. "Emory is a special girl. She is intelligent and resourceful. Much more so than I was at her age, far more than most. As long as she keeps up with her studies, there is no reason to cross her."

Nash's face was red. "Cross her? Who the hell is in charge here?"

Burrow had had enough. "Detective Nash, ultimately I work for Mr. Talbot. The extent of my duties ends with that girl's grades. If he wished for me to fulfill some type of parental role, I would be more than willing to do so, but that is not what he wanted when I was hired, nor is it a role he wishes me to perform now. If you have questions or concerns regarding Emory's upbringing or her environment, I suggest you express those concerns directly to Mr. Talbot. Do not expect me to sit here and be berated for circumstances beyond my control. I am speaking to you voluntarily, and you are giving me little reason to continue."

Nash was ready to open his mouth and retort when Porter squeezed his shoulder. "Why don't you take a little walk and blow off some steam? I'll finish this up."

Nash gave them both a frustrated glance, then stormed out of the room.

"I apologize, Ms. Burrow. That was unprofessional and completely unwarranted."

She rubbed her chin. "I understand his concerns, but without knowing Mr. Talbot or Emory—"

Porter raised his hand. "There's no need to explain."

"I do care for her, I really do. It pains me to think she may be in trouble."

"When did you first learn she had been abducted?" Porter asked.

"Mr. Talbot reached me about an hour ago," she replied. "He was upset, near hysterics. He said he was golfing with his attorney and two detectives tracked him down to tell him the news." She paused. "Because it's my personal day, my phone was switched off. Otherwise, I'm sure I would have heard sooner. I came straight back after receiving the news." She took a deep breath. "Had I heard earlier—"

Porter placed a hand on her shoulder. "It's okay, Ms. Burrow. You're here now."

She nodded and forced a smile.

"How is her relationship with her father?"

Burrow sighed. "You know, until this morning the only emotion that man has ever expressed was anger. Normally he is very distant, guarded, particularly with Emory. He rarely comes by to visit her. I'm required to complete weekly progress reports regarding her studies. That is how he monitors her, always from a distance. I understand there is a certain need for discretion, but he is still her father. You would think he would wish to be more involved."

"They speak on the phone, though, right?"

She shrugged. "They do, but their conversations do not sound like a father and daughter. That girl has a benefactor, nothing more, and she is very much aware of that fact. She fears him and wishes to please him, but there is little love there. That is why his reaction surprised me so."

She bent forward and lowered her voice. "Had you asked me a week ago, I would have told you that man was more likely to smile than shed a tear at the news of her abduction. Having an illegitimate daughter hanging over his head all these years, it's a problem money can't necessarily fix, and that eats at him. He is not fond of anything he cannot control. He can be a cold, cold man."

"Do you think he could be involved?"

She thought about this for a moment, then sat up straight. "No. He's a heartless bastard of a man, but I don't think he'd be willing to hurt his own flesh and blood, or anyone else, for that matter. If he wanted her out of the picture, he would have done something years ago. That girl wants for nothing. He ensures she has the best this world has to offer."

"In exchange for silence?" Porter asked.

"In exchange for cooperation," she replied. "I've never heard him ask her to keep their relationship a secret. There is an understanding between the two of them, simple as that."

From the doorway, Murray crunched on a potato chip. Porter shot him a nasty look, and the officer raised his hands in surrender and left the room. He returned his gaze to Ms. Burrow. "Did you see anything strange in the days or weeks leading up to her abduction yesterday? Did she mention anything? Somebody following her, or strange calls on her phone? Anything out of the ordinary?"

Burrow shook her head. "I do not recall anything."

"Would she tell you?"

"Contrary to what your partner may believe, Emory and I were,

I mean *are,* close. She has confided in me regarding other matters. If something were troubling her, I think she would have mentioned it."

"Other matters?"

Her face grew red. "Girl issues, Detective. Nothing worth mentioning."

"There's a good chance the man who took her may have observed her for some time. Is there anyone new in her life? Have you seen anyone in the building lately you didn't recognize? Or maybe someone you saw here, and again someplace else, like the grocery store today?"

"You think he followed her?"

Porter shrugged. "We don't know. I can tell you he's extremely careful. He doesn't leave anything to chance. I don't think nabbing her in the park was a spur-of-the-moment decision. Most likely he kept tabs on her, learned her routine, plotted out where she'd likely be and when. Most likely he followed you too."

She looked down at her hands, shaking her head. "I don't recall anyone like that. This building is extremely secure. Do you think he could have gotten inside?"

"He has breached far more secure buildings in the past. I think if he had reason to get in here, he would find a way."

Ms. Burrow pursed her lips. "The book."

Porter frowned. "What book?"

Burrow stood and pushed past him through the doorway, nearly running into Murray in the hallway. As Porter followed quickly after her, he couldn't help but marvel at her speed. She was a rather large woman, after all. He found her standing at the desk in the den. She was holding the calculus book they had found earlier.

"I saw this three days ago and asked Emory about it. She completed calculus two years ago. I thought it odd she would purchase a book on the subject, particularly one this trite. Her studies progressed far beyond whatever this text has to offer. She told me she didn't buy it, she didn't know where it came from."

Porter eyed the text warily. "Please put the book down, Ms. Burrow."

29

Diary

The screen door at the back of the Carters' house had been left open. The wind owned it now, banging it against the white-paint-flaked frame. I reached for the handle and held it still for Mrs. Carter. She walked past me into the dark kitchen. She hadn't said a word the entire walk back. Neither of us had. If it hadn't been for the sound of her sniffling, I wouldn't have known she was behind me.

I pulled the door shut and flipped the lock. The wind outside howled in protest.

Mrs. Carter pressed her hands on the countertop and bowed her head, facing the sink. Her eyes glossed over, lost in thought. I spied a bottle of bourbon on the kitchen table next to a glass with Snoopy and Woodstock emblazoned on the side, the colors faded and worn after years of washes. I walked over and poured about an inch of bourbon. Two fingers, Father would have said.

"Aren't you a little young for that?" Mrs. Carter said. She had turned and was facing me now.

I handed the glass to her. "It's for you."

"Oh, I couldn't."

"I think you should."

Father never shied away from a drink after a long day at work. I knew a cocktail or two helped him relax. If anyone needed to relax, it was Mrs. Carter.

She hesitated, eyeing the brown liquid, then took the glass and brought it to her swollen lips. She swallowed the bourbon in one swift gulp before setting the glass down hard on the counter. Her entire body shivered, and she let out a soft gasp. "Oh my."

I couldn't help but smile. We were sharing a rather adult moment. Just a couple of drinking buddies knocking back a few in the kitchen. I had a hankering to give it a try, but I told myself now was not the time. I had to keep my wits about me. The night was far from over.

"Would you like another?" I asked her.

When she nodded, I poured her another glass, adding another finger or so.

She put this one away even faster than the first, this time without the shiver and with a little bit of a smile, then sat at her table. "Simon was a good man, most of the time. He didn't really mean to hurt me. It is . . . was . . . all the pressure, that's all. He didn't deserve to . . ."

I took a seat beside her.

In school it could take me an hour to summon the courage to ask a girl if I could borrow a pencil. There was something about Mrs. Carter, though, something that set me at ease. There was no sign of the usual churn in my stomach or fever on the back of my neck. I reached up and touched the bruises on her cheek. They had darkened considerably in the past twenty minutes or so. "He would have hurt you more, maybe even killed you."

She shook her head. "Not my Simon. He wasn't like that."

"Sure he was. Look at what he did to you."

"I deserved it."

The image of Mrs. Carter with Mother flashed in my mind. Did she know I witnessed that? "Nothing you could have done was deserving of a beating like the one he put on you. A man should never lay hands on a woman. Not a real man."

She snickered. "Did your father teach you that?"

I nodded. "Women are to be respected, cherished. They are gifts be-stowed upon us." He also told me they were weak and incapable of de-

fending themselves against a beating, physical or verbal, but I left that part out.

"Your father is a sweet man."

"Yes."

Mrs. Carter reached for the bourbon and refilled her glass, then slid the bottle over to me. "Why don't you give it a shot? Have you ever drunk alcohol before?"

I shook my head. This was a lie. My father made me a martini for my last birthday. Mother poured a glass of her favorite red wine, and we toasted in celebration. I spit most of it out on the table, and the rest burned at my throat so badly, I dared not finish. Mother laughed and Father patted me on the back. "It's an acquired taste, champ. One day you'll love it. I'm afraid that day is not today, though!" Then he laughed too. "Perhaps you're more of a beer man," he joked.

She gave the bottle another nudge. "Come on, don't be afraid. It won't bite. You're not going to make me drink alone, are you? That would be so rude." Her voice had lost the sharp edges of earlier. She wasn't slurring her words yet, but even a boy with limited experience such as myself could tell she was well on her way.

Puzzle it out, champ.

I took the bottle and removed the cap. EVAN WILLIAMS KENTUCKY BOURBON, the black label read. The light above the table made the brown liquor glisten like liquid candy. I raised the bottle to my lips and took a small drink. It burned, but not as much as the martini had. Perhaps I was prepared this time, or maybe I'd built up a tolerance. It wasn't . . . bad. It wasn't my first choice of beverage, but I wouldn't call it bad. In fact, it warmed me up a little, a heat growing in my belly. I took another drink, this one a little more than the last.

Mrs. Carter laughed. "Look at you! You're like an old pro. If I gave you a cigar and a nice newsboy cap, you'd be all set for poker night with the boys."

I smiled and tipped the bottle back at her. "Want some more?"

"Why, are you planning to get me drunk?"

"No, ma'am. I just thought—"

"Give me that," she said, reaching for the bottle. This time she didn't bother with the glass. She drank straight from the bottle, as I had. When she set it back down on the table, her whole body shivered again.

"Candy is dandy, but liquor is quicker," I said.

She laughed. "Where did you hear that?"

"Father said it once. He got quite drunk that night."

"This father of yours seems like a very interesting man."

I considered another drink. The first had made me feel warm, calm. Calm was good. I nodded toward the bottle, and she handed it back to me. A grin filled her face, and she burst out laughing.

"What is it? What did I do?"

She waved her hand at me, her laughter growing to a cackle. I felt a smile at my own lips and couldn't help but laugh along with her, even though the joke was lost on me. "Tell me!" I said. "You gotta tell me!"

Mrs. Carter placed both of her hands palm down on the table and stopped laughing, her lips pursed tight. Then she said, "I was thinking, if I send you home drunk, your parents might kill me."

I stared at her for a moment, my eyes locked with hers. Then we both burst into a round of roaring, tear-filled laughter, the kind that makes your belly hurt.

She picked up the bottle and took another drink. "This was Simon's favorite, but bourbon always made him so mean. It doesn't make you mean, does it?"

I shook my head.

"It doesn't make me mean, either. So why did it make him so mean? Why did he have to get angry and hurt me whenever he touched this bottle? Why couldn't it have been like it is with us right now? Fun. Oh God, he's really dead. My Simon is really gone. They really killed him, didn't they?"

Perhaps the second drink was a bad idea. Two Mrs. Carters sat across from me now. If I squinted just right, they merged back together into one, but then there were two again. I covered one eye, then the other, then back to the first.

Mrs. Carter quieted, then suddenly spoke in a low voice. "I know you saw me the other day, out by the lake."

Adrenaline burst through me, and the two Mrs. Carters became one and stayed that way. "You . . . you do?"

She nodded slowly. "Uh-huh."

My face flushed. My eyes fell from her and landed on the table, on the bourbon. I reached for the bottle, but before I could grasp it, Mrs. Carter's hand took mine. She was shaking. "I think I wanted you to see. I watched you walk out there with your fishing pole. I knew you'd be there."

"Why would you—"

"Sometimes a woman wants to be desired, is all." She took another drink. "Do you think I'm pretty?"

I nodded. She was one of the prettiest women I had ever seen. And she was a woman. Not like the girls at school, barely out of training bras and princess parties, and passing notes and lusting after the latest and greatest pop band. She was a woman—a woman talking to me, about this. That feeling down below returned, warm blood rushing. I knew she couldn't see under the table, but I grew embarrassed nonetheless. I pulled my hand out from under hers and lifted the bottle to my lips; there was no burn this time. I found it simply delightful.

I handed the bottle to her, and she didn't hold back. Nearly a quarter of the bottle disappeared before she finally tried to set it down on the table, missing entirely. It crashed to the floor and burst with a bang, glass and bourbon spreading out at our feet.

"Oh my, I . . ." she said. "It's a mess I made. Bad."

"It's okay, I'll clean it." I stood up, looking for a dishrag. The room spun around me. I steadied myself on the back of my chair and took deep, slow breaths until the kitchen righted itself. Mrs. Carter watched me from her yellow vinyl and metal chair, then laid her head down on the table within her folded arms.

I stood there in complete silence. I remained still until I heard her breathing fall into the rhythm of sleep. Then I pushed out the door into the ever-increasing cold of night.

I had to get Mother and Father. I would need help tying her up.

30

Porter

Day I • 4:49 p.m.

"It's old. Out of print." Watson was reading the tiny display on his iPhone as he, Porter, and Nash hovered over the book on Emory's desk. "*Calculus in the Modern Age* by Winston Gilbert, Thomas Brothington, and Carmel Thorton. First published in 1923, looks like the final edition went out in 1987."

He leaned down to the black Pelican case at his side and came back up with a small brush and fingerprint powder. He dipped the brush into the powder and began to run the bristles over the top of the text, his hand twisting in a circular motion, spreading the dark powder evenly over the cover.

"Good luck returning that to the library," Nash frowned.

Watson ignored him.

Reaching back into the bag, he withdrew a large flashlight, flicked it on, and crouched back over the book.

"Is that standard issue?" Porter asked.

Watson shook his head. "It's a Fenix 750. Has an LED array capable of putting out twenty-nine hundred lumens. That's nearly twice the brightness of the ones we get from Supply. It also does infrared and has a strobe function."

Nash whistled. "That's one fancy fucking flashlight. I guess we cops ask Santa for a new gun at Christmastime, you guys ask for flashlights. Makes perfect sense to me."

"Anything?" Porter asked.

Watson leaned in closer. "I only see one set of prints, probably Burrow's. I'll need a sample to rule her out. And check out the spine." He pointed at the edge of the book. "There's not a single crease. I'd say this book has never been used. It's in remarkable condition."

"Not to sound all conspiracy theory, but do you think it could be rigged?" Nash asked.

Porter frowned. "Rigged?"

"Yeah, like a bomb or something. Maybe hollowed out?"

Watson began to open the cover.

"No, don't—" Nash shouted, before backing up into the wall.

The cover flapped against the desk with a soft thud. Nash squeezed his eyes shut.

Porter read the first page. "It's just a book. No boom."

"I'm getting some water," Nash said, before disappearing down the hallway toward the kitchen.

Porter flipped through the pages. Watson was right—for a book last published in 1987, it looked new. The glossy pages stuck together. That "new book" smell still lofted from it, bringing back memories of third-grade English class—the only time he ever received a new text-book. "If 4MK placed this here, what do you think it means?"

Watson sighed. "I don't know. Has he ever left a clue behind?"

"Not one."

"He's clearly trying to tell you something. Why else would he bother?"

"Where do you think he got it?"

Watson thumbed through the pages. "The city has its share of vin-tage bookstores, but I don't know of any dealing in textbooks."

"Who would want an old math book?"

"A math teacher?"

"Do you think it came from a school?"

Watson thought about that for a moment, then shook his head. "If this book ever circulated through the school system, it wouldn't be in this condition. Textbooks don't just sit around. They get used and abused."

"Okay, how about a supplier?"

Watson flipped back through the pages at the beginning. He skimmed some text on the second page, tapped it with his finger, then spun the book around so Porter could see. "It was manufactured here in Chicago. That address is less than three miles from here—in Fulton."

Porter frowned. "Did you dog-ear that page?"

"No, sir."

Somebody had. The corner of the page had a soft crease, barely visible but there nonetheless. 4MK wanted them to find this.

Porter pulled out his phone, dialed Kloz, and read the address off to him. He hung up a moment later. "The address belongs to a condemned warehouse scheduled to be torn down day after tomorrow."

Porter and Nash understood the significance. The Four Monkey Killer had left the body of his third victim, Missy Lumax, under a tarp at the center of an abandoned warehouse. It too had been set for demolition. It too had been in the Fulton River District.

31

Diary

I don't recall falling asleep, but I must have drifted off at some point because I found myself in bed wearing my best pajamas, with the headache to end all headaches throbbing at my temples. The morning sun squeezed between my blinds and pecked at my eyes so ferociously, I thought the light would render me blind.

Last night, Father scolded me for drinking and I tried to explain why I had done so, but he wasn't willing to listen. Or maybe he did. Much of the evening was a blur.

Peeling back the blankets, I lowered my feet to the floor.

Although I did so with the most tender of motions, the impact radiated through my body and went straight to my aching head. I considered climbing back under the warm sheets and sleeping for perhaps another year or so, but I knew if I didn't rise soon, my parents would surely come in search of me. In our house, if you weren't at the breakfast table by nine, service would close and you'd find yourself standing at the refrigerator with nothing but an empty plate and a grumbling tummy. Mother locked it, you see. Promptly at nine, she would latch the refrigerator closed and fasten the door tight with a shiny new Stanley padlock. It would remain locked until lunchtime, and the process would repeat again for supper. While I was perfectly capable of fasting until the noon hour, something told me a little sustenance in my belly would help with the lingering effects of the previous night's bender and possibly set me right for the remainder of the day.

Yesterday's clothes were piled at my feet, and I considered putting them on until the scent of vomit drifted up from my T-shirt. I didn't recall throwing up, but I had no reason to believe the foulness came from anyone but me. Why would someone else take the time to vomit in my room? The thought was ludicrous. No, most likely I had gotten sick. Apparently some of the bourbon felt the need to vacate my small premises via the entrance ramp.

I left the pile of clothes on the floor, making a mental note to burn them at my first chance, and pulled a clean shirt and pair of jeans from my dresser. Then I made my way down the hall to the kitchen.

"There's my boy!" Father beamed from behind a heaping plate of eggs and sausage. "Take a seat, son. A little greasy food will help settle that angry stomach of yours. You're a little young for a hangover, to be sure, but a hangover is surely what ails you if you consumed the amounts of alcohol you boasted about last night."

I found my way into my chair and did my best to hold back the contents of my churning stomach. Bourbon was a man's drink, and I had put away every drop like a man. I had no intention of showing weakness under Father's watchful eye.

He reached across the table, picked up a carafe of orange juice, and filled a glass for me. Then he produced a shot glass from beneath a napkin with the fanfare of a magician pulling a bunny from his black felt hat. "I prepared this just for you. This is Kentucky's finest, and perhaps the fastest method for banishing a hangover known to the civilized world." He slid the glass over to me with a Cheshire grin.

I stared down upon the shot glass no doubt with bloodshot eyes and pale cheeks, waiting for him to follow up with a punch line to his little joke, but none came. He nudged the glass closer. "Drink up, champ. I promise a little 'hair of the dog' will make you feel better."

"Really?"

He nodded.

I reached for the glass and gently raised it to my lips, my head throbbing. The scent of warm caramel and toasted vanilla tickled at my nose.

"Quickly now. Real men put away a shot in a single gulp without a drop spilled."

Taking a deep breath, I dumped the glass into my mouth and forced a swallow, wincing as the burn worked down my gullet to my stomach. I found it odd how I could feel it every inch of the way. Never before had I thought about the journey taken by my meals and drink. Alcohol was strange indeed.

"Now, slam the glass back down on the table," Father instructed with glee.

I did as I was told, ramming the shot glass against the wood so hard, I thought for sure it would shatter in my hand.

Father clapped with joy. "That's my boy!"

I wiped my mouth on my sleeve, the bourbon lingering on my breath. It reminded me of burnt toast and molasses.

Father took up the glass and poured another shot. He drank this one himself, then also brought the glass down hard on the table. He let out a grunt and shivered with an audible sigh, then turned to me, his face suddenly serious. "I want you to remember this moment as your first drink. Do you think you can do that, champ? When you grow older and reminisce back upon your life, I want you to think of our little moment as your first taste of the forbidden fruit juice, a simple shot with your old man. A true father and son moment. Forget last night. Forget the drinks you shared with our lovely little neighbor. Forget the reason for those drinks. When you grow old, I don't want you to think about getting drunk with Mrs. Carter. I don't want you to think about her at all, I only want you to remember this. What do you think, champ? Can do, or no way, nohow?"

I thought on his words and nodded my head. "Can do, Father," I said with a grin. "Can do for sure."

"Pinky swear?"

I held up my tiny hand to his, and we swore on it.

"Good, because that is how your first drink should be remembered —a happy moment with your pops, not drinking yourself silly with the crazy bitch neighbor." I had never heard him use foul language before; Mother either. They never cursed. The word wasn't new to me; I had heard it many times before at school and from other adults, but never from Father, never in his voice.

"Oh, I'm sorry, champ. I probably shouldn't use such terms around you. You should never call someone such things, particularly a woman. I'm setting a horrible example. As I've often said, women should be cherished and treated with the utmost of respect."

I glanced around the room. I hadn't seen Mother yet this morning.

"She's downstairs with our guest," Father said. Sometimes he seemed to read my mind.

I had wondered if Mrs. Carter was still alive. Frankly, the fact that she was surprised me. Although Mother and Father weren't in the best of mind last night, they were typically careful when it came to their indiscretions. They didn't leave loose ends.

"Will Mrs. Carter be staying with us awhile?"

Father pondered this. "Yes, champ, I think she will. You see, we can't blame Mrs. Carter for her husband's actions, not really, but she must have done something to put him into such a tizzy. If she hadn't, he would have never come over here and threatened your mother, and she wouldn't have found herself in that little predicament. Your mother wouldn't have had to hurt him. Mr. Carter would probably be sitting on his porch right now enjoying the summer breeze with his lovely wife, and Mother wouldn't be spending the morning on her hands and knees scrubbing the basement floor of all things nasty." He shook his head and laughed. "That man sure was a bleeder, wasn't he?"

I couldn't help but agree. I found myself smiling.

Father ran his hand through his hair. "Now, the question is, just what did Mrs. Carter do to make her husband so upset? Did he see something? Did you see something, champ?"

He spoke the words so fast, they took me by surprise.

The breath seized in my throat, and when I tried to speak, nothing wanted to come out. I shook my head and finally said, "I don't think so, Father."

He narrowed his eyes. "You don't think so?"

To this I said nothing. My tongue felt like it was swelling in my mouth, blocking the words that wanted to come out. Father stared at me intently. There was no anger in his gaze, but he read every blink of my eyes and every twitch of my nose. I did not look away, for he would surely take that as a sign of forthcoming lies. "I meant I don't think he saw anything, Father. I certainly haven't."

He tilted his head and stared at me for a long while. Finally, he smiled and patted my hand. "Well, the truth will come out soon enough. It always does, and at that point I will deal with the situation posthaste. For now, though, the sun is shining, the air is alive, and I do not intend to waste such a glorious summer day."

I reached across the table for a piece of toast. It wasn't hot anymore, but it was good to get something in my stomach.

"How's your head?"

I realized that my headache had nearly retreated, gone now but for a dull thump behind my left eye. The queasiness too. "Much better!"

He reached over and ruffled my hair. "There you go. Eat up. When you're done, I want you to take a plate downstairs to our guest. Perhaps a glass of orange juice as well. I imagine she's worked up quite an appetite. I'm going to take a walk over to the Carter house and straighten up a bit. I think I'll pack her a bag. Best if it looks like they went on a little road trip, should someone take it upon themselves to check in on them."

"Maybe you should move their car," I suggested, nibbling on my toast.

He ruffled my hair again. "You sure are a chip off the old block, aren't you?"

I grinned.

32

Emory

Day 1 • 5:00 p.m.

The music stopped.

Just like that.

One second, "Sweet Home Alabama" beat at her head with the ferocity of a storm shutter caught in a hurricane, then nothing.

The room wasn't silent, though. A loud ringing had replaced the music, and although Emory knew the tone existed only in her mind, it might as well have been blaring from the largest of speakers. The tone didn't increase or decrease in volume; it remained steady.

Tinnitus.

Ms. Burrow had taught her all about the dangers of loud noises nearly three years earlier before sending her off to her first concert, Jack's Mannequin at the Metro. She'd wanted to scare her; looking back, Emory could see that that was obvious. Ms. Burrow had told her how easily prolonged exposure to loud music might lead to permanent problems, particularly in a closed environment. Something about the tiny hairs in your ear getting damaged like frayed wires, causing your brain to perceive sound that wasn't there. Most of the time the condition was temporary.

Most of the time.

When Ms. Burrow handed her a pair of earplugs, she gladly accepted them before heading out the door. She hadn't used them, of course. She refused to let her friends see her with those silly pink things sticking out of her head. Instead, they remained in her pocket, and she had finished the night with a ringing in her ears much like now.

That was nothing like now, sweetie. Don't you remember? That was barely audible and only lasted a little bit. After all, the concert wasn't loud, not long, either. Not like the barrage you were just subjected to. How long did that music blare? Five hours? Ten? You're down one ear already. I'm sure that doesn't help.

"Shut up!" Emory tried to shout. Instead, the words came out in a muffled garble, her dry throat protesting each syllable.

I'm only saying, an earplug might do you some good. The one side is wrapped up good and tight. If that dreadful music comes back, you should consider taking a little piece of that bandage and shoving a wad into the ear canal. Better safe than sorry, right? If you get out of this pickle, you'll be a one-eared Jane—best you keep the other one in tip-top working order, don't you think? You know what's worse than a girl with one ear? Do you?

"Please be quiet."

Do you know what's worse?

Emory closed her eyes, plunging from black to blacker, and began to sing "It's My Party" by Jessie J.

The only thing worse than a girl with one ear is a girl with one ear and no eyes. I think that may be the next stop on your little journey, my love, because if the music stopped, that means somebody stopped it.

Emory's breath caught in her throat, and her head swiveled quickly from right to left, then back again, as she peered at the wall of darkness.

Her eyes tried to adjust to the black, but they were losing the battle. Emory sat perched atop the gurney with her knees pulled up tight against her chest, and she couldn't even make out her own feet. The shiny silver of the gurney appeared to be nothing more than a dim blur. That didn't mean there was no movement, though. Things moved all around her. The dark swirled in waves, floating through the air with a murky thickness she could almost taste.

He might be in the room with her right now, and she wouldn't know. He might be standing a foot or two away with a knife in hand, ready to plunge the tip into her eyes and pop them out with a twist. She wouldn't have time to react or fight him off, not until after he began to carve the sight from her.

Emory continued to sing, but the rhythm and cadence of the song were all wrong.

"I keep da-dancing alone, da-dancing," she sang softly. "Da-dancing till I say stop." She reached her free arm out in front of her and slowly swiped back and forth, groping at the darkness. "Are . . . are you there?"

In her mind's eye, she saw him. A tall, thin man leaning against the far wall with a knife in one hand and a spoon in the other. His fingers flexed against the handle of the knife as he ran the blade against the edge of the spoon. Both were caked with dried blood, remnants of those who had come before her. Even through the darkness, she knew he could see her. He could see her perfectly. A white box rested on the floor at his feet, a black string waiting at its side. With his right hand, he spread his index finger and middle finger in the shape of a V, pointed at his eyes, then pointed at hers, a grin edging his lips — chapped lips all dry and cracked from lack of water. His tongue ran across them, slow and deliberate. "There's nothing left worth seeing," he told her in a low voice. "Your young eyes have been tainted by the evil in the world, and they need to come out. It's the only way to unsee — the only way to cleanse you, make you pure."

Emory backed up, scooting closer to the wall. "You're not real," she told herself. "I'm alone in here."

She wanted the music to come back.

If he was here, if he truly stood in this room ready to hurt her, she didn't want to hear him coming. It would be better that way.

The ringing in her ears had lessened, and she forced herself to ignore the pounding of her heart at her damaged ear; she forced herself to listen to the room around her.

Would she hear him breathing?

"If you're going to hurt me, get it over with, you sick shit!" she shouted. Only it wasn't a shout — her throat had gone so dry, her voice came out high and cracked.

A sound came.

Had that been there earlier?

A steady *plop, plop, plop* every second or so.

Where, though?

She had walked around the room when she first woke. She'd checked every wall. She was barefoot—if there was a leak, standing water somewhere, she would have found it, right?

Her throat ached at the thought of water.

You might be hearing water because you're so thirsty, dear. The mind is funny like that. I think if he wanted you to have water, he would have given you water.

Emory closed her eyes and tried to listen harder. She knew it was silly; she couldn't see anyway, but somehow closing her eyes helped. Sounds became a little louder, a little clearer.

Plop . . . plop . . . plop.

She tilted her head, positioning her good ear, turning slightly with each drip until it was at its loudest. When the sound began to fade again, she stopped and turned slowly back.

It came from her left.

Emory slid off the gurney and stood on the icy concrete. Goose bumps ran over her skin, and she wrapped her left arm around herself in an attempt to warm up. Her right hand tugged at the gurney.

Don't forget the rats, dear. Those little guys are probably scurrying around you right now. They probably found the water a long time ago; now they want a little dinner to wash down with it, a little chunk of girl-meat. If I were a rat, I'd probably set up base right next to the water. I'd protect that water too; I'd protect it with my life.

Emory took a step forward, followed by another, the gurney dragging behind her.

She didn't want to abandon the wall. The wall brought her comfort, like a big safety blanket, but she left anyway. She left the wall behind her and took another step, a little step, more of a shuffle. Without knowing what was in front of her, she couldn't permit herself any more than that.

Can you imagine if he scattered broken glass? Or rusty nails? What about a hole in the floor? If you fell and broke your leg you'd be in all kinds of trouble—much worse than your current predicament, that's for sure. By the way, not to be a pest, but I feel this is worth mentioning. Have you figured out who turned off the music yet? Because if he's nearby, then fetching a drink shouldn't be your number one priority right now.

"If he plans to hurt me, he'll hurt me," Emory shot back. "I'm not going to sit around and wait for him to make a move."

She shuffled forward, her toes growing numb with each step.

Was the concrete getting colder?

"He's not going to let me die, not until he's done with me. He kept the girls in the news alive at least a week before he killed them. I've only been down here a day at the most. He still needs me."

I suppose there's something to that, but there are so many things he could do to you, so many unpleasant things, things that wouldn't kill you. He already took your ear. You know your eyes are next. Would that be so bad, though? I mean, you can't see now, right? Honestly, I would be more worried about losing my tongue. You can always fumble around in the dark, but to lose the ability to speak? Oh my, that would be rough. You've always been such a talker.

Emory listened. She was close now, only a few more feet at best.

A rat scurried over her toes, and she let out a shriek, nearly falling back over the gurney.

She forced herself to take a deep breath. She had to stay calm. Again a pair of little feet ran over her toes. This time when she screamed, her voice was loud; dry throat or not, she didn't hold back. Her throat felt as if she had vomited glass, and she wanted to stop but the scream kept coming anyway—the scream to end all screams. It wasn't about the rat anymore or being kidnapped and trapped in this place, it was about her father and the people around her, it was the frustration of homeschooling and the limited number of friends in her life. The pain at her ear, the numbness in her feet, and the vulnerability of being naked in a strange place all came to a head. It was about the unknown eyes on her. It was about the man who took her—a man who could be miles away or inches from her, lost in the dark. It was about her mother dying and leaving her to suffer all of this alone.

When she finally stopped, her throat burned as if she had swallowed hot lead and scraped the residue away with a rusty blade, but she didn't care. The scream cleared her head. She needed clarity.

She needed to think.

The ringing in her ears was gone.

Emory forced her good ear to listen, past the rushing blood pumping through her other one.

Plop.

At her left came a soft scratching. Nails against concrete. Tiny nails. Digging.

Ignore them, she told herself.

Just ignore them.

She forced herself forward, inching along, first one step, then another. Then an—

Her toe jabbed into something. The surface seemed colder than the concrete. Cold and damp. She kneeled down awkwardly to touch it, her right arm trailing up behind her. She tugged at the gurney, pulling it closer, giving her a little more slack.

A metal plate? That was it, a rather large metal plate. She traced the edge and estimated the plate to be about three feet wide. About every four inches or so, threaded bolts poked through it, securing it to the concrete.

Emory slipped her hand over the surface—damp for sure.

Plop.

This time the drop hit so close that droplets sprayed up at her, sprinkling a fine mist against her skin. She ran her finger over the metal plate and brought it to her lips. Even before she tasted it, she smelled the metal—rust or some kind of residue. She tasted anyway, her brain telling her if she didn't get water soon, nothing else would matter.

It was awful, but it was wet and she wanted more.

Emory lowered her head toward the metal plate, pulling at the gurney to get a little more slack. When there was no more, she stretched her neck and stuck out her tongue. She might not be able to see, but water was right there, inches away. She sensed it—the tip of her tongue reaching, groping the air, stretching.

She heard the scratching again. Tiny little claws digging at—

I'd put that tongue back in your head, if I were you. Water or not, it seems like a delectable little treat for a big hungry rat, don't you think? At the very least, you're making things easy for your host to cut the little bugger right out of your mouth.

Emory pulled back. With her damaged ear, she couldn't pinpoint the source of the scratching. One moment it sounded like it was right next to her. Then, if she tilted her head, the sound seemed as if it originated across the room.

Plop.

Droplets of water sprayed her hand and cheek.

"Fuck it." Emory leaned forward again as far as she could, pulling at the handcuffs behind her. She stretched until it seemed her neck would snap under the strain. The metal of the cuffs chewed at her wrist, and she forced herself to ignore the pain, her thoughts on one thing and one thing only — water.

She tugged forward.

Her tongue brushed the surface of the metal plate for a second, only a quick second at best, and the taste of rust found her lips. It happened so fast and the metal was so cold, she couldn't tell if she had actually gotten any water or simply imagined the cold metal to be water. Certainly it wasn't enough to quench her thirst. The little sample only made her thirst worse.

She wouldn't cry. She refused to cry.

She leaned in as far as she could and pulled at the handcuffs with all her strength. The metal cut at her wrist, and she didn't care. Emory used all her weight to pull forward. Something gave and her face went forward. Her tongue found the water — icy, refreshing, dirty, rusty water pooled at the center of the plate. Her tongue dipped into the puddle for only an instant before the gurney tipped and crashed down on her back, slamming her head against the floor, sending all to an even deeper black.

33

Diary

I located a breakfast tray in the cupboard and loaded it up with a few slices of toast, a banana, orange juice, and a cup of Cheerios (my personal favorite breakfast selection). I wanted to add milk, but when I checked the refrigerator I only found a cup or so left in the carton. Father happened to be fond of milk, and I would never consider crossing him by taking the last of it, knowing full well Mother had not purchased a replacement when she last went to the market.

The steps leading to the basement seemed steeper since I'd last descended them. I eyed the tall glass of orange juice perched precariously on the tray, the liquid sloshing back and forth, pausing as it reached the lip and racing back to the other side with my next step. If the juice were to find its way up and over the lip of the glass, the resulting spill would surely dampen the toast, and I couldn't have that. I felt guilty enough for tricking Mrs. Carter last night. I had no intention of compounding that guilt by serving soggy toast.

Mother started up the staircase as I neared the bottom. She was carrying a bucket, a few rags, and a large scrub brush. Her hands were dressed in long plastic yellow gloves that went nearly to her elbows.

"Good morning, Mother."

She glanced up at me and grinned. "Well, aren't you a kindhearted little soul! Our guest will be tickled pink when she sees you. She's been mumbling so. I can only imagine she has a hankering for a nice meal and a little something to moisten her palate."

As she slipped past me, she took a nibble from one of the toast slices and placed the remainder back on the plate. "Make sure she understands the rules. I'd hate to see her get off on the wrong foot so early in her stay."

I had to agree.

"Not too many lights, either. We don't want to aggravate your father with a hefty power bill."

"Yes, Mother."

I watched her ascend the stairs, my keen sense of smell taking in the mix of damp copper and bleach hanging in the air.

I spotted Mrs. Carter a moment before she saw me. Mother (or possibly Father) had handcuffed her left hand to the same water pipe her husband had been attached to only hours earlier. Rather than sitting on the floor, she was perched on Father's old cot. Her right hand was cuffed to the opposite side. He once told me he brought the cot back from the war. It seemed like the rickety old thing had seen its share of fighting in days long past. The thick canvas was tattered and worn, and there were several holes in the faded green material. The metal legs, no doubt shiny when new, were now dull and covered in rust. The frame creaked under her weight as she shifted slightly to her left.

She was lying down, whether out of comfort or necessity, I couldn't be sure. There was little light. Mother had extinguished all the bulbs except one, which hung bare from a wire at the center of the basement. Although the air was still, the light swung gently back and forth, casting thick, dancing shadows along the walls and floor.

Mother (or Father) had the foresight to place her on the right side of the pipe, leaving the space on the left previously occupied by Mr. Carter free from obstructions. The bright red blood that flowed so freely last night was now gone, replaced by a dark stain on the concrete. I imagine Mother had scrubbed at the mess with the same enthusiasm she applied while creating it, but blood was a stubborn mistress and not one to release her hold once she got her snarled old hands wrapped around something she liked. I made a mental note to suggest Mother apply cat litter. Not only was litter absorbent, but it would help mask the odor.

I couldn't help but wonder if Mrs. Carter recognized the scent of her husband's blood and sweat.

I nearly dropped the tray when she sat up and stared at me, her eyes bloodshot and large. She cried out from beneath a gag, but I couldn't make out what she said.

"Good morning, Mrs. Carter. Would you care for some breakfast?"

She struggled to draw breath through her gag. Her nose was no doubt mucked up with snot from all the crying, but I tried not to think about that. Despite enduring what was surely not the best of nights, she was still rather pretty. I could see past the bruises and the right eye that had gone black. Her left seemed better, not yet normal but no longer as swollen as it was only a few hours earlier.

Setting the tray down on the edge of her cot, I considered the headache that welcomed me this morning and imagined her head was most likely worse. Aside from the beating, she'd drunk far more than I, and although she seemed experienced, I seriously doubted she'd escaped without a hangover. "How about some of the dog's hair?"

Her gaze became puzzled and I realized my error. "I'm sorry, a little hair of the dog?"

She continued to stare at me with bewilderment, her head cocked slightly to the left. At least the screaming had stopped.

"For your headache? Father has bourbon upstairs, and a little sip did wonders for me. I know the time may be early, but there is no reason to spend the day in pain."

Mrs. Carter shook her head slowly, her eyes fixed on me.

I nodded at the tray. "Left to our own devices, Father and I aren't the best of cooks. Perhaps tomorrow Mother will prepare something. I'm sure that would prove to be a treat indeed. Would you care to eat?"

She nodded and tried to slide into a more comfortable sitting position. The handcuff tugged at her left wrist. She shot an angry glance at me and mumbled something behind the gag.

I edged closer. "If I remove the gag, do you promise not to scream? I wouldn't blame you if you did. I would, but it would be fruitless. Honestly, you can never make out the screams upstairs. There's no way anyone outside would hear you." I slipped my fingers beneath the edge of the gag and pulled down. There was something about her skin; that quick touch made me feel all tingly. I'm not afraid to say my cheeks may have blushed and my heart pattered.

As the gag dropped around her neck, Mrs. Carter sucked in a deep breath, then let the air out before pulling in another and another after that. I thought she might hyperventilate and considered running upstairs for a paper bag, but then she spoke, her voice muted and raspy, no doubt from a dry throat.

"Screams?"

I cocked my head.

"You said 'you can barely hear the screams upstairs,' as in plural. Have your parents done this before?"

"Done what?"

"This." She tugged at the handcuffs, causing them to rattle against the water pipe.

"Oh." My gaze fell back to the breakfast tray. "I don't know."

She frowned. "You don't know if your parents have ever chained a woman up in their basement before?"

I reached for the orange juice. "You must be parched. This juice is delightful, like sunshine in a glass."

"I don't want any juice, I want you to let me go. Please, just let me go."

"How about a banana, then? I think I may eat one myself. We bought them two days ago, and they're right at that stage between green and yellow, with a little tang of unripeness, just enough to put a pucker on your lips."

"Let me go!" Mrs. Carter bellowed, the words scratching at her dry throat. "Let me go! Let me go! Let me go!"

I sighed. "I'm going to replace your gag for a second while I explain the rules to you. I'm sorry, Mrs. Carter."

She tried to pull away, but I was ready for her. I grabbed a handful of her hair and tugged her head back sharply. I didn't want to hurt her, but she left me little choice. My knife was tiny, a Ranger buck knife I easily concealed in my right palm. I had it out in an instant, the blade snapping open with a quick flick. I pricked her neck in the blink of an eye and held the bloody tip out in front of her to be sure she could see. It wasn't a deep wound. I only wished to draw blood and help her understand I could do significantly more damage should I desire to do so.

Mrs. Carter whimpered, her eyes on the blade.

With my free hand, I maneuvered the gag back into place and released her. It was all over so fast, but I had made my point (pardon my silly little pun). With another flick of my wrist, the blade slipped back inside the sheath and out of sight as I dropped the knife into my shirt pocket. "The rules are simple, Mrs. Carter. They'll only take a minute to explain, then I can leave you to your breakfast. I'm sure you're famished."

Her face grew red with anger.

"Do you promise to behave while I explain the rules?"

"Fuck you!" she shouted from behind the gag.

I was taken aback. I mean, how rude! Wasn't I trying to help her?

"We don't tolerate that kind of language in our house, Lisa. Not even from our guests," Father's voice boomed at my back.

I turned to find him standing at the base of the stairs, a steaming cup of coffee in his hand. He stepped closer. "It starts with language like that. Such talk is quickly followed by rudeness, then anger and hate . . . There is simply no need for it in a civilized society. Before you know it, we're all running naked in the streets, swinging axes. We can't have that, can we? We're trying to raise our boy right. He looks up to the adults around him. He learns from the adults around him." He stepped forward and ruffled my hair. "This little guy is growing up quickly, and he picks up on things like a sponge. His mother and I want to be sure we instill the best values in him before we release him out into this big, nasty, beautiful world of ours. That's where the rules come into play."

"The rules come from the three monkeys." I said. I couldn't help but clap my hands with excitement. "Some people call them the three mystical monkeys but there was actually a fourth. He was called—"

"Slow down, son. When you tell a joke, do you skip to the punch line?"

I shook my head.

"Of course not," he continued. "The same is true of a good story.

First you begin with a little backstory, some history if appropriate, then you get to the nut of the tale, and finally you finish with a neat little bow to tie the package all off. You mustn't rush. You should savor the telling like you would a good steak or sweet cone of your favorite ice cream."

Father was right, of course. He always was. I had a tendency to be a little impatient, a fault I fully intended to work on. "Why don't you tell her, Father? You tell the story so much better than me."

"Than I, son. Than I."

"Sorry. Than I."

"If our guest promises to behave, I'm sure I could spend a few minutes with the two of you and run through it. After all, it's best she understands the rules from the start, don't you agree?"

I nodded.

Mrs. Carter stared at us both, stonefaced, her cheeks red behind the black and blue reminders of the previous night.

Father pulled over an upside-down bucket and sat beside me, setting his coffee down on the concrete floor. A little spilled over the side and sank deep into the bloodstain. "The wise monkeys are depicted in a carving above the door to the famous Tosho-gu Shrine in Nikko, Japan. They were carved by Hidari Jingoro in the seventeenth century and are believed to depict man's life cycle . . . well, all the panels depict the life cycle, only the second one includes the wise monkeys. The life cycle is based on the teachings of Confucius."

"Not the one from fortune cookies — the real Confucius," I blurted out. "The real one was a Chinese teacher, editor, politician, and philosopher. He lived somewhere between 551 BC and 479 BC."

"Very good, son!" Father said, beaming. "He authored some of the most influential of Chinese texts and codes of conduct still utilized today, not only in China but in much of the modern world. He was a wise man indeed. Some people also say the idea of the monkeys came to Japan from a Sendai Buddhist legend. If you ask me, nobody knows for sure. Such a strong proverb simply endures. I wouldn't be surprised if one day we learned both Japan and China obtained the wisdom from an even more ancient source, and perhaps that source got it from something older still. The wise monkeys may date back to the dawn of man."

Mrs. Carter continued to stare as Father went on. "The life cycle carving at the Tosho-gu Shrine is made up of eight panels in all. The monkeys appear in the second panel. Can anyone tell me their names?"

I, of course, had the answer, and I raised my hand earnestly. If Mrs. Carter also knew, she chose not to participate.

Father looked to me, then Mrs. Carter, and back to me. "Well, you did get your hand in the air first. Why don't you tell us their names?"

"Mizaru, Kikazaru, and Iwazaru."

"You are correct! Give that boy a well-deserved prize." Father grinned. "Bonus points if you know the meaning of their names . . ."

Surely he knew that I knew, but Father was fond of games, so I played along. "Mizaru means see no evil, Kikazaru means hear no evil, and Iwazaru means speak no evil."

Father nodded his head slowly and tapped Mrs. Carter's knee. "You've probably seen the depiction. The first ape is covering his eyes, the second his ears, and the third has a hairy paw over his mouth."

"So when Mrs. Carter used a bad word, she violated Iwazaru's rule," I said confidently.

Father shook his head. "No, son, although foul language is bad and a sign of lesser intelligence, she would need to say something bad about someone else to violate Iwazaru's rule."

"Ah." I nodded.

Mrs. Carter growled and tugged at her handcuffs.

"There, there, Lisa. You'll get your turn, but you must be faster with your hand," Father told her.

She yanked at the handcuffs again. They clattered against the pipe and the cot. She groaned in frustration.

"Perhaps your foot, then?"

"There is a fourth monkey, but nobody really knows about him," I explained.

Father nodded. "The first three monkeys define the rules we should all live by, but it's the fourth that carries the most importance."

"Shizaru," I said. "His name is Shizaru."

"He stands for do no evil," Father said. "And that, of course, is the rub. Should someone see or hear evil, there is little one can do. When someone speaks evil, there is fault to be had, but when they do evil . . . well, when they do evil there is no room for forgiveness."

"Those people aren't pure, are they, Father?"

"No, son, they most certainly are not." He turned back to Mrs. Carter. "Unfortunately, your husband fell into the latter group, and there is simply no need for people like him on this great planet of ours. I would have preferred to rid the world of his filth with a little more discretion than my wonderful wife deemed appropriate, but what's done is done and there is no use fretting over that which we cannot control. I'd also prefer you did not discover our shenanigans last night, but alas, your detective skills were exceptional, and discover you did. Hence, our current predicament: What to do with you?"

"Is she pure, Father?" I had to ask, for I did not know the answer. Surely she had seen and heard evil, but Father had told me before that those offenses were forgivable. Had she spoken evil? Had she done evil? I did not know.

Father brushed a strand of Mrs. Carter's hair from her eye. He stared at her for a long time in silence, then: "I don't know, son, but I plan to find out. Mr. Carter was an unsavory man, there is no question of that, but something set him off—something pushed a final button and caused his steam to come billowing out." He reached up and touched Mrs. Carter's black eye with the tip of his index finger. "I can't help but wonder what that little something was, and whether or not our dear Mrs. Carter here was behind it."

My mind shot back to the image of Mother with Mrs. Carter. I couldn't tell Father. Not yet. If Mrs. Carter's actions caused Mr. Carter to break the rules, then wouldn't it stand to reason that Mother was partly responsible for the actions of Mrs. Carter? If Mother broke the rules . . . I couldn't bear the thought.

Father watched me closely. Did he know? Had I given it away? He didn't delve deeper, though. Instead, he stood and gestured to the breakfast tray. "Now I'm afraid your breakfast has gone cold. I guess it will have to do. Perhaps next time you will accept such a gracious meal with a smile rather than such harsh negativity." He patted me on the shoulder. "Remember, son, no utensils for our guest."

"I know, Father."

"Atta boy."

He retreated up the stairs.

I turned back to Mrs. Carter and reached for her gag. "How about we give this another go?"

She nodded, her eyes fixed on Father's back as he disappeared.

34

Porter

Day I • 5:23 p.m.

Located just northwest of the Loop and bordering downtown Chicago, the Fulton River District was at the center of the city's urban renewal, with old warehouses converted to high-rent lofts and former shoe factories now turned to spas and coffee shops. Scattered among these hipster meccas stood the occasional condemned building. If they had thoughts, Porter supposed they were nervously monitoring their neighbors and waiting their turn at a facelift, hoping the reprieve would come before the wrecking ball arrived, ready to make room for something altogether new.

Such was the case for 1483 Desplaines.

Squat compared with the surrounding structures, it was only three stories tall and maybe ten thousand square feet at most. Upon closer inspection, the original red brick veneer poked out here and there but for the most part was lost beneath layers of paint—colors ranging from green to yellow to white. Most of the windows were either boarded or broken.

At one point it had probably stood proud, but history had not been kind to it. This building had lived through the worst of times. Prohibition had grown from the bowels of politics only to be snuffed out by the gangsters who had once stood in its windows. It witnessed the birth of the city and watched the Great Chicago Fire as neighboring buildings across the river burned to the ground. Porter swore he could still smell the flames and soot in that neighborhood, even though a hundred winters had tried to wash the stink away.

A single sign adorned the rooftop in faded wooden letters, reading MULIFAX PUBLICATIONS, all that remained of its former glory.

"Not much to look at," Nash said from the passenger seat of Porter's Charger. They were parked on the corner across the street with a direct view of the building. His phone buzzed with a text message, and he glanced down at the screen. "Clair is two minutes out, with SWAT at her back."

Porter checked his rearview mirror; Watson was busy typing away on his own phone. Porter had never seen fingers move so fast. "Christ, Doc, that thing is going to catch fire."

"Mulifax Publications shut their doors in 1999. This building has been empty ever since," Watson said without looking up. "Apparently their parent company kept up with the bills until 2003; then they went bankrupt and the city took possession. They tried to rent the place out but couldn't find a taker; the city condemned it in 2012."

"Why not renovate, like these other buildings?" Nash asked. "This neighborhood has gone ritzy. We're not getting in on a cop's salary, that's for damn sure."

Porter nodded at Mulifax. "Can your magic phone tell us what's inside that building?"

Nash answered. " I can tell you what's not inside—the Four Monkey Killer. 'Cause he's resting comfortably down at the morgue." His gaze played up and down the street. "That brings me to the ten-thousand-dollar question. Why are we waiting on SWAT anyway? No killer means there's nobody left to shoot at us."

Porter shrugged. "Captain's orders."

"Did he say why he wanted SWAT to go in first?"

"He thinks this might be a trap. Leaving the book like that . . . that's not like him. Something's not right."

"What do you think?"

"I don't know what to think."

"Look at this." Watson handed his phone to Porter. The browser window was open to a Wikipedia page. "They used to run bootleg booze out of here. There are secret tunnels running in and out of all these buildings."

"He could have used those to get around here unseen."

A green Honda Civic pulled up behind them. Clair Norton climbed out and ran low around the back of Porter's Charger to Nash's window. He rolled it down.

"See anything?" she asked, nodding toward the building.

"Nothing. It's been quiet."

"What about that white sedan?"

Porter had spotted the car when they arrived. A late-model Buick with a nice Bondo patch on the rear driver's side fender. "No sign of the driver."

Watson retrieved his phone from Porter. "Do you think he's using the tunnels?"

"The bootleg tunnels?" Clair glanced out at the surrounding buildings, then returned her gaze to the car. "I worked a trafficking case on the East Side a few years back, and the perps used the old tunnels to get around. I heard the phone company expanded them to run cables way back, even created a rail system down there. They were able to get from the river to nearly the center of the city without breaking daylight. Some of the tunnels are wide enough for a truck to pass," she explained. "You can get around the entire city if you know your way. It's cold as a witch's tit down there too—a few of the movie theaters downtown still use working air shafts to bring the cold air in from below to keep the theaters cool."

"Can you get from A. Montgomery Ward Park to here?"

"I see where you're going, Sam, but I doubt that would work," Nash said. "He took her out of there in a car. If he had tried climbing down a storm drain with our girl in tow, I think somebody would have stopped him."

Clair rolled her eyes. "You didn't see that crew."

Porter continued to brainstorm. "Okay, so he takes her in a car. Where next? A. Montgomery Ward Park is less than a block from the North Branch of the Chicago River. Can you enter the tunnel system from there with a car?"

Watson was tapping at his phone again. "I'm going to guess that you can, but I can't find any detailed pictures. Makes sense, right? The builders would have wanted access from every major waterway. He could have disappeared underground with her and carried her here without the risk of being seen even if he made part of the trip on foot."

"It's possible he transported all the victims that way. That would explain how he got around the city for so long without a trace," Nash added.

"So, she could be here," Clair said softly.

"Yeah," said Porter.

A dark blue van with TOMLINSON PLUMBING stenciled on the side in bright yellow letters crossed the intersection and pulled into the space directly behind the sedan.

"That our boys?" Porter asked.

"Yes, sir. Figured best to keep quiet." Clair's phone rang and she plucked it from her pocket and answered. She nodded several times, then: "Copy that, go in three." She turned back to Nash and Porter. "Ready to gear up? We go in behind them. They'll clear the building, then we follow on their six."

Nash pointed his thumb at the back seat. "What about him?"

Porter turned back to the rearview mirror, eyeing Watson. "You're not carrying, right?"

Watson shook his head. "No, sir."

"Any chance you brought a vest?" Department policy prohibited anyone from entering a hot crime scene without a bulletproof vest.

"They're not standard issue in my department."

"Then I guess you're waiting out here. Sorry, kid."

Porter and Nash climbed from the car and walked around to the back. From the trunk, Porter retrieved two bulletproof vests, a shotgun, and a large Maglite. He handed the shotgun along with one of the vests to Nash and donned the other. Nash snapped open the shotgun, checking the breech that sealed the barrel back in place. Porter then pulled a nine-millimeter Beretta 92FS from beneath the spare tire and checked the magazine. A pull of the slide confirmed that one round readied the chamber.

"Backup piece?" Nash asked, checking his own gun, a Walther PPQ.

Porter nodded. "I haven't seen the captain yet. He still has my department-issued."

"Technically, you're not back on the job yet. Probably best you don't get yourself shot. *Injured tagalong civilian* carries much more paperwork than *injured partner.*"

"Glad you've got my back."

Clair's phone buzzed with a text message. "Go in ten seconds." She pulled the slide on her Glock and chambered a round.

The Tomlinson Plumbing van rocked for a second, then the back doors swung open and men dressed in full riot gear began pouring out. The first two carried a large black metal ram, the others held AR-15 assault rifles at the ready. They moved in swift unison to the building.

Nash darted across the street after them, with Porter at his side and Clair on their heels.

The ram made quick work of the front doors—one hit and they were in. The padlock ripped from the metal frame and clattered to the ground, only to be kicked aside by booted feet as they rushed through. The men holding the ram fell to the side to allow the others to stream past, then they plucked their own rifles from their backs and went in behind them.

A concussion grenade detonated. Muted shouts of "Police!" and "Clear!" sounded as the team disappeared inside. Porter's grip tightened on his Beretta as they crossed from the sunlit street to the black void of the building's entrance.

"I can't see shit in there," Nash groused, staring inside.

"All the windows are sealed. It's like a tomb," Clair said.

Porter peered around the door frame. The light from the street seemed to pool inside the entrance, nothing more than a ten-by-ten square edged by the blackest of black. The shadows seemed to push back, forcing the light out.

He snapped on the Maglite and swept the beam over the interior, expecting a wide-open warehouse. Instead, the light played across a narrow entranceway of rotted wood. The acoustic-tile ceiling was crumbling, the plaster walls were chipped and cracked, and the floor was covered in the debris that had broken away over the years.

Porter heard the team deep inside the building, their boots pounding against the concrete as they swept room after room.

Then silence.

"You hear that?"

"Hear what?"

"SWAT stopped moving."

"They might be too far into the building. You just can't hear them anymore."

"No, that's not it. They stopped moving."

"Maybe they found something?"

"Maybe."

"It's too quiet," Clair said.

"Let's go," Porter said. "Stay close."

They moved slowly, the beam of the Maglite slicing through the gloom. The entryway turned into a hallway that turned into a narrow path as they made their way through boxes, crates, and other assorted items stacked against the wall. Porter counted no fewer than five mattresses within the first fifty feet, the cloth rotted and worn, damp with mildew and insects crawling in and out of the fabric. The concrete floor was a cesspool of dirt and grime dotted with small puddles of piss-scented water. The sound of needles crunching underfoot was enough to wish his attention elsewhere. He pictured tiny rodent skeletons snapping under each step.

There were doors every ten feet or so, the wood frames cracked and splintered. Porter knew the SWAT team had made quick work of them either with a kick or the battering ram they had used on the front door. Porter shined the Maglite through each room as they passed, even though he knew he wouldn't find anything worthwhile —a cautionary move at best.

At the third door he stopped and forced his ears to listen.

He heard the steady drip of water.

Nash and Clair, breathing, a few paces back.

The ticking of his watch.

He couldn't hear the SWAT team, though. Not a single sound came from up ahead.

Porter slowed down enough to allow Nash and Clair to catch up. "Something's wrong; I don't like this."

A loud crash followed by two quick gunshots came from deep within the building.

"Go!" Porter ordered, rushing toward the gunfire.

Clair and Nash chased after him, following the bouncing Maglite.

Moving fast, Porter followed the sound. He felt as if he was going to choke on the mildew. They came upon a broken freight elevator with a set of stairs trailing down to the left. Voices rose from below.

Without hesitation, they descended the steps two at a time, avoiding the trash and debris, careful not to slip.

"What the fuck!" someone shouted.

"Where are they coming from?"

"I can't tell!"

"Pull back!"

"No, wait!"

A bright red light illuminated the doorway at the base of the stairs. Someone had set off a flare. Porter squinted against the bright light. He raised the muzzle of his gun so it pointed to the ceiling. He wasn't about to risk an accidental discharge.

From below: "They're scattering!"

"Set off another one. Over there, in the corner!"

Nash grabbed Porter's shoulder and held him still a few steps from the bottom, then shouted, "Espinosa? It's Detectives Nash, Norton, and Porter. We're at the stairs. Hold your fire!"

"Hold on, Detectives!" Espinosa shouted back.

"Clear!" someone else cried out.

"Fucking things are everywhere!"

Another flare burned to life with a loud sizzle and landed at the base of the steps.

At least half a dozen rats darted past, their tiny feet clambering over Porter's and Nash's shoes. Clair let out a yelp.

"Fuck!" Nash shouted, jumping back against the wall.

Porter stared in awe as six more ran by.

"All right—you can come down; just stay in the light," Espinosa told them.

"I ain't—" Nash said.

Clair gave him a push. "Move, you baby."

They stepped out into a large basement, which appeared to span the length of the building. Illuminated by the red flares, concrete floors and redbrick walls spread out as far as Porter could see. The floor was littered with trash: boxes, loose paper, soda cans, and—

"I've never seen so many rats," Porter said, his eyes locked on the ground just beyond the flare's reach. The floor shimmered and moved. A living blanket of rodents. They crawled over one another in an attempt to retreat from the light, only they had no place to go. Little nails clicked against the concrete, digging into the backs of others as they scrambled back.

"I told you guys to wait outside," Espinosa said, frowning. "At least until I know what the hell we're dealing with down here."

"We're dealing with a damn infestation," one of the other SWAT members grumbled, before tossing another flare deep into the back of the room.

"You throw them back there, the rats are gonna come out this way. We need to force them back."

"Force them where?"

"You're shooting at rats?" Porter asked.

"That was Brogan, fucking idiot."

"Hey!"

"Damn things are everywhere. Gotta be a thousand of them down here," Espinosa said, kicking one off his boot. The rat sailed through the air and bounced off a far wall, then shook it off and ran toward the far corner of the room.

Nash stood perfectly still, his face pale white as rats scurried around their feet, running past in blind panic with their tiny yellow teeth bared.

Clair told them about the tunnels, suggesting that was probably how they got in and out of this basement.

Espinosa nodded and pressed a button on the radio at his shoulder. "Check the perimeter walls. We're looking for some kind of tunnel entrance."

"We don't need to search," Porter said, his eyes following the rodents as they crossed the floor, darting around the trash. "Just follow them." His eyes went to the far back corner. They weren't running in random patterns but streaming in that direction, a river of disease and filth. "Can I have a flare?" he asked.

Espinosa pulled one from his belt and handed it to Porter.

Porter tugged off the cap, ignited it, and launched the canister toward the back. It arched through the air and landed with a thud sixty feet away.

"Whoa! You've got a hell of an arm on you, Detective!" Espinosa exclaimed.

Porter chased after the flare.

Although the rats gave the flame a wide berth, they continued toward a singular spot, toward a closed door with a small hole at the bottom right corner, a hole large enough for them to squeeze through. And that was precisely what they were doing. In neat single file, they pushed through the opening, one after another.

Porter reached for the door, and Espinosa grabbed his hand. "Step back, Detective. We need to clear that room." His voice was low, barely audible.

Porter nodded and moved to the side.

Gesturing with his free hand, Espinosa directed two team members to flank the door. He stood ten feet back with his weapon trained on the opening, then counted down from three with his fingers.

At zero, one of the SWAT team kicked in the door and ducked inside, moving swift and low to the left. The other officer trained his weapon above him and swept the barrel across the room before following his partner. Two other men streamed in behind him.

"Clear!" Muffled, distant.

Then another: "Clear!"

Weapon at the ready, Espinosa moved quickly and disappeared. A moment later the bright light of a red flare burned from inside.

"Porter—get in here!" Espinosa shouted.

Porter looked back at Nash and Clair, then stepped through the doorway, avoiding the rats running both in and out at his feet.

The room was colder than the rest of the basement, damp with mildew and decay. He recognized the scent immediately, the sickly sweet odor of rotting flesh. His hand went to his nose and mouth in an attempt to block the stench, but it did little good.

The five men stood before him, their eyes fixed, staring.

"Everyone out," Porter ordered through muffled breath.

Espinosa turned, ready to argue, then thought better of it. He went back through the shattered door, motioning for his men to follow.

Porter stepped deeper into the room.

Hundreds of candles lined the walls and floor, most burned to nothing but piles of wax. The few that remained sputtered their pale light, a weak dance at best against the bright illumination of the flare.

He wanted to put it out. The flare, the candles.

He wanted to extinguish all of it and plunge this place back into darkness.

He didn't want to see.

None of it.

Toppled on its side at the center of the room lay an old hospital gurney, its metal rails covered in crimson patches of rust.

Under the gurney, a naked body was handcuffed to the frame— a body that had been devoured by the thousands of rodents rustling hungrily about.

A bony pile of tattered meat.

35

Diary

Mrs. Carter must have understood the rules, because she didn't scream this time when I removed the gag. She didn't curse. If hateful thoughts floated through her head, she kept them to herself. Instead, she looked at me with tired eyes. "Thirsty," she said.

I held the orange juice to her parched lips and tipped it just enough to allow the (now warm) liquid to fill her mouth, then gave her a chance to swallow.

"More, please."

I gave her more. When she finished the last of it, I set the glass down beside her cot. "Banana or Cheerios?"

She took in a deep breath. "You have to let me go."

"I know dry Cheerios may not seem very appetizing, but I guarantee you, they are. Those little round oats are a wondrous treat, perhaps one of my favorites." I was tempted to eat some of them myself, but she needed the nourishment. I would reward myself with a bowl when I went back upstairs.

Mrs. Carter leaned closer. I felt her warm breath on my cheek. "Your mother and father are going to kill me. You understand that, right? Is that what you want? I've never been anything but nice to you. I even let you see me . . . you know, out by the lake. That was a special moment between you and me. Something only for you. If you let me go, I

promise you there will be more of that, much more. I'll give you anything you want. I'll do things no girl your age could possibly know. You
just have to let me go."

"Banana or Cheerios?" I repeated.

"Please."

"Okay, banana then," I peeled the banana and held it up to her
mouth. Her eyes fluttered for a moment, then she leaned forward and
took a bite.

"I told you it was good."

"You're good," she told me. "You're a good boy, and I know you're
not going to let anything happen to me, right?"

I thrust the banana back at her. "You need to eat."

She took another bite, slower than the last, her red lips slipping
over the banana and lingering for a moment before pulling away.

36

Porter

Day I • 5:32 p.m.

As Espinosa and his team filed out the door, Porter stepped deeper into the room.

"Nash, Clair, grab a flashlight and get in here!" he shouted over his shoulder.

Kneeling down beside the body, he clapped his hands with as much force as he could muster. The loud crack echoed through the room, sending rats scurrying out from under the body. He clapped again and two more bolted for cover. His palms red and pained, he clapped a third time, and another shot out, bits of flesh dangling from clenched teeth. It looked like part of an ear.

A beam of white light danced across the far wall. Porter turned to find Nash standing behind him, the sleeve of his jacket covering his mouth. "Holy Christ," he said.

"Let me see that," Porter said, gesturing to the light.

Nash stretched and handed the flashlight to him, his legs firmly planted in place.

"Oh, bloody hell." Clair coughed, covering her mouth. "Is that Emory?"

Without turning: "Clair, head back topside. Tell Watson to call in CSI and get down here. ME's office too."

"Yes, sir," she replied before heading back the way they'd come.

"Brian, you don't need to stay in here. I understand."

Nash shook his head. "I'll be all right . . . give me a minute."

Porter turned the beam to the body.

Flies buzzed around the pale mound wedged beneath the gurney and the concrete floor. As he leaned in toward the head, he noticed a fracture in the skull a quarter inch below the hairline. The skin around the fracture had been picked clean. Most likely the injury had bled and the rats honed in on the scent. "I think they fell off the gurney and split their head open on impact. No telling how long they were down here."

Nash pointed farther down. "The right arm is handcuffed to the gurney. I think they pulled the whole mess down on top of them when they fell. Is it our girl?"

Porter ran the light up and down the body, then moved in close at the head again. "No, this person has short brown hair. I think they're older. I see specks of gray, heavy wrinkling under what's left of the chin. Emory is much younger, and her hair is darker."

"Is it a woman?"

"Hard to say. Help me roll the body."

Another rat pushed out from under the left leg and ran for the door. "Motherfuckers—" Nash jumped back.

Porter rolled his eyes at him and thrust out the flashlight. "Christ, I'll do it. Hold this and follow my hands."

Nash took the light and held it forward. "Sorry, damn thing spooked me, that's all."

"Didn't you ever own a pet hamster or gerbil when you were a kid? They're no different, just a little bigger."

"They eat trash and carry more diseases than a Kardashian at Mardi Gras," Nash replied. "One of those little fuckers bites you, and you'll spend the rest of the night down at the ER getting rabies shots in your gut. No thanks."

"In your arm," Porter said as he reached into his pocket and pulled out a pair of green latex gloves.

"What?"

"The shots, they don't get you in your abdomen anymore; they inject them into your upper arm."

"Ah, progress."

"They don't typically carry rabies, either. There's never been a recorded case of rabies resulting from a rat bite in the U.S. That's a myth. Makes us feel better about killing them. Can you imagine how filthy this city would be without rats running around eating our waste? People are the real infestation, if you ask me. People do things like this." His eyes were fixed on the body. "I need you to pick up the gurney while I roll the body. Get on the other side."

"I never took you for a rat sympathizer." Nash pinched the flashlight under his arm while pulling out a pair of his own gloves and snapping them on, then walked around the body and took hold of the frame. "On three?"

"On three."

He counted them down. As Nash lifted the gurney, Porter took hold of the shoulder with his left hand and reached around to the back of the body's leg with his right and pulled toward him, his aging back fighting the movement with a bolt of pain down his thigh. The body made a sick sucking noise as it pulled away from the concrete floor. The smell lofted up in a wave of stink both sweet and sour, rotten and damp. As the body fell onto its back, Porter realized half the stomach was missing. There was only a large cavity where the intestines and lining had been, pink and oozing melted fat infested with maggots.

Nash rolled the gurney aside, barely missing Porter's head as he dropped the frame to the ground and doubled over, half-digested Kit Kat remnants splashing against the cinder block wall. The flashlight turned with him, and Porter was thankful for the moment of darkness. He needed those seconds to prepare himself before he could look back.

When Nash righted himself and turned back, he tried to apologize but Porter waved him off. "Give me the light."

Nash nodded and handed the flashlight to him before wiping the corner of his mouth on his jacket sleeve.

The beam rolled over the body, slowly, from what remained of the face to the toes and back again. "Male, probably fifties."

"Christ, how can you tell?"

The rats had made off with his genitals. Most of the meat had been picked clean, leaving bones, sinewy muscle, and an empty space where they had once been. It was an odd color, a mix of dark green, white, and maroon. Maggots wiggled and writhed through the layers, slowly digesting what remained of the rat's feast.

"They made off with the eyes," Nash said.

Porter directed the light back to the head. They had taken more than just the eyes. The empty sockets stared back at him with an unfaltering gaze. The white of the optic nerve at the center and the missing eyelids gave a cartoonish appearance—Little Orphan Annie from the old comic strips.

"How long do think he's been down here?"

Porter sighed, regretting the deep breath the moment the putrid air entered his lungs. "Couple days, at least. I think he was alive for at least two before he passed."

"Why?"

Porter pointed at the man's neck. "See the beard stubble? He's got at least a couple days' worth. His hair is short, well kept. He even trimmed his eyebrows. A man like that shaves once, sometimes twice a day. He hadn't shaved at least two days, maybe three. I'm sure the medical examiner will be able to get us something more precise."

"Any idea on the cause of death?"

He ran the light over the body again. "No obvious wounds. I'm going to guess he was stabbed in the stomach area. That's where the rats seemed to do the most damage."

"They went for the blood from the wound first, like the crack to his skull."

"Uh-huh."

Nash took a step closer and pointed at the victim's left hand. "What's that?"

Porter followed his gaze. The hand was balled up into a fist, clenching something. He reached down and tried to pry open the fingers.

"Rigor?"

"It's already passed. The rats chewed at the fingers, and the dried blood glued them together. Hold this again." He passed the flashlight back to Nash.

Both hands free, he pried open the fingers. There was a piece of glossy paper clutched in the victim's grasp. About five inches long, rolled up like a handmade cigarette. Porter plucked it free and delicately unrolled the thick paper. "It's a brochure."

"For what?"

Porter held the colorful brochure up to the light.

Nash leaned in closer and read aloud. "The Moorings Lakeside, a Talbot Estates Development. Where yacht and country club living combine."

"Talbot's real estate company?"

"Or his construction company, possibly both." Nash reached for the brochure. "I've seen commercials for this place. They bulldozed dozens of warehouses and industrial facilities on the lake, buildings just like this one, and they've been replacing them with McMansions. The houses are huge, but on zero lot lines. It's crazy. If you've got the kind of coin to afford a place like that on the water, why would you want to live right on top of your neighbor? I've got a buddy who works down at Harbor, and he said the water lots come with docks, but they didn't dredge them out deep enough — you can't get much more than a troller in there. If you want to bring in a bigger boat, they upsell you into paying a ridiculous fee to go deeper. Doesn't do much good, though, unless your neighbors do the same; the sediment washes right back in. A couple years' time and you'll need to do it all over again."

Porter forced his tired body to stand, his knees creaking under the strain. "We need to get outside and call Hosman. 4MK targeted Talbot for a reason; it must be tied to this development."

"Maybe something sketchy with the accounting?"

"Big project like this? Could be anything. You step on a lot of toes pushing a large real estate project through."

"Porter?"

Both men turned. Espinosa was standing at the entrance. "My men located the tunnel you mentioned. It was boarded over at some point, but someone busted through recently and covered up the opening with a few crates. The tunnel breaks off from the subbasement and heads north. Unless you need me here, I'm going to take a team and follow it, see where it leads."

Porter wanted to get back outside. This room, the body, the rats, everything about this mess was making him claustrophobic. "Nash, wait here for the medical examiner. Get Watson to process the scene. I'm going with Espinosa's team. I'll touch base when we figure out where the tunnel leads." He turned back to Espinosa. "Lead the way."

37

Diary

"Hey, champ. Can you give me a hand with these?"

Father stood near the back stoop, my little red wagon beside him, piled high with small parcels about one foot square wrapped in black plastic bags and sealed with duct tape.

I must admit, I hadn't used that wagon in a number of years. The last time I saw it, it was buried far back in our toolshed under assorted lawn care products and an old barbecue Father purchased on clearance at Sears many summers ago. Father liked the grill because it used gas; Mother disliked it because it did not use charcoal. To me, a burger off the grill was a burger off the grill, and I had zero preference as to how it was grilled as long as that burger ended up on my plate—perhaps with a dab of ketchup, a smear of mustard, and a little mayonnaise.

I didn't like Father using my wagon without asking me.

I knew this was a silly thought. He'd purchased the wagon, but still, it was mine and it was rude to borrow someone's wagon without first seeking permission. I would never do such a thing, and even at such a young age, I was bothered.

"I need you to do me a big favor, buddy. I need you to take these packages down to the lake, tape some heavy rocks to them, and throw them out into the water as far as you possibly can. Think you can do that for me? Can I count on you?" He handed me half a roll of duct tape. "I planned to do it, but I got called into the office. I'm afraid if I let this little task go until later tonight, we might find a tad of a stink permeating the house, and we don't want that, particularly since we have a guest."

I picked up the wagon's handle and gave it an experimental tug. "It's heavy."

Father smiled. "It's about a hundred eighty pounds of bad beef—should make our little fishy friends very happy, don't you think?"

Do fish eat beef? I'd heard of exotic fish such as piranha that love to dine on a pound of flesh, but I was fairly confident there were no piranhas in our lake. Our lake had plenty of trout and bass, though I hadn't been schooled on their dietary habits. I still harbored suspicion about whether or not they even ate worms.

"Do you still have your knife with you? Maybe cut a small slit in each package before you toss it into the water. Give them a little taste of the feast to be found inside. That would be splendid."

"Yes, Father."

"Oh, fiddlesticks." He glanced over at the Carter house. "We still need to pack a couple bags and stage the house."

"I can do it," I told him earnestly.

He looked down at me and cocked his head. "Yeah?"

I nodded. "Absolutely, Father. You can count on me!"

His eyes grew narrow as he contemplated this. Then he nodded. "Okay, champ. I'll leave this man's work in your capable hands. Load some stuff in their car, and I'll get rid of it tonight."

"Where are you going to leave it?"

Father shrugged. "Not sure yet. The airport is a bit of a drive. I was thinking about the bus depot over in Marlow. I'll come up with something."

He started toward the front of the house, then paused. "One more thing, champ. Can you keep an eye on your mother? You know how she gets after . . ."

I nodded. I did, in fact, know how she gets.

He grinned. "My little boy is almost a little man. Who'da thunk it? Surely not me." He turned and rounded the corner. "Surely not me, no sir," he said as he disappeared from sight.

Mother tended to get a little emotional after a kill. She could be unpredictable. Sometimes she would shut down completely, just disappear into her room and not come out for days. When she did emerge, she would be right as rain, but for those few days it was best to leave her alone. Other times she'd overflow with joy, laughing and joking in the merriest of ways. She would dance in the kitchen and skip down the street. I liked this Mother best—Chipper Mother, Elated Mother, the Mother of Many Smiles. We never knew which Mother would emerge after a kill, only that one of them would, and no less than a handful of days would pass before Original Mother returned from her mental journey.

I considered checking on her before I left for the lake but decided against it. If today was the day for Chipper Mother, hearing what I was about to do might cause her to revert to one of the others, and nobody wanted that. Best to leave well enough alone until I completed my morning chores, then devote the remainder of the day to her company, helping her cope with the events of last night.

With a rough tug, the wagon fell into step behind me and I started down the path to the lake while whistling a merry little tune by Eddie and the Cruisers. Luckily, it was downhill. Mr. Carter had been a large man.

38

Porter

Day 1 • 6:18 p.m.

Porter followed Espinosa out of the kill room to the main subbasement. Three of Espinosa's men were huddled in the far right corner, a stack of crates at their side. As Porter approached, he took note of the names stitched into their uniforms: Brogan, Thomas, and Tibideaux.

Tibideaux spoke first. "It was just like you said. We followed the rats, and most of them made a beeline from the body to this corner. They disappeared behind this mess of crap, so we figured something must be back here. We found the tunnel opening buried behind the crates." He gestured to a wide mouth carved into the cement wall.

The rounded opening was about seven or eight feet tall and six feet wide, reinforced with a stone parameter. Small railroad tracks started just inside the passage and disappeared down its throat.

"My grandfather told me about these. They used them to transport coal from the river to buildings downtown in the early 1900s," Brogan said. He shined his light into the opening, revealing a small railcar a little larger than a shopping cart. Although the car must have been a hundred years old, the wheels glimmered with newly applied oil.

"Do any of you have a printing kit? Someone's been using that."

Thomas nodded. "I'm on it." He pulled a small pack from his belt, knelt down beside the cart, and began brushing powder. His fingers moved with the dexterity of a seasoned professional. Porter couldn't help but wonder what previous assignments the man held before finding his way into SWAT.

Porter had lived in the city for more years than he cared to count, and before today he had no idea these tunnels existed. His mind began to race back through 4MK's previous victims, where they were abducted, where they were found. If these tunnels did run throughout the city, it was feasible he had been using them this entire time to transport the bodies. It made sense. They'd never determined how he moved through the city unseen. After all, he deposited some of the bodies in heavily trafficked areas without a single witness. Susan Devoro had been positioned on a bench near the center of Union Station, covered in a filthy blanket. The odds that one of these tunnels intersected with Union was high. To get her body there aboveground, he would have passed through security, a dozen vendors, and who knows how many pedestrians. Even in the middle of the night the route was bustling. Underground, though? That had to be it.

"It's been wiped," Thomas said. "But I've got a partial down here at the left rear wheel. Should be enough to make a match if he's in the system."

"4MK never left a print behind. I guess if you're planning on stepping in front of a bus, stealth no longer matters."

Thomas lifted the print and handed the latent preservation tape to Porter in a plastic bag. "Here you go, sir."

Porter held it up to the light—more than half of a fingertip. Enough for an ID. "Nice job, Thomas." He dropped it into his pocket and turned to the sergeant. "Espinosa, is your radio working?"

The large man glanced down at his receiver and shook his head. "We lost communication the moment we descended those stairs. No cell service, either."

"If we follow that tunnel, how do we keep from getting lost?"

Porter imagined dozens or more tunnels breaking off in numerous directions—an underground maze. He supposed the city had maps, but how accurate would they be? Particularly if some tunnels were constructed for bootlegging. There may be no record of them at all.

Espinosa pulled a small can of spray paint from a pouch on his pack. "Did I mention I used to be a Boy Scout?"

"All right then, lead the way."

Espinosa went first, followed by Thomas and Tibideaux, then Porter with Brogan at the rear. Together they filed into the tunnel, squeezing past the railcar. The air immediately felt damp and cool. Porter figured the temperature must be in the mid-fifties. The tunnel walls were smooth, carved out of limestone. Even in today's world, digging something like this would prove to be a difficult task. How had they managed such a feat more than a hundred years ago? How many men died down here?

At least one more soul joined them this week, Porter thought.

Water dripped from the ceiling in places. Not enough to be worrisome, but enough to make the ground slippery. Porter hadn't dressed for spelunking; his black loafers offered little traction.

Twenty minutes later, when they arrived at a bend followed by an intersection, the five men stopped. Espinosa lifted his light high and pointed the beam down the three possible paths. "Any suggestions?"

Porter knelt down at the center. "Shine that down here?"

The light redirected, joined by flashlights from the others. Porter studied the tracks. Only one bore signs of recent use: the one veering off to the left. "That way."

Espinosa gave his paint can a quick shake and drew an arrow on the wall pointing back the way in which they had come; then they continued.

Porter peered into the darkness at their backs. Pitch-black. Not a single hint of light poked through. He imagined the entrance to hell was something like this. What would happen if the tunnel collapsed behind them? The air felt thin, desperate. How cut off from the real world were they?

He looked down at his iPhone. No signal.

Espinosa raised his right fist and froze, pointing his weapon ahead. "I see light up there," he told them in a low voice.

"Outside?" Thomas asked.

"I don't think so; not bright enough. Come with me. The rest of you hold here for a minute."

Porter crouched low, pulled the Beretta from his shoulder holster, and disengaged the safety, pointing the barrel at the ceiling.

What if bullets started flying around in here? The ricochet off these stone walls would be deadly. Although he wore a vest, that left plenty exposed for a bullet to wreak havoc. A quick inventory of the other men's eyes told him they were having similar thoughts. Brogan had pulled a large knife from a sheaf on his thigh, favoring the close-quarters weapon to the MP5 slung over his back. Tibideaux held a Glock.

"Porter!"

From up ahead, Espinosa's voice echoed off the smooth stone.

Porter rose and sprinted down the tunnel toward the light, the other men at his back. They found Espinosa and Thomas standing at the center of some type of chamber. A floodlight illuminated the space from high atop the wall, somehow tapped into city power. In the far corner, a ladder was bolted into the limestone. A manhole cover rested at the top. Espinosa was pointing his weapon at the ground. "There."

Porter followed his gaze.

Three white boxes stood side by side, each sealed with a black string. A single word was scrawled into the top of the middle box. PORTER.

"Gloves?"

Tibideaux pulled some from his jacket pocket. Porter slipped them on and carefully pulled the string on the first box. Then he removed the lid—

A human ear lying on a bed of cotton.

"Oh, that's foul," Brogan said, taking a step back.

Porter opened the next box, revealing a pair of eyes. Blue. Part of the optic nerve still dangled from the end of one of them, shriveled and crusted, dried and stuck to the cotton by a thin trail of blood.

The final box contained a tongue.

Porter hadn't checked the body at Mulifax for a tongue. The eyes and ear were both missing, but he assumed the rats had gotten them. "I'm guessing these belong to our victim back in the basement. We'll have to get them back to the medical examiner to find out for sure."

"Not it," Brogan spat. "I'm not carrying those."

"Me either, boss. That's bad juju right there," Tibideaux said.

"Fucking pansies," Thomas said. He pulled three plastic bags from his pack and handed them to Porter. "If you bag them, I'll carry them."

Porter shook his head. "Leave them as is for now. I'll get CSI to run this entire room."

He stood and gestured at the ladder. "He wants us to go up there. No other reason to place them here. X marks the spot."

"On it." Espinosa slung his weapon over his shoulder and started up the ladder. "Cover me, Brogan."

"Yes, sir." Brogan knelt down at the base and pointed his MP5 at the manhole.

When he reached the top, Espinosa pushed at the metal cover. It was difficult to get leverage on the thick steel from that position. Porter knew from experience that they weighed about a hundred pounds. With a loud grunt, he slid the cover to the side. Daylight streamed in. Porter shielded his eyes.

Espinosa pulled a Glock from a thigh holster and readied the weapon, then in one quick, fluid motion he pulled himself through the hole and rolled off to the right.

Brogan stood at the ladder's base, his weapon pointed at the sky.

"Clear!" Espinosa's voice came back.

"Go ahead, Detective," Brogan said.

Porter pulled his tired frame up the ladder, the warmth of the sun forcing the cold from his bones. As his head broke the surface, he found himself at the center of a residential intersection. There was no traffic, the houses still in various stages of construction.

"The Moorings Lakeside, I presume."

39

Diary

The cat no longer smelled, which was a welcome surprise. As I approached, I gave the furry remains a little tap with the tip of my shoe. An assortment of flies took wing, and a couple of creepy-crawlies darted out from the carcass. What little meat remained had the appearance of rotten jerky matted with black and white hair. The skull appeared smaller, as if shrunken by the elements. That was silly, of course. Cats don't shrink, even when exposed to water. But smaller it appeared, defying such logic. Something had absconded with the cat's tail. Of all things, why would something want its tail? Mother Nature and her critters never failed to surprise me.

I tugged at the wagon, the precariously stacked parcels threatening to tumble as one of the wheels bounced over an exposed root. I reached for them and held them in place. The contents were squishy under my touch, like the surface of a water balloon. My mind's eye sent me the image of my finger bursting through and sinking into one of the bags, and I cursed myself for not taking a moment to fetch a pair of gloves. I considered running home for some but realized Father probably preferred that I complete this task barehanded. If I wore gloves, evidence might gather on them or because of them, then the question of disposal would come into play. I couldn't bring gloves home and chance the wrong person finding them (never mind the large Mr. Carter stain drying into our basement floor), nor could I throw them into the lake and risk someone finding them there and tracing them back to me. Father had once told me the police could lift prints from the inside of a pair of gloves. Best to go without and simply wash my hands of whatever muck happened to accumulate.

Reaching the water's edge, I dropped the wagon handle and peered out around the lake. Fishermen, swimmers, or some other spectators might be wandering about, none of whom were welcome at my little party. The lake appeared quiet, though— not another soul to be found either in the water or along the edge.

Satisfied I was alone, I withdrew my knife and snapped open the blade, then picked up the first package. I sliced it open and turned my head as the putrid aroma crept out and tickled at my nose.

Well, Father, here's to hoping the fish enjoy a yummy snack. I heaved the package toward the middle of the lake with all the strength I could muster. I would never make the school football team, but it sailed a respectable distance before plunging into the water and disappearing beneath the surface.

"Skipper doodles!" I cursed. I'd forgotten to tape rocks to it.

I watched the lake, expecting the plastic-wrapped parcel to float back up, but it never did. A few minutes passed and the water grew still.

Turning back to the wagon, I counted at least thirty more packages. I would need rocks, many rocks. I began to gather a pile beside my wagon. Once I had enough, I secured them to the packages with the duct tape, double-wrapping to ensure they would remain together. Then, one at a time, I cut the packages open and heaved them out toward the center of the water. The extra weight limited my distance, but they still traveled far enough. I had swum here before (and I was fairly certain after today, I never would again), and I knew the bottom dropped off significantly just a few feet from shore. I didn't know how deep the lake was at the center, but I could only walk out about ten feet before the water reached my chin—another step and I would be forced to swim or sink. The packages were landing anywhere from fifteen to twenty feet out and no doubt sinking to the bottom.

It took me nearly forty minutes to complete my assignment. By the time I looked down at an empty wagon, my shoulders and back were both screaming from the exercise, and my knife was shiny with crimson. I dipped the blade into the water and rubbed it off with my thumb and forefinger, scrubbing until the metal glistened. I dropped it into my pocket and took one last gander out at the lake. I was fairly confident none of the bags would float back up, but I'd be lying if I said that very first bag didn't concern me. Perhaps I would take a walk back out here later today for a little double check.

Dropping the remainder of the duct tape into my wagon, I scooped up the handle and started back down the path toward home, where the Carter house awaited.

40

Porter
Day 1 • 9:12 p.m.

Porter emerged from the dark, cavernous mouth of the Mulifax Publications Building with Nash at his back. Both men drew in long breaths of fresh air, tasting the acidic scent of fish rolling in from the lake, decaying trash in the alley to their right, and a damp sleeping bag left to rot outside the door.

It was wonderful.

It was the best air Porter had ever breathed.

After reaching the end of the tunnel and the manhole, he instructed Espinosa and his team to search the Moorings housing development from top to bottom. He retraced his steps back to the kill room in the subbasement, where he found Watson diligently processing the scene while the medical examiner looked over the body.

He'd spent an additional three hours inside the building, and Porter had no intention of stepping back inside in the foreseeable future.

Clair had her back to him, pacing as she spoke into her phone. "It all revolves around Talbot; we've got to bring him in. There's more than—" She lifted her phone up over her head and swore a string of words Porter wouldn't have anticipated coming from a longshoreman.

She rolled her eyes and brought the phone back to her ear. "But Captain, I—"

"Could the captain really be fighting her on this?" Nash asked, his eyes locked on Clair.

Porter wanted to talk to Talbot—not a chat on the golf course but a sit-down, bright-light-in-your-face, one-way-mirror-at-your-side kind of talk. The man was clearly in the middle of all this. Not only had 4MK kidnapped his illegitimate daughter, but now he linked that kidnapping directly to the Moorings Lakeside, one of Talbot's real estate developments. As much as Porter despised the killer, he knew the man didn't operate without a plan, without reason. Every previous victim had been kidnapped as retribution for some illegal activity perpetrated by a family member.

Talbot was dirty.

If they determined how dirty, they had a chance of getting to his daughter while there was still time.

Part of him hoped Espinosa would find her in one of the houses back at the Moorings, tied up and blindfolded in a basement or unfinished bedroom, but the chances of that were small. 4MK wouldn't stash her someplace where she could easily be found. On a construction site, a worker might stumble onto her. Hell, even a homeless person—God knew there were plenty of them squatting out there.

4MK wanted them to find Talbot, not the girl.

She had been missing for more than a day now. Most likely without food or water. He couldn't begin to imagine the pain she must be in. Even if 4MK gave her something after severing her ear, the drugs would have surely worn off by now.

"Yes, sir. I'll tell him," Clair said into her phone. "Yes, I'll make sure of it. You too, Captain." She disconnected the call and dropped the phone into her pocket. "That fucking spineless piece of shit!"

Nash handed her a cup of coffee he pilfered from one of the uniforms. "Let me guess. The captain plays golf with the mayor, who is close friends with the Talbots, and none of them wish to put a hole in the donation boat."

If a black woman could turn red, Porter imagined Clair was doing so now. For a second he thought she might throw the coffee back at Nash. "Cock-sucking little pissant ass clown."

"You're so hot when you rant," Nash said, squeezing her shoulder.

Finally she sighed. "He's got twelve more patrol cars on the way here and ten more heading to the Moorings. They're going to search both locations from top to bottom—all the structures and the tunnels. The captain wants us all to go home, get a good night's rest, and start fresh in the morning. Thinks if we stay out here all night, we'll be useless by tomorrow, walking zombies. He said if they find something, he'll notify us so we can come back out, but he doesn't want us standing around here. He also said he's not willing to bring in Talbot for an official sit-down, not yet. Says we're better off waiting for Hosman to finish digging through his financials than bringing him in because of this." She spread her arms out, gesturing toward the building. "He owns this place too, by the way. Bought it three weeks ago at auction."

"There's a shocker. I'm fairly certain he bought my house during the three minutes we've been standing here," Nash said.

"I'm not going home, fuck that," Clair said. "The captain is a tool."

"I think the captain's got a point on Talbot. Better to get the full picture on the financials than tip our hand on circumstantial evidence. We don't have enough to hold him." Porter ran his hand through his hair, his eyes wandering over the development. "Not yet, anyway. We'll probably only get one shot at him."

"So what do you want to do?" Nash asked.

"Clair, you head out to the Moorings and stay on top of the search. Nash, you do the same here. I'm going to take a ride out to Talbot's house and keep an eye on him. We may not be able to talk to him, but we can watch him. Besides, I'm not active right now. The captain doesn't get to tell me where I can and can't park. We'll regroup at the war room at first light." He glanced around at the growing crowd of officers. "Where's Watson?"

"He's still down in the tunnel, processing the chamber where you found the boxes," Nash replied. "Said he's got at least an hour to go."

Porter reached into his pocket and pulled out the bag with the fingerprint lift. "Can you give this to him? Better yet, catch a ride with one of the uniforms and drop it at the lab when you're done here. Ask them to process it. No need to add one more person to the chain of custody."

"Where'd you pull it?"

"Off the railcar back at the subbasement."

Nash held the bag up to the light for a second before shoving it into his pocket. "Will do." He turned toward Clair's car, hesitated, then leaned into Porter. "It's good to have you back, Sam."

Porter gave him a nod.

"I agree with Shrek. Good to have you back," Clair offered with a smile.

Porter watched Nash disappear in the crowd and Clair climb into her Civic and speed away, then crossed the street to his Charger.

41

Diary

Mr. Carter's car was still parked in their driveway. I'm not sure where else I expected it to be—Mr. Carter's time behind the wheel had come to an end, and Mrs. Carter would not be driving in the immediate future—yet seeing the car there made me feel as if someone occupied their house, even though I knew the place to be empty.

I left the wagon in our driveway and walked over.

As I pulled open the screen door, I couldn't shake the feeling someone was inside. The door had not been locked, so I suppose someone may have ventured in, but I had no legitimate reason for believing so. Our neighborhood was quite safe, the kind of place where doors were never locked and friends and family alike came and went from the various houses with little deterrent. In fact, I suspected Mr. Carter left the keys in his car yesterday; my parents typically did.

Something felt off, though.

The screen door squeaked ever so slightly as I pulled it open and stepped inside, just loud enough to alert a trespasser of my arrival.

The kitchen was quiet and seemed untouched since last night, the remains of the shattered glass still on the floor in an evaporating puddle of bourbon. It was crawling with ants. Did ants get drunk? I imagine they did. I watched as they scurried over the sticky mess, zigzagging with such purpose. They didn't appear any different from any other group of ants you might find outside on a sidewalk or lurking under a rock, yet they were saturated in alcohol. A couple of glasses had put me in a tizzy; surely swimming in booze would send them on a one-way trip to Drunksville. They seemed normal, though, unaffected.

I wanted to take a match to the whole lot of them. I'd set them ablaze and watch them burn. Their little bodies would crackle and pop with an alcohol-saturated fury. Alive one moment, charred dust the next. I would play God.

I made a mental note to conduct an experiment at a later date; I'd come here for a reason, and Father would be disappointed if I allowed a gaggle of ants to pull me astray.

I glanced over at the small table where Mrs. Carter had passed out. I could still picture her sitting there, her eyes glassy and speech slurred as she told me she had intended for me to see her naked that day at the lake. "A woman just wants to be desired, is all," she had said.

The thought sent my blood rushing.

Focus. I needed to focus.

The noise came from deep within the house.

A rattle of sorts, or perhaps a clank.

It wasn't the type of sound made by a house alone, not the creak or groan of a house settling or flexing as houses are known to do. This was something different.

I heard it again, louder than the first time. It came from the other side of the house, beyond the kitchen and down the hallway to where the bedrooms and a bath were no doubt located. I'd never ventured that far into the Carter home, and I didn't know exactly what lay beyond the kitchen. I could only speculate based on the layout of our own home, which was of similar size and style.

Reaching into my pocket, I withdrew my knife. I dared not flick the blade, for that would make a sound all its own and possibly betray my position to whoever (or whatever) was back there. I held the blade with one hand and pressed the button, slowly releasing the blade while maintaining pressure against the spring until the blade fully engaged and locked into place, the recently cleaned and sharpened metal shimmering in the dull light inching through the curtains and grasping at the interior of the Carter home.

Another clank.

Whoever (or whatever) was back there didn't know I was there. I had been noisy when I entered the house, carelessly so, but I must not have been heard. A burglar would have surely come running to see what was what.

Father had taught me to hunt when I was little. He'd taught me to walk on the tips of my toes so as not to make noise and to move with the grace of an elk slipping through the forest. I called upon that skill now, and without the slightest sound to betray me, I made my way across the kitchen and leaned against the door frame in order to get a view down the hallway.

The living room fell off to the right with a small bathroom across on the left. There were two other doors down at the end of the hall—no doubt belonging to the two bedrooms.

I closed my eyes and listened.

Rustling.

The shuffling of papers.

A drawer sliding open.

More rustling.

The noise came from the bedroom on the right. I didn't know if that was the Carters' room or their guest room, not from this distance.

My palm was sweaty from holding the knife too tightly.

I knew better.

A sweaty knife would be difficult to control. It might slip, miss its mark.

I wiped my hand on my jeans and took a deep breath, willing my pulse to slow, calming my body. I surrendered to my instincts.

I surrendered to the hunt.

I began down the hall, with my knife hand pressed against my chest, the blade facing forward. Father taught me this particular grip. If necessary, I would launch the knife forward with the full strength of my arm muscles and the accuracy of a loaded gun. Unlike an over-hand thrust, a jab would be difficult to block. This hold also allowed me to go directly for the heart or the stomach, with either an upward or downward motion, respectively. With an upper-hand grip, coming from *above, you could only strike down—such an attack was more likely to glance off your victim than penetrate deeply.*

Father was very skilled.

I pressed tightly against the wall, melding with the plaster as I moved, inching closer to the open door.

More rustling, then a hushed curse.

I saw a shadow moving within the room, a glimpse in the early light as the intruder shuffled about.

I reached the edge of the door frame.

Father once told me if you sneak up on someone, you have a second or more to attack before they are able to react. The human brain processes this activity slowly; your victim freezes for a moment as they try to comprehend the fact that you're standing there, particularly in a room where they believe they are alone. He said some victims will continue to freeze, just watching you as if they were watching a television program. They stand there, waiting to see what happens next. Sometimes, not knowing what comes next is better.

The sound of one drawer closing and another yanked open.

With a deep breath, I tightened my grip on the knife and swung through the open doorway, rushing toward the intruder.

Mother sidestepped me, her right hand crashing down on my arm while her left snagged the knife from my hand. I tried to stop moving, but my momentum was too strong; I slammed into the bed and tumbled over the side, finally coming to a stop against the far wall.

"Always best to sneak up slow and steady," Mother said. "Particularly when you have surprise working for you. Slow and steady, and you may have gotten me. As it stands, I heard you huffing and puffing long before you started your little gallop at me. Sure, some might not have time to react, but anyone with a bit of reflex in their step wouldn't find it much of a bother."

I had banged my head on the floor, and my earlier headache came back with a vengeance. I gathered myself and stood, wiping my hands on my jeans. "I didn't know it was you. I didn't expect anyone to be over here."

She tilted her head. "And what exactly did you expect to find? A house empty for the pilfering?"

"Father asked me to pack a bag, make things look like the Carters went away. I'm supposed to put some stuff in their car. He's going to move it somewhere when he gets home tonight."

Her eyes narrowed. "That's all, huh?"

"Honest Injun."

"Well, get to it, then. Don't let me stand in your way."

I rubbed the back of my head; a nice-size lump was making an appearance. "Can I have my Ranger back?"

"You need to earn your knife back. Maybe next time you won't part with something precious so easily."

"Yes, Mother."

There was a closet to my left. I pulled open the bifold door and found a battered suitcase tucked into the corner. "Perfect!" I heaved the bag up onto the bed.

Mother had returned to the dresser drawers. She carefully sorted through the contents of the third one of five in a large, dark oak bureau. It contained sweaters. "What are you looking for?"

She closed the drawer and opened the fourth. "Never you mind." She glanced at the suitcase on the bed. "Be sure to throw some shoes in there. Women travel with shoes, at least two pairs, sometimes more. Unlike men, who are comfortable with only the ones on their feet, regardless of their destination. Perhaps a jacket too."

"A jacket? But it's summer. It's too hot for a jacket."

Mother grinned. "That's the beauty of packing one. If you find a suitcase with a jacket packed inside during the middle of summer, you gotta wonder where the owner is running off to, don't you think? Keep it random and you keep people guessing. If I found a suitcase like that, I would think they were off to someplace exotic, like Greenland."

"Or Antarctica."

She nodded. "Or Antarctica."

"I should throw in a bathing suit too; that would really be confusing."

"Well, that would be silly. Nobody goes to a place where you need a jacket and bathing suit."

"What if the hotel in Antarctica has an indoor pool?" I countered.

She thought about this for a moment. "I don't think you'd find a hotel like that in Antarctica. Maybe in Greenland, though."

I started pulling random articles of clothing from the closet and adding them to the suitcase—shirts for Mr. Carter, some dresses from Mrs. Carter's side, a few pairs of slacks, a tie.

"Don't forget their unmentionables. And socks, lots of socks. People always overpack socks."

"Which drawer?"

She nodded to a small dresser beside the closet. "Second and third in that one."

I walked over and tugged at the drawers. Both were stuffed full—one his, one hers. I grabbed an armload from each and dumped them in the suitcase. I was nearly out of room.

"Leave a couple of the drawers open; disorganization will give the impression they left in a hurry," Mother suggested.

"Bathroom stuff?"

Mother nodded and pulled open another drawer. "Toothbrushes, razors, deodorant . . ."

I found a small travel bag in the closet, then made my way back down the hall to their bathroom. Mrs. Carter kept a tidy house—not a speck of toothpaste on the sink, and the mirror was spotless. Everything was neatly arranged on the vanity.

I plucked both toothbrushes and a tube of paste from a green ceramic cup and dropped them into the bag. Then I added an electric razor, a can of Right Guard deodorant, a pink roll-on that smelled slightly of lilacs, a jar of Noxzema face wash, dental floss, and a women's razor I found on the bathtub's edge. From inside the medicine cabinet, I also pilfered some aspirin, two bottles of multivitamins, and three prescription bottles—lisinopril, Imitrex, and a blister pack of birth control.

I left the medicine cabinet open and carried the smaller bag back to the bedroom, dropping it next to the suitcase.

"I can help you search, Mother. You just need to tell me what you're trying to find."

She waved an impatient hand in the air without looking at me, and continued shuffling through the clothing stacked neatly on cedar shelves.

A copy of A Caller's Game by Thad McAlister lay on the night-stand.

People read on vacation, don't they? I was sure they did.

I tossed the book into the suitcase and noticed the edge of a photograph sticking out from the pages.

It was a picture of Mrs. Carter and Mother. Both were naked, their limbs twisted together in an embrace while they held each other in a passionate kiss. It was taken in the Carters' bed, Mother and Mrs. Carter lying atop the same comforter that covered the bed now.

I stared down at the photo in disbelief, my mind flashing back to what I'd seen yesterday. I thought that had been the first time something happened between the two of them. Clearly I was wrong.

When had this been taken? Nothing in the image offered a clue. It must have been recent, though. Then my mind offered a question of its own.

Forget when it was taken. I was more curious to determine who had taken it.

I didn't hear Mother come up behind me. Until she snatched the photo from my fingers, I didn't know she stood there at all. "I don't believe that belongs to you," she said before tucking the picture into her pocket. She pointed at the bags on the bed. "Get those into their car."

My mouth hung open. What would Father think?

"Don't even think about telling your father," she breathed.

42

Porter

Day 2 • 4:58 a.m.

Porter found a parking space three blocks from his apartment and started toward his building. He had sat outside Talbot's house for the better part of the night, and aside from Carnegie stumbling in at a little past two, there was no movement. No sign of Talbot at all.

Both Clair and Nash had checked in with him; neither search party found any sign of Emory at the Mulifax Building or the Moorings construction site.

Dead ends.

From his vantage point at Talbot's house, he had read more of the diary—that yielded nothing either, just more childhood ramblings. He was beginning to think it was nothing more than a fiction crafted solely to waste his time.

Another dead end.

Emory was lost out there, and they had nothing.

As Porter came upon his "secure" building, he found the door wide open and flapping in the wind. There was also a rather large pile of dog excrement steaming at the base of the steps, no doubt from the pit bull in 2C. He didn't blame the dog, but he'd have no problem rubbing the owner's chubby face it in if he were to find him alone outside. The entire building knew the guy let his dog do his business right outside in this very spot; they also knew the man never picked up after his dog.

Carmine Luppo.

The fifty-three-year-old former bathtub salesman sat around all day playing video games and only left the building long enough to cash his disability check, replenish his beef jerky stock, and coax his lovely dog to shit on the stoop.

Last month, six of his neighbors took shifts to try to catch him in the act, and yet he somehow slipped past all of them. He looked as if he weighed four hundred pounds—not exactly like a man who could move stealthily, but somehow that magic pile of dog shit appeared out of nowhere.

There was talk of installing a camera.

Porter suggested they buy the domain www.poopertv.com and stream the feed, maybe charge for advertising.

He slipped his key into his mailbox, pulled out the stack of envelopes, and quickly sifted through them. Three bills, a mailer for a dry cleaning service, and the *TV Guide*.

Porter threw away everything but the *TV Guide*. He loved *TV Guide*. He never watched television, didn't need to—he got everything he needed from the magazine. As far as he was concerned, television had lost its luster when they canceled *The Incredible Hulk* in May of 1982. The three flights of stairs proved a little more difficult to ascend than they were to descend, and he found himself nearly out of breath when he finally reached his floor. Heather was vegan and swore if he changed his diet, he'd drop some weight and gain some energy. He figured she was right, but when he watched her eating a bean burger and sprouts while he put away good old-fashioned red meat he knew the vegan road was not one he'd meander down anytime soon. He'd sooner tote his growing gut than give up cow flesh. He'd come to terms with his decision, accepted the consequences. Hence, the bag in his hand containing two cold Big Macs and a large order of fries.

Through a feat of digital dexterity, he unlocked the apartment door and managed to get inside without dropping a single item. He set the McDonald's bag down on the counter, peeled off his coat, and went into the bedroom.

The note from Heather sat on the side of the bed, where he'd left it the previous morning.

Went to get milk.

Porter lowered himself beside it and took a deep breath, then picked up his phone and dialed Heather. Her voice mail message played, followed by a beep.

"Hey, Button." The words came out in a voice much weaker than he hoped. A lump grew in his throat. "It's been a crazy day. I doubt I'll get much sleep, but I'm going to try anyway. There's this girl, Emory Connors. She needs me to find her. She's only fifteen, Button. The Monkey Killer took her. Fucking bastard. That's what Nash called about this morning. That's why I left so—" The air left him. Tears welled up in his eyes, and he wiped them away with his shirtsleeve.

When the first sob hit, he tried to choke it down, but the next one was more insistent. Grown men weren't supposed to cry. He wanted to stop, but a rush of emotion surged through his tired body. His stomach rolled and the tears came, soft at first, then louder, then louder still as he finally gave in, collapsing into his hands, the phone falling to his side.

43

Diary

Father was pleased with my packing skills.

When he arrived home about an hour earlier I was waiting outside, a baseball in my hand.

I didn't particularly like baseball; I wasn't really a fan of sports in general, but Father had taught me the importance of appearances and I fully intended to keep them up. Mother had me on lookout duty, and I couldn't stand outside staring at the ground, now, could I? So, baseball it was. I tossed the ball in the air and caught it with my left hand, then my right, then my left again—an old pro having a grand old time.

I tried hard not to think of the picture. The image remained, though, every time I closed my eyes. Mother and Mrs. Carter, all naked and twisted together. I tossed the ball back up and began to count each catch—a little something to tie up my thoughts so they couldn't linger on that image, the elephant in the room (or Mother's pocket, unless she'd found a good hiding place).

When Father drove up, he gave me an appreciative nod and held up his hand. I threw the ball to him. His arm shot up and snatched it from the air with the skill of a major-leaguer. He spun the ball between his fingers and walked over to me. "Busy day today?"

Father often spoke in code, another trick he and I were practicing.

We could conduct a complete conversation on one topic while knowing full well we were talking about something completely different.

"You know, a little of this and a little of that," I said, trying not to smile.

Between blinks, my eyes darted to the Carters' car and back again so quickly as to be practically imperceptible, but Father caught it. I could tell by the slight smirk edging his lips.

He turned to the sky. The sun was setting, preparing for the night's slumber. "I think we've got the makings of a fine night, champ. I think I'll ask if your mother wants to go for a little drive, a date night in the big city. Think you can keep an eye on the house while we're gone?"

The words hiding between the lines were quite clear. Father was going to drive the Carters' car somewhere and dispose of it. He needed Mother to follow him so he could get back home. He was going to trust me to monitor Mrs. Carter while they were gone.

"Sure thing, Father! You can count on me!"

He tossed the baseball back to me and ruffled my hair. "Ain't that the truth?"

I watched him disappear into the house and emerge ten minutes later, with Mother on his heels. She gave me a worried glance as she walked past and got into the Carters' car. The door slammed with a squeak. She adjusted the rearview mirror, her eyes peering back at me. Father was standing at his Porsche, twirling the key between his fingers. "Shouldn't be gone too long, champ. Couple hours at the most. I'm afraid I grabbed your mother before she could get dinner going. Think you can rustle up a little something on your own?"

I nodded. Mother had baked a nice peach pie earlier in the day and set the tin out on the windowsill to cool. We also had peanut butter and jelly in the cupboard. I would be fine. "You two have fun!" I told him in my best adult voice.

He smiled, donned his favorite hat, and dropped down behind the wheel. The engine roared to life, and he eased out the driveway and down the street, disappearing over the hill at Baker Street. Mother didn't follow at first. When I turned back to the Carters' house, she hadn't even started the car. She sat in the driver's seat, her eyes fixed on me. She glared at me something fierce. It almost hurt. I'm not lying; it was as if tiny little laser beams shot from her eyes and burned at my skin. I tried to hold eye contact. Father had always told me it was important to hold eye contact no matter how uncomfortable a situation may be, but I couldn't—I had to turn away. When I did, she started the Carters' car, shifted into first with a grinding of gears, and rushed out down the road after Father.

The dust lingered in the air above the Carters' driveway. The setting sun seemed to catch it just right, a shimmer above the gravel.

I dropped the baseball and went inside.

I could hear the banging before I passed through the kitchen doorway, a loud metal-on-metal clanging coming from the basement.

I reached for the knob, part of me expecting the basement door to be locked. It wasn't, though; the brass knob turned and the door popped open. A steady clang, clang, clang echoed up from below.

I descended the steps.

Mrs. Carter was standing beside the bloodstain on the floor. Somehow, she had wrapped her arm around the metal frame of the cot and was busy swinging it like a bat against the water pipe. Each swing was followed by a grunt; then she lowered the cot, swung it back to her side, and twisted back around, using her body weight to help propel the cot back again. Considering one wrist was still handcuffed to the water pipe and the other fastened to the side of cot, it was a wonder she didn't break her arm.

As the cot slammed into the pipe, I saw the jolt rumble through her body; the vibration alone had to be painful.

If she saw me, she didn't say anything. Her hair was askew, and sweat dripped down her forehead.

"The basement would flood, you know," I pointed out. "If you were somehow able to break a big pipe like that, the water would probably fill up this basement inside of an hour, and there you'd be—chained to the pipe and the cot, bobbing along below the surface."

She inhaled deeply and repositioned the cot, preparing to take another swing. "If I break the pipe, I'll be able to slip the cuff off the end and get upstairs."

"The pipe would rupture long before it would break clear through. Then all the water would come rushing out. It's hard enough to swing the cot like that now. Can you imagine the difficulty gallons upon gallons of icy cold water rushing out at you would create? I'm not saying you've devised a bad plan. I just think it's a little flawed, is all. Perhaps it needs a little more thinking through before you continue. You seem like you need to take a break anyway."

She dropped the cot at her side. The handcuffs tugged at her wrist, threatening to pull her down, but she held firm. "You're not going to try and stop me?"

I shrugged. "I kinda want to see what happens."

She glared at me, her eyes red and glistening with tears. She was breathing hard. I couldn't help but wonder how long she had been working at this little project. Mother had probably ignored her. I bet she'd been beating on that pipe for hours.

"So you don't care if I die down here?"

I said nothing.

"If I drown or your parents kill me, it doesn't matter to you? What did I do to deserve this? I didn't hurt anyone. My husband beat me, remember?"

She plopped down on the edge of the cot, sulking.

It was funny. Although she was older than I, sometimes I caught glimpses of a much younger girl in her expressions and movements. Sometimes I spotted a girl much younger than I, one who was afraid and unsure, one who expected an adult (or a boy) to sweep in and save the day.

As an adult looking back on this moment, I now realize I've seen that same expression countless times. When someone is in trouble, they expect, they wait, for someone of authority to help them. I think it's because that is how these things play out in the movies and on television. The hero always arrives at the last minute, foils the crime, and rescues those in distress from certain death as all other options are exhausted. The tears come after that, possibly a hug, followed by a commercial break before they wrap up the program.

Real life doesn't work that way. I've seen more lives end than I can count, and they all seem to hold that same expectation at the end, their eyes glancing at the door, waiting for their savior to arrive. He doesn't, though. In real life, the only true savior is oneself.

She had succeeded in chipping away the paint on the pipe, nothing more. Not even a dent. She had tried, though, and that is what I found to be important. The game got boring when they eventually gave up.

And she would give up. Eventually. They always do.

"If you let me go, I won't say anything," she said. "I promise I won't. Simon was a bad man—he had it coming to him. Your parents did me a favor. They set me free. I owe them. They don't have to worry about me. I promise. We can all walk away from this."

"You broke the rules," I said softly. "Unfortunately, there are consequences."

"And how did I do that? By letting my husband beat me?"

"Better to consider why your husband beat you, don't you think?"

Another tear fell from her eye and started down her cheek. She tried to wipe at it, but the cuffs held both her hands. She couldn't reach her face.

Sitting on the edge of the cot, I pulled the handkerchief from my back pocket and blotted it away. She stared at me but said nothing.

"I found the picture."

"What picture?"

"Oh, I think you know what picture."

With that, the color left her face. "You've got to hide it."

"Mother was with me; she has it now. I don't know what she did with it."

"Your father hasn't seen it?"

"Not yet," I told her. "But that doesn't mean he won't."

"But you won't tell him, right?"

I didn't answer, which I guess gave her an answer.

"If he sees that picture, not only will he hurt me, he'll go after your mother too. Is that what you want?"

Again, I said nothing.

44

Porter

Day 2 • 6:53 a.m.

When Porter arrived in the war room, Nash, Clair, and Watson were standing around one of the desks, staring at a laptop screen. Nash looked up and beckoned him over. "Get any sleep?"

"Couldn't. You?"

He knew by their red, puffy eyes that none of them had. Porter dropped his coat at his own desk and walked over. "We get something?"

"Oh, we got something. We got a few somethings. Eisley's girl-friend came through, for starters. Check this out." He turned the laptop so it was facing Porter.

"Is that a head from Madam Tussauds wax museum?"

Watson pointed at the image. "She boiled the skull, then applied spacers to simulate muscle and tissue depth—twenty-one specific places—then used clay to fill in the mass. I've heard of forensic anthropologists reconstructing facial renders like this, but I've never seen it. It's quite impressive. To do it so quickly . . . Eisley said she didn't even start until last night."

Porter frowned. "Wait, this is 4MK?"

Watson went on, oblivious. "She already had his hair. That wasn't damaged nearly as bad as the face. Even his dental held up, so she had that too. Eye color was already known . . . I can't imagine this is far off. I checked out her website, and she usually works with Native American skulls found at archeological dig sites—many more unknowns with those, a lot of guesswork. With this, she may be dead-on."

"I think Watson has a hard-on for Eisley's girlfriend," Nash said.

Watson shot him a sideways glance. "I'm merely pointing out I believe this is an accurate representation of the Monkey Killer, one she created in record time, that's all. The artistry and skill are amazing. You couldn't get this kind of detail with a computer rendering. This kind of accuracy takes a special hand."

"It skeeves me the fuck out," Nash replied. "Looks like it's watching you. Like one of those paintings where the eyes follow you around the room. Creepy."

"Clair, I want you to get some pictures of this and hit all the cancer treatment centers we talked about yesterday. Between the drugs and this image, we may be able to ID him," Porter said.

"Oh, we got more, big guy," Clair told him. "While you slept in until all hours, the rest of us have been working."

Porter glanced at his watch. "It's not even seven."

"You damn near wasted half the day."

He rolled his eyes. "What else did you find?"

"Our vic from the Mulifax Building? He was Gunther Herbert, CFO for Talbot Enterprises, which includes the Talbot Estates Development, the Moorings, and about a dozen other ventures. His wife reported him missing five days ago. Left for work and never arrived. Eisley identified him about an hour ago. He also put time of death around five days too, so he was most likely snatched on his way to the office."

"Did you tell the captain yet?"

"There's more, Sam," Nash said. "Tell him, Clair-bear."

Clair beamed. "The shoes dead guy number one was wearing when he kissed the bus? The prints Nash lifted came back from the lab with a match."

"Who?"

Nash drummed his fingers on the edge of the desk. "Arthur Talbot."

"Did you call me Clair-bear?"

Porter silenced Nash before he could respond. "The shoes belong to Talbot?"

"He seems like the kind of guy to buy fifteen-hundred-dollar shoes, right?"

"Why would 4MK be wearing Talbot's shoes?"

"Same reason he took Talbot's daughter. The man did something bad, and 4MK wants us to know. This is his last hurrah, his swan song. He doesn't want us to drop the ball, so he's lining everything up nice and neat for us," Nash said. "Somehow he snagged Talbot's shoes, stuffed some newspaper in them so they'd fit on his wee little feet, and put them on before stepping out into traffic."

"Clair, try and get Hosman on the phone. Find out where he is on the financials. We need to speed this up," Porter instructed.

Clair grabbed her cell phone off the desk and walked toward the corner of the room, dialing.

Porter turned to Watson. "Anything on the watch?"

Watson shook his head. "I showed my uncle a photo, but he said he needs to see the real thing to provide any real help. I tried to sign the watch out of evidence, but I was told they would only release it to you or Nash."

Porter rolled his eyes. He really didn't need department policy slowing him down right now. "When we're done here, I'll walk up there with you."

"One other thing," Nash said. "The feds want in on this case; the local field office has been calling all night. Emory is over twelve, and there's no proof of interstate transport, so it's our call."

"Let's see where Hosman is. They may be able to help with Talbot's books. Anything else on the Moorings or Mulifax after I talked to you?"

Nash shook his head. "They walked every house, found evidence of a couple squatters but nothing else. If 4MK had her there, she's gone now. They're still combing the tunnels, but those things go on for miles, all over the city. We're not going to find her down there by wandering around in the dark. We need a bread crumb. Aside from the body, Mulifax was a bust."

"4MK led us there. There's a reason. It's probably—"

"In the financials, I got it," Nash interrupted. "Feds, Hosman, financials—I'm all over it."

"Porter? Can I speak to you for a second?" Captain Henry Dalton was standing in the doorway. Nobody had seen him come in. His thinning hair was slicked back, still damp from a shower, his suit clean and pressed.

Porter gave Nash and Watson a quick glance. "Excuse me."

The captain put a hand on his shoulder and steered him out into the hallway. He glanced in both directions, then spoke quietly after confirming that they were alone. "Listen, the guys down at the Fifty-First picked up a kid last night on an attempted burglary. He tried to hold up a 7-Eleven on the East Side with a .38. An off-duty uniform happened to be in the store and got the better of him, took him down without a single shot fired. They processed the gun, and it's a match to the one from, well . . . the gun from Heather."

Porter's stomach twisted into an ache so powerful he thought he might double over. He drew in a deep breath and tried to fight it back. He felt the weight of his own gun under his shoulder, the gun he wasn't supposed to be carrying right now. Technically, he was still on leave. They wouldn't allow him a gun until he completed an evaluation and the shrink signed off, until they thought he was ready. If the 4MK case hadn't broken, he'd still be home, waiting for news, any news, something to help carry him through the day. But the case had broken and they'd called him in. He had welcomed the distraction, anything was better than all the waiting, all the waiting and the solitude.

He slipped his hand into his pocket and wrapped his fingers around his cell phone. He wanted to call her. He wanted to hear her voice.

You've reached the phone of Heather Porter. Since this is voice mail, I most likely saw your name on caller ID and decided I most certainly did not wish to . . .

"I need to go down there," Porter said. His voice sounded like a little boy's. The voice he'd had when he was a child, the voice he'd had when there was no bad, only life and good things ahead.

"I know," said Captain Dalton. "I already told them to expect you."

A tear welled up in Porter's eye, and he quickly snatched it away before shoving his shaky hand back into his pocket.

Dalton had noticed and offered a concerned smile. "Maybe someone should drive you."

Porter opened his mouth to argue with him, then thought better of it. He didn't want to pull Nash or Clair off the case, not now.

"I'll get Watson to take me over."

Captain Dalton glanced into the room and nodded. "They got him dead to rights on the attempted burglary last night, but nobody's told the perp they matched the gun. I explained your situation, and they agreed to hold off until you got there to observe. I promised that is all you're going to do: observe. Stay on the right side of the one-way and let them do their job. They'll get a confession out of this kid."

"Yes, sir."

Dalton put a hand on his shoulder. "I'm sorry you're going through this, I truly am."

"Thank you, sir."

Dalton pulled in a breath, nodded, and started for the door of the war room. "Nash! Where the fuck is your latest report? I got a dozen reporters camped outside my office. I gotta feed those dogs some scraps."

Nash shrugged his shoulders. "You told us to go home and rest— no time for paperwork. You're welcome to sit in while we hand out assignments."

Dalton paused at the door and turned back. "Oh, and Porter?"

"Yeah?"

"Leave your spare piece in the car. I don't want a record of you carrying right now. They'd try and log it at the lineup."

Porter nodded. "Yes, sir."

Clair hung up and walked over. "Hosman may be on to something; he wants us upstairs."

"Go with Nash; I need to take care of something down at the Fifty-First. I'm commandeering Watson too."

"You're going to leave me alone with that Neanderthal?"

Porter's eyes watered up. He turned away. Clair glanced back at the captain. "Oh," she said quietly. "Okay. Just . . . just call me if you need anything."

Porter forced a smile and nodded. "Thanks, Clair-bear."

She punched him in the arm. "Don't you start too. Assholes, the both of you."

Porter winked at her and stuck his head back in the war room. "Watson? Let's go see about that watch."

Evidence Board

Victims

1. Calli Tremell, 20, March 15, 2009
2. Elle Borton, 23, April 2, 2010
3. Missy Lumax, 18, June 24, 2011
4. Susan Devoro, 26, May 3, 2012
5. Barbara McInley, 17, April 18, 2013 (only blonde)
6. Allison Crammer, 19, November 9, 2013
7. Jodi Blumington, 22, May 13, 2014

Emory Connors, 15, November 3, 2014
Left for a jog, 6:03 p.m. yesterday

TYLER MATHERS
Emory's boyfriend

ARTHUR TALBOT
Finances?
Body found in Mulifax Publications Building (owned by Talbot)
    identified as Gunther Herbert, CFO Talbot Enterprises
Something fishy with the Moorings Development (owned by
    Talbot)

N. BURROW
~~Housekeeper? Nanny? — A little of both~~ Tutor

ITEMS FOUND ON 4MK
Expensive shoes — John Lobb/$1500 pair — size 11/UNSUB
    wears size 9 — have Talbot's prints on them
Cheap suit
Fedora
.75 in change (two quarters, two dimes, and a nickel)
Pocket watch
Dry cleaner receipt (ticket 54873) — Kloz is narrowing down
    stores
Dying of stomach cancer — meds: octreotide, trastuzumab,
    oxycodone, lorazepam

Tattoo, right inner wrist, fresh — figure eight, infinity?

Calc book — left by 4MK — leads to —

MULIFAX PUBLICATIONS WAREHOUSE
Partial print found on railcar at tunnel mouth. Probably used to
  transport the body.
Ear, eyes, and tongue left in boxes (Gunther Herbert) — brochure
  on body AND boxes lead to —

THE MOORINGS LAKESIDE DEVELOPMENT
Extensive search — nothing found

Video footage — Appears 4MK committed suicide, no clear visual
  on face

Info needed:

- Background on Emory's mother
- Facial reconstruction — <u>Done</u>

Assignments:

- Nash and Clair going to see Hosman
- Clair — Organize canvass of cancer centers with image of
  UNSUB
- Kloz, research dry cleaner's ticket
- Watson, visit uncle regarding the watch with Porter

45

Diary

I was asleep when Mother and Father returned. Well, truth be told, I was pretending to be asleep, otherwise I wouldn't have heard them.

At first there was shouting, but I couldn't make out the words. Mother and Father never ever fought, and I couldn't imagine them arguing outside where a neighbor might listen, but there they were— yelling in the driveway.

I couldn't help but think about Mr. Carter yelling at Mrs. Carter and Mother yesterday.

They must have caught themselves, because all went suddenly silent. The door opened and closed, and angry steps pounded through the living room. I think Father tossed the car keys. They clattered across the counter and fell to the floor. Mother simply said, "Do what you want. I won't be party to it," then stomped past my door and down the hallway to their room, the door slamming behind her.

Silence.

The loudest silence I have ever heard.

I could picture Father standing in the kitchen, his face aflame. His fists clenched tight, opened, and clenched again.

I peeled back the sheets and climbed out of bed. I walked on the tips of my toes and pressed my ear to the door.

"Champ?" Father's voice bellowed from the other side.

I nearly tripped over my own feet as I jumped back, my heart pounding as I considered diving for my bed and the safety of the sheets.

I'd never make it.

"Champ? You up?"

I reached for the doorknob, twisted, and pulled the door open, sure and swift. Father's frame filled the opening, his features dark and shadowed with the kitchen light burning at his back. His hand was still positioned where the doorknob had been a moment earlier, the other holding something behind his back.

"Burning the midnight oil, buddy?"

The anger I'd heard in his voice with Mother was either gone or cleverly masked, because now there was no trace. His face held nothing but a smile, his eyes twinkling.

Father once taught me the importance of projecting emotion. He told me I should always determine the emotion expected of me under a given circumstance and ensure it stood tall and true at the forefront, regardless of what I really felt on the inside. We practiced numerous times. Once, our dog, Ridley, had puppies of her own, and he snapped the neck of one right in front of me, then forced me to laugh. When I wasn't able to do what he asked, he picked up another puppy, and I let the laughter flow rather than watch another die. That wasn't enough, though; he said I didn't sound sincere. By the fourth puppy I learned control. I was able to go from happy to sad, angry to somber, solemn to giddy with the snap of his fingers. Ridley went away soon after that. To where I do not know. I was only five at the time, and my memory of that age is spotty at best.

Father grinned like the Cheshire cat, and I had no way of knowing how he really felt, nor did I want to. If he suspected I thought he was anything but happy, the evening would not go well for Mother or me.

"I didn't want to go to sleep until you got home. In case you needed help with anything."

He reached out and ruffled my hair. "You are my little soldier man, aren't you?"

I nodded.

"As a matter of fact, I'd love for you to help me out with a little something, if you think you're up for it. Feel like having a little fun?"

Again I nodded.

"Grab your mother's big plastic salad bowl from the kitchen cup-board, and meet me down in the basement. I've got a little surprise for our guest." He pulled a paper sack out from behind his back and held it up, then gave the bag a little shake. From inside, something scratched. "This is going to be great!" He smiled.

This time I knew he really was happy.

46

Clair

Day 2 • 7:18 a.m.

"Did he say why he had to go down there?" Nash asked, staring at the elevator floor number display.

Clair rolled her eyes. "I told you three times already. He just said he had something he had to take care of down at the Fifty-First, nothing else. No secret handshake, no passing of notes, no nothing."

"It's got to be something about Heather, though, right?"

"If he wanted us to know, he would tell us."

The elevator doors opened on the fifth floor; they stepped out into a mess of cluttered cubicles and rickety metal desks topped with computers old enough to still house floppy drives.

Nash took a quick glance around before negotiating the narrow pathway cluttered with file boxes and stacks of folders. "And what's up with him taking Watson? Why wouldn't he take one of us?"

"We don't even know if it's about Heather."

"It's got to be about Heather."

Clair knew he was right. The captain never came down to the basement. "Yeah, probably."

"So why Watson?"

"According to the hunk of metal they let you carry around, you're a detective. Why do you think he didn't want to take one of us?"

"I'm his best friend."

Christ, was this man going to cry? "Maybe he wanted to be around someone who doesn't know. Less pressure. I mean, I haven't brought it up, but he knows we know and that creates all kinds of tension. It's got to be hard for him to be back on the job, surrounded by all this, knowing he can't do anything. I think he's handling everything the best he can. Sure as shit better than I would. I'd be a fucking mess."

They found Hosman's office, two doors down from the end on the left side. His door was open and he waved them in. "Who's ready to do some math?"

Clair pointed at Nash. "Here's your guy. Nash won the state math championship in high school, three years in a row."

Hosman looked up at Nash with raised eyebrows. "You did?"

"Sure did. Right after I won the gold in pole vaulting," Nash replied, nodding his head. "I also bake a mean cherry pie. You should see all the ribbons I've received."

"So. No math fans, then?"

"Nope."

"Do you know what a Ponzi scheme is?"

Clair raised her hand. "It's when a person or business pays returns to its investors from the capital raised from new investors rather than profits earned."

Nash whistled. "You're hot when you know stuff."

Clair punched him in the shoulder.

Hosman tapped a stack of papers on his desk. "I think that's what we've got going on here; not only with the Moorings but across all of Talbot's holdings."

Clair frowned. "How is that possible? He's one of the richest men in the city, possibly the country."

"He's rich on paper. Crazy rich on paper, but he's got some serious problems. Things started going south with the Moorings about two years ago. He bought all that land, and a week before his company was supposed to start bulldozing buildings, the Chicago Planning and Development's Historical Preservation Division won an injunction and blocked the project. They felt the neighborhood should be preserved. During the heyday of Prohibition, at least a dozen speakeasies popped up in that area. Planning and Development felt the city would be better served if they rejuvenated the neighborhood with everything intact, turn the waterfront into a tourist mecca. One of them used to be frequented by Al Capone; the gangsters are always a good draw."

Clair tilted her head. "He had to see that coming, right? Run-down shitholes or not, Planning and Development has been preserving pockets like that all around the city. I imagine a savvy real estate developer pads his budget and timeline to deal with those groups."

Hosman tapped at one of his spreadsheets. "You're right; he put twenty million aside in an escrow account specifically to fight these guys. Not only did he see it coming, his attorneys were waiting at the courthouse the day the injunction was filed with a claim of their own."

"He planned to sue Planning and Development?" Nash asked.

Hosman grinned. "Better than that. He filed a suit against the city. His attorneys claimed the speakeasies were built without permits, and not only was it illegal to preserve them, the city was obligated to either bring them up to code or tear them down."

Clair whistled. "Wow. How did that fly down at city hall?"

"Well, they weren't pleased, and the county filed a counterstrike. The next day they halted construction on two skyscrapers he had going up downtown. One office building, the other residential. Apparently a whistleblower came forward and claimed his company was using substandard concrete. When they tested the mix, it turned out to be true. Too much sand or something. I'm still trying to get the details. The office building is forty-three stories and is estimated to cost six hundred eighty-eight million dollars, and the residential tower is sixty-four floors with a price tag hovering around one billion."

"So what does that mean? He's got to demo and start over?" Nash asked.

Clair was studying a picture Hosman had printed of the office building. "Do you think the city knew about the bad concrete all along and only brought the infraction up to retaliate?"

Hosman raised both his hands. "Dunno on both counts."

"We saw houses at the Moorings, so they must have worked out some kind of resolution, right?" Nash pointed out. "I mean, the buildings are gone, replaced with plush single-family homes, so somebody blinked."

Hosman was pointing at another spreadsheet. "Well, that's the mystery of the hour. I found nearly four million dollars leaving his accounts last May, and I've had zero luck tracking the recipient. Shortly after, though, construction started back up at the Moorings, and the city allowed him to move forward with the two skyscrapers by approving a very costly reinforcement retrofit."

"So he bribed a city official?"

"That would be my guess. The lawsuits were dropped all around too."

Nash frowned. "I'm not a financial analyst, but none of this sounds like a Ponzi scheme to me. Sounds more like a rich guy using his riches to get richer."

"Not exactly getting richer," Hosman replied, shuffling through various stacks of paper. When he found the sheet he wanted, he handed it to Nash.

Nash took a quick glance and handed it back to him. "Not a financial analyst, remember?"

Hosman rolled his eyes. "Talbot has sixteen large-scale projects going on right now, everything from residential construction to retail, to condos and luxury office space. All of them are months away from completion, and they're bleeding money—the towers with the structural problems in particular. As soon as his backers got wind of the problem, they started pulling out. He's paid back more than three hundred million in the past month. He owes another hundred eighty million in the next two weeks, and from what I can tell, he doesn't have it. It appears he's been using the money coming in from new investors to pay out the old while attempting to float loans to cover the construction."

"Okay, so Ponzi scheme," Nash said.

"No, that's not a Ponzi scheme," Hosman replied.

"Then what is a—?"

Clair placed her hand over Nash's mouth. "In order for this to be a Ponzi scheme, he'd have to solicit funds for a bogus project and use the proceeds to pay off the investors of the other projects."

"That brings us back to the Moorings." Hosman produced a copy of the brochure found on the body of Gunther Herbert, Talbot's CFO. "This place is a sham."

"But he's building out there," Nash pointed out.

"You saw houses in phase one, six in total, none of which have sold yet. The real problem is in phase two. He's been selling lots, future homes, even stakes in an upscale golf and country club with an estimated completion date of fall of next year. I called Terry Henshaw at FBI White-Collar, and he said they've been monitoring Talbot for a few months now. He's been routing the money from phase two through a series of sub accounts overseas, then bringing it back in under the Talbot Enterprises umbrella in order to pay back investors from the other projects."

Clair was shaking her finger. "That's still not a Ponzi scheme. It may be unethical, but if his corporation owns all these projects and they're legit, he probably covered his ass with some fine print in the paperwork."

Hosman spun his chair in a slow circle, a grin playing at his lips. "You'd be right, but I found one other thing."

"What?"

"The land where they plan to build phase two, he doesn't own it. He's selling a development on somebody else's land."

"If he doesn't own it, then who does?"

A grin spread across Hosman's face, and his eyes darted back and forth between the two detectives. "Wait for it . . ."

Nash's face grew red. "Spit it out, math boy."

"Emory Connors." Hosman slapped his hand on the desk. "Her mother left it to her in her will. That little girl is worth some serious coin. Since she owns the land, not Talbot, we've got something worse than a Ponzi scheme. There's more, look at this." He pointed to a highlighted paragraph in a legal document.

Nash read it and whistled. "Think the captain will let us bring him in now?"

47

Diary

The steps creaked as I descended with Mother's large salad bowl in one hand and a glass of water in the other. Mother had watched me intently as I went about the business of collecting these items; at one point she even mouthed the words "Don't let him do it." Of course, I paid her no mind because I didn't "let" Father do anything and I wasn't about to ruin his good mood by passing on such a message from Mother. He had asked me to bring the bowl, and I knew Mrs. Carter hadn't drunk anything in hours. I imagined she must be parched, so I brought water too. If Mother took pause at anything that was about to happen, she was perfectly capable of communicating her position. Father was already downstairs, kneeling next to the cot. As I drew closer, I realized he was tying Mrs. Carter's feet to the frame with a length of three-strand nylon rope. He had already secured her free hand. She yanked at the bindings to no avail. Father knew how to tie a strong knot.

A rag was stuffed in her mouth, held in place by a gag made from a piece of Mr. Carter's shirt. Little crimson specks were caught up in the cloth.

Father tugged at the last knot and patted Mrs. Carter's leg. "Snug as a bug." He turned to me, his eyes shining like a child's at Christmas. "Do you have your knife on you?"

Mother still had my knife. I had searched the house high and low but found no sign of it. I shook my head.

Father frowned. "You should always carry your knife." He reached into his back pocket, retrieved his own, and handed it to me.

"Are we gonna kill her?"

"You should say 'going to,' not 'gonna.' Smart boys don't use language like that."

"Sorry, Father."

"The only time you should talk like that is when you want those around you to think you're less intelligent than you are. Sometimes it's best not to be the smartest guy in a room. Some people are scared of those with a higher intellect. If you dumb yourself down to their level, they'll accept you. Makes it easier to blend with the crowd. No need for false pretenses when it's just your old man and our lovely neighbor, though. If you can't be yourself around friends and family, what's the point, right?"

I couldn't help but agree. "Are we going to kill her, Father?"

Father took the knife from my hand and held the blade up to the light. "That's an excellent question, champ, but it's not mine to answer. You see, Mrs. Carter holds the cards for that particular game of chance, and she's playing them close to the vest. Personally, I'd rather not kill her. I'd prefer to keep her around for a little while. I hear Mrs. Carter is quite the party girl, and I have yet to experience her virtue firsthand." He tapped her leg again. "Isn't that right, Lisa? You're a little burst of pleasure?"

Her eyes were locked on the knife blade. It shimmered nicely under the glow of the sixty-watt hanging from the ceiling.

Father's paper bag sat on the floor at his side, skittering softly against the concrete. He handed the knife back to me. "You're a big boy now. How about you take the honors?"

Mrs. Carter squirmed, her feet kicking and eyes bulging. She shouted something behind the gag, but it was impossible to make it out. I wasn't sure why Father had gagged her. Wasn't half the fun in hearing the reaction?

Father tugged Mrs. Carter's white blouse out from her jeans. "I

want you to cut this off her. It's a shame to ruin such a pristine gar-
ment, but unfortunately there's no other way to get the job done with
her secured to the cot like this. Too bad she didn't wear a nice but-
ton-down."

Mrs. Carter was shaking her head furiously, but she didn't get a
vote where Father was concerned. I gave her my most reassuring smile,
then slipped the blade into the thin fabric of her blouse and gave it a
little tug. The sharp edge cut through the cotton with little effort, and
I pulled it along. My knuckles brushed against the smooth skin of her
belly, and I felt my face flush. I couldn't look at Father or Mrs. Carter
for fear of revealing the flood of emotions surging through me. I'm sure
I was warm to the touch—my temperature rose by the second. When
the back of my hand rubbed against her brassiere, I thought I might ex-
plode. I forced the knife past and sliced until the blade came out at her
collar—the blouse split in two. Mrs. Carter was crying now.

"Cut off the arms and shoulders too. Get that pesky thing out of the
way," Father instructed.

I did as I was told, and soon the blouse was lying in a tattered pile
at my side. Mrs. Carter grew increasingly anxious, her breathing labored by the gag. Her chest rose and fell with increased urgency. Would
she pass out?

"Should we take the gag off?"

Father glanced down at Mrs. Carter for a brief second before shaking his head. "A person screaming in fear is one thing, but someone
screaming in pain? That's a whole other animal. And this is going to
hurt. I'm quite certain of that." He took another length of rope and
wrapped it around her stomach just below her breasts, then circled the
cot and tied a tight knot. He repeated this four more times until he ran
out of rope.

This did nothing to calm Mrs. Carter. She kicked at her restraints
and bucked at the cot with renewed vigor. Father placed his large hand
on her knees and forced them down before tying them to the cot as well
with another length of rope. When he was through, Mrs. Carter could
no longer move. "Best to get on with it. Can you hand me that bag and
the salad bowl?"

I nodded and reached for the paper sack. It was heavy. Whatever was inside weighed at least half a pound. I felt it sliding around inside. It had peed too. The bottom of the bag was soaked in urine and stank of warm ammonia.

Father took the bag from me and set it on Mrs. Carter's stomach. She drew in a deep breath and tried to sit up as the soaked sack touched her skin, but the rope held her firm. She craned her neck enough to see the bag, but she couldn't hold the awkward position for long before falling back.

Father peeled back the top of the sack and let in some air, then quickly placed the salad bowl on top, sealing the bag between the dome of the bowl and Mrs. Carter's stomach.

He produced a roll of duct tape, tore off a few strips, and taped the bowl to her chest. It was clear plastic, so we could see the happenings inside very nicely.

He tapped at the top of the bowl. "This little guy is your typical field rat. I scooped him up right outside without much trouble after feeding him a piece of cheese laced with methyl trichloride. It's starting to wear off, though, and when he wakes up he's going to be angry and battling an epic headache. Rats aren't fond of confined spaces, so I'm fairly certain he is going to want out of this bowl. He may try clawing at the plastic, but the surface is too smooth to get any kind of worthwhile purchase. Once he gives up on that route, I think he's going to turn his attention to what lies beneath, and that's when the real fun will start. Unlike plastic, his sharp, pointy nails will have little trouble tearing through your tender torso, and if he gets his mouth into the game and starts chewing . . ." Father smiled broadly. "Well, let's just say teeth like those were made to devour much more difficult substances."

Mrs. Carter was squirming again, and breathing had become a battle. She tried to suck in air but couldn't get enough through her nose. Tears streamed down her cheeks. Her eyes were red and puffy.

I leaned closer. The rat was curled up in the bag, barely moving, but it was clear the drug was wearing off. When the black little rat poked its head out of the top of the sack, I nearly jumped out of my shorts.

Father laughed. "Don't worry, champ. He's not coming after you. If he gets out of there, his belly will be so full, another meal will be the last thought on his little mind."

"She's going to pass out."

I'm sure Father already thought about that possibility, but his expression said otherwise. He appeared puzzled at first, then frustrated. "You may be right, champ. I guess this may be a little overwhelming. We're almost done, though." He ran his hand through Mrs. Carter's hair. "You can hold it together for a few more minutes, can't you, Lisa? You're tough enough to do that, right?"

Her head bobbed and I couldn't tell if she nodded in agreement or shook out a vigorous no.

The rat climbed from the bag and fell over the side before scrambling to its pink feet. Its balance was off, and it was clearly groggy but slowly finding its way back to the land of the living. It sniffed first at the bag, then the bowl, then Mrs. Carter's belly button, its little snout disappearing before poking back up.

"There's our little friend." The rat scuttled around the edge of the bowl. "I think my son may be right. That gag is making it difficult to breathe, so I'm going to remove it to give you a chance to catch your breath. I'd also like you to answer a simple question, one that could put an end to all of this if you're honest with me. Would you like that?"

This time, Mrs. Carter most definitely nodded.

Father considered this, then leaned in close, his lips pressed against her ear. "Was your husband sleeping with my wife?" The words came out in a hush, barely audible from where I stood.

Mrs. Carter's eyes went wide, staring back at him. Father reached for the gag and pulled the cloth from her mouth. She spat out the wadded-up piece of cloth lodged in her mouth and gasped up the air, as if she had been submerged for hours. "Get that thing off of me!" she shouted. She bucked again, but it did little good. Her torso moved no more than an inch before the bindings snapped her back. She craned her neck but couldn't raise her head enough to see what was going on.

I could see, though. I could see plenty.

The rat was coming around fast, shaking off the sleepy time and finding its sea legs. If rats were capable of suffering a panic attack, I was fairly confident this furry wonder had one in its immediate future. It circled the edge of the bowl, its twitchy little nose pressed to the space where the plastic met Mrs. Carter's skin, pausing every few steps to inspect the plastic before returning to the perimeter search. The rat circled the bowl again, then again, each pass more frantic than the last.

"Oh boy, I think he may be claustrophobic. What do you think, champ?"

I nodded. "He sure is, Father! Look at him go! He's getting angry!"

"None of God's creatures enjoy captivity. Doesn't matter if it's a worm, a rodent, or the strongest of men. You lock up a living creature, even if you fill its cage with the most delectable of treats and a comfy place to rest its head, it'll want to get out. This little bugger will tunnel right on through our dear neighbor for a shot at freedom. Can you imagine that? A hole running right through the middle of her. I bet it wouldn't even kill her, at least not for a little while. I once witnessed a man live three days with a gunshot wound through his gut—I swear if the light caught it right, you could see clear through. Of course, this hole will be much bigger, so I don't expect her to live on for days, but I bet twenty or thirty minutes wouldn't be out of the question." He shivered. "Can you imagine the pain of something like that? A hole as big as a man's fist." He raised his own fist and held it above her.

Mrs. Carter pulled at her bonds and kicked her feet with what little play in the rope she had, though this only made the rat more agitated. "Please get it away from me! Please! I'll tell you whatever you want!"

Father leaned back in close. "The question I asked you was simple enough, but maybe in all the excitement you forgot or didn't quite hear me, so I'll repeat it—was your husband sleeping with my wife?"

Mrs. Carter shook her head. "No! No, no, no!"

Father gave me a wink. "What do you think, champ? Is she being honest with us or spinning a little untruth?"

"Ahh!" Mrs. Carter screamed, her eyes bulging and her face going flush.

I looked down at the rat. It had taken the tiniest of bites at the corner of Mrs. Carter's belly button. Not enough to draw blood, but certainly enough to bring on the red and puffy. His head was raised and his little mouth twitched as he sampled his findings the way one might assess a fine wine.

Father clapped his hands, and the creature turned up to him, forgetting about his meal for a moment or two. "The little bugger is getting hungry. And he's got a hankering for flesh. That sure is a good sign! I bet you must taste sweet—just the right amount of tender and tang."

"You're fucking nuts!" Mrs. Carter blurted out. She was gasping for breath again. Removing the gag was a good call. She surely would have passed out by now if Father left it in place.

"Please, get it off of me," she said, tears streaming down her face. "I answered your fucking question, now get it off."

"Language, my dear, language."

"I'll do whatever you want. I'll tell you anything, just please—"

The rat bit down on her an instant before she howled the ugliest of screams. This time the rodent didn't hesitate. Unlike the first bite, which had simply been exploratory, this one was driven purely by hunger. Father was right—the little critter had developed a taste for flesh. He took a quarter-inch chunk out of her abdomen. I stared in awe as the spot first turned pink, then red, then filled with blood.

"Oooh!" Father crooned. "Now we've got a ball game."

Mrs. Carter gripped the sides of the cot, her fingers white as she tugged at the frame. She sucked in a gulp of air. I had heard the expression bulging eyes before, but until this instant I had never witnessed such a thing. Her eyes were bulging, though; they really did look as if they might pop right out of her head.

Then Father noticed the glass of water.

"Champ, watch this." He tipped the glass and spilled the littlest of water drops on the bowl. It dripped down the side and pooled where the plastic met her skin. Not even a second passed before the rat sensed the water—it jumped from the opposite side of the little cage and shoved its snout at the edge of the bowl. It couldn't reach the water, though—Father had taped the makeshift dome thoroughly in place. This seemed to frustrate the rat, and it began to dig, tiny claws slicing at Mrs. Carter's belly with little concern for the woman's screams. And scream she did. I thought the bite was bad, but—

Father ruffled my hair. "How's that for fun!" Turning back to Mrs. Carter: "You see, Lisa, I know she's been going over to your house, sometimes for hours at a time, and she comes home stinking of sex. She comes home stinking with the filth of sex, and she smiles at me as if nothing were wrong, as if she did nothing wrong. Well, we both know that's not true, don't we? I think we both know what's going on here. When she killed him, she wasn't trying to protect you, she was trying to protect herself. Am I right?"

I don't think Mrs. Carter heard him. She drew breath in long, lingering gasps. Each one made wet, slurping noises as the air mixed with the tears and snot clogging her throat. Her eyes were fixed on the ceiling; she didn't see me or Father at all anymore.

"I think she's going into shock," I said.

The rat had stopped digging, but it had made a bit of a mess. Aside from the last bite, the wounds weren't deep, but they were plentiful. Scratches covered the area surrounding the water, little marks as if someone took the edge of a razor blade to her abdomen with thin slices.

Father tugged off the tape and batted the bowl aside, sending it and the rat flying across the basement. "Damn rodent . . . too far . . ." he muttered, snatching up the water glass and dumping the contents on Mrs. Carter's face. The gasps stopped. She glared at both of us and shrieked.

Father slapped her, his open palm leaving a bright red mark on her face. She fell silent, her body shivering in violent spasms. "Oh come now, that wasn't so bad." He dabbed at the wound with the paper sack. "See? Just a little scratch. Nothing to write home about." He leaned over her again, his lips at her ear. "If I wanted to hurt you, I mean really hurt you, I could do much worse. I once took a knife to a man's fingers and cut off the skin clear to the bone. First I sliced down the center, then I began cutting away thin little strips. I took nearly an hour to finish with the first one. He almost went into shock only a few minutes in, so I gave him a shot of adrenaline. Not only did that wake him right back up, but it amplified the pain." He reached down and caressed the back of Mrs. Carter's hand. She jerked away, tugging at the handcuff. "Do you know there are twenty-seven bones in the human hand? Some big, some small. They all break, though. I'm not sure if he was able to feel much at that point, since I cut away most of the skin, tissue, and tendons, but he sure did squeal. I bet if I did that to you, if I skinned your fingers one at a time, you'd tell me the truth fast, don't you think?" He traced the back of her hand and circled her wrist before grabbing her tight. "I bet if I sliced just right, if I started here and worked my way around to here, circled the dorsal branch right here at the ulnar nerve, I bet I could peel your skin off like a wet glove. I'd need to be careful not to nick the vein, but I think I could do it." He turned back to me. "What do you think, champ? Should we give it a try?"

The picture popped into my head.

Father pressed his palm against the wound in Mrs. Carter's abdomen, and this time she didn't scream. Her eyes rolled so far back into her head, they went white, then her head fell to the side.

"Is she dead?"

Father touched the side of her neck. "No, she passed out. I suppose it was bound to happen." He rose and started for the stairs. "You can untie her, but leave the cuffs on. Then get upstairs and get some shuteye. This has been a long night. I need to have a talk with your mother."

"What about the rat?" I called after him. He was gone, though, and I was alone with our guest.

48

Emory

Day 2 • 8:06 a.m.

Sweetie? You really need to get up. All this napping isn't healthy, not in the least.

Emory swatted absently at the air around her, at the thick fog that had settled over her thoughts. When her eyes blinked open, they saw nothing. She was only able to tell they were open because of how dry they were—the cool air on her pupils felt so gritty, she had to pinch them shut again. She tried to roll over but couldn't.

Somebody was holding her down! Somebody pressed down on her back and shoved her into the concrete floor. *God, don't let him take my eyes! Don't let him take my tongue!* She braced herself, waiting for the pain of a blade to dip into her cornea and pluck out her eyes, or a hand to grasp at her throat and apply enough pressure to force her mouth open and—

Relax, sweetie. It's just the gurney. Don't you remember? That metal monstrosity fell down on you when you tried to lap up a little gutter water like a stray dog.

Everything came back in one quick flash, which was followed by an ache in her temple so great, she thought she might pass out again. Emory touched her forehead; her fingers came away sticky with drying blood.

Did you at least get a drink of water before all hell crashed down on you, dear? I don't know about you, but I'm parched.

Judging by the state of her throat, she had not.

At first her wrist didn't hurt. She felt nothing until she shifted her weight and tried to climb out from under the gurney, but when the pain did come, it came quickly. It felt as if her hand were separating from the rest of her arm at the wrist, seeming to cut through skin and bone like angry teeth. She tried to scream, but all that came out of her dry throat was a soft grunt.

Between the wrist and her battered head, dark semiconsciousness threatened to take her again. She fought it, though. Emory told herself that as long as she felt pain she was still alive and as long as she lived, she would recover regardless of what her current situation threw at her.

Oh, you go, girl. Girl power and all that. Nothing will play out on national television better than a girl missing her ear, with a stump for a hand, telling the world how she's a survivor. Matt Lauer will eat that up. "How did you keep it together when your hand came off and all the blood started spurting out? I guess it felt good to be free, but hell, I bet it hurt something fierce, right?"

Was she bleeding?

With her good hand, Emory reached back and touched the extremely swollen muscle and tissue at the handcuff. There was blood, but not a lot. The cuffs had peeled back the skin nearly all the way around, but that wasn't the part that bothered her most. She reserved that particular panic for the wrist bone protruding at such an odd angle under her touch. It hadn't pierced the skin, but not for lack of trying. When she tried to move her wrist, it howled back at her and she went limp, sucking in a deep breath between her teeth.

Her wrist was broken for sure. For once, she was glad she couldn't see.

Something told her she needed to stand up, and before another something talked her out of this course of action, she did just that, dragging the gurney up by her shattered wrist with a weak grasp until it was firmly balanced on four wheels. Then Emory stood, waiting in perfect silence bracing her shaking frame against the gurney, for the pain that was bound to follow.

The pain washed over her in a wave. Not only at her wrist but at her legs and arms as well. She wasn't sure how long she had been out, but clearly it leaned more toward hours than minutes. Every inch of her body burned with numbness, then with pins and needles, finally with a deep throb that settled in, determined to stay awhile.

This time she didn't scream. She was too shocked to realize she'd wet herself, the first time since waking here. The warmth trickled down her leg and puddled at her toes.

Emory stood there as Rod Stewart's voice suddenly began to shout from above, the chorus of "Maggie May."

She stood there and wondered how much longer it would take for her to die.

49

Diary

I applied a cold, damp cloth to Mrs. Carter's wounds. They didn't look quite as bad as I expected. Nothing a little Neosporin and a Band-Aid couldn't handle. Unfortunately, I had neither, so the damp cloth would have to do.

I thought she would wake up, but after twenty minutes she was still sound asleep. I was convinced that's all this was, sleep. Shock is nothing more than a defense mechanism orchestrated by the body. Things get a little hairy, and the body flips the off switch to compensate. Combine that with the enormous amounts of adrenaline released by the medulla just before, which caused her metabolism to go into overdrive, and you have got a recipe for an epic crash.

She would rest, then she would wake.

I found a blanket atop the washing machine and draped it over her small frame, then went upstairs.

I found Father passed out on the couch, a bourbon bottle lying empty on the floor beside him. I crept past without so much as a squeak of the floorboards, ducked into my room, and closed the door.

I stood there, my forehead resting against the door, eyes closed. I had never felt so tired.

"Did you tell him about the picture?"

I spun around and found Mother standing in the corner, her features obscured by shadows, her body a mere outline in the dark.

"Did you tell him about the picture?" she asked again, her voice low, full of gravel.

"No," I said, my own voice sounding far more timid than I intended. "Not yet," I added, attempting to sound tougher than I felt.

She stepped toward me, and I realized she carried a knife, one of the large ones from the butcher block in the kitchen. I wasn't allowed to play with those.

"What did she tell your father?" The blade caught the moonlight and glistened as she twisted it in her hand. "Does he know?"

I shook my head. "He thinks you were sleeping with Mr. Carter."

I'm not sure where I learned the term sleeping used in this manner, and even though I was certain I used the word properly, it felt funny coming out of my mouth. "He was . . . persuasive, but she didn't tell."

"What did he do?"

I told her, leaving out the fact that a rat was still running around the basement. Can rats climb stairs?

"And you won't tell him, will you? It will be our little secret?"

To this I said nothing.

Mother raised the blade and stepped into the moonlight. Her eyes were red and puffy. Had she been crying?

"If you don't tell him, I'll let you do things to Mrs. Carter. Private things. Things boys your age only dream about. Would you like that?"

Again I said nothing. My eyes were fixed on the blade. "You know what your father will do to me if he finds out, right? What he'll do to Mrs. Carter? You don't want to be responsible for that, do you?"

"I cannot lie, Mother." The words came from my mouth before I realized I spoke them, before I realized my error.

Mother lunged at me, the knife held high, stopping mere inches from my face. "You will keep this from him, or I will gut you like a fucking pig while you sleep. Do you understand me? I will carve out your eyes with a sugar spoon and shove them down your little throat until you swallow them whole, like two ripe grapes fresh off the vine."

The knife was so close to the tip of my nose, I saw two of them.

Mother had never touched me before.

Never hurt me.

But I believed her now.

I believed every word of it.

She went on, her voice hushed, yet so, so loud. "If you tell him any-thing, I'll tell him you were there too. Many times. I'll explain how you stood in the corner with your man parts out like a monkey at the zoo, drooling over your dear Mrs. Carter. How you watched your own mother through her bedroom window in the most secret of moments. You should be ashamed for your behavior, you despicable, deplorable child."

I wasn't about to let her intimidate me. Not this time. "Who took the picture, Mother?"

"What?"

"I think you heard me. Who took the picture? Was it Mr. Carter? Is Father right? Was there something going on between the two of you be-fore yesterday? Is that why he followed you so easily?"

The hand wielding the knife shook as her anger grew. I knew I was pushing her, I knew I should stop, but I could not. "Somebody had to work the camera, and I'm willing to bet it was Mr. Carter. Is that why you killed him, Mother? You didn't lure him over here to protect Mrs. Carter. You just wanted to cover your own tracks. Father will find the truth—you'd best prepare for that. You know he won't stop until he has all the answers. You're supposed to be faithful, Mother— that's what married people do, not sneak around doing who-knows-what with who-knows-who."

Her face was flushed. "Speak no evil, my son."

"Do no evil, Mother," I retorted. "We've all broken rules tonight."

She flipped the knife over and dropped it. The blade missed my foot by less than an inch and buried itself in the floorboard, then she pulled open my door and stormed out into the hallway toward her room. Fa-ther remained motionless on the couch, oblivious to all, snoring deeply.

I plucked the knife from the floor, closed my door, and shoved my desk chair under the knob, securing it as best I could. The door had a lock, but Father had taught me to pick it when I was only five, and I was sure a simple Kwikset lock wouldn't slow Mother, either, as she was no doubt a recipient of the same lessons. I closed and locked my windows as well. It was a sweltering night, but I had little choice. My mind's eye could picture Mother climbing in and crossing to my bed, a spoon in one hand and the knife in the other. "Good morning, champ. Ready for breakfast?" I heard her say before she thrust the spoon into my eye socket while plunging the large blade into my abdomen with a twist. "We're having your favorite."

I shook away the thought, then pulled the blanket and pillow from my bed and carried them over to my closet, where I curled up on the floor amid the clutter of tennis shoes, soccer ball, and assorted odds and ends of a young boy.

I didn't want to sleep but knew I should. This was far from over, and I needed the rest.

I couldn't sleep with my eyes open, but I sure did try, dark dreams finding me as I stared blankly at my bedroom door, waiting for the monster to return, the butcher knife held firmly in my grasp.

50

Porter

Day 2 • 8:56 a.m.

"You can ask me, you know."

Watson turned to Porter, then returned his gaze to the road ahead. "I figured if you wanted to talk about it, you would. You don't have to." He paused for a long moment, then hesitantly went on. "I heard bits and pieces, from Nash mostly. I've been meaning to tell you how sorry I am, but the right opportunity hasn't come up. I'm sorry."

"You're sorry you didn't get to tell me, or you're sorry my wife is dead?"

Watson turned pale. "I'm just—"

Porter slumped, shaking his head. "No, wait—that came out wrong. I'm on edge. They've been pushing me to see a shrink, and I know I should, I know I need to, but every bone in my body objects. It's like when you're a kid and your parents tell you to do something and you do the opposite because you don't want to do whatever it is they asked you, even if it's the right thing. It's the stubborn ass in me."

Watson gave him a slight nod. He fidgeted with the evidence bag in his hands, the pocket watch rattling around inside. "Nash said she was shot."

Porter nodded once. "We always made coffee in the morning before we headed off to work. That night we ran out of milk, so she went to the store to get a carton so we'd have some the next day. I had fallen asleep watching TV in the bedroom. I didn't hear her leave. She probably didn't want to wake me. I got up and found a note on her pillow telling me where she'd gone. It was only about eleven thirty, and since I had been sleeping, I wasn't sure if she'd left five minutes earlier or two hours, but I had been out for nearly three hours. This job will do that to you—you run and run, and when you finally get a chance to breathe, it catches up to you and you collapse. Anyway, I got up and went out to the living room to read a book, figured I'd wait up for her. Another twenty minutes went by, and I started getting nervous. We usually go to this little corner market about a block away, five minutes each way tops, maybe another five or so inside the store. She should have been back. I tried her cell phone and got voice mail. Ten minutes later I decided to walk down myself."

He paused, his eyes fixed on the road.

"I saw the lights. As soon as I rounded the corner onto Windsor, I saw the lights and I just knew. I knew it was my Heather. I started running. When I got to the store, the building was all taped off. Half a dozen patrol cars were blocking the street. I ducked under the tape and started for the door, and one of the uniforms must have recognized me because I remember hearing my name. Then someone grabbed my arm, then someone else, and someone else . . . It seems more like a bad dream than something that actually happened."

"You were probably in shock."

Porter nodded. "Probably."

"Robbery?"

"Yeah. Just some kid. According to Tareq, the night cashier, Heather was in the back of the store when this banger came in and shoved a gun in his face. I've known Tareq for going on four years now. Good guy, late twenties, wife and two kids at home. Anyway, Tareq said the kid pointed the gun at him, asked him to clear out the register. Tareq had been robbed before and knew better than to put up a fight, so he started bagging the cash in the till, thinks he had around three hundred and change. Tareq said the kid was shaking something awful, and you know that's the worst kind of robber. The calm ones treat it almost like a business transaction—everybody plays their role and everybody walks away. The nervous ones, though, they're another story. Tareq said he could barely hold the gun straight, and he thought for sure it would go off. And that's exactly what it did, only he didn't shoot Tareq. He shot the woman he glimpsed from the corner of his eye, the woman he didn't spot when he came into the store. She startled him. He spun around and clipped the trigger. The bullet caught Heather below the right breast, passed right through the subclavian artery, a through and through."

Watson lowered his head and stared at his hands. "She would have bled out fast. Nothing you can do for that."

Porter sniffed and pulled a hard left onto Roosevelt. "The shooter took off, didn't take the money. Tareq dialed 911 and tried to stop the bleeding, but like you said . . . nothing you can do for that."

"I'm so sorry."

"You wanna know the real kicker? When I was heading home that night I remembered we were nearly out of milk. I was gonna stop for some, but the market looked busy when I got close, so I let it go, figured I'd head back out a little later. Do you believe that shit? I lost . . . because I was too damn lazy to spend a few minutes in line."

"You can't think like that."

"I'm not sure what to think right now. I don't know what I'm supposed to do. I don't think I could have sat around that apartment one more day—neighbors all staring at me in the hallway, everybody treating me with kid gloves. Everything is off. Even this—" He waved his hand between them. "I figured bringing you along would be easier than Nash or Clair, but it's no different. Part of me wants to talk about this with someone who doesn't"—he cleared his throat—"who didn't know her. Another part doesn't want to talk about it at all, and the rest of me has no idea what I should be doing. Working Homicide, I've had to tell so many families about the death of a loved one. I became numb, detached. Twenty-three years of telling people, breaking that news. That kind of hurt became systematic to me. Would you believe I've got two or three speeches down cold? One to fit each scenario. Nash and I used to flip a quarter—loser had to give the death speech. I'd tell them what happened, explain how their loved one is in a better place, how they should move on and get past their personal tragedy, how time will heal. Now, though, all of that seems like complete bullshit. When I lost . . . I lost Heather . . . Christ, I can't even say it out loud without getting choked up. She wouldn't want me to get choked up. She'd want me to focus on all the good memories and forget about these past few weeks, not let them define the relationship we had. But I can't do that. I want to do that. Every time I see something of hers—the book she was reading that she'll never finish, the toothbrush that will never be used again, her dirty laundry, her mail. We played Scrabble once a week, and the last game is still set up on the board; I can't bring myself to put it away. I keep looking at her tiles, wondering what her next word would have been. I wake in the middle of the night and reach for her side of the bed, and just find cold sheets."

He downshifted again and swung around a taxicab slowing for a right turn, then yanked the wheel hard to the left to avoid a minivan pulling out from a Burger King.

"Maybe we should put the light on," Watson suggested. "Or I can drive, if you want."

Porter wiped his eye on his shirtsleeve. "No, I'm okay. I'll be fine. I guess I should have warned you before you got in the car. All of this should be coming out in therapy, not on a rookie CSI. You didn't sign on for this."

"You need to talk to someone. That's how we heal. Keeping it bottled up isn't healthy. It'll grow in you like a cancer if you keep it all inside."

Porter chuckled. "Now you sound like a shrink. That may be the longest spiel I've heard you string together since we met."

"One of my degrees may be in psychology," Watson said sheepishly.

"Are you serious? Wait, *one* of your degrees?"

The kid nodded. "I'm working on my third right now."

Porter blew through a very yellow light and swerved to avoid a Volkswagen Bug merging into traffic.

Watson's knuckles were white as Porter dropped the Charger into third and made a right-hand turn from the far left lane, nearly clipping a red Buick. "I think I should drive. The captain wanted me to drive."

"We're almost there."

"I'm not even sure going there is the best thing for you."

"Not going isn't an option. If it's him, I need to see."

They turned onto Fiftieth Avenue and skidded to a stop at the station. Porter negotiated the Charger into a handicapped spot and put his police placard on the dash. Reaching into his shoulder holster, he pulled his Beretta and slipped it under the seat. He eyed the watch in Watson's hand. "Where did you say your uncle's shop was?"

"It's called Lost Time Antiques and Collectibles, on West Belmont."

"Let me hold it," Porter said. "I don't want to leave evidence unattended."

Watson handed him the watch, and he dropped it into his pocket.

"Are you sure this is a good idea?" Watson asked.

"I think it's a horrible idea, but I need to see this kid."

51

Diary

I woke to a loud knock.

My neck and back ached from sleeping in a sitting position on the cold wood floor. I forced myself to stand and tried to stretch the pain from my limbs. My fingers still clutched the butcher knife. They were wrapped so tight around the handle I practically had to pry them apart with my free hand.

I set the knife on my nightstand. I still wore the clothing I had on the previous day. The sun was out and I had no idea of the time.

Another knock, heavier than the first.

It came from the front door.

I pulled the chair out from under my doorknob and pushed it aside, opened the door a crack.

Father (and the empty bourbon bottle) were both gone. At the other end of the hall Mother and Father's bedroom door stood open, the bed made. If anyone had slept there, they were gone now too. The house felt oddly quiet.

"Mother? Father?"

My voice seemed louder than I intended against the stark silence.

Was Father at work? I'd lost track of the days. Today felt like Monday, but I wasn't sure.

The knock again.

I went to the door and pulled the curtain aside at the side window. A heavyset man of about seventy stood on the porch in a beige trench and rumpled suit. He looked down at me and raised a badge in his left hand so I could clearly make out the shiny silver.

I released the curtain, took a deep breath, and opened the door.

"Morning, son. Are your parents home?"

I shook my head. "Father is working, and Mother set off to the store to get fixings for dinner."

"Mind if I wait for her to return?"

Considering I had no idea where either of them went, it didn't seem wise to say yes. Mother could have been in the basement, doing who knew what to (with?) Mrs. Carter. How would she react if she came upstairs and found a stranger in the house? A stranger with a badge?

"I don't know how long she will be," I told him.

He sighed and wiped at his forehead with the sleeve of his coat. I found it strange he would wear not only a suit jacket but a coat atop it while he was clearly hot. Perhaps it was to hide his gun? I pictured a .44 Magnum tucked under his meaty arm in a shoulder holster, ready to be drawn and fired at the drop of a pin like the one Dirty Harry carried in those old movies. Didn't all cops secretly want to be Dirty Harry?

This particular cop didn't resemble Dirty Harry in the slightest. He was severely overweight, and his hair had deserted him some time ago, leaving nothing but a large head covered in wrinkles and age spots. His eyes had probably been blue at a younger age but now appeared the color of diluted Windex. He had a several chins, the skin rumpled like that of a shar-pei or an apple forgotten in the sun.

"Maybe I can help you with something?" I made the offer knowing full well he would turn me down. Adults rarely accepted help from kids. Many adults didn't notice kids at all. We were lost to the background of life, much like pets and old people. Father once told me there was a sweet spot to life between the age of fifteen and sixty-five when you were fully visible to the world — any older and you fade from sight, dimming to obscurity. And the young? Well, the young started out invisible and gradually took form, solidifying till those mid-teen years when we joined the rest of the world in the visible spectrum. Poof! One day you were there and people held you accountable, people saw you. I knew that day was coming for me, but it hadn't quite arrived yet.

"Well, maybe you can," the man said, much to my chagrin. He raised his sleeve to the side of his head and blotted a trickle of sweat inching down his ear. He nodded toward the Carters' house. "When was the last time you saw your neighbors?"

I turned toward the house with as much disinterest as I could muster. "Couple days ago. They said they were going on a trip, and I promised Mrs. Carter I'd water her plants."

This was a good story. A plausible story. There was a flaw, though. As soon as the words left my mouth, I couldn't help but wonder: Does Mrs. Carter own any plants? Although I hadn't been looking, Father taught me to capture my surroundings with my mind's eye, and I didn't recall any plants, not one.

"Are you a budding botanist?"

"A what?"

"A botanist. It's someone who studies plants," he replied. More sweat dripped down the side of his head, and I tried not to stare. I tried not to look at all.

"No, I don't study plants, I just water them. Not much science in that."

"No, I suppose not." His eyes flitted past me into the small living room.

Was Mother there? Had she been in the basement after all and come up?

"Can I trouble you for a glass of water?"

The sweat dripped from his jaw, rolled down all his chins, and fell to his shirt. I felt a sudden urge to reach up and wipe the salty trail of yuck from the side of his head before it dripped again, but I did not. "Okay, but you should stay outside," I said. "I'm not allowed to let strangers into the house."

"That's very heedful of you. Your parents taught you well."

I left the man standing at the door and went to the kitchen to fetch a glass of water. Before I reached the sink, I realized I hadn't closed the door. I should have closed and locked it tight. He could walk right in if he wanted to. After such an egregious trespass, he would surely go down to the basement, where Mrs. Carter eagerly waited to tell him all about everything that had happened over the past few days.

What if she screamed?

Don't let her scream, not now. He would hear her from the door for sure.

I don't want to have to hurt him. But I would. If I had to, I knew I could.

I fought the urge to turn and look back. If I did, he would surely read the worry in my eyes. Father taught me to hide such things, but I wasn't sure I could. Not well enough to fool a police officer, not even this one with the beady eyes and pudgy belly.

I plucked a glass from the drying rack, filled it with cold tap water, and walked back toward the front door, doing my best to hide the relief I felt when I found him still standing on the porch, writing in a small notebook.

"Here you go, sir," I said, handing him the glass.

"So well-mannered," he replied, taking the glass. He pressed it against his forehead, rolling it gently against his rumpled skin. Then he lowered it to his mouth, took the slightest of drinks, and smacked his lips. "Ah, just what I needed," he said, handing the glass back to me.

Did he really need a drink, or had he taken the opportunity to get a better look at the inside of our house?

"Did they say where they were going?"

I frowned. "I told you, Father is at work and Mother went to the store."

"No, your neighbors. You said they went on a vacation. Did they say where?"

"I said they went on a trip. I don't know if they went on a vacation. I guess they might be on vacation."

He nodded slightly. "Right you are. I suppose I shouldn't jump to conclusions like that."

That is right. I read a lot of Dick Tracy comics, and I knew a good investigator never jumps to conclusions. He follows the evidence. The evidence leads to facts, and facts lead to the truth.

"You see, we got a call from Mr. Carter's employer. He didn't make it to work and didn't call, and he's not answering his phone . . . They're worried about him, so I told them I'd come out here to check things out, make sure everyone was okay. Doesn't seem to be anyone home, though. I took a quick peek in a few of the windows and didn't see anything worthy of sounding the alarm, nothing out of the ordinary, really."

"They went on a trip."

He nodded. "They went on a trip. Yeah, you said that." He peeled off the coat and folded it over his arm. There were large sweat stains under his arms. No gun, though. "Thing is, seems a little odd to me they would ask you to water their plants but not pick up their mail or their newspapers. I couldn't help but notice their mailbox is overflowing, and there are two papers in their driveway. When people go away, that's usually one of the first things they take care of—find someone to pick up the mail and the paper. Nothing tips off thieves to an empty house faster than correspondence piling up."

"Their car is gone," I blurted out, not sure why. "They left in their car."

He glanced back at their empty driveway. "Did they now."

This was not going well. This was not going well at all. I slipped my hand into the pocket of my jeans searching for the familiar hilt of my buck knife, but it was not there. If I had it, I could slash this man across the neck. I'd cut right through all his chins and let his blood loose as if from a faucet. I was fast. I knew I was fast. But was I fast enough? Surely I could kill him before this overweight waste of a man could react, right? Father would want me to kill him. Mother too. They would. I knew they would. But I didn't have my knife.

He leaned in close. "Do you have a key?"

"To what?"

"The Carter place. You need to get inside, right? To water the plants?"

I felt my stomach roll. "Yes, sir."

"Think you can let me in? Just for a second, to poke around?"

I supposed I could. Wasn't that what Father wanted? Wasn't that the reason we'd staged the place? Only one problem—I told him I had a key, and I didn't. I was putting the cart before the horse, as Father would say. Talkin' without thinkin' is a surefire way to dig a hole waist-deep.

"People are worried about them. What if something happened?"

"They went on a trip."

He nodded. "As you said."

"You're a cop. Why don't you bust the door down and go on in?" I asked him.

The man tilted his head. "Did I say I was a cop?"

Had he? Now that I thought about it, I didn't think he had. "You look like a cop."

He reached up and rubbed his chin. "Do I now."

"And you said someone called because Mr. Carter hadn't been to work. Who would somebody call, if not the police?"

"Looks like you're a budding botanist and detective."

"So why don't you bust the door down?"

He shrugged. "We cops, we need probable cause. Can't go in without probable cause. That is, of course, unless you let me in. If you let me in through your own volition, we're all covered and nobody gets in trouble. I take a quick peek, and I'm on my way."

"Just like that?"

"Just like that." He winked. The sweat had stopped, though his face was all blotchy red.

I thought about it for a second. It was a sound offer. A prudent offer.

If he was a cop, why wasn't he carrying a gun?

"Can you show me your badge again?" Now that I reflected on it, the thing he'd produced looked like a badge, the right color and shape, but how could I know it was real? I had never seen a real-life police badge before, only the ones they used on television. Usually they're in a spiffy wallet with an identification card. His badge had not been in a wallet. His badge might have been real, or it might have been one of those toy badges you can pick up at the five-and-dime.

He cocked his head, his lip curling up at the corner. He reached for his back pocket, hesitated, then dropped his arm to his side. "You know, I think I'm gonna come back a little later, when your parents are home, and have a little talk with them. Find out where the Carters went on their . . . trip."

Something changed in his expression. His face hardened, his eyes went a little darker. I fought the urge to step back. "That may be for the best."

He gave me a quick nod and started back toward his car. An old Plymouth Duster. Emerald green. Not a cop's car, my mind pointed out. A classic car though, for sure, one of Detroit's finest.

Halfway across the Carters' lawn, he stopped and called back over his shoulder, "Best you pick up these newspapers and check their mailbox. Wouldn't want the wrong element to stumble upon this place and realize they're not home. Worse yet, they might realize you're home alone right next door. There're some nasty people out there, my little friend."

I closed the door and locked it tight.

52

Clair

Day 2 • 9:23 a.m.

From behind the one-way mirror, Clair watched Talbot shuffle nervously in one of the interrogation room's aluminum chairs. He tried to pull closer to the table, but the chair was bolted to the floor. Clair had often wondered if the designer did that on purpose—placed the chairs a little farther back from the table than would be comfortable to add to the unease of being locked in the small room. Louis Fischman, the attorney Nash and Porter had met the day before out at Wheaton, sat beside him. The golf clothes were gone, replaced with a crisp dark gray suit that probably cost more than her Honda Civic on its best day. Talbot wore a white dress shirt and khakis along with one of the shiniest Rolexes she had ever seen.

"Porter should be here for this," Nash said beside her, his eyes fixed on Talbot.

"Yeah."

Fischman leaned over and whispered something to his client, then glanced up at the one-way with a wary eye.

"Think he knows why he's here?" Nash asked.

Clair shrugged. "All the shit a man like that is probably guilty of? I bet he's running a laundry list through his head right now. His attorney is salivating over the future legal bills. He's probably already picked out a new summer house on Lake Geneva."

At a table crammed into the small observation room, a tech gave them both a nod. "We're recording. Ready whenever you are."

Nash nodded back and turned to Clair. "How do you want to play this?"

"Same as usual—good cop, crappy cop," she replied, pointing a thumb first at herself, then back at him. Before he could respond, she picked up a large file box and carried it through the doorway into the interrogation room.

Talbot and his attorney both glanced up at her.

"Gentlemen, I appreciate you coming in on such short notice," Clair said, setting the box down on the table before taking a seat across from them. Nash sat down beside her.

"Did you find Emory?" Talbot blurted out.

"Not yet, but we've got a lot of people searching for her."

Fischman eyed the large box. "Then why is Mr. Talbot here?"

"When was the last time you saw Gunther Herbert?"

Talbot tilted his head. "My CFO? I don't know, a few days ago. I haven't been in the office. Why?"

Nash dropped a manila folder onto the table and flipped it open. Glossy photos stared back at them. "We've seen him recently, and he ain't looking too good."

"Oh, God." Talbot turned his head to the side to avoid looking down.

Fischman glared at Nash. "What the hell is wrong with you? Is that even Gunther, or is this some kind of sick joke?"

"Oh, that's Gunther."

"What happened to him?" Talbot turned back to them, eyes forward, unwilling to look down at the images.

Clair shrugged. "We're still waiting for the medical examiner to pinpoint cause of death, but I'm fairly confident he didn't kill himself. Are you familiar with the Mulifax Building down by the waterfront, Mr. Talbot?"

Fischman raised his hand, silencing his client. "Why?"

Nash leaned in close. "Because your CFO was feeding the rats in the basement."

Talbot looked pale. "Is that what . . . what did that?"

Fischman shot him a look and turned back to Nash. "Mr. Talbot's company purchased that building from the city. If he visited at all, and I'm not saying he did, it was simply to evaluate the building's worth."

"Is that true, Mr. Talbot?" Clair asked.

"I told you it was," Fischman barked.

"I'd prefer to hear it from your client."

Talbot turned to Fischman. The attorney considered this and nodded.

"I was there with Gunther a few months ago. Like Louis said, we were thinking about buying it, along with a few other buildings on that block. The city had it set for demolition. We needed to determine if the structure could be salvaged and turned into loft apartments, or if we'd be better off letting the city tear it down and buying the land," he explained.

"Can you think of any reason he'd go back alone?"

"Did the Monkey Killer do this?"

"You didn't answer my question, Mr. Talbot."

"If he did, I didn't ask him to," said Talbot. "If he went back, it was of his own accord."

"Was it the Monkey Killer?" Fischman repeated his client's question.

Clair shrugged. "Maybe, maybe not."

"What's that supposed to mean?"

"It means your client may have reasons of his own for wanting his CFO out of the picture. His daughter too, for that matter," Nash said.

Talbot's mouth dropped open. "That's preposterous! Why would I—"

Clair cut him off. "Why have you kept Emory hidden all this time, Mr. Talbot?"

Fischman raised his hand. "Don't answer that, Arthur."

Clair noted how he had dropped the less formal *Arty* Porter mentioned from yesterday.

"I didn't *keep* her hidden," Talbot replied, eyeing his attorney angrily. "Emory had a hard time getting on after her mother died. I figured it would be best if she wasn't attached to me. I'm constantly in the press. Reporters would put her picture on the front of every tabloid. 'Billionaire child born out of wedlock' and all that. They'd chase her all over town, harass her at every opportunity. Why subject her to such a sideshow? Bad enough Carnegie has to deal with that. I wanted to give Emory a chance at a normal life. Get a good education, start a family, make something of herself without the added pressure of my shadow." He looked Clair directly in the eyes. "Bottom line, though, if she wished to go public, I would have supported her in a heartbeat. Damn the consequences to me. Do you have children, Detective?"

"I do not."

"Then I can't expect you to understand. When you have a child, life ceases being about you and becomes wholly about them. You'll do anything for them. I spoke to Ms. Burrow about it once, and she asked me a simple question. 'If Emory were standing in the middle of the street about to be hit by a car, would you sacrifice your own life to save hers?' Without hesitation, I knew the answer was yes. When she asked me the same question about my wife, I found myself hesitating. This was very telling to me. You can never love someone as much as you love your own child, including yourself. And you will do absolutely anything to protect them."

"Why do you think someone would take her?" Clair asked.

Fischman narrowed his eyes. "Don't you mean, why would the Monkey Killer take her?"

"Sure, let's go with that." Clair shrugged. "Why would the Monkey Killer take your illegitimate daughter?"

Talbot's face flushed but he replied evenly. "You're the detective. Why don't you tell me."

Clair rested her hand on the white box. "If there's one thing we've learned about the Monkey Killer over the years, it's that he doesn't do anything without purpose or a clear endgame in mind. He targeted you because he feels you did something wrong, something worthy of punishment. Rather than hurt you directly, he kidnaps your daughter. What I find odd is that he went with a daughter nobody has ever heard about, someone completely isolated from the Talbot empire, over the Talbot family heiress. Your other daughter, Carnegie, she's a bit of a socialite. A spoiled little rich brat who—"

"Watch it, Detective," Fischman said.

"A spoiled little rich brat who galavants around the city, spending her daddy's money. Kidnap her, and you're guaranteed media sensationalism. He'd draw so much attention to this case, you couldn't buy a paper in the Philippines without stumbling on an article or two. That's what he usually wants, right? If you examine any of the other cases, he went for big impact, blood to feed the media machine. Here, though, he breaks MO and takes the unknown daughter. One you've locked away in an ivory tower and hidden from the world. Why do you think that is?"

Talbot looked to his attorney, then back to Clair. "Maybe he thinks when the press finds out about Emory, who she is, the story will blow up bigger than if he had taken Carnegie."

Clair tilted her head, considering this. "Sure, that would be my first guess, but I think he's smarter than that. I think he had a very specific reason for choosing Emory over Carnegie, one that may explain why he targeted you in the first place." She reached up and tapped the lid of the box. "Why don't you tell me what's going on with the Moorings, Mr. Talbot?"

Talbot shifted uncomfortably in his chair. He exchanged a look with Fischman, then glared at the box. "The Moorings?" he said, his voice cracking.

"Don't say a word, Arthur. Not a single word," said Fischman. "Detective, we're here to help you find Emory. Mr. Talbot came down willingly. If this is going to turn into some kind of witch-hunt, then I'll put an end to this interview right now."

A mischievous grin found the edges of Clair's lips. "Oh, I think this has much more to do with Emory than your client initially told you, Mr. Fischman. Look at him. See how the gears are turning?" Standing, she walked around behind them and faced the mirror. She leaned down to whisper in Fischman's ear. "He's trying to figure out how he's going to convince you he still has the funds to pay your firm after you see his latest bank statements."

Nash approached the table, his eyes falling to the box. Both Fischman and Talbot swiveled their head back at him. "Your buddy Arty couldn't finance a Snickers bar. Isn't that right, Arty?"

"He's been shuffling assets between his various projects like a shell game," Clair said. "His accounts are tapped, loans are due, and the investors are starting to knock on his door. He probably has a packed bag in the car right now, ready to skip town. Then there's the little problem with phase two down at the Moorings." She tilted her head at Fischman. "Aren't you an investor in that project?"

Fischman frowned. "How is that relevant?"

"As an investor, wouldn't it bother you to learn Mr. Talbot doesn't actually own the land he's attempting to build on?" Clair asked.

"What?"

"I just want you to find my daughter," Talbot murmured.

"I bet you do, Arty," said Nash.

"What are they talking about, Arthur?"

"Carnegie doesn't own any real estate, does she, Mr. Talbot? Not like Emory, anyway," Clair said. "Why don't you tell your friend here exactly why the Monkey Killer picked her over Carnegie?"

Fischman glared at him. "Arthur?"

Talbot waved a hand at him. "Emory's mother originally owned the waterfront development land from Belshire to Montgomery. When she died, she willed it to Emory." He turned back to Clair. "It's only a formality, though. Emory agreed to sell it to me. She completely supports this project."

Fischman grew red. "She's a minor, Talbot. She can't sell you anything for another, what, three years? The development is supposed to be finished in fifteen months."

Talbot was shaking his head. "We can get around that. I've been working with her trust. The paperwork was drawn up months ago. As her legal guardian, I can sign for her at any time."

Nash pulled the legal document Hosman had copied for him from his pocket and handed it to Talbot, pointing at the highlighted paragraph. "Your CFO is dead. That's his signature as witness on the lien transfer. The one man in your organization who could expose this problem is out of the picture. Doesn't that seem a little convenient? As Emory's father, if she dies, you take complete control of her assets. The trust becomes irrelevant. You take over the land and move forward with the Moorings without missing a beat. I'm beginning to wonder if the Monkey Killer has anything to do with this. To me, it seems like everything that has happened benefits you."

"That's motive, Mr. Talbot," Clair pointed out. "You clearly have the means."

Talbot was shaking his head. "No, no, you've got it all wrong. It's not like that."

"I think it's exactly like that."

"No, I mean the trust doesn't work that way." Talbot took a deep breath, attempting to calm himself. "If Emory dies, the land reverts to the city."

Clair furrowed her brow. "What?"

Talbot rolled his eyes. "It was her mother. When she drafted the trust, she was very clear on this point. If something happens to Emory, if she dies before her eighteenth birthday, all real estate reverts to the city, and remaining assets will be distributed to various charities. The only way I can obtain the land is with Emory's consent." He smiled. "You see, Detective, if anyone has a vested interest in seeing my daughter returned safely, it's me."

Clair turned to his attorney. "Is that true, Mr. Fischman?"

Fischman raised both his hands and shrugged. "My office doesn't handle the trust. I wouldn't know."

"We'll need to see a copy," Clair told Talbot.

He nodded. "I'll ask my secretary to e-mail it to you." Glancing at both detectives, he added, "If there is nothing else, I need to return to my office. Unless, of course, you plan to charge me with something? Then I imagine I'll need to post bail."

"You're broke, Talbot," Nash said. "How do you plan to do that?"

Talbot only glowered, tightlipped.

Clair grunted, turned, and went into to the small room next door, leaving Nash with Talbot and Fischman. The recording engineer glanced up at her. "That went smoothly."

"Fuck off," she said. Scanning the counter, she picked up a photograph and stomped back to the interrogation room. She dropped the photograph on the table in front of Talbot. "Do you recognize those?"

"Should I?" He frowned. "They look like John Lobbs, black leather."

"Do they belong to you?"

"I don't know. I own many shoes. If you'd like a pair, I can recommend a nice store downtown."

"Smart-ass," Nash said. "The Monkey Killer was wearing these shoes yesterday morning when he stepped in front of that bus. We lifted your fingerprints. How do you explain that?"

Fischman raised his hand again and leaned over to Talbot, whispering in his ear.

"I can't," Talbot said. "Perhaps someone stole them from one of my residences. I own dozens of John Lobbs. They're quite comfortable."

A condescending smirk had filled his face. Clair wanted to hit him. "What size shoe do you wear?"

Talbot glanced at his attorney, who nodded, then looked back to Clair. "Eleven."

"Same size as these."

Talbot picked up the picture and tossed it aside. "You're wasting your time chasing me on this, Detectives. Whether you believe it or not, I love my daughter and I would never do anything to put her in harm's way. If you'd prefer to think of me as some kind of heartless bastard, then rest easy in the fact I need her alive in order to complete the Moorings project successfully. Either way, as long as you're in here with me, you're not out there trying to find her, and that is not acceptable."

Fischman squeezed Talbot's shoulder. "That's enough, Arty."

Arty again.

"I think you've wasted enough of my client's time, Detective Norstrum," said Fischman.

"It's Norton."

"Yes, well, forgive me," he replied. "Are you filing charges? If not, we'll be leaving now."

Clair let out a frustrated sigh and motioned for Nash to follow her into the adjoining room. He closed the door as he stepped in behind her. "Not a fucking word out of you," she said to the engineer.

He raised his hands and held back a smile.

"It wasn't a total loss," Nash said. "At least he's going to hook us up with a good shoe store."

Clair punched him in the chest.

"Christ, Clair-bear!" He guffawed. "I'm one of the good guys, remember?"

"Waste of fucking time," Clair said. "He's in on it . . . has to be."

Nash was shaking his head. "You're getting too wrapped up in this. You've gotta step back. I think 4MK is playing us. Talbot is *his* target. That doesn't necessarily mean he should be ours. If what he said about the trust pans out, I think he's off the hook. Do you think that guy killed his CFO? Like that? I don't. The boxes were the same ones 4MK has used from the beginning. How would somebody like Talbot even know what kind to get? If he wanted to kill his CFO to cover something up, he would hire someone to take him out, make it look like an accident, a drowning or a car wreck, maybe even a heart attack. I'm willing to bet Hosman will link the CFO to the financial crimes—that's reason enough for 4MK to move on him. We've seen him kill for less."

She knew he was right, but she sure as shit wasn't about to admit it.

"We'll still get Talbot on the financial crimes, just not on this. We've got to stay on track, focus on finding Emory."

"We're no closer now than we were twelve hours ago. That girl is going to die of dehydration before we find her," Clair said quietly. "We're running out of time."

Nash nodded at the white box on the interrogation room table. "What about that?"

Clair shrugged. "It's empty. I figured it would put him on edge."

He rolled his eyes. "Let the feds book him on the financial crimes. We should head back downstairs and run the board."

Clair's phone buzzed and she glanced down at the display. "It's Belkin." She hit the Talk button and put the call on speaker.

"Detective? I'm down at University of Chicago's Medical Center. A nurse here ID'ed 4MK from a photo of the reconstruction."

"Is she sure?" Clair said.

"Positive. Said he always wears the fedora and mentioned he stares at an old-fashioned pocket watch for the duration of his treatment. It's our guy. His name is Jacob Kittner. I've got an address. I'm texting it to you now."

"Send it to Espinosa with SWAT, and tell them to meet us there. We're on our way." She disconnected the call and smiled at Nash. "I'd kiss you right now if you weren't such an ugly son of a bitch."

53

Diary

"Pass the potatoes, please," I asked of nobody in particular.

Mother had returned home about two hours earlier and immediately started on dinner. Father walked in and sat at the table without so much as a hello to her. He rubbed my head with a "How's my little man doing?" but I could tell it was forced.

There was tension in the air, and it was thick.

When the potatoes didn't arrive at my plate, I reached across the table and grabbed the bowl myself, procuring a generous helping. Neither Mother nor Father said anything when I avoided the greens entirely this evening, leaving the broccoli for the adults while grabbing an extra slice of meatloaf.

The unsteady clink of our forks against porcelain seemed so loud, I was fairly certain our neighbors would have heard them if one wasn't dead and the other chained up in the basement.

I reached for my milk, chugged it, and wiped my chin with the back of my hand.

"A man came by today. He was looking for the Carters. At first I thought he might be a cop, but now I'm not so sure."

Father peeked up from his meal and glanced at Mother. When their eyes met, he turned to me. He was eating the broccoli, a piece of it stuck between his two front teeth. "You shouldn't call him a cop. You should refer to him as a police officer. Calling him a cop is disrespectful."

"Yes, Father."

"Did he say he was a police officer?"

Earlier, I had pondered this long and hard. "He had a badge, but no, sir, he did not. But he acted like one. At first anyway, then not so much."

"What do you mean?"

I ran through the conversation as best as I could recall.

"A Plymouth Duster?" Mother said when I finished. "Are you sure?"

"Yes, ma'am. My friend Bo Ridley's father has one just like it, except his is yellow. I'd recognize that car anywhere."

Father turned to her. "Does that mean something to you? Do you know him?"

Mother hesitated for the briefest of seconds, then shook her head. "No." She stood and started clearing the dishes.

Father and I looked at each other. He saw too.

She wasn't telling the truth.

54

Porter

Day 2 • 9:23 a.m.

Porter and Watson followed the uniform through the halls of the Fifty-First and paused outside a second-floor door. "The investigating officer's name is Ronald Baumhardt. He's waiting for you inside." He looked down at his shoes for a second, then back at Porter. "For what it's worth, I'm sorry about what happened."

Porter gave him a nod and entered the small room.

Baumhardt was a stocky man in his mid-forties with graying hair and a goatee. He was sitting on the edge of a table, reviewing a file. Porter offered him a hand. "Detective, thanks for allowing me access today."

Baumhardt shook his hand. "I can't imagine what you're going through—it's the least we can do." He eyed Watson. "You are?"

"Paul Watson. I'm with the crime lab downtown. I'm assisting Detective Porter on another case."

"The Four Monkey Killer?" Baumhardt whistled. "Ain't that the shit. You've been chasing him for what? Five or six years? And he steps in front of a city bus. Saved the taxpayers all kinds of money. I hope the driver threw it in reverse and went back over that piece of shit."

"He was thrown clear, but quite dead," Watson said. "Not much more the driver could have done."

"Ah, right," Baumhardt replied, giving him a funny glance.

Porter nodded at the file in his hand. "So, where do we stand?"

Baumhardt motioned them back toward the table and spread the file across the top. "His name is Harnell Campbell. He walks into a 7-Eleven about a block from here last night at quarter past ten and shoves a .38 into the cashier's face, demands the contents of the register and the safe. Same old bullshit, only his selection of venue is piss-poor. Half the force hits that store before and after their shift. It's practically kitty-corner with the carpool lot. An off-duty officer was back at the beer cooler, he pulls a can of Coors Light from the six-pack he was about to purchase, shakes it up real good, then beams it across the store at the door. Our would-be robber turns toward the mess and gets caught up watching the exploding can just long enough for the officer to sneak up behind him and press his piece into the guy's head. First takedown by beer I've ever heard of."

"Don't know if Coors Light is really considered beer."

"Yeah, my wife calls it training beer," said Baumhardt. "But it's clearly got use as a tactical weapon. Anyway, we ran a slug from the .38, standard protocol, and got a match to—"

"The bullet that killed my wife," Porter said.

Baumhardt nodded. "I went to the academy with your captain, so I called Dalton straightaway and told him what was going on."

"I appreciate the chance to sit in. Thank you for that."

A phone on the wall rang. Baumhardt picked up the handset and pressed it to his ear. "Baumhardt. Okay, send him in."

A moment later the door to the observation room opened and Tareq was led inside. His face tightened when he saw Porter. Then he thrust out his hand. "I'm so sorry, Sammy. If I had thought the kid was going to really shoot, I would . . . I don't know, have done something differently. They never shoot, though. They're usually in and out. Christ, I . . . I'm so sorry . . ."

Plenty of guilt to go around, it seemed.

Porter shook his hand and squeezed his shoulder. "I don't blame you, Tareq. They told me what you did, how you tried to help her. Thank you for being there for her. I take solace in the fact that the last face she saw was a friendly one. She didn't die alone."

Tareq nodded and wiped his eyes with the back of his sleeve.

Baumhardt came over and introduced himself, then explained what was about to happen. "We're going to bring out six guys, they're going to line up right out there, and each will be holding a number." He glanced down at the paperwork on the table. "According to your statement, the guy who robbed you told you, 'All the cash in a bag, now.' I'm going to ask each of them to step forward and repeat that phrase. I need you to check out each person very carefully. Keep in mind the man who robbed you may not even be here, so don't feel like you have to pick one. I want you to be one hundred percent sure we've got the right guy. If you have any doubts, if none of them look right, that's okay, just tell me. Got it?"

Tareq nodded.

"They can't see us, so don't worry about that either. Don't worry about anything but looking out for your guy," Baumhardt instructed.

"Okay," said Tareq.

Baumhardt pressed the intercom button on the wall. "Go ahead and bring them in."

Porter stood at the back of the room. His hands were cold and clammy. He rubbed them on his pants. He could feel his heart throbbing at the side of his neck, hear the pulse behind his ears. Beside him, Watson stared into the white lineup room as a door swung open and six men were ushered inside by two uniforms.

"Number four," Tareq said. "That's him, I'm sure of it."

Baumhardt glanced at Porter, then back to Tareq. "Do you need them to run the line? You've got to be certain for this to stand up."

Tareq nodded. "I'll never forget that kid's face. That's him."

Porter stepped forward to get a better look.

A little shy of six feet tall, according to the height markers on the wall, he was a white kid barely out of his teens with a shaved head and multiple piercings lining both ears. His right arm was covered in a sleeve of tattoos ranging from a dragon at his shoulder to Tweety Bird on his forearm. His left arm was oddly bare. He stared back at them with a firm jaw and fixed eyes.

Baumhardt was sifting through the folder again. "You didn't mention anything about tattoos in your statement."

"He was wearing a jacket—I couldn't see his arms," Tareq replied. "He had a tattoo on his right ear, though. I remember that. I know I told the investigating officer."

"You said he was shaking so bad he could barely hold the gun straight. He doesn't seem very nervous now," Baumhardt pointed out. "Looks stone cold right now."

"That's him. Check the ear."

Baumhardt pressed the intercom button again. "Number four, please step forward and turn to your left."

Porter swore he saw the kid smirk before doing what he was told, as if he was somehow enjoying this. As he turned, Porter spotted the dark text on his inner lobe. "There, I see it."

"Where? I just see a shit-ton of piercings," Baumhardt said.

"No, on the inside. Under the piercings, black ink."

Baumhardt stepped closer to the glass and squinted. "Shit, you can see that? I can barely make it out." He retrieved a booking sheet from the table. "According to this, the ink says *Filter.*"

Tareq turned to them. "That's it! I told you that was him."

Baumhardt let out a sigh.

Porter put a hand on Tareq's shoulder. "Thank you."

Tareq turned to him, his eyes sharp. "I wish there was something more I could have done."

"You can't blame yourself."

Any more than I blame myself.

Baumhardt motioned to one of the uniformed officers. "Put number four in an interview room. We're about to have a very long talk." Turning back to Tareq: "We'll get you out of here as quickly as possible. We just need you to fill out some paperwork."

Porter nudged Watson. "Let's go see your uncle about that watch."

Watson frowned. "You don't want to witness the questioning?"

Porter shook his head. "My blood's boiling right now. I can't stay here. I thought I needed to see this, but I don't. It's better I go."

Baumhardt, standing only a few feet away, began packing up his papers. "Do you want me to call you? Let you know what happens?"

"I'd like that."

"He's putting up a tough front, but he'll cave. Even if he doesn't, we've got the ballistic evidence and Tareq's testimony. I've seen juries convict on much less."

Porter reached out and shook his hand. "Thanks again."

Watson was frowning at him.

"What?"

"You're a little pale, that's all."

"I'll be all right. I just need to get some air," Porter replied. "Let's go."

Pushing through the doorway, he stepped out into the busy hallway and slammed into a bulky detective carrying a four-pack of Starbucks coffee. The hot liquid exploded over both of them and rained on the floor. Watson jumped out of the way.

"What the fuck!" the detective growled. "You don't watch where you're going?"

"I'm so sorry, I—"

"I don't give a shit. You trying to send someone to the burn ward?" He frantically dabbed at the stain on his shirt with a single napkin.

Porter hadn't fared much better. Coffee dripped from his sleeve and jacket, and there was a large stain on his pants leg. It felt as if his shoe had captured half the spill and his sock was soaking it up. He reached into his breast pocket and pulled out a damp business card. "I work Homicide downtown. Send me the cleaning bill, and I'll take care of it."

"Damn right, you will," the man said, snapping up the card. "You're lucky I don't make you hit an ATM right now and send you off to Starbucks for replacements." He stomped down the hallway, muttering something about the state of cafeteria coffee.

"Let's go," Porter told Watson. "My place is on the way to your uncle's shop. We'll swing by and I'll change."

55

Clair

Day 2 • 10:59 a.m.

"We should call Porter," Nash said.

They had arrived at Kittner's apartment building, a nondescript squat three-story brick structure with fifteen units, to find Espinosa and his team already in position, preparing to enter. Donning their own vests, they followed SWAT through the main entrance and up two flights of stairs. Kittner's apartment was the last door on the right.

Clair checked the magazine in her Glock and positioned herself beside him against the hallway wall. "I don't think we should bother him right now."

"He'd want to know what's going on," Nash said.

"We gotta give him a little space."

"Prepare to breach in five," Espinosa's voice barked in Clair's earpiece.

"Go time," she said.

Nash peered down the hallway and watched Brogan and Thomas slam Kittner's door with the ram. It flew open with a splintered howl and crashed against the wall on the other side.

"Go! Go! Go!" Espinosa shouted before darting through the opening.

"Let's go," Clair told him before running down the hallway with her weapon held out before her, pointing toward the ground. As she reached the door, voices crackled in her ear.

"Brogan, clear."

"Thomas, clear."

"Tibideaux, bedroom is clear."

"Espinosa, all clear. Sort of."

Nash stepped inside the apartment with Clair on his heels. "Holy hell."

If the living room held any furniture, you couldn't tell. Newspapers stacked floor to ceiling cluttered the space, dozens of piles. Some were yellowed and faded with age; others were crisp and new. The newspapers were offset by stacks of books in both hardcover and softcover. "They're organized by genre. This pile is westerns, then we've got romance and science fiction. These look like horror. How the hell does someone live like this?"

"It's like that show, *Hoarders*," Clair said. "People start collecting little things here and there, and they escalate over time. I picture your porn stash to look something like this." She cocked her head. "Do you hear a cat?"

"I *smell* a cat," Brogan said.

"It's coming from back here," Tibideaux said. "The litter box hasn't been emptied in a few days."

"How does it even find the litter box?" Nash asked.

Espinosa came out from the bathroom. "The clutter seems to be contained to the living room. The rest of the apartment is fairly clean."

Tibideaux walked out of the bedroom holding a rather large Russian blue. The cat meowed in his arms and licked at the black plastic of his Kevlar vest. "Poor thing must be starving."

Nash stepped back from him. "Keep that thing away from me—I'm allergic."

Clair was digging through a stack of newspapers. She held up a copy of the *Tribune*. "This one is six years old."

"Judging by these piles, he may have a decade's worth in here," Espinosa replied. "What are we looking for?"

"Anything that might tell us where we can find Emory," Nash instructed.

Clair's phone rang. "It's Kloz." She put the call on speaker.

"So, this is strange," Kloz said, without a hello.

"What's strange?"

"I pulled Kittner's bank records—Porter, before you get on my ass, I got a warrant."

"Porter's not here right now."

"Where is he?"

Clair rolled her eyes. "Busy. What did you find?"

"I found a wire in the amount of two hundred fifty thousand dollars that came into his checking account five days ago. That's not the weird part, though—another quarter million hit up yesterday afternoon after he died," said Kloz.

"Can you tell where the funds originated?"

"A numbered account in the Cayman Islands. I'm trying to pull a name, but they're not very cooperative down there. I've got a buddy at the Bureau who may be able to put a little fear into them. I'll call him as soon as we hang up."

Nash nudged Clair. "Think the money is from Talbot?"

"For what purpose?"

"I don't know, some kind of payoff maybe?"

Clair turned back to the phone. "Kloz, does Talbot hold any accounts in the islands?"

"He has accounts everywhere. The money came from RCB Royal, and I was able to find wires both incoming and outgoing from several of Talbot's businesses to that particular branch, but the account numbers don't match up. That doesn't mean we should rule it out, though." He fell silent for a second; only the sound of a keyboard clicking came from his end of the phone. "Huh."

"What?"

"I found another wire. Fifty thousand came into Kittner's account exactly one month before the first two hundred fifty thousand was deposited five days ago. If this is some kind of payoff, it started at least a month ago."

"What can you tell us about Kittner?" Clair asked.

"Fifty-six years old. He worked for UPS up until a month ago, then took an extended leave of absence. I requested his employment file, but I imagine it's related to the cancer diagnosis."

"Did he own a cell phone? Can you retrace his steps?"

"Nada. I can't find one registered in his name, and UPS didn't provide him with one. If he had a cell at all, it was a prepaid. There's a landline in the apartment there. I'm running the logs now."

"What about relatives? Anybody?"

More typing. "He has a younger sister, but she was killed in a car accident five years ago. Amelia Kittner. Married name Mathers."

Nash perked up. "Mathers?"

"Yeah, why?"

"Emory has a boyfriend named Tyler Mathers. He goes to Whatney Vale High School."

"Hold on a second. I'm trying to pull up her file," Kloz said.

Clair's eyes were wide. "Emory is dating 4MK's nephew?"

Kloz returned. "Bingo. That's him. Sixteen years old. He lives with his father downtown."

"Detectives?"

Clair and Nash turned to find Espinosa holding up a cell phone at the bedroom door. "It's Emory's."

"Kloz? I'll call you right back," Clair said, disconnecting the call. "Let me see it."

Espinosa handed her the phone; she took it in gloved hands and tapped the screen. Nothing happened. "How can you tell?"

"He pulled the battery. I ran the serial number, and it came up under Talbot Enterprises with her listed as the designated user. The phone went offline night before last at forty-three past six," Espinosa explained.

Clair dropped the cell into an evidence bag and turned back to Nash. "We need to pick up the nephew. He may know where she is."

56

Diary

The next morning was a truly beautiful summer day, and so I decided
to take a walk rather than spend it cooped up within the confines of
the house. I hadn't been gone long, an hour at most—just long enough
to check on my cat, skip a few rocks, confirm Mr. Carter's burial at sea
was of a permanent nature, and return.

The green Plymouth was back.

Parked in the road in front of the Carters' home, it sat empty. I drew
close. The engine was still warm enough to tick, and exhaust lingered
on the air. There was no sign of the man from yesterday.

Careful to remain concealed behind the thick shrubs and trees of the
woods, I made my way closer.

The keys twinkled in the sunlight, dangling from the ignition.

He was a trusting man.

If the keys were in the ignition, it would stand to reason the car was
unlocked.

I poked my head up high for the briefest of seconds and glanced
back at the Carter house.

The front door was closed, but something didn't seem right. The
house didn't feel empty.

He must be in there; where else would he be?

The car's driver-side door faced the Carter house, while the passenger door sided with the street.

With nothing more than a deep breath and a dare, I darted out from my hiding spot and slid to a stop in the gravel at the passenger door. I had a clear view through the car to the Carter house—this meant someone exiting the Carter house would be able to spot me too. I had little choice, though; I would have to move fast.

I lifted the handle and pulled the door toward me with the utmost care. It let out a shrill squeak in protest. At first I thought the racket was loud enough for the man to hear, so I left the door open and ducked back down, peering at the house from under the car. When a minute passed and he didn't come out, I got back on my feet and leaned inside.

The Duster had a black leather bench seat with a tall gearshift knob poking up from the floorboards topped by a black eight ball, possibly the coolest gearshift knob I ever saw in all my years on this planet, and then and there I vowed to purchase one the moment I bought my first automobile. Such a transaction was still far off at this point, but proper planning is a must in all things from car purchases to breaking and entering.

I did not have time to properly plan this particular break and enter, and as I reached for the glove box, I prayed silently to the gods above it would be unlocked. If it wasn't, I wouldn't be getting in without my picks; I left them in the top drawer of my nightstand under the latest issue of Spider-Man.

The glove box opened with a pop.

I had hoped to find a registration slip or some type of documentation to help identify the strange man, but first glance revealed I would have no such luck. The glove box didn't contain any paper. However, it did contain a rather large gun. I do not know guns, and I'd be lying if I said under normal circumstances I could identify any weapon at first glance. I did recognize this gun, though, because I did a Dirty Harry movie marathon a few months earlier and this was clearly the same pistol favored by Clint Eastwood's character in that chain of films.

A .44 Magnum, the most powerful handgun in the world, the kind

of gun that could blow your head clear off, especially if you were an
unlucky punk.

I was not an unlucky punk. I was a smart punk. I reached for the
gun, pushed out the cylinder, and tipped it back, dropping the bullets
into my hand. I placed them in my pocket, returned the cylinder, and
put the Magnum back into the glove box exactly as I'd found it.

When Mr. Stranger decided to pull his gun (an event I was fairly
certain would come to pass in the near future), I'd revel in knowing
that the weapon would be about as effective as a water pistol. If I'd
had my tools, I would have removed the firing pin and left the bullets—
and I considered doing just that, but it would have meant a trip to the
house and back, in direct view of the Carters' house. Such a risk wasn't
in the cards. If the opportunity arose, I would reconsider.

The gun safely disabled and tucked back where I'd found it, I closed
the glove box and searched under the seat. Aside from an old sandwich
wrapper, which still stank of mustard, I found nothing. The back seat
was empty as well.

The man who might be a cop but probably wasn't was still a mystery, one I was determined to crack.

I wanted to search the trunk, but my sense and sensibilities told me
I was already pushing my luck, so I eased out of the car, gently closed
the passenger door, then made my way back to the safety of the woods.

Careful to remain between the largest of the oaks, I neared the Carter house. When I was parallel to the front porch, I ran across the grass
and knelt down below the living room window.

I closed my eyes and listened.

Father once told me our senses worked in tandem with one another
during the normal course of a day, but if you blocked out one or more
of your senses and focused on those remaining, they were that much
keener. I often found this to be true, and simply closing my eyes seemed
to give my ears an added little boost otherwise untapped.

I heard Mr. Stranger shuffling around inside; that much was clear. I
was fairly certain he was in the living room directly above me.

I heard a loud crash.

It sounded as if it came from the living room, but I didn't recall anything in that space that could make such a noise, and I had an excellent memory. Father often made me step into an unfamiliar room, then immediately close my eyes and recite everything I could recall, and exactly where each item was placed. To practice, we would visit houses for sale on open house day and move from room to room. When we finished with one house, we'd move on to the next, and if there was enough time, we would find another after that. We once stopped at six houses all in one day. My ability to remember the contents of a room was near photographic, Father told me with pride. His, however, was even better—at dinner after the six-house marathon, he asked me to recall the contents of specific rooms in the second house. I hadn't been prepared for this secondary exam, and although I remembered some, I could not recall all. Father, however, seemed to remember everything. He seemed to—

"Here to water the plants?"

The voice startled me, and I nearly jumped out of my skin as I spun around to face the source. Mr. Stranger was standing directly behind me, his eyes narrow and face awash with frown lines that seemed to have seen their fair share of use during this man's lifetime. He twirled a hammer between chubby fingers.

"The Carters are on vacation, and I thought I saw someone moving around inside their house," I blurted out quickly. This seemed like a viable reason for being over here. Sometimes the simplest answers are the best because if you lie and get deeper into a conversation, those lies can start to twist around your throat and cut off your breath.

"That would be my business associate, Mr. Smith," Mr. Stranger replied. "Like myself and my employer, Mr. Smith is equally concerned because your neighbor hasn't reported to work in a few days. I think I mentioned that Mr. Carter didn't put in for time off before leaving on this vacation. It's all very worrisome."

I couldn't remember if he had said that when we spoke the other day, but I nodded anyway. "You shouldn't be in their house. Maybe I should call the police."

"I think that's an excellent idea," Mr. Stranger said. "Would you like to call from inside or from your house?"

Rats.

Mr. Stranger's free hand rushed at my shoulder. I ducked, swirled, and came up beside him.

He let out a chuckle and tapped on the window, then curled his finger in a come hither motion. "Relax, kid. I'm only asking Mr. Smith to step outside."

A rumble filled the air from the direction of my house, and I spotted Father's Porsche pulling into the driveway. He climbed out of the driver's seat, and Mother exited the passenger side. Speaking to each other in a hushed tone, they stared at Mr. Stranger and me. They approached, Father with a smile that could light a room and Mother with her arm folded through his. She was wearing a lovely green floral dress that hugged her legs with each whimsical step. They belonged in a magazine.

Father offered his hand and what was sure to be a firm handshake. "How do you do, kind sir? Friend of the Carters'?"

Mr. Stranger offered a smile in return. "I work for his employer, actually. He hasn't been at work since Tuesday, and talk around the water cooler is getting a little worried. Thought I'd take the drive on out here and see what was what."

The screen door at the front of the Carter house slammed, and we all turned. A wiry man with long blond hair and thick glasses stepped down off the porch. Rather than approach, he leaned against the railing and pulled out a pack of Marlboro Reds. I watched as he flicked the tip of a match with his right thumb, setting it ablaze, then lit a cigarette that had found its way into his mouth, though I hadn't seen him remove it from the pack.

"That's my coworker, Mr. Smith."

Mr. Smith tipped a nonexistent cap and continued to survey us from afar. His eyes lingered on Mother a little longer than they should have, and I knew this probably angered Father, although he didn't show it. Instead, he cordially said, "Pleased to meet you," and returned his attention to Mr. Stranger. "I didn't catch your name."

Mr. Stranger smiled. "No, I don't suppose you did. I'm Mr. Jones."

"And you're a police officer, Mr. Jones?"

Mr. Stranger tilted his head. "Why would you say that?"

Father's eyes didn't break contact with Mr. Stranger. "My son said you had a badge yesterday."

Mr. Stranger did break eye contact, and he did look down at me. "I'm not sure why he would say such a thing. He must have been mistaken." He offered a quick wink, then ruffled my hair before returning to my father. "Did the Carters tell you where they were going?"

Father shook his head. "We aren't that close."

"Did they say when they would be back?"

"Like I said—"

"You're not that close."

"That's right."

From the porch, Mr. Smith let the remains of his cigarette fall to the floor and crushed the butt under a black boot that belonged on the foot of a motorcycle rebel, not the little man standing before us. He wasn't much taller than I. But his voice was much deeper than one would expect, raspy. "Mr. Carter was working on a rather sensitive project for our employer, and since he didn't clear this vacation with the office and he appears to be unreachable, we have to assume he has skipped out on his duties. That in mind, all associated work papers, the property of our employer, must be returned immediately. We hoped those work papers would be here in his home, but that doesn't appear to be the case. At least, if they are here, they are not readily visible. Did Mr. Carter ever speak about work? Perhaps he mentioned what he was working on?"

"We aren't that close," Father repeated again. "I am sorry to say I'm not even aware of Mr. Carter's profession."

"He's an accountant," Mr. Stranger said.

I saw his eyes shift over to Mother for the briefest of seconds, and she looked back. Something was communicated with that simple glance, but I did not know what that was.

Mr. Smith was holding his hands out before him. He traced a square in the air.

"He stored his work papers in a beige metal box about a foot tall and two feet wide, fireproof, with a key lock on the lid. Similar to a large safe-deposit box. I found it under their bed, empty as a drunk's shot glass. I'd like to know what he did with the contents."

Mother, who had remained silent up until this point, spoke up in a firm tone. "I don't believe the Carters would be happy to learn you rummaged through their things without prior permission in search of such a box, regardless of its contents. I think it would be best if you gentlemen were to leave. When the Carters return, I will personally see to it Mr. Carter contacts his office. I imagine his failure to properly request this time off was simply an oversight, and this can all be straightened out with a very boring explanation."

Mr. Stranger smiled, but it was a forced smile, the kind you spread across your face to be polite when fed a bitter dessert. "I am sure you are right and we are all overreacting." He lowered his head in a mock bow. "It was a pleasure to meet you both." He ruffled my hair again. "You have a fine boy here. Please tell Mr. Carter to phone the office the instant they return."

"Absolutely," Father replied.

With that, the two men walked at a leisurely pace back to the Plymouth at the curb, neither looking back. Father, Mother, and I held our ground until the car disappeared from view, leaving nothing behind but a dusty rooster tail.

57

Emory

Day 2 • 11:57 a.m.

Emory pulled her knees to her chest and wrapped her free arm around her body in an attempt to warm up. She shivered uncontrollably, her teeth chattering in her skull. Earlier she felt her broken wrist with her good hand and had to pull away. It had swollen so thick the skin seemed to wrap around the edges of the handcuffs, the metal digging in. Her pulse beat against the sharp steel, all warm and wet. She feared she might lose the hand if she didn't find a way out soon, but she didn't know what to do.

There was no way out.

No door.

No ceiling.

Nothing but cold concrete surrounded her.

Music blared, a song she didn't know.

Putting a coherent thought together had become difficult too. She knew this stemmed from lack of food and water, but telling herself that did little to help. Her head throbbed with pains of its own, and her mind seemed muffled, lost on the other side of the fog.

She had gotten drunk once.

She and Colleen McDoogle.

They found a bottle of Wild Turkey under the kitchen cabinet at Colleen's house and decided to try it. After all, if they didn't practice drinking, how would they know how much they could safely drink at a party without getting wasted? In the end it took very little, and Colleen's mother was far from thrilled when she walked in on them, arriving home a full hour earlier than expected. Emory couldn't remember how much they'd drunk, but the next day she was left with a special kind of headache, one that seemed to start behind her eyes and intensify as it worked its way back.

She had such a headache now.

I remember when that happened. You couldn't walk a straight line if your life depended on it. You tried, though, you and Colleen both, hoping her mother couldn't tell.

"It was last year, Mom. You were dead."

That doesn't mean I wasn't watching, honey. How I would have grounded you! I would have taken away your computer and your phone and your television. I might have done what my mother did when she caught me drinking for the first time with my brother. You remember your uncle Roger, right? She caught Roger and me with a fifth of vodka and made us finish the entire bottle between us. I was sick for days, but I didn't touch alcohol again for nearly three years. How is Roger these days?

"Who is Roger? I don't remember an Uncle Roger."

How could you forget Uncle Roger? He lived with us for nearly a year after you were born.

Then Emory did remember Roger. Slightly overweight, dark hair disheveled in a vain attempt to hide the bald spot slowly accumulating real estate at the top of his head. He fixed the sink once when Ms. Burrow stuffed the disposal up with pasta. He also helped her get a new access card for the elevator when hers died from sitting under her cell phone in her purse. Wait . . . "I don't have an uncle Roger. Roger is the building superintendent."

Did I say Roger? Oh dear, I meant your uncle Robert.

"I don't have an uncle. If I met any of your relatives, I don't remember them," Emory said quietly. She could have shouted if she wanted to, and nobody would hear over the thundering sound of Cream singing "Born Under a Bad Sign."

You don't remember your uncle Steve? He would be very upset.

He used to love rocking you to sleep when you were a baby. He used to sing you that song . . . How did it go? Do you recall? Something about the day the music died . . .

"Drove my Chevy to the levee but the levee was dry," Emory croaked, her lips dry and chapped. She ran her tongue over the cracks. ". . . this'll be the day that I die . . ."

That's it! Uncle Ryan loved that one.

"I don't have any uncles. I don't have a mother, either. You don't exist. Please stop talking to me."

Do you think today is the day?

"What?"

You know, the day you're going to die.

Emory pressed the fingertips of her good hand against her temple and ground them into the soft skin.

I think it's best you come to terms with your limited future. Really, dear, even if that Monkey Killer doesn't kill you soon, you haven't had food or water in weeks. How much longer do you think you can last?

"It hasn't been weeks. It's only been two days, three at most."

Oh, I think it's been at least a week, sweetie.

Emory shook her head, cringing as the motion rocked her damaged ear. "I think the music is on a timer. If it is, I think it's coming on once a day. That would make today the second day."

Even if your little theory turned out to be true, and I don't believe it is, just how long can you last without food or water?

"Gandhi fasted for twenty-one days," Emory said.

Twenty-one days without food, but he had water.

"Did he?"

Oh, I'm sure of it. I wouldn't be surprised if someone snuck him a candy bar or two along the way. You know how those celebrities are.

"He wasn't a celebrity, he was a . . ." Why was she talking to her? She wasn't real. It was just her mind. She was losing her mind. She would snap long before the lack of water did her in. Her brain was slowly dehydrating like a sponge left out in the sun—her organs too. She felt like she needed to pee, but when she tried there was nothing. She could almost picture her kidneys and liver shriveling up inside her. How long before they failed? Even though she wasn't moving, her heart was speeding up, pounding in her chest. At first she thought it was only her imagination, but when she'd taken her pulse a few hours ago, she measured nearly ninety beats per minute. Very high. When she ran, her pulse rarely broke eighty.

Emory pressed her finger into her neck and took her pulse again, counting the beats over fifteen seconds — twenty-six. Twenty-six times four is . . . Crap, she couldn't focus. Twenty-six times —

It's nearly two hundred, dear. That's fast.

"One hundred four," Emory said, ignoring the voice. Her resting heart rate normally ran around fifty-five. She was doing nothing right now, and her heart was racing. Emory didn't know exactly what that meant, but she knew it wasn't good.

When the Monkey Killer comes back, maybe you can ask him to kill you quickly. That would be so much better than the business with the eyes and tongue, don't you think?

Emory ran her tongue around the inside of her mouth. She had lost most of her sense of taste, but what little remained reminded her of sawdust. A mouthful of sawdust.

She wanted to cry but had no more tears. Her dry eyes burned against the darkness.

From somewhere up above, Jimi Hendrix picked up his guitar and began to wail.

58

Diary

The rat was dead.

As I chased Mother and Father down the steps into the basement, it was the first thing I noticed. Its little black body resembled a soggy dishcloth with eyes. The rat's head faced its back, and its legs were splayed this way and that. The mangled rodent rested in a small puddle of blood beside the cot where Mrs. Carter now sat, her free hand red with death.

She smiled up at us as we came down. Any fear that had filled her eyes a few hours earlier had vanished, replaced with a cold, icy stare.

"He'll kill us all, you know." Her voice was different too, calm and collected. Sure.

"Who?" Father replied, although I was pretty sure he knew exactly who. How Mrs. Carter knew who or what we were coming down to discuss was the question that filled my mind, but evidently she did. She knew exactly why we were down here.

"Did he leave? Because if he did, I wouldn't expect him to stay gone for very long." Mrs. Carter wiped her bloody hand on the bottom of the cot, then kicked the dead rat, sending it sliding across the basement floor, leaving a red stripe in its wake. "You really shouldn't have killed my husband."

Father drew his hand back, and I thought for sure he was going to hit her. I couldn't imagine him doing such a thing; he had always told me never to hit a woman even if she hit you, even if she hit you with something heavy—there was never an excuse to hit a woman. Never.

He drew his hand back, grabbed a towel from the top of the washing machine, and tossed it to her.

She smiled a thank-you and wiped the blood off her hand as best she could without water. "If you let me go, I can try to explain what happened, but I don't think he'll believe me. Even if he does, I doubt that he'll care."

"He wants your husband's work papers. He said he works for your husband's boss," Father said.

She tilted her head. "Well, that's not a lie."

"Do you know where they are?"

Mrs. Carter smiled again but said nothing, then tugged at the handcuffs.

Mother, who had remained silent through this exchange, charged at her. Father grabbed her as she jumped through the air in an attempt to tackle Mrs. Carter. Mother squirmed in Father's grasp, her hands clawing at the air, reaching for Mrs. Carter. "What did you bring into my house!" she shouted.

Mrs. Carter scowled. "You brought me into your house. I didn't ask for this. I didn't tell you to kill my husband, you crazy bitch."

That set Mother off, and for a second I thought Father wouldn't be able to hold her back, but somehow he did. He wrapped his arm around her neck and put her in a sleeper hold, not tight enough to knock her out but enough to let her know that he could if he wanted to, and that was all it took because Mother finally relented and went still. Father didn't relax his grip, though, and I knew exactly why—when he had taught me how to use a sleeper hold, he said the victim would sometimes pretend to fall asleep or pretend to cooperate, and the second you loosened your grip, they would strike. He told me this not only so I would know how to properly execute a sleeper hold, but also so I would know to try it should I ever find myself locked in one. He had even taught me to feign passing out. Father was extremely wise.

"If I let you go, you need to promise me you'll behave," Father said softly at Mother's ear.

When she nodded, he slowly unwrapped his arms. He remained ready to grab her again if she made another move, but she did not. Instead, she leaned back against the washing machine and glared at the other woman.

Father returned his gaze to Mrs. Carter. "Who does your husband work for?"

"Don't you mean, who did my husband work for?"

He waived a dismissive hand through the air. "Semantics."

Mrs. Carter fell silent, and for the first time since we had come down here, I saw the previous fear creeping back into her eyes. She tried to hold it at bay, to appear tough, but it was there, no mistaking it. Father saw it too. When she finally spoke, her voice was softer, fragile. "We need to leave, all of us."

Father kneeled down beside the cot and placed his hand on hers. "Who did he work for?"

She looked at Mother for a moment, then at me, then back to Father. "Criminals. A dozen of them, maybe more. Even a few members of the Genovese family. He helped them hide their money."

Father didn't miss a beat. "What did he take from them?"

Mrs. Carter took in a deep breath, closed her eyes, and let it back out. "All of it. Every last penny."

59

Porter

Day 2 • 12:18 p.m.

"Just make yourself at home," Porter told Watson as he dropped his keys on a small table near the front door. "You're welcome to root around the fridge. I'm not sure what I got in there."

The ride from the Fifty-First back to his apartment had been quiet. Watson had fidgeted in his seat, and Porter had done his best to try and forget the face of the kid who had shot and killed his wife.

It wasn't working.

Every ounce of his being wanted to drive back down, shove his Beretta under the kid's chin, pull the trigger until the last bullet exited the chamber, then beat him over whatever was left of his head.

He wasn't proud of these thoughts. He didn't want them. He wasn't a violent man, and Heather would scold him if she knew he harbored even an ounce of hate for that young man. She would tell him to rise above, not give in to the anger. She would tell him that anger and hatred wouldn't bring her back and such thoughts did nothing but blacken his soul.

She was right, of course. Heather always seemed to be right, but knowing that changed nothing.

"You okay?" Watson was staring at him.

Porter nodded. "I will be. I just need to catch my breath, regroup." He hesitated, then said, "Thanks for going down there with me."

"Anytime. Is that her?" He gestured toward a photo on the end table.

Heather, taken about a year earlier.

Porter reached over and picked it up. "Yeah. I was so proud of her that day. She always wanted to be a writer, was constantly scribbling in a notebook, always writing. I submitted one of her short stories to the Shirley Jackson Awards, and she actually won. I took that photo right after the award ceremony."

Porter was grateful when Watson didn't push for more information. "I'll be right back. Help yourself to some food." He nodded again toward the kitchen and watched Watson walk off in that direction.

His phone vibrated in his pocket as he entered the bedroom, and he considered letting the call go to voice mail, then changed his mind. A quick glance at the display told him it was Kloz. He hit the Talk button and brought the phone to his ear.

"Sam?"

"Yeah?"

"We've got a serious problem."

"What's up?"

"Remember the print you pulled yesterday off the railcar down in the tunnels?"

"Yeah."

"It came back with a match."

Porter walked over to his closet and pulled off his jacket, then started on the buttons of his shirt. The coffee was cold and sticky and went halfway up his arm. He'd probably have to toss it.

"Sam, the print belongs to Watson. Only it wasn't Watson. The name on the ID from ViCAP was Anson Bishop. I just got off the phone with the crime lab—at first glance his file seems legit, but once I started digging I found some holes. His ViCAP record is a fake. There is no Paul Watson. It's an alias for this Anson Bishop. I'm still trying to piece things together, but he touched that railcar sometime before you and SWAT got down there. That means he's somehow involved. This is bad, Sam. Real bad. Whoever this guy is, he's not law enforcement. Where did you say you and Nash found him?"

"Uh-huh."

"Shit. He's with you right now, isn't he?"

"Yep."

"Where are you? Are the two of you alone?"

Porter poked his head out the bedroom door and glanced back down the hall toward the kitchen.

"Sam, are you there?"

"Watson?" Porter said loudly. "Do I have any beer left in the fridge?"

"Your apartment? You're home?"

"Yes, sir. That is so true."

He could hear Watson in the kitchen or the living room, but the man didn't answer.

Porter removed his shoes and stepped silently out his bedroom and into the hallway, his eyes dancing quickly over the empty living room, then toward the open kitchen door.

"Watson?" Porter slowly reached up and unsnapped his holster's leather strap. His fingers coiled around the grip of his Beretta as he drew the weapon. "I know it's early, but I could really use something to take the edge off."

He heard Klozowski faintly barking orders on the other end of the line. "Keep him there, Sam. I've got units on the way."

"Sure, Kloz. Come on over. Watson and I are heading to his uncle's watch shop after this; you can ride with us."

"Closest car is four minutes out. Where is he? Do you have visual? Can he hear us?"

"Watson, if you're eating all the leftover pizza, I'm not going to be happy."

With the gun at point, Porter burst through the door into the small room.

Empty.

The large knife slipped into his thigh a moment before he saw Anson Bishop from the corner of his eye. "Don't move," Bishop whispered into his ear from behind. "The knife is right on your common iliac artery—that's one of the largest in the pulmonary system. You attempt to pull out this knife, and you'll bleed out in seconds. I'm going to help you to the floor. Drop the gun."

"Who are—" Porter managed to say, the words slipping out from behind gritted teeth.

"Drop the gun. The phone too."

Porter did as he was told and remained still as Bishop kicked the gun away, then stomped on his phone, crushing it under the sole of his shoe.

"Watson?"

"Shhh, don't speak," Bishop said. "Now, easy. Knees first, then lie down on your stomach . . . that's it. Mind the knife."

Porter let the man help him down. He could feel the weight of the knife in his leg, but Bishop held the blade still with his free hand until Porter was facedown on his hardwood floor.

"I imagine your friend has help on the way, so you won't have to wait long. If you notice, there isn't much blood. It will stay that way as long as you leave the knife in the wound. Wait for the professionals; they'll know how to take it out. Then a couple of stitches and you'll be right as rain. I'm sorry I had to hurt you, I truly am. I hoped we would have more time together; I was having such fun. As with all good things, though, they must come to an end at some point, and we are fast approaching the endgame."

"Where is Emory?"

Bishop smiled. "Please give my best to Nash and Clair. For what it's worth, I am very sorry about your wife."

Porter twisted his head just enough to watch him round the corner and disappear into the hallway. In the distance, sirens wailed.

60

Diary

"Well, that was the plan, anyway. Steal it all and get away. I don't know if he pulled it off, though. Simon talked a big game, but his follow-through left a little something to be desired."

"They found a beige metal box under your bed. Is that where he put it?" Father asked.

Mrs. Carter shrugged. "Dunno."

Mother charged at her again, and this time she was faster than Father. Her hands reached for the woman's hair, grabbed a handful, and pulled hard. Mrs. Carter squealed and swatted at Mother's arm with her free hand, her nails leaving a quick red slash across Mother's forearm.

"Enough!" Father bellowed, pushing his way between them.

Mother released her grip and snorted, taking a step back. "This woman is going to get us all killed."

"What specifically did he take?" I asked. This was a valid question, and one I hoped would break the tension.

Mrs. Carter touched her scalp tenderly and winced. She narrowed her eyes at Mother. "We're all good as dead now."

Father pushed her down onto the cot. "Answer my boy's question."

She smirked at him. "Aren't you tough, shoving around a woman handcuffed in your basement." Some blood had dried on her fingernails, and she began picking at it. "Simon knew their business better than they did. If they think he's run off, they've got to be worried." She gave Father and Mother an accusing glance. "Sounds like the two of you did an excellent job of making it look like he's in the wind, so I'm sure they're worked up plenty. You brought them right to you."

"What did he steal from them?" Father asked again, the anger rising in his voice. He wouldn't ask a third time, not nicely anyway.

Mrs. Carter gave up on her fingernails and drew a deep breath. "About a month ago, he said the two owners of the firm began acting strange, secretive—more so than usual, anyway. They left him out of a few meetings he felt he should have attended. They began working odd hours. A few times he thought someone had gone through his things. He felt like people were whispering behind his back, preparing to force him out, or worse. He began taking files home and making copies. I told him he was crazy. If they caught him, there was no telling what would happen, but he did it anyway; dozens of them. He told me it was insurance. If they tried to hurt him or cut him out of the business, he'd go public with the records."

Father ran his hand through his hair. "That sounds like a very dangerous game."

Mrs. Carter nodded. "Last week, when they pulled him from his largest account, he said that he was going to use the information he had gleaned to embezzle money into an offshore bank so we could run off, just disappear."

"But you don't know if he did it?"

She shook her head. "If he did, he didn't tell me. We've been fighting so much this past week, I don't know that he even would."

Tears had filled her eyes, and I felt uncomfortable watching her. I looked down at the floor and kicked at the dust.

"What did he do with all the documents he copied?" Father asked.

Mrs. Carter shrugged. "I don't know. He didn't tell me. And now he's gone."

Father turned to Mother. "People like this, they'd sooner kill us all than risk their dirty laundry getting out. Maybe we should leave."

"Maybe we should kill them first," Mother replied quietly.

"I know that man. This is just the beginning," Mrs. Carter said. "He'll be back, probably soon, probably with others. Running is the only option."

61

Clair

Day 2 • 1:23 p.m.

"What the hell is going on here?" Steven Mathers's face was flushed as he stormed into Principal Kolby's office.

Kolby raised both hands. "Calm down, Steven. I called you as soon as they arrived."

Steven Mathers's eyes fell on his son sitting in the far corner of the room, his head down and clasped between his hands. He turned to the detectives. "What do you want with my son?"

Clair motioned to an empty seat in front of the large oak desk. "Why don't you sit down, Mr. Mathers."

This only seemed to anger him more. "What I'm going to do is take my son out of here, lock him in our apartment, and send three of my attorneys down to your boss's office for a chat. That's what I'm going to do."

Clair took a deep breath and let it out. "Your son may be involved in the kidnapping and possible murder of Emory Connors-Talbot."

Mathers frowned. "Talbot? The real estate guy?"

Nash nodded. "Your son is dating his daughter."

"Dating is far from kidnapping, Detective."

"Please take a seat, Mr. Mathers," Clair asked again.

This time Mathers complied, dropping his briefcase at his side.

"What can you tell us about Jacob Kittner?" she asked.

"My wife's brother?"

Clair nodded.

"I haven't talked to him since my wife, Amelia, died a little over five years ago."

"What about your son? When was the last time he spoke to Mr. Kittner?"

"He hasn't had any contact with him, either. We don't talk to her side of the family," said Mathers.

The three of them looked over at Tyler in the corner; his face was still buried in his hands.

"Isn't that right, Tyler?" Mathers said.

When Tyler glanced up, it was from behind red, swollen eyes. "This is my fault, all of it. I didn't think anyone would get hurt."

Mathers stood up and walked over to his son. "What are you talking about?"

"Uncle Jake said she wouldn't get hurt."

Clair and Nash looked at each other, then back to Tyler.

"Uncle Jake? Since when do you have any kind of relationship with that guy?"

Tyler sighed. "Mom and I used to see him all the time. We didn't tell you because the two of you never seemed to get along and she didn't want to fight. When he told me he was dying, I started helping him out around the house—little things after school, that's all."

"He was dying?"

Clair glanced up at the principal, who was watching from behind his desk. "Mr. Kolby, do you think you could excuse us for a little while?"

Kolby frowned, prepared to protest, then thought better of it. "I'll be right outside if you need anything."

Once the man left, Clair returned her attention to Mathers. "Your brother-in-law had advanced stomach cancer. He probably would have died within weeks."

Mathers was shaking his head. "Wait a minute, what do you mean by 'would have'? What happened?"

Nash ran his hand through his hair. "Yesterday morning, at a few minutes past six, Jacob Kittner was struck and killed by a CTA bus while walking to a mailbox at Fifty-Fifth and Woodlawn. We think he was attempting to mail a small white box. That box contained a human ear . . . Emory's ear. Your brother-in-law was the Four Monkey Killer."

Mathers's face went pale and he shuffled in his chair. "Jake? He couldn't be."

Nash nodded. "He kidnapped Emory, and she's still out there somewhere. Without food or water or someone to take care of her —she doesn't have much time. Your son may be the only person left alive who knows where to find her."

Mathers appeared worse than his son now, his face pale, breath shallow. "Tyler, is this true?"

Tyler drew in a breath. "He's not the Four Monkey Killer. It's not what you think."

Clair crossed the room and knelt at his chair. "I understand you cared for him, but he did some terrible things. Right now, though, we need to focus on Emory, and if you know where he took her, you need to tell us."

"He's not the Four Monkey Killer," Tyler repeated.

Mathers rose and went to his son. "What are you trying to say?"

"Uncle Jake was just trying to help us."

"Help you how?" Clair asked.

Tyler looked up to his father, then returned his gaze to the floor. "My father has been having money trouble. He got downsized at work last year, and since then he's had a tough time covering expenses, and he dipped into my college fund."

"How do you know about—"

Clair raised her hand. Tyler continued.

"Based on my grades, I've got a good shot of getting into an Ivy League school, but I'm not doing well enough for a scholarship. Dad still makes too much to qualify for grants, so we'll need to pay out of pocket. The student loans won't cover everything. Uncle Jake said the only way to make that happen is if I let him help me. When he found out he had cancer, he tried to get a life insurance policy, but they denied him as soon as they learned about his diagnosis. Then he told me he had another way.

"About a month ago, a man approached him and told him he could make a lot of money if he helped him out with something. He told Uncle Jake it wasn't illegal—well, not very illegal. He said he knew Uncle Jake was sick and he didn't have much time left. This was a way for him to help not only me but a whole bunch of people. He said Uncle Jake couldn't do it alone, though, that I would need to help."

Mathers was turning red again. "What did that bastard make you do?"

"Mr. Mathers, please," Clair said.

Tyler sighed. "He didn't make me do anything, Dad. Nothing I didn't want to do, anyway. He said I had to get close to Emory Connors, maybe even take her out a few times. She's hot, so I figured, why not? We went on a couple of dates, then I took her to homecoming . . ." His eyes drifted back to Clair's. "At first I only wanted to see if I could get her to go out with me, but once I got to know her, I really liked her. We had a lot of fun. I could talk to her, you know? And she's so smart. She even helped me with some of my classes. Things were going good. That's when Uncle Jake told me to get the shoes."

"Mr. Talbot's shoes?" Clair asked.

"Yeah. Last Thursday we were hanging out watching a movie, and Mr. Talbot came by for about twenty minutes. His clothes were covered in dirt. He didn't say why. He said he needed to take a quick shower and change, then he was off. He left his dirty clothes in the guest room for the maid. About twenty minutes after he left, I got a call from Uncle Jake. He told me I needed to bring him Mr. Talbot's shoes. Didn't say why, only that the man had told him to get them. I have no idea how he even knew Mr. Talbot had come by, let alone left some clothes behind. Kinda weirded me out. I thought he had cameras in the place. When Em got up to use the bathroom, I slipped the shoes into my backpack. I brought them over to Uncle Jake's the next day. He didn't say what the man wanted with them, only that he'd transferred enough money to cover my tuition and then some. For a pair of shoes! I couldn't believe it. We expected the money to get pulled back out, but it wasn't. The next day, Uncle Jake received a calculus book from the man. He told me I had to leave it at Em's apartment.

That seemed weird, but I figured, why not? If some strange guy wants to pay hundreds of thousands of dollars for a pair of shoes and for me to—"

"How much?" Mathers blurted out.

Tyler turned to his father. "Uncle Jake said he initially gave him fifty thousand when he agreed to help, then another two hundred and fifty when we got the shoes with more—"

Mathers turned to the detectives. "I don't think we should say anything else until my lawyer gets here."

Clair rolled her eyes. "Tyler, where is Emory?"

"I don't know."

"Detective, didn't you hear me?" Mathers said.

"What did this man look like?"

Tyler shrugged. "I never saw him. I don't think Uncle Jake ever did, either. He only talked to him over the phone."

"We have rights, Detective!"

"Give us a minute." Grabbing Nash by the shoulder, Clair pulled him out of the cramped office into the hallway. "Are you buying this?"

"I don't know what to believe anymore. Nothing about this case makes sense."

Clair's phone vibrated. She glanced down at the screen and read the text message:

CALL ME! — KLOZ

62

Diary

We left Mrs. Carter in the basement.

She had said they would come back, and they did. Less than an hour later, we heard the rumble of the Duster coming down the road. Mr. Stranger pumped the gas three or four times before letting the engine fall idle; he wanted us to know they were out there.

The three of us gathered at the window and watched the green car for nearly five minutes before Father let out a gruff breath and pushed out the kitchen door, heading for the road.

I stood in the open doorway with Mother behind me as Father plodded across our grass, heading straight for the Plymouth parked in the street between our driveway and the Carters'. He was about ten feet from the car when Mr. Stranger dropped into gear and sped away, kicking up dirt and gravel in his wake.

Father stood and stared at the space where the car had been for a long while before returning to the house. He closed the door at his back and twisted the deadbolt. We rarely closed the wood door during the summer months. Without air conditioning, our little house grew stifling hot, and the circulation of open doors and windows was one of the few ways we battled the heat.

He saw Mother and me watching him. "This is going to end badly."

"They don't know she's here," Mother replied.

"They know," he said. "I don't know how they know, but they know."

"Then why don't we just give her to them? Let them do what they want?"

Father thought about this for a moment, then shook his head. "I think she knows exactly where her husband's work papers are hidden."

Mother crossed the room to the coffeepot and clicked the power switch. From inside the cupboard she retrieved a brown bag from PT's Roasting Company, added two scoops to the filter, and pressed the Brew button. A minute later the scent of finely roasted happiness filled the room, and although Father said I was far too young to drink coffee (Father said caffeine would stunt my growth and increase my chances of insomnia as an adult), I appreciated the smell. I found it to be soothing, creating a calm that settled over the room. Mother retrieved two mugs, filled them, and carried them to the kitchen table, where she and Father took a seat.

"Perhaps we should march her out to the lake and drown her, make it look like an accident," Mother suggested.

"That might open a larger can of worms. Mr. Carter is feeding the fish at the bottom of that lake. I don't think we should risk drawing anyone's attention to that particular body of water," Father replied.

"Her own bathtub, then?"

Father took a drink of his coffee and set the mug back down, twisting it in his hands. "Those men already searched their house and know she's not home. Since it appears the Carters left in a hurry, I doubt the missus would come back to take a bath."

An idea popped into my head. From where, I am not sure, but it was a worthwhile idea, so I presented it. "You could strangle her and put her body in the trunk of their car. If you stage things right, it will seem like Mr. Carter killed her and ran off somewhere."

Both Mother and Father turned to me with blank stares. I was in trouble. I shouldn't have said anything. Maybe I should go to my room and—

"An excellent idea, champ!" Father said. "We left the car at the train station; that may be the perfect setup for a husband on the run."

Mother was nodding in agreement. "We should find out where they hid the work papers first, though."

Father's eyes were fixed on his coffee. "Insurance?"

Mother nodded. "Insurance. If these men don't believe this little ruse, it wouldn't hurt to have a little something of value for bargaining purposes. What if he stole the money too? The funds could come in handy."

"We're not thieves," Father said.

"If we have to relocate, we're going to need that money. Who knows how the rest of this debacle will play out. It's their fault we're involved. They owe us."

Considering Mother had killed Mr. Carter and we now had Mrs. Carter chained up in our basement, I failed to see how this was "their fault," but Father must have agreed to some extent, because he offered no further objections.

Mother finished her coffee, stood, and set her empty mug in the sink. "Should we do it tonight or tomorrow?"

"Better to go during the daytime. The train station gets a little too quiet at night, and I think we're more likely to be seen," Father said.

Mother asked, "How do you plan to get her to tell us where to find the work papers?"

Father finished his own coffee and placed his mug next to Mother's. "There's the rub. She's a tough cookie. Perhaps you'd like to give it a go?"

The broadest of smiles crossed Mother's face. "Oh, I would indeed!"

63

Clair

Day 2 • 3:56 p.m.

Clair crushed an empty Pepsi can and tossed it into the wastebasket next to Nash. "How long has it been?"

"Since he went in, or since the last time you asked me?" Kloz replied.

She shook her head. "Either . . . both . . . I don't know. Why is this taking so long?"

"Twelve minutes since you last asked me. Three and a half hours since he got to the hospital. Three hours and twelve minutes since they brought him in to surgery."

"This is my fault," Nash said to nobody in particular. "I assumed the kid was CSI. He was photographing the scene; he had all the right credentials. There were a dozen other CSIs floating around, and nobody singled him out as some kind of imposter."

"He wasn't an imposter," Kloz said. "On paper anyway, he was legit. I checked with his supervisor. HR records had him transferring in from Tucson two months ago. Nobody verified the transfer by phone. They relied on the electronic records."

"Which were faked?"

Kloz nodded. "Some of the best hacking I've ever seen. According to his lieutenant, Watson—I mean Bishop—worked a dozen or more cases since he got here. Half his unit swore he was some kind of super-CSI. He solved two murders with only a cursory review of the blood splatter. Hell, if he had stuck around, he'd probably be running the department in a couple years."

Clair looked confused. "But you said his fingerprints came back under a different name. How did you catch that and the crime lab or HR didn't?"

"His fingerprints came back as two different people. One set backed up the Paul Watson persona, but a juvie record came back as Anson Bishop. I think he hacked ViCAP and created the adult match in order to fool the background checks. They wouldn't have had access to the juvenile record."

"But you did."

Kloz rolled his eyes. "Well, not officially. The juvenile record was sealed. You just need to know where to look. Forget how I got it. The point is, you can't see the name on a juvie record until you access the file, so they probably assumed it belonged to Paul Watson. It was coded as a shoplifting, not a serious enough offense to block entrance to the crime lab, so whoever reviewed his file when he first started probably wrote off the charge and moved on. That's if they were able to see the record at all. That's a big *if*. I honestly doubt anyone dug that deep, especially since he came in on transfer papers."

"What do we know about Anson Bishop?" Clair asked.

Kloz snorted. "We don't know shit. As soon as I figured this out, I called Porter." He drew in a deep breath. "Crap, do you think this is my fault? I mean, if I hadn't called Porter, they'd still be out running around chasing leads. Bishop wouldn't have had a reason to hurt him. Fuck, I did this."

The room went quiet.

Kloz looked around at their faces. "Come on, guys, you're supposed to say this wasn't my fault. That something like this would have happened anyway."

Nash punched him in the shoulder.

Kloz jumped up, his hand rubbing the spot. "What the fuck?"

"If Porter dies, I'll kick your fucking teeth in," Nash growled.

"Quit being a Neanderthal," Clair said. Turning to Kloz, she added, "Of course it's not your fault. You tried to warn him. Any one of us would have done the same."

A doctor with wiry glasses and dark hair entered the room from the hallway behind them, gave the two men a peculiar glance, and turned to Clair. "Detective Norton?"

Clair stood. "Yes?"

"Your friend came out of surgery without any issues. He's a very lucky man. That knife was within an eighth of an inch of a major artery. The slightest deviation in the knife's trajectory, and he would have bled out within a minute. As it stands, though, the wound is fairly superficial—nothing more than tissue damage. We'll probably keep him overnight, but I see no reason for him to stay longer."

Clair wrapped her arms around the man, nearly knocking the clipboard from his hand.

"Can we see him?" Nash asked.

The doctor pulled awkwardly away from Clair and nodded. "He just woke up, and he's been asking for you. Normally I would never allow visitors this soon after surgery, but he made it clear you're involved in an open investigation and he'd come to you if I didn't bring all of you in there. I can't have him wandering the hospital, so I'm making an exception. Please try to keep it brief. He needs his rest." He gestured toward the hallway. "Come with me."

Room 307 was semiprivate, and the bed nearest the door was empty. Clair felt her heart skip a beat as she rounded the corner and spotted Porter in the second bed, wired to a heart monitor with an IV line in his wrist. He turned toward them as they entered the room, his eyes glassy and distant.

"Ten minutes," the doctor said before turning and heading back toward the nurses' station.

Clair walked up to the bed and took Porter's hand. "How are you feeling, Sam?"

"Like someone stabbed me in the leg with my own kitchen knife," he replied. His voice sounded rough, congested.

"We're going to get him," Nash said.

Kloz approached hesitantly, his head held low. "I'm sorry, Sam."

"Not your fault," Porter said. "I should have seen the signs. There was something off about him."

"There wasn't anything off about him," Nash said. "He fooled all of us."

"What do we know about him?"

Kloz explained about the fingerprints and the juvenile record. "Aside from that, we've got nothing. We pulled his photo from his ID and put the image out to the press. They're airing his mug every chance they get. The captain has done three press conferences, and he's got another scheduled for the six o'clock news."

Clair's cell phone buzzed and she looked down at the screen. "Tyler Mathers is down at Central Booking. They're holding him as long as they can, but he'll probably be out in a few hours. He insists he doesn't know any more than he told us. They showed him the picture of Bishop, but he didn't recognize him."

"Tyler Mathers?" Porter frowned. "How does he fit into this?"

Clair told him what they had learned—how Kittner was paid off to take his own life, how Tyler stole Talbot's shoes and planted evidence.

"Watson is 4MK," Nash said quietly. "Or Bishop, or whoever. The little fucker has been orchestrating this entire thing from right under our noses."

Porter tried to take it all in, his mind fighting against the drip of painkillers. "I know you want to be here, but I really need you back at the station researching this guy." He shifted his weight to the right. "He still has Emory, and now that his cover is blown I imagine he's going to speed up his plans. She's running out of time. *We're* running out of time. Did he put an address on his paperwork with HR?"

Kloz nodded. "Yeah, but it came back as Kittner's place."

Porter twisted in his bed and immediately grimaced.

"Careful, Sam. You don't want to aggravate the wound," Nash said, concerned.

"That bastard knew exactly how to stick me. It only took seven stitches to close back up. Hurts like a son of a bitch, though."

"If he wanted to kill you, he would have. He just wanted to slow you down," Kloz said.

Porter shifted his weight again. "I should have taken one of you with me. I've had a tough time with this, and I don't know what I'm comfortable talking about yet. I guess taking the kid with me to the Fifty-First was an easy way out."

Clair took his hand. "We're all family, Sam. You can talk to any one of us or none of us. Just know that we're all there for you when you're ready."

Porter said, "They caught him, the guy who shot her. They busted him on another burglary, and the cashier from the market ID'ed him. It's over."

Clair squeezed his hand. "We figured you went down there for something like that. If there's anything you need, just ask. Okay?"

Porter agreed. "Let's get back on track and go over what we know."

"Are you sure you're up for that?" Nash asked.

"I'm still a little groggy from the anesthetic, and they've got me on some wonderful painkillers. I guess that dumbs me down to your level, and you seem to function okay."

"Smart enough to not get stabbed."

Porter waved him off. "Clair, think you can run the board from here?"

She nodded and held up her phone. "I've got everything on here." She clicked away for a moment and brought up her notepad app. "All right, our man in the morgue is not the Four Monkey Killer. Instead, we've got the elusive Anson Bishop." She turned to Kloz. "I want you to get back to the station and dig up anything and everything you can on him. Particularly his movements through the city. We might get lucky and find Emory based on his cell phone GPS data. I'll get a warrant."

"He probably used a throwaway," Kloz pointed out.

"Maybe, maybe not. He didn't expect us to figure out who he was, at least not yet. You may want to dig into the Paul Watson identity as well. There could be something there."

"We need to check the log," Porter said.

Clair frowned. "What log?"

"We had to sign in at the Fifty-First. That means he wrote down a contact phone number and address."

Nash pulled out his own phone and began to dial. "On it."

Clair went on. "We know Bishop planted the shoes on Kittner. He wanted him to die in those shoes so we'd trace them back to Talbot. That means every other item he had on his person is a potential clue."

"Some change, a dry cleaner receipt, a fedora, the pocket watch . . . what does it all mean?"

"Puzzle it out," Porter muttered.

"What?"

Porter shook his head. "It's just a phrase he used a few times in the diary. Can you hand it to me? It was in my pants pocket when they brought me in."

Clair scanned the room and spotted Porter's possessions in a sealed plastic bag on a shelf in the closet to the right of the bathroom. She retrieved the diary and handed it to him.

"Since I'm stuck here, I'll finish this up. I don't have much left to go."

Nash disconnected his call and returned to Porter's bedside. "He wrote down an address on LaSalle—not Kittner's address, this is someplace new: Berwyn Apartments."

"Okay, that's got to mean something. Get Espinosa to meet you and Clair out there," Porter said.

"What do you think his endgame is?" Nash asked. "We've got a lot of information on Talbot, but nothing damning enough for hard charges. I'm guessing that means Bishop isn't done yet. We're still missing something."

"Talbot needs Emory alive in order to complete his waterfront project," Clair said.

"How so?" Porter asked.

She told him about their interview with Talbot.

"That doesn't mean Bishop needs her alive," Nash countered. "If anything, he may kill her just to take down the project."

Porter thought about this for a minute. "I agree with Nash. 4MK always kills the loved one of the person committing the crime. I don't think he gives a rat's ass about Emory as long as he can bring Talbot down. My guess is he left my place and went straight to wherever he's been holding her. He wants to finish this. In his eyes, I think everything ends with her."

Evidence Board

4MK = PAUL WATSON = ANSON BISHOP

Victims

1. Calli Tremell, 20, March 15, 2009
2. Elle Borton, 23, April 2, 2010
3. Missy Lumax, 18, June 24, 2011
4. Susan Devoro, 26, May 3, 2012
5. Barbara McInley, 17, April 18, 2013 (only blonde)
6. Allison Crammer, 19, November 9, 2013
7. Jodi Blumington, 22, May 13, 2014

Emory Connors, 15, November 3, 2014
Left for a jog, 6:03 p.m. yesterday

TYLER MATHERS
Emory's boyfriend — nephew to —

JACOB KITTNER — man hit by bus

ARTHUR TALBOT
Finances?
Body found in Mulifax Publications Building (owned by Talbot)
    identified as Gunther Herbert, CFO Talbot Enterprises
Something fishy with the Moorings Development (owned by
    Talbot)
Emory owns land/Moorings Development

N. BURROW
~~Housekeeper? Nanny? — A little of both~~ Tutor

ITEMS FOUND ON 4MK — KITTNER'S
Expensive shoes — John Lobb/$1500 pair — size 11/UNSUB
    wears size 9 — have Talbot's prints on them
Cheap suit
Fedora
.75 in change (two quarters, two dimes, and a nickel)
Pocket watch

Dry cleaner receipt (ticket 54873) — Kloz is narrowing down
stores

<u>Dying of stomach cancer</u> — meds: octreotide, trastuzumab,
oxycodone, lorazepam

Tattoo, right inner wrist, fresh — figure eight, infinity?

Calc book — left by 4MK — leads to —

MULIFAX PUBLICATIONS WAREHOUSE
Partial print found on railcar at tunnel mouth. Probably used to
transport the body. Print = Watson/Bishop/4MK
Ear, eyes, and tongue left in boxes (Gunther Herbert) — brochure
on body AND boxes lead to —

THE MOORINGS LAKESIDE DEVELOPMENT
Extensive search — nothing found

Video footage — Appears 4MK committed suicide, no clear visual
on face

Assignments:

- Clair and Nash to go to address on LaSalle (4MK/
Bishop's apartment)
- Kloz, research Watson/Bishop/4MK
- Porter, finish diary

64

Emory

Day 2 • 4:18 p.m.

Emory's world went silent.

A silence so deafening it tore at the space behind her eyes with a red heat, rushing through her good ear and into her brain, then out the other side with the ferocity of boiling oil. She pressed at the side of her head with her free hand and cursed the one that was bound.

Why wasn't this nightmare over?

"Please just kill me," Emory whispered in a voice that wasn't her own. A thin, dry voice that sanded the back of her throat. It was the voice of a girl she didn't want to know.

The music was gone, replaced with a loud ringing she knew was only in her mind but seemed to echo off the walls anyway. It fed the migraine, which grew from a headache that grew from her singular desire to just die rather than endure another hour of this hell.

The music was gone, again. But it would be back. The music always came back.

The last song to play was "Whole Lotta Love" by Led Zeppelin. She knew the song but had no idea from where. That the name of the band came so easily when she couldn't recall the day of the week surprised her. They sang "Stairway to Heaven," and she had been waiting for that one. She had heard the song four times already since waking in this place, and she was beginning to think of the little tune as her official marker of another day past, but it hadn't played today. Or had it? When did it play last? She couldn't remember. She couldn't remember anything.

You're dehydrated, dear. I think your hand is infected now too. You're quite the mess. Nobody is going to ask you to prom in this state, that's for sure.

Her hand probably was infected. The pain throbbing at her wrist nearly matched that of her head.

She refused to touch the wrist again.

She wouldn't do that.

No, sir.

The last time she touched the wrist, it didn't feel like part of her at all. It felt like a stuffed glove. It was so swollen—at least twice its normal size—and the flesh around the cuffs had become all damp and mushy. Oddly, that part didn't hurt as much as the wrist itself, and she couldn't help but wonder why that was. Had the cuffs severed the nerves?

The bones sat at the oddest angle too, her fingers pointing back in a direction they were not meant to point, the kind of gesture only cartoon characters seemed to make. It wasn't good; it wasn't good at all.

She should take her pulse again, but such things didn't seem important anymore.

I bet you could eat a rat.

"I'm not going to eat a rat," Emory replied, rubbing her temple. "I'd rather die."

Would you, dear? Because I would rather eat a rat. I would eat a rat without giving it a second thought, if I happened to be in your position. You could snap its little neck and use the sharp edge of the gurney to slice it open. If you do it quick, the meat would still be warm. It would be like eating leftover chicken from the bucket. You've done that; I've seen you.

"I will not eat a rat," Emory said again, this time louder, more defiant.

It's so dark, you could pretend you were eating just about anything. How about ribs? You love ribs.

Emory's stomach gurgled.

It's not like your friends would find out, and even if they did, do you think they would blame you? I bet they would congratulate you on your bravery and resourcefulness.

Although Emory couldn't see any rats, she was sure more than one occupied her cell. On occasion they ran across her feet and legs when she was lying on the ground. Even now, as she sat on the top of the gurney, she felt something watching her. The hair on the back of her neck stood on end. Can rats see in the dark? Had she pondered that already? She no longer remembered.

Of course, you'd need to catch one first. Oh, I think you should try, don't you? It would be our little secret. I promise, I won't tell anyone. A little meal would do you so much good. You'd get your strength back, you'd be able to concentrate. Maybe you'd be able to revisit this little dilemma and come up with a way to get out. I hear rat is excellent brain food, good for the memory.

Emory closed her eyes and took a deep breath, then began counting backward from ten in an attempt to shut out the voice. When she reached one, all was silent.

I bet their eyes taste like candy.

"Shut up!" she shouted. *"I. Will. Not. Eat. A. Rat!"*

Suit yourself, sweetie. I'm pretty sure they won't hesitate to eat you, though, when you finally starve to death. They're probably drawing straws right now to see who gets the first nibble.

A loud click.

Emory's vision went blinding white. She squeezed her eyes shut, and when that wasn't enough, she pressed her face into her leg and covered it with her arm. It didn't help, though. She saw pink through it all, she saw the blood vessels of her eyelids. Her surroundings flooded with light, and it was so bright, it burned.

She heard someone shriek, a horrible cry echoing all around her. It wasn't until she gulped a breath that she realized the scream came from her. She swallowed it back and went silent, save for the pounding of her heart and the wheeze of each drawn breath.

Emory forced herself to open her eyes, and through the tears she could tell the bright light came from far above. She arched her back and faced up, looked toward it.

A shadow moved high above, impossibly high above, and with the shadow came a voice, a voice that echoed down to her and reverberated off the walls, sounding as if he stood only a few feet away.

"Hi, Emory. Sorry it took me so long to visit. I've been a very busy boy."

65

Diary

I don't recall sleeping, but I must have drifted off at some point because I had lain down on my back and was now on my side with a little pool of drool on the pillow beside me. I still wore the clothes I had worn yesterday, with the exception of my tennis shoes, because shoes should never be worn while lying on a bed, whether above the covers or not. Father told both Mother and me it would be best if we remained dressed so we could act quickly should Mr. Stranger return during the night.

According to the clock on my nightstand, it was nearly eight.

I rose, stretched, and went to my door.

I had placed my chair under the knob again last night. I was fairly certain Mother no longer wished to hurt me, but I figured it was better to err on the side of caution.

The chair groaned as I pushed it aside, opened the door, and stepped out into the hallway.

I found Father asleep on the couch again. Perhaps he was passed out. An empty bottle of Captain Morgan spiced rum lay on the floor at his side, and he was snoring rather loudly.

The door to my parents' room was closed. Mother was most likely sound asleep as well. Both had been up late into the night, discussing our current situation. I wanted to stay with them, but Father insisted I get some rest. I think he also wanted to speak to Mother alone.

While I am fully aware that eavesdropping is not the proper behavior of a budding young gentleman, I listened anyway. Unfortunately, they anticipated my actions, because they kept their voices to a low muffle completely indecipherable from my location. I imagine it didn't end well if Mother slept alone in the bedroom and Father found himself on the couch for the second night in a row. Unless, of course, he'd decided to stand watch. Had he assigned such a task to himself, he was doing a poor job.

If Mother was still in the bedroom, that meant she had yet to speak to Mrs. Carter. This was good too, for I wanted to take part in that discussion, providing I was permitted.

Father would probably wake soon, and I knew he would likely have a tremendous headache with an appetite of equal proportion following quickly on its heels, so I set upon the kitchen to make breakfast. Twenty minutes later I had a plate of toast slathered in butter, sliced oranges, and a skillet of eggs scrambled with American cheese on our little table.

As a child to the pied piper, Mother emerged from the bedroom with a yawn and took her seat. "Did you make coffee?"

I had, in fact, made coffee, so I set a cup in front of her and filled it to the rim. Added two lumps of sugar and a hint of cream.

"Thank you."

From his spot on the couch, Father groaned and awoke. He lowered his feet to the floor and wiped at his tired, red eyes. "What time is it?" His voice was hoarse, filled with gravel.

"Eight oh seven," I told him. "Would you care for breakfast, Father?"

He nodded and stood, stretching before the large living room window. "Oh, my."

Father was staring outside, his face slack and pale. "Take a look at this."

Mother and I walked over and joined him. I felt a fist reach around my heart and squeeze.

The Carters' Dodge Aries was back in their driveway. Both doors were open, and the clothing I had so carefully packed was strewn around the yard and driveway. Not just their yard and driveway, but ours as well. I spotted a shirt hanging from the large hackberry tree on the corner of our property; tennis shoes and flip-flops adorned Mother's prize rosebush, and—

Oh my. Father's Porsche. The black convertible top was down, and the passenger door stood ajar. Father would never leave his top down overnight unless the car was garaged, and leaving the door open under any circumstance was unacceptable.

Father pushed past us and ran outside. I tried to stop him, fearful that whoever had done this (most likely Mr. Stranger and his friend, but I wasn't one to jump to conclusions) may still be out there, but I was not strong enough to hold him back.

As I approached the car, I realized the top wasn't down—it was no longer there. Someone had cut it away with ragged strokes of a blade and shoved the remains of the cloth behind the driver's seat.

The damage didn't stop there.

All four tires were flat. I inspected the one nearest to me and had no trouble discovering where the knife had entered the rubber. There were two punctures directly in the sidewall, eliminating any chance of patching the tire. It would need to be replaced. I assumed the others were in similar condition.

Both headlights were smashed. Bits of glass littered the bumper and the driveway. The taillights too. Someone had kicked them in or hit them with a bat. It was hard to tell which.

How had they done such a thing without making any noise? Surely we would have heard something like this?

Words were scrawled into the paint, foul words, nasty words. And the seats? The knife that had made quick work of the top and tires had found its way into the plush black leather and sliced it away in thin strips, releasing a flurry of stuffing upon the interior.

I noticed that the hood of the car was slightly ajar at about the same time Father did, and both of us reached for it and lifted it up. The wires leading to the battery had been pulled and reversed, all but guaranteeing that every electrical component in the car had been destroyed. I could still smell the sulfur in the air. The damage from such a maneuver would have been instant, but the culprit had taken the time to tighten the wires back down in their reversed position anyway, ensuring the most destruction. The battery had burst under the stress, and sulphuric acid had boiled out from the casing vents at the top, dripping down over the spare tire and toolkit Father kept in the front trunk.

The rear trunk was open too. The oil fill cap was missing, as was the one that belonged on the coolant tank. Nearly a pound of sugar coated the surface of both. No doubt it had been poured in each tank.

We found more sugar around the lip of the gas tank.

Father could only stare.

His eyes were fixed on his beloved Porsche, and his hands trembled at his sides.

Mother's car hadn't fared much better. Her Ford Tempo had four flat tires, and the hood was up.

I looked around for the green Plymouth, but there was no sign of it.

Mother was facing the Carter house. The front door was open.

66

Porter

Day 2 • 4:40 p.m.

The phone on the table beside Porter's hospital bed came to life, ringing so loudly he flinched. His leg barked in pain. He cringed and rubbed at the fresh stitches in his thigh, then reached over and picked up the receiver. "Hello?"

"How you feeling, Sam?" the man who had been Paul Watson and was now Anson Bishop asked him. There was a strange confidence in his voice that hadn't been there before. Porter knew this was the real man, that the Watson persona had been nothing more than a façade.

"I feel like someone tried to kill me," Porter replied, his free hand unconsciously returning to the wound on his leg.

"I didn't try to kill you, Sam. If I had, you'd be dead. Why would I try to kill my favorite player in the game?"

Porter looked around the hospital tray and nightstand for his cell phone, then remembered Bishop had stomped it to pieces back at his apartment. If he could dial headquarters, he could initiate a trace.

"I'm on a burner, Sam. One of those cheap disposables you can pick up at the drugstore. I activated it with a gift card purchased with cash more than a month ago. I imagine you could trace the call if you tried, but what's the point? In a few minutes the phone will be floating down the Chicago River with all the other trash, and I'll be miles away."

"Where's Emory?"

"Where *is* Emory?"

"Is she alive?"

No answer.

Porter forced himself to sit up, ignoring the pain. "You don't need to hurt her. Just tell us what you've got on Talbot, and we'll put him away. You have my word."

Bishop chuckled. "I believe you would, Sam. I really do. But we both know that's not how this game is played, is it?"

"Nobody else has to die."

"Of course they do. How else will they learn?"

"If you kill her, you're doing evil, Bishop. That makes you no better than the rest of them," said Porter.

"Talbot is scum. He's a green, oozing infection on this world, something that should be cut away and discarded before it destroys the surrounding tissue."

"Then why hurt Emory? Why not just kill him?"

Bishop sighed. "Pawns must be sacrificed for the king to fall."

"This isn't a game."

"*Everything* is a game, Sam. We're all players on the board. Haven't you learned anything from my diary? I thought the pop psychologist in you would have pieced this together by now. I learned a long time ago that to best punish the father for his sins, he must be made to experience the pain of his child. Somebody like Talbot expects to pay for his crimes at some point—he's mentally prepared himself. He's waiting for the day to come. If you throw him in jail, he won't learn, he won't evolve, he won't reform. He'll do his time, get out, and do something worse. But you take away that same man's child as punishment for what he's done? Well, that's a whole new ball game. He'll spend every waking moment of his remaining days cursing his actions. Not an hour will pass where he won't realize his child died for his sins."

"Emory is innocent," Porter said.

"She's very brave. I've told her how her sacrifice will bring on a change for the better. I've explained how her father brought this upon the two of them, and I think she understands."

He spoke of her in the present tense. Was she still alive?

"I urge you to try and understand too. It's important to me that you understand. Piece together everything I gave you. Puzzle it out. You hold the answer in the palm of your hand, or rather, you did."

"You said everything I needed could be found in the diary."

Bishop let out a breath. "Is that what I said?"

Porter thumbed the pages of the small book. "I'm nearly done."

"You are, Sam. Nearly done." He took a deep breath and let it out slowly. "I imagine your friends are at my apartment by now. Perhaps that will shed some light?"

"Where is Emory, Bishop?"

"It's elementary, as you might have said yesterday. Too bad we had to cut that farce short. I was having such fun playing detective with you and your friends. I'll miss my colleagues down at the crime lab too."

"Why did you do that? Why pretend to be a CSI? Why talk Kittner into killing himself? What was the point?"

Bishop laughed again. "Why, indeed." He paused for a moment. "I suppose I was curious about you, Sam. You've been chasing me for over five years now, this little cat-and-mouse game of ours. I wanted to better understand you. Father once said, 'It's better to dance with the devil you know.' I needed to know you. I'm not going to lie; the challenge intrigued me too. It's good to challenge one's self, don't you think?"

"I think you're fucking crazy," Porter replied.

"Now, now, there's no need for profanity. Heed my father's lessons. To speak evil only leads to more evil, and we have so much in this world already."

"Let her go, Bishop. Walk away. End this."

Bishop cleared his throat. "I have a few more boxes for you, Sam. Fresh boxes. I'm afraid I won't have time to mail them, though. You don't mind if I just leave them out for you, do you? Someplace where you'll find them?"

"Where is she?" Porter asked again.

"Maybe I already left them out. Perhaps you should check in with Clair and Nash."

"If you hurt her, I will kill you," Porter growled.

"Tick tock, Sam. Tick tock."

Click.

The line went dead.

Porter held the phone for a moment, the sound of his own breathing playing back over the tinny speaker. He placed the handset back in the cradle.

Tick tock.

Bishop was playing another game.

Porter rose from the bed, moving slowly, his hand held over his wound. The stitches tugged at his flesh but held tight. He crossed the room to the closet and retrieved the plastic bag containing his shoes. No sign of his clothes. They had cut away his pants; they were probably in a dumpster right now with his shirt.

Shit.

He pulled open drawers until he located a set of green surgical scrubs and pulled them on—a little tight, but they would have to do. He reached for his shoes and paused when he noticed the hint of plastic peeking out from inside: the evidence bag holding the pocket watch.

It glistened under the fluorescent lights.

His heart thumped and a breath caught in Porter's throat.

Could it be that simple?

67

Diary

The grass was still moist with morning dew and felt spongy under my shoes. I started for the Carter house without much thought, and even though I couldn't hear them, I knew both my parents were only a few paces behind me. I expected one of them to tell me to stop or wait or get behind them, but such instruction never came. I guessed Father was in shock, and I could only imagine what thoughts drifted through Mother's head.

As I passed the Carters' car, I realized it wasn't in quite the same condition as Father's Porsche. Yes, they'd rendered the car completely immobile, but the destruction wasn't as personal. They didn't slash the seats or smash the lights or glass. They limited their carnage to things that would prevent the vehicle from running, and they stopped there. With Father's Porsche, they not only attacked the car—they attacked him. They sent a message.

The travel bag I had not so carefully packed had been torn open and the contents spilled out on the Carters' front porch: medications, toothbrushes, deodorant—someone had crushed the tube of toothpaste under their foot and sprayed Crest across the floorboards. The ants were thrilled and had already started the laborious process of hauling it away to some unseen colony somewhere between the planks of the porch. I wanted to stomp them but thought better of it. "Try not to step in the toothpaste. We don't want to leave shoe prints," I said in a hushed tone.

Father grunted behind me. I'm sure he appreciated my caution, but I couldn't fault him for not offering up praise.

The inner door as well as the screen door stood open. I could see directly into the kitchen.

I turned back toward the street to confirm the green Plymouth hadn't returned, then stepped inside.

The puddle of bourbon was dry and riddled with the bodies of dead, drunken ants. The trail thinned to a single line and disappeared beneath the kitchen sink. Somebody had swept the broken glass into a small pile in the far corner.

Laid out neatly on the kitchen table were six photographs—photographs I had never seen before but that looked familiar nonetheless. Photographs of Mother and Mrs. Carter naked in bed.

68

Clair

Day 2 • 4:47 p.m.

Clair pressed the accelerator to the floor as her Honda Civic raced down West Van Buren, the blue and red of her bubble light bouncing off the whitewashed concrete of the tunnel walls.

"What are the odds he's got her locked up in his apartment?" Nash asked, his fingers gripping the door handle so tightly that they'd turned white.

Clair snorted. "Not a fan of my driving?"

Nash's face flushed and he released the handle, flexing his fingers. "You're doing eighty through the Loop at the start of evening rush hour. I'm surprised you haven't jumped up on the sidewalk and mowed down a few pedestrians yet."

Clair swerved, cutting off a middle-aged man in a black BMW. He held down his horn and slammed his middle finger against his windshield. "Emergency vehicles get right of way, asshole!" Clair shouted at her rearview mirror, holding her own finger out the window.

"You didn't answer my question," Nash said.

"You want my opinion? I think Watson or Bishop or whatever the hell his name is is playing us. We're going to bust down that door, and the whole damn place is going to blow up in our faces, that's what I think," Clair said. "You know what else? If there's a chance she's in there, I think it's worth the risk. This has been a game to him from the start. We've been like mice running through his maze. We're going to his apartment because he wants us to, plain and simple. Why else would he write down the address? I guess —"

"Shit!" Nash shouted.

Clair pulled hard at the wheel, jumped the curb, and missed a garbage truck by less than four feet. As she tugged the wheel to the left, the car bounced back onto the road, avoiding a hot dog stand by a distance so snug, Nash could have reached out the window and grabbed dinner. "I guess as long as he's yanking our strings, Emory is still alive somewhere."

"You're going to pretend that didn't just happen?"

Clair nodded. "Yep."

Nash rolled his eyes. "Kill the siren and lights — we're getting close. Bishop's building should be right up ahead."

"There's Espinosa." Clair pointed at the dark blue Tomlinson Plumbing van about two blocks ahead. She parallel parked three cars behind it and called Espinosa on speaker.

Espinosa's voice crackled back. "It's the two-story building with the red Camry out front."

Clair and Nash both looked up at once. "Got it."

"My men are in position. Bishop's apartment is on the first floor, second door from the right facing the street. We've been watching for about twenty minutes now. The blinds are drawn. We're not getting any heat signatures from inside, but it's tough to get a good reading through that brick. We're going to breach, clear the space, then give you the go-ahead to follow. Copy?"

"Copy," Clair replied. "Ready whenever you are."

Espinosa began barking orders. Three men left the van in a quick run. Espinosa and another went for the front door, and the third rounded the side of the building heading toward the back. Arriving at the door, the first man shouted, "Police!" then broke it open with a small ram while the Espinosa covered him. They both ducked inside and disappeared in the shadows.

Espinosa's voice came back on the line. "All clear, Detectives."

Clair and Nash exited the Civic and bolted down the street, weapons drawn.

As they approached the front door, Espinosa stepped back outside. "He knew we were coming. He wants us here."

"Why? What's inside?"

He nodded back over his shoulder. "Take a look for yourself."

Clair frowned and stepped through the doorway into the apartment.

It wasn't very large, maybe eight hundred square feet or so. The door opened on a living room with a small kitchen to the side, a bathroom to the right, and another door toward the rear. There was no furniture, and the kitchen appeared unused. The walls were bare.

In the center of the room stood a white file box tied off with a black string.

69

Diary

I scooped up the photos and shoved them into my pocket just as Mother and Father stepped into the kitchen behind me.

"It smells something fierce in here," Mother exclaimed, wrinkling her nose.

Father pointed at the refrigerator. "Somebody left the door open. Everything has probably started to spoil."

My hand was still deep in my pocket. I was afraid to look down, half expecting to see the photographs floating to the floor, but they stayed safely tucked away in my pants.

Father let out a whistle. "They did a number on this place."

They had. All the kitchen drawers and cabinets were open, the contents littering the floor and counter. In the living room, the couch was a tattered mess. The cushions had been sliced and gutted, their innards drifting around the room like white tumbleweeds. They had scratched a large X into the television screen. The books from Mrs. Carter's collection had been pulled from the shelves and torn to pieces, pages scattered everywhere. Not a single item had been left untouched.

"This doesn't feel right," Mother said. "We should go."

Father took a quick peek down the hallway into the master bedroom, then returned to the kitchen. "If whatever they're looking for was here, they must have found it. They hit every room, every possible hiding spot."

"I want to leave." Mother shuffled her feet.

I heard the car right before Father did, but he still beat me to the screen door. I drew next to him and watched the green Plymouth Duster as it left the road and started down the gravel driveway toward the house. The morning sun glared off the windshield, and I couldn't see inside.

"Back home, now!" Father ordered.

The three of us bolted out the front door and across the lawn in a dead run, with Mother in the lead and Father behind me. I half expected him to stop and exact some kind of revenge for his Porsche, but he did not. Father was very smart and not one to let his anger take charge.

I bounded up the steps into our house as the Plymouth slid to a halt somewhere behind us. A car door squeaked open, quickly followed by the distinctive clunk of a rifle bolt. Mr. Stranger's voice boomed: "Howdy, neighbors! Did you miss us?"

70

Porter

Day 2 • 4:57 p.m.

As Porter exited the hospital's main entrance, he spotted a young woman climbing out of a cab at the curb. With two fingers pressed between his lips, he let out a whistle loud enough to startle an elderly gentleman at his right. He forced a smile, nodded at him, and hobbled toward the taxi.

When Porter fell into the back seat, the driver snickered. "Are you escaping?"

Porter pulled the door shut and winced as the motion tugged at his stitches. "What?"

"You're wearing scrubs and you look a little rough to be on staff."

"No, nothing like that. One of my coworkers stabbed me in the leg with a kitchen knife, then left me for dead in my kitchen. I couldn't find my clothes, so I took these."

"Smart-ass." The man smirked. "Where we heading?"

"A place called Lost Time Antiques and Collectibles, on Belmont," Porter told him.

"Address?"

Porter realized he didn't have an exact address. He reached for his phone and remembered again that Bishop had crushed it. "I don't know. I was told it was on Belmont."

The driver rolled his eyes, reached for his own phone, and tapped away at the screen. "316 West Belmont. Looks like it's across the street from the Belmont Edge apartments."

"That sounds right." Porter glanced out the window at the thickening rush hour traffic. "If I told you I'm a cop, I don't suppose you'd get us there any faster, would you?"

The driver eased the cab out into traffic and glanced at him in the rearview mirror. "Let me see your badge."

Porter started to reach for his back pocket, then remembered that he was wearing the scrubs. "It's in my—"

"It's in the pants with the knife sticking out of them?"

"Yeah."

"I'll see what I can do."

Porter pulled out the diary and picked up where he'd left off.

71

Diary

I think I felt the bullet before I heard the blast of the gun. The projectile whizzed past my head and thwacked into the door frame about six inches to my right, sending little shards of wood flying through the air. One of them caught me in the cheek and tore at my skin. Before I could reach up and assess the damage, Father crashed into my back and shoved me forward. I lost my balance and flew across the floor, sliding into the side of the couch. I rolled over to find Mother crouching at the couch, her wild eyes bouncing from me to the front door and back again. Behind me, Father kicked at the door, slamming it shut.

Father was on the floor. I watched as he reached up and twisted the deadbolt before sinking back down.

"He shot you!" Mother shrieked.

I shook my head. "No, Mother, it was just a splinter, nothing serious. I'll be okay."

It took a moment before I realized she wasn't talking to me. I followed her eyes to Father. His left hand was pressed against his right shoulder. A growing red stain peeked out between his fingers.

Mother stood and went to him.

"Stay low," Father said.

She knelt down beside him. "Let me see."

"He nicked me. I don't think it's bad."

Mother unbuttoned his shirt and examined the wound. "Get me the medicine kit and a damp towel, and keep your head down," she told me.

I shuffled to the kitchen and retrieved the little red box from beneath the sink. We kept identical kits in each bedroom as well as the bathroom. Mother typically used this particular kit on me when I scraped a knee or dinged an elbow, which was fairly often, and I wondered if it was fully stocked. I considered getting one of the others but decided it was best to get this one to Mother and go back for more if necessary. I found a clean hand towel in the drawer beside the sink and ran it under the water, getting it good and wet, then raced back into the living room.

Sweat glistened on Father's forehead. I couldn't remember the last time I had seen him sweat.

Mother took the kit, flipped open the latch with one hand, and pulled out the alcohol bottle. She wiped away the excess blood with the towel and poured alcohol on the torn flesh. Father inhaled with a deep hiss.

The bullet had not passed through his skin but had grazed it, leaving a red trench in its wake. I leaned in close to get a better look, and Mother batted me away. "You're blocking the light."

"Sorry, Mother."

She dabbed at the scrape again and retrieved a roll of gauze with her free hand. A minute later she had the wound wrapped. The bandage turned pink, but the blood had already slowed. Father would be okay.

He smiled up at her. "Thank you."

Mother nodded and dropped the remaining alcohol and gauze back into the first aid kit, then slid the box to the side. "Now what?"

"Now we end this."

72

Clair

Day 2 • 5:09 p.m.

Clair stepped closer. "Did you open it?"

Espinosa shook his head. "I wanted to save you the honors. If you think it could be something dangerous, I can get the bomb squad over here."

Nash knelt down in front of the white box, slipped on a pair of latex gloves, and tapped at the black string tied at the top. "That's not our guy's style. He tends to leave body parts inside his boxes. Nothing ever this big, though."

"Open it up, Nash," Clair said.

"Maybe we should flip for it. I had to open the last one."

"No, I insist. I saw *Seven*—if Gwyneth's head is in there, the image will be stuck in my mind for months. This is all you. Be a man."

Nash rolled his eyes and turned back to the box. "For the record, it's a standard file box, the kind you can pick up at any office supply store." He knelt closer. "I don't smell anything, and there's no sign of dampness or leakage—nothing written on it."

He tugged at the string, releasing the knot; it fell to the sides. When he reached for the lid, both Clair and Espinosa took a step back.

"Maybe we should wait for CSI to get here," Nash suggested.

"Open it. It may tell us where to find Emory."

Nash nodded reluctantly, peeled off the lid, and leaned over the top, peering inside. "Huh."

73

Diary

I flinched as someone pounded at the front door.

"Did I get you?" Mr. Stranger asked from the other side. "Sorry about that. I guess I got a little carried away. It's been so long since I've been out hunting, and I've been all giddy about firing my peashooter since we left the city."

"Stay away from the windows," Father said softly.

I nodded and drew closer to the corner of the couch. I wasn't scared, though. Okay, maybe a little, but I wasn't about to let Mother or Father know. I wanted my knife.

Another loud bang as Mr. Stranger struck the door again. I couldn't tell if he used his fist or the butt of the rifle, but I jumped just the same.

Mr. Stranger's muffled voice said, "I tried asking nice, I did. Now I'm going to ask not so nice. I need the paperwork your lovely neighbor stole. I know you've got it, so let's forgo the pretense that you don't. I'm not sure what is going on over here, and frankly, I don't care all that much. You give us those documents and point us toward whatever rock the Carters are hiding under, and we'll be on our way, no further questions. That's not a bad deal, right? I think I'm being nice and fair about the situation."

"He thinks they're both still alive," Mother said quietly. She had edged away from Father and was trying to peek out the side window.

"Course, if that rock is in there with you and you're hiding them, well, that's another story entirely. You don't really want to harbor criminals, do you? That's what he is, you know. Anyone who steals from their place of business, even if it's only information, that puts you clearly in the criminal camp in my book, right next to the rapists and murderers. His wife ain't no better, either. She's got a whole box of scruples stacked away in her closet."

His voice was loud but steady. I got the impression he was standing right there on the porch, right on the other side of our door. If we had a gun, we could shoot him clean and true through the wood. A bullet at the center would probably do the trick. He probably thought we had a gun, a big one, otherwise he would have busted the door down by now. I know I would. Father didn't believe in guns, though, and he would never let such a weapon into the house. "Accidents happen with guns," he always said. "Knives, on the other hand—you don't stab somebody by accident. There's no accidental discharge on a knife." I wondered if he was rethinking that whole stance. I couldn't read his face. He had barely moved. It wasn't the bullet wound holding him still—that was just a nick—he was concentrating. I imagined he was formulating a plan. Father didn't panic. Nor did he overreact. He always seemed to know exactly what to do and when.

Mother crawled over to the window behind the couch, the one with a view of our side yard, and raised her head, peeking over the sill. When a face appeared, she jumped back and let out a shriek. The man with the long blond hair and thick glasses stood on the opposite side of the glass, a grin growing across his thin red lips. He mouthed the word hello and pressed his palm to the windowpane. I watched the moisture build around it, and when he pulled away, a perfect palm print was left behind. He then brought up the barrel of a rifle and tapped it against the glass. His grin widened even more as he ducked from sight. Mother and I looked at each other, then back to Father, searching for some kind of guidance.

Another pound at the front door. "You still in there?"

Father raised a finger to his lips.

Mr. Stranger continued. "I found the whole business with their

car a little perplexing. I guess leaving it at the train station like that
makes perfect sense—make things seem like they took off on a trip.
But why leave their suitcases in the car? Who goes on a trip and for-
gets their bags? When we found the car, when I saw the bags, it was
clear to me somebody had staged the scene. At first I thought the Carters were trying to create a little head fake, throw the foxes off their
scent so they could zig while the rest of us zagged. Once I thought it
through, though, I dismissed that idea. Simon isn't all too bright. Sure,
he's a whiz with numbers, but like most book-smart people, he's got
no common sense, no street smarts. If he were to run, he'd run. That
means if he had really abandoned the car at the train station, the bags
would have boarded with him. Once I figured out that little ruse, it
didn't take long to piece together your involvement. You've got the only
two houses down this godforsaken stretch of road. Where else would
they go? Your kid about shat his britches when I stopped by the other
day. He's a bright one, I'll give him that, but he needs some work in
the lying department. Nothing a few more years under life's big top
won't cure."

Father pointed at Mother, then toward the kitchen, and made a
stabbing motion in the air. Mother understood and crawled past me in
search of knives.

"Anyway, my mouth is running off. It doesn't matter how I ended
up on your porch, only that I'm here and you're there, and the things
I need are somewhere in between. I imagine you're not willing to risk
your lives over a few papers, probably not even to harbor your criminal
neighbors. I mean, why die for them, right? Why let your kid die over
somebody else's problem? That's what's going to happen if you don't
come out soon."

Mother returned, holding two large chef's knives from the wood
block on the counter. She handed one to Father and kept the second for
herself.

Mr. Stranger cleared his throat. "Like I said, I asked nicely. Now I'm
going to ask not so nice. While you and I have been chatting, my friend
Mr. Smith has been circling this beautiful house of yours with a couple cans of gasoline. It stinks to high heaven out here! He spread it nice

and high on the walls, under the crawlspace, even got a couple of your trees so we can light this place up real good and bright."

Something crashed on top of the roof, then rolled for a few seconds before coming to a stop.

"Whew! I wish you could see this! He tossed a full can up on your roof, and it's pouring out all over the place. Hell, it's coming out the rainspouts. He soaked this place from top to bottom with ninety-three octane." Mr. Stranger was chuckling, his voice rising with excitement. "This is the part where I ask not so nice. You've got five minutes to come out with the Carters, or we start dropping matches and have ourselves a little bonfire. Of course, that means we lose the paperwork and your neighbors, but I'm okay with that. I'll sleep like a baby knowing this ends right here. If you try to run, we'll pick you off like pigeons at the range. Five minutes, people. Not a second more."

74

Porter

Day 2 • 5:12 p.m.

The cab squealed to a halt on West Belmont east of Lake Shore Drive, across from the Belmont Edge apartments. The cabdriver pointed a thumb toward the building at their right. "There it is. I believe that was record time."

Porter slid over in the seat and peered out the window. The building was fairly typical for this area: brick, probably built around the turn of the twentieth century, with a glass storefront on the ground floor and what appeared to be residential space on the second floor. Many of the shop owners in this part of town lived on premises. For those who did not, the apartments rented for a small fortune. They were within a stone's throw of Lake Michigan, and waterfront views were always at a premium. Walking distance didn't hurt, either.

Porter reached for the door handle and started to climb out.

"Hey!" the driver shouted. "You owe me $26.22!"

"I don't have any money," Porter replied. "But Chicago Metro thanks you for your assistance."

"The hell it does!" The driver unfastened his seat belt and opened his door.

Porter raised a hand. "Relax, I'm kidding. I'll call my partner from inside and get some cash. Give me a minute."

The driver prepared to argue, then shifted abruptly and said, "Your leg is bleeding."

Porter looked down at his thigh, where a dark stain about two inches around had formed. "Crap, I think I pulled a stitch."

"You really did get stabbed?"

Porter reached down his thigh and pressed at it tenderly with the tip of his finger. It came away damp with blood.

"I should take you back to the hospital."

He shook his head. "I'll be all right."

The man nodded reluctantly and leaned against the side of his car. Porter turned back to the storefront.

Lost Time Antiques and Collectibles appeared dark. He limped to the front door and tried the handle—locked. Cupping his hands, he pressed his face against the glass.

"They're closed," the driver said from behind him. "Their hours are posted by the door," he said. "They lock up at five. We missed them by about fifteen minutes."

Porter took a step back and found the small red sign with the posted store hours. He was right. He went back to the glass and peered inside. The walls were covered in clocks. Everything from small digital models to freestanding grandfather clocks. The pendulums swung back and forth tirelessly, some moving in sync, others independent of the group. It was mesmerizing. He could only imagine what it sounded like inside when they struck at the top of the hour.

Porter pounded his fist on the door, then stepped back and eyed the apartment upstairs. Maybe the owner lived up there?

"I don't mean to tell you how to do your job, but if you got some urgent business with this place—and I'm guessing you do, considering you're willing to stand there and beat on the door while bleeding on the sidewalk—maybe you could ask next door? They might know how to reach the manager or the owner."

Porter turned and followed the man's gaze. A woman exited the shop next door, holding three dry cleaning bags. She nearly tripped off the curb as she circled the parking meter to get to the trunk of her car.

Porter felt his heart pound. He stepped up to the parking meter in front of the cab and read the rate card.

$0.75 per hour.

"Can I borrow your cell phone?"

"You're kidding, right?"

Porter's face must have said he was not, because the man shrugged his shoulders, walked around to the driver's door, and pulled his cell phone from a clip on the dash. Porter punched in a number.

"Klozowski," came the voice on the other side.

"Kloz, it's Porter."

"Did you get a new number?"

"Long story. Are you near the evidence board?"

"Yeah, why?"

Porter took a deep breath. "How much change did we find in the bus victim's pocket?"

"You mean Kittner, AKA no longer 4MK? Seventy-five cents. Why?"

He started toward the cleaners next door. "What was the receipt number on the dry cleaning ticket?"

"What are you doing? Shouldn't you be resting?"

"Kloz, I need that ticket number." He pushed through the door and went straight to the counter.

An overweight man with dark hair, thick glasses, and two large laundry bags gave him a dirty look. The kid behind the counter had no such scruples. "Back of the line, buddy." Then he saw the blood-stain on Porter's pants. "Shit, do you need a doctor?"

Porter reached for his back pocket to retrieve his badge and re-membered for the second time he didn't have it. "I'm with Chicago Metro. I need you to pull up a ticket for me." Back to the phone: "Kloz, the ticket number?"

"Ah, yeah, it's 54873."

He repeated the number back to the clerk, who eyed him suspi-ciously, then punched it into his computer. "Give me a second." He disappeared through a doorway, heading toward the back of the store.

Behind him, Porter heard the overweight man drop both laundry bags on the floor and let out a sigh.

"Sorry."

The man grunted but said nothing.

The kid returned, holding three hangers all bunched together. He hung them on a hook attached to the side of the counter.

Porter peeled back the plastic, revealing a pair of women's jogging shorts, a white tank top, socks, and undergarments. All had been cleaned and pressed. White and pink Nikes were in another bag fastened to the hangers.

The kid pointed to the shoes. "I told the guy when he dropped those off that we don't clean shoes, but he insisted we keep it all together."

"Porter? Talk to me," Kloz said. "What's going on?"

"I've got Emory's clothes."

75

Diary

"Get Lisa and bring her up here," Father instructed Mother.

She nodded and disappeared into the kitchen. I heard the squeak of the basement door and her steps as she descended. He turned to me. "Champ, go in the kitchen and pull out Mother's soup pot—you know which one I mean? The big one with the glass lid?"

I nodded.

"Fill the pot about an inch with vegetable oil, and put it on the stove, full heat. Think you can do that?"

I nodded again.

"Okay, hurry up now."

I ran into the kitchen, pulled the soup pot out from the lower cabinet, and placed it on the burner. I found the vegetable oil in a cabinet next to the stove, nearly a full gallon. I twisted off the cap and poured about a quarter into the pot, then spun the burner control knob to the highest setting. Nothing happened. A second later I smelled gas. "Poppycock," I said to nobody in particular, then dug out the box of matches from the drawer beside the stove. The pilot light always seemed to go out; Mother probably went through a box of matches each week. I struck one on my jeans and watched it flare to life, then guided the flame under the pot. The gas caught with a poof. Blue flames licked out across the bottom of the metal. I dropped the box of matches into my pocket and went back out to the living room, giving Father a thumbs-up.

He nodded.

Another knock at the door. "It's awfully quiet in there. Everything okay? Four minutes left by my watch."

"Simon Carter is dead!" Father shouted back.

Only silence on the other side of the door for a moment, then: "What happened?"

"Unfortunate things sometimes happen to unfortunate people."

"That they do," Mr. Stranger replied. "Didn't much care for him anyway. What about the missus?"

Mother and Mrs. Carter appeared in the living room. Mother had draped a towel over the woman's shoulders in an effort to cover up her bared chest. Her hands were cuffed in front of her. I couldn't help but blush at the sight of her. Even after days in the basement living in her own filth, she still looked beautiful. The tip of Mother's knife was pointed an inch below her rib cage, pressing into the naked flesh.

Father eyed her, then returned his attention to the man on the front porch. "She's been a houseguest of ours for the past few days, but I'm afraid she's overstayed her welcome. I'm perfectly willing to send her on out there to you, providing you load her up into that fancy car of yours and head back to the city. My family and I have nothing to do with this and just want to be left alone. You leave us peacefully, and I see no reason for any of us to ever mention this to anyone. You get what you want, we get what we want, everybody wins."

"Is that a fact?"

Mrs. Carter shook her head urgently. "You hand me over to those men and they'll kill us all, including your boy. They're not the kind of people to leave loose ends. You can't trust them."

"Three minutes!" Mr. Stranger shouted.

"She doesn't know anything about this missing paperwork. Whatever her husband was up to, he didn't share the details with her," Father said.

"I'm supposed to believe that?"

"It's the truth," Mrs. Carter said loudly.

"You in there, Lisa?" Mr. Stranger called. "Did you promise some of the money to these fine folks if they watch over you? Is that it? Why don't you come on out so we can talk things over? I'm getting hoarse shouting through this door."

Father turned back to the door. "Like I said, I don't mind turning her over. I don't care what you do to her, as long as you leave us out of it. Your problem is not our problem."

"Oh, I disagree with you there."

"Tell your boss Simon is dead!" Mrs. Carter shouted back to him. "Whatever secrets he may have died with him."

"I'm afraid I wouldn't be doing my job if I took your word for it."

Glass shattered behind us, and we all turned to the kitchen. A hand poked through the narrow window beside the back door and fumbled with the lock. Father darted toward it. He raised his knife and brought the blade down across the intruding fingers in one quick, fluid motion, splitting two or three of them open. Blood gathered at the wound in an instant before the man on the other side shouted in pain. The hand disappeared. Father plucked the boiling pot of vegetable oil from the stove as he passed on his way back to the front door.

Mr. Stranger was laughing. "You got Mr. Smith good! I told him he'd never get in fast enough like that, but he didn't listen, wanted to do things his way. Isn't that like the younger generation? They don't heed their elders anymore, not like when you and I were young, right, hoss? They don't have the kind of respect we were taught, the kind instilled in us from the get-go. Your boy might—he seemed to mind his p's and q's. I bet he'd grow up into a pillar of society, if given the chance. Of course, whether or not that happens is really in your hands at this point."

"I'm gonna kill that fucking bastard!" Mr. Smith shouted from somewhere behind Mr. Stranger.

I crawled to the window that overlooked the front yard and spotted the man with the long blond hair and glasses standing at the edge of the porch, blood pooling at his feet. He tore off a length of cloth from the bottom of his T-shirt and wrapped it around his damaged hand. It immediately turned red.

Mr. Stranger spotted me and winked. "In all that excitement, I completely lost track of time," he said loudly. "I'm going to guess you have about thirty seconds left. Does that seem about right to you?"

I ducked and scurried away from the window. "There's only two of them, Father. If some of us go out the back and the rest go out the front, they can't stop everyone."

"And where do we go? They destroyed both cars."

"We take his."

Father was already shaking his head. "This needs to end here, or we're forever on the run."

"They have guns."

"We're smarter than they are. We need to think this through, puzzle it out."

Mother had been oddly silent, calm. "We kill Lisa and toss her body out to them."

With that, Mrs. Carter struggled, but Mother held her knife to the woman's eye. She fell still and stared at the silver tip. "My husband moved nearly fourteen million dollars into offshore accounts. I've got all the numbers and passwords. Half of that money is yours if you get me out of here alive."

Father left the door and walked over to her. "What about the paperwork? That's what they really want."

Mrs. Carter let out a deep sigh. "Safe-deposit boxes at Middleton downtown. Four of them. Enough information to access another hundred million easy."

"Where are the keys?"

Mrs. Carter said nothing.

Father grabbed her by the hair, jerking her from Mother's grasp, and pulled her over to the boiling pot of vegetable oil. He pushed her head down toward the pot. Mrs. Carter fought, arching her back and trying to kick at him, but Father was too strong. He held her face inches above the steaming liquid. "I'm going to ask you one more time, then you're going in. Where are the keys?"

Mrs. Carter shook her head and reeled back, but Father held her tight, impervious to her kicking. With her hands cuffed in the front, they were of little use. "No . . ." she managed to say.

Father shrugged and pushed her closer.

The oil fizzled and popped, and little drops struck her skin, leaving tiny red welts. She shrieked and pushed back with all her strength. Drops of oil sizzled in her hair. "Under the cat! God, stop! They're under the cat!"

"What?" He loosened his grip, putting a few inches between Mrs. Carter's face and the pot.

I knew what she meant, though. I knew exactly what she meant. "By the lake? My cat?"

Mrs. Carter nodded quickly.

"You know where she's talking about?"

"Yes, Father."

Father turned to Mrs. Carter, his eyes narrow. "You're going to do exactly what I say. Do you understand?"

There was another loud bang at the door. "Time's up, people!"

76

Clair

Day 2 • 5:12 p.m.

"What is it?" Clair asked.

"A lot of paperwork and a note," Nash replied as he reached into the box. He pulled out the sheet of stationery resting atop thousands of documents all bundled together neatly with elastic bands.

Clair leaned closer. "What does it say?"

Nash read aloud.

Ah, my friends!

It is good to know you finally found your way here! I had hoped to be there with you when this moment came, but alas, it was not meant to be. I take solace in the fact that this material has found its way into your capable hands, as I am sure you will take it to your compadres in financial crimes so they may add it to the mounting pile of evidence against Mr. Talbot and company. While I believe this box contains more than enough information for a substantial conviction, I'm afraid I couldn't wait for the trial portion of the program and went ahead and passed a sentence I believe to be more than fitting for the crimes at hand. Much like his longtime business partner, Gunther Herbert, Mr. Talbot will meet with justice face-to-face today, and he will answer for his actions on the swiftest of terms. Perhaps I will allow him to give his daughter one last kiss before goodbyes are said? Perhaps not. Maybe it's best they just watch each other bleed.

Truly yours,
Anson Bishop

Nash's eyes narrowed. "Do we still have a car tailing Talbot?"

Clair already had her cell phone out. "I'm on it."

Nash returned to the box and pulled out one of the document bundles. The ream was about two inches thick and contained about three hundred sheets of paper. The topmost sheet was white lined in green, each line filled with tiny, neat handwriting. "This looks like some kind of ledger. Old too. This page is dated nearly twenty years ago. Who the hell keeps their books on paper anymore?"

Clair waved him off, turned her back, and began pacing the room with the phone to her ear.

Nash shrugged and went back to the paper. The first line read *163. WF14. 2.5k. JM.*

"Is it some kind of code?"

He reached inside and began removing the other ledgers, twelve in all. Each contained similar entries. Nash stacked them neatly at the side. At the very bottom of the box was a manila envelope. "Now we're talking," he said to himself before plucking it out.

Clair hung up the call and walked back over. "I'm getting voice mail on the patrol car. Dispatch can't reach them, either. We need to get over to Talbot's house."

Nash gestured to the box. "What about this stuff?"

"Have someone run everything back to Kloz," she instructed.

He nodded and opened the envelope. It was full of Polaroids. He reached in and pulled one out—a snapshot of a naked young girl of no more than thirteen or fourteen.

77

Diary

I opened the door—not Father, not Mother, and certainly not Mrs. Carter, but me. I opened the door to find Mr. Stranger standing on our stoop wearing the same jacket he had been wearing on that first visit only a few short days ago. Sweat trickled down his forehead, and he dabbed at it with a white handkerchief in his left hand. In his right, chubby fingers wrapped around the grip of the .44 Magnum I had found in his glove box yesterday. The barrel was pointed at my head.

"Howdy, friend. I hope you've been well."

Behind him, Mr. Smith cradled his injured hand in the now soaked scrap of cloth, a small puddle of blood pooling on the tip of his shoe and the ground around him, a rifle held loosely between his arm and his side. His face was blotchy, burning with anger. "I'm going to gut your fucking father for this." He raised the bloody hand in case I didn't know what "this" was and shook it, sending little droplets of blood across the white boards of our pristine porch. Mother wouldn't be very happy about that.

"Now, now," Mr. Stranger said. "No need for hostilities. You can't blame these kind people for simply defending their home."

"The fuck I can't."

Mr. Stranger dabbed at the sweat again; the collar of his shirt was soaked.

I could smell the gasoline, the fumes wafting off the porch in a thin haze. Streaks of it dripped down the siding. Four gas cans stood in our driveway.

"Why are you wearing a jacket if you're hot?" It was a simple question, one I felt needed to be answered regardless of current circumstances. Sometimes I find it difficult to move forward if open issues are nagging at me.

Mr. Stranger's lips stretched into a wide grin. "Why, indeed. You are an interesting little fellow, aren't you? So inquisitive. What if I told you it was my favorite jacket, one I've owned more years than you've probably graced this planet. What if I told you it was also my lucky jacket and today just felt like the kind of day that called for a little luck all around so I plucked it from the closet and donned it for the duration, temperature be damned. What would you say to that?"

"I would tell you it's an ugly jacket and it probably stinks to high heaven 'cause of all the sweating you're doing."

Mr. Stranger's grin held still but his eyes grew dark. "I'm experiencing a bit of déjà vu from this little back-and-forth of ours, son, so I'm going to ask you the same question I did when I first made your acquaintance. That way we can bring this full circle. Are your parents home?"

He knew full well that they were, so I thought this was a stupid question. But I nodded anyway and gave the door a little push so it swung open.

Mrs. Carter stood a few paces behind me. Father stood behind her, one arm wrapped around her waist and the other draped over her shoulder. He held one of the kitchen knives against her neck, the sharp tip pressing into her jugular. Her head tilted at a slight angle away from the blade, her gaze fixed on the men at the door.

"Lisa." Mr. Stranger nodded. "My condolences on your husband."

She said nothing. Her cuffed fists curled over her bra.

Mr. Stranger looked past us to Mother, who leaned against the side of the couch, her hands at her sides. "Nice to see you again, ma'am."

Mother snickered but said nothing in return.

Mr. Stranger tucked the handkerchief back into his pocket and pointed the .44 at Father. "Drop the knife."

Father shook his head. "Nope."

"What then?" Mr. Stranger asked.

"The papers are in a safe-deposit box. My boy knows where she hid the keys, so he's going to go fetch them while the rest of us wait here. I'm going to keep this knife right where it is, and if you or your friend try anything I find remotely threatening, I'll slit her throat. It won't take much. I'm right at the artery. You shoot me and I could tear it wide open on my way to the ground. You hurt my wife or son, and she's dead. I do that, and nobody will be alive to tell you what bank holds the box."

Mr. Smith opened his mouth to protest, but Mr. Stranger silenced him with a raised hand. "How do we know he's not running off to call the police?"

Father shrugged. "Because we killed Simon; we all have skin in the game. He'll fetch the keys and be back inside of thirty minutes."

Mr. Stranger's gaze fell on Mrs. Carter.

"These people are fucking crazy," Mrs. Carter told him. "They killed him and had me tied up in the basement for nearly a week."

The knife was pressed tight against her neck. Just the movement of speech was enough to send a trickle of blood down the blade.

Mr. Stranger turned back to Father. "So your kid runs off somewhere while we all stand around with weapons pointed at each other till he comes back with the safe-deposit box keys. At that point, you hand over Lisa there and my friend and I walk away, leaving your family to live out the rest of your days. Nobody else has to die? What keeps us from killing the lot of you as soon as we get the name of the bank?"

Father gave a slight shrug. "I guess at some point we're just going to have to trust each other."

Mr. Stranger thought about this for a second, then shook his head. "No, I don't like that plan." He leveled the .44 at Father's head.

"It's not loaded!" I screamed. "I took out the bullets!"

Father shoved Mrs. Carter at the man, his hands—

The Magnum went off with a deafening roar.

78

Porter

Day 2 • 5:22 p.m.

"What do you mean, you've got Emory's clothes?" Kloz asked.

Porter pulled the hangers off the hook and started back for the door.

"Hey! You've gotta pay for that!" the kid behind the counter shouted. "Get back here!"

"Porter? Are you there?"

"I'm at a dry cleaner down on Belmont. The ticket was a match, and—"

"Wait. You're not in the hospital?" Kloz asked. "Porter, please tell me you didn't leave the hospital."

The clerk from the cleaner burst through the doorway, holding a box cutter. "You need to get back inside and pay for those, or we're going to have a serious problem, my friend."

Porter watched as the cabdriver came around the car and walked up behind him. He plucked the blade from the kid's hand and slapped him on the back of his head. "That man's a cop, you idiot. You really feel like going to jail today?"

The kid rubbed at the back of his head. "He's a cop? Why's he wearing pajamas?"

Porter nodded back at the dry cleaner. "Get inside, now."

The kid turned on his heels and pushed through the doorway.

"Porter?"

He pressed the phone back to his ear and told Kloz about the call from Bishop and his hunch to follow up on the watch. His head was spinning. "The parking meter costs seventy-five cents per hour, and there's a dry cleaner next door. He told us how to get here from the beginning; we just didn't see it."

"Okay, but where is *here*? Where is Emory?"

Porter pulled the watch from his pocket and held it up, twisting the timepiece between his fingers. He pressed the button on the top, and the cover snapped open, its movement hindered by the bag. The hands on the face were stopped, frozen in time.

3:14.

He turned back to the cabdriver. "What is the address of this place?"

"316 West Belmont."

Porter turned to his left. Construction barricades blocked off the building next door, a tall skyscraper, fifty or sixty stories at least. "Kloz, who owns 314 West Belmont?"

"Hold on." Porter could hear him pecking away at his keyboard. "It's office space bought last year by Intrinsic Value LLC, which is owned by CommonCore Partnerships, a wholly owned subsidiary of A. T. The Market Corp, one of Talbot's companies. They're currently going through a complete renovation, set to open in the spring."

"Get SWAT down here, now."

79

Diary

I watched Father as he soared through the air, his hands reaching for Mr. Stranger's throat. Openmouthed and red-faced, Father was burning anger as fuel.

When the gun went off, when the barrel of the weapon bucked and the bullet took flight, the world slowed to a crawl. I could see the projectile as it passed the tip. I watched as the bullet crept across the air. I saw it enter Father's forehead above his left eye, leaving a tiny red dot. I saw the shock as it registered on his face. Then I watched the back of his head as it exploded in a cloud of red mist.

Father fell to the ground in a motionless heap.

"Father?"

I didn't recognize my own voice; it sounded thin and frail, distant, like someone shouting underwater. "I . . . I took out the bullets."

Mr. Stranger popped the cylinder out, then back in. "A good soldier always checks his weapon before battle, kid." He pointed the gun at Mrs. Carter, now sprawled on the floor at his feet. "Get up."

Mrs. Carter slowly rose to her feet.

Mother stood motionless, her mouth agape as she sucked in a deep breath.

My eyes were locked on Father's lifeless body. I knew he was dead, but I couldn't bring myself to admit that fact. I expected him to stand up, to finish the man who had threatened his life, this man invading our home.

A scream rose from my throat.

It was a scream so shrill and sharp, I felt the vibrations at my very core. My fingers dropped into my pocket and wrapped around my knife, the comforting handle and silver bolsters warm to the touch, hot even. I gripped the Ranger with a ferocious strength, pulled it out, and flicked the blade open with a single fluid motion. Then I was on him. He tried to raise the gun, but I was too fast. I swung the knife up and buried the blade in the soft skin under his chin, forcing through the flesh and bone until it punctured into his mouth and tore through his tongue. When it finally stopped as it embedded itself in the roof of his mouth, I yanked the knife back out and slit his throat, tearing through the muscle, tendons, and arteries. The blood sprayed out onto my face, into my hair, my eyes. I didn't care. I sliced him again. When his body began to crumple to the ground, I rode it down and plunged the knife into his chest, again and again. I stabbed dozens, possibly hundreds, of times. I stabbed him until—

My eyes snapped open and I was staring at father's lifeless body again. I hadn't moved, not an inch. My hand dropped into my pocket in search of my knife, but it wasn't there. Mother had taken my knife. My fingers found nothing but the small box of matches and the photographs I had taken from the Carters' house.

"Hand out of your pocket slowly, kid," I heard Mr. Stranger say. I felt the barrel of his .44 Magnum press against the side of my head. It was still hot.

I removed my hand, leaving the matches and photos behind.

The barrel pressed hard against my head.

The shot rang out and my eyes pinched shut. My body stiffened, waiting for the bullet to tear through my skull like it had Father's, to tear the life from me and plunge me into a darkness where I would be united with him once again.

The darkness didn't come.

Mr. Stranger collapsed at my side, smoke rising from a large hole in the back of his head.

80

Clair

Day 2 • 5:26 p.m.

The patrol officers were dead. Both shot. The driver, at point-blank just below his left temple. His partner took three rounds to the chest. As far as Clair knew, 4MK had never shot anyone before. A nine-millimeter Beretta 92FS lay on the dash. Porter's backup weapon.

Endgame, she thought.

Nash tapped Clair on the shoulder, and she turned from the car. He pointed at the front of Talbot's house, his own weapon drawn.

The front door was cracked open a few inches.

The sun was setting, and the shadows crawled across the expanse of the front yard. No lights burned inside, although it was dark enough now to call for it; no sound escaped, either. There was only that door, open just enough.

"He may still be in there," Clair said, drawing her Glock.

"Porter and I were here yesterday. Talbot has a wife and daughter, at least one housekeeper in there too, possibly more."

Clair called dispatch. When she hung up, she was shaking her head. "Cars are on their way, but they've got rush hour traffic. They're at least ten or fifteen minutes out. Espinosa's team is still at the apartment."

Nash started for the door. "Watch my back."

Clair nodded grimly. They couldn't wait. If Bishop was still inside, there was no telling what he was doing to that family. The deaths of those officers landed squarely on the heads of their task force. She didn't care for Talbot in the slightest, but she wasn't about to let anything happen to him and his family if she could prevent it. Neither was Nash.

They reached the door.

Nash leaned against the frame and angled to get a glimpse inside. After a moment, he shook his head. "Shades are drawn," he mouthed.

Clair nodded and held her finger up to her lips.

Nash eased open the door, cringing as a low squeal escaped from the hinges.

The streetlights came to life, and Clair welcomed the light until she saw her own shadow stretch across the floor with Nash's beside it. He must have spotted it too, because he ducked through the doorway and rounded the corner in an instant, concealing himself within the dark foyer. Clair followed close, her eyes scanning the darkness for any sign of life.

A muffled groan came from down the hall.

Nash moved quickly, his gun held in a firm grip pointing down and forward. He clearly remembered the layout, because he maneuvered around a small table in the hallway with little effort. Clair would have bumped it for sure; the light from outside seemed to halt at the threshold, unwilling to step inside.

Past the small table, they came upon a large opening and what appeared to be a library or some kind of sitting room. The remains of a fire crackled and popped on the hearth of a stone fireplace. A small end table lay in splinters surrounded by broken glass—the remains of a crystal decanter or maybe a vase. The couch had been overturned and settled on its side. A woman lay sprawled across the center of the rug.

Nash scanned the room and knelt beside her. The housekeeper, Clair assumed from the uniform. She watched them from the corner of her eye while training her gun on the hallway.

The woman's hands and feet were tied with a phone cord, and

she had been gagged. Clair could see her eyes shifting quickly in the dim light as she stared up at the two of them. Nash signaled for her to keep quiet, then pulled the gag from her mouth. She coughed and her eyes watered.

"Is he still here?" Nash asked her in a hush.

81

Diary

"I should have popped that fucker twenty minutes ago," Mr. Smith said. He stood in the doorway with the rifle in his good hand.

"Why didn't you?" Mother asked.

"I wasn't sure what to do about your husband. It wasn't supposed to go down like this."

"Sometimes you have to improvise," Mother told him. "Let me see that hand."

Mr. Smith started toward her, and I watched as Mrs. Carter slapped Mother across the face with both hands still cuffed together, nearly knocking her down.

"What the hell?" Mother spat. The corner of her lip was bleeding.

"You could have ended this days ago. Do you know what he did to me with the rat? He could have killed me!"

Mr. Smith reached down and pulled Mr. Stranger into the house toward the basement door. "Quit the bickering, we don't have time. Briggs called for reinforcements on the way out here."

Father's lifeless body still sprawled on the floor.

I hadn't moved.

I couldn't move.

Mrs. Carter walked over slowly and ran her hand through my hair. "Are you okay?"

I nodded. My head was foggy, thoughts moving through taffy. I pulled the photographs from my pocket and handed them to her. "These are yours."

She took the photos, flipping through them deliberately, her face turning red. "Where did you find them?"

"On your kitchen table this morning. Someone left them there."

Mr. Smith snickered. "Briggs did, that sick fuck. He found them on top of the fridge in a cookbook and left them out."

Father's body.

I heard a moan and realized it came from me. A dark sob from deep in my throat.

"I told you the boy was broken. He's not right, never has been," Mother said. Her eyes so cold and dark. This was not the Mother I needed right now; this was the Other Mother. She didn't see the bodies on the floor. She looked right through them, as if they weren't there at all.

Mrs. Carter frowned at her. "You shouldn't say things like that."

Mother walked over, lifting my head up by the chin. "When was the last time you took your medication?"

"I . . . I don't know."

"I don't know, I don't know, I don't know," she mimicked in a sing-song voice. "I want you to run out to the lake and fetch the keys from the place Mrs. Carter hid them. Do you think you can do that?"

I nodded. "Yes, Momma."

"Don't call me that. You know I hate it when you call me that."

"Sorry, Mother."

"Go, then. We need to hurry. We need to leave before this guy's friends show up." She nodded toward Mr. Stranger's body.

I pushed past Mr. Smith and Mrs. Carter. When I glanced back, Mother was working the locks on Mrs. Carter's handcuffs. They clattered to the floor and she rubbed at her wrists. The two women exchanged a whisper, their eyes on me. Mr. Smith was moving Father's body.

Without another word, I ran off toward the small path leading into the woods.

82

Porter

Day 2 • 5:27 p.m.

Porter took the box cutter from the cabdriver and dropped it into his pocket. "What's your name?"

"Marcus. Marcus Ingram."

"Do you own a gun, Marcus?"

Kloz's voice grew loud enough to hear, even though the phone wasn't on speaker. "You are not going in there, Sam. Wait for backup. You just got stabbed, remember? You shouldn't be on your feet, period. Clair is liable to put a bullet in you if you try."

"Do you own a gun, Marcus?" Porter asked again.

The cabdriver shook his head. "I don't like guns. I got this, though." He reached under the driver's seat and pulled out a small baseball bat with CHICAGO CUBS stamped in colorful letters on the barrel. "Got this in 2008 when they went up against the Dodgers for the division. They lost, but this little guy has helped me beat down my share of muggers and deadbeats. It's not one of those cheap souvenir bats; this one is made of northern white ash. It won't crack."

"Porter? I spoke to Dispatch. They have cars en route. Stay put."

Porter took the bat and measured the weight in his hand. It had a little heft. "What about a flashlight?"

Marcus nodded. "Yep." He reached into the car and came out with a small LED flashlight. "It's tiny but bright." He handed it to Porter.

"Kloz? I'll keep you on the line as long as I can, but I'm going to put the phone in my pocket so I can use both hands. Try to keep quiet. If he's in there, I don't want him to hear me coming."

Bishop knew he was coming, though; Porter was sure of that. The man who used to be Watson had left a neat little trail of bread crumbs, and not only did he know Porter was coming, he would be waiting.

"He wants me to come alone, Kloz. If that girl is alive and she's in there, our only shot at getting to her is me doing this alone, just the way he wants it," Porter said.

Kloz sighed. "He'll kill you. You understand that, right?"

"He could have killed me already. He wants me to see this through to the end."

"So he can kill you," Kloz retorted. "This is his final act, and he wants you to play a part. That's the only reason he's kept you around. Once that curtain falls and your part is done, he's done with you. Wait outside for backup. They'll be there in less than ten minutes. You go in there alone, and you're committing suicide."

Porter didn't need to think about it for a moment. Without Heather in his life, he had nothing else worth living for anyway.

"Tell them to watch out for Marcus. He's going to stand right outside and wait for SWAT. He can show them where I went." Then, before Kloz had time to respond, Porter dropped the cell into his pocket and crossed the sidewalk to 314 West Belmont, flashlight in one hand, the small baseball bat in the other.

83

Diary

The lake seemed oddly still as I approached, the water unmoving save for the slight ripple caused by a duck floating lazily across the surface near the middle. I ran the entire way and nearly collapsed at the water's edge, my breathing heavy and labored. I hoped running would clear my head. I hoped it would help me forget what I had just seen, what had just happened, but the moment I closed my eyes, I saw the bullet tear through Father. I saw Mother watching, watching but not acting, Mother standing as still as I while Father was killed. I bent over at the waist with my hands on my knees until my strength returned, then scanned the bank for the cat.

Nothing remained but fur and bones; the little meat I spied on my last visit had been picked clean. Not even a single ant crawled over the body. They had moved on to bigger and better things, I supposed. There was always something dying in the forest, just as sure as new life was born.

I poked at the cat with the toe of my shoe, half expecting to see a beetle or some other straggler come running out, but nothing did.

Mother had told me to hurry.

Dropping down to my knees, I pushed the cat aside and began digging at the dirt beneath the frail frame. I noticed a slight odor, a mix of onions and rotten spinach, and tried not to think about the melted fat and bile that probably soaked into the earth as the cat decayed. I tried not to think of such things at all because they made me feel like I might get sick, and knowing that the body of Mr. Carter lay at the bottom of the lake beside me, I could not leave a pile of vomit on the shore for the authorities to find, should they ever happen upon his final resting place.

About six inches down, my fingers brushed against a plastic bag, the kind with a zip lock on the top, and I tugged it out and shook the dirt off.

Inside was my knife.

No safe-deposit box keys.

My Ranger buck knife, nothing else.

A lump began to grow in my stomach, a painful fist clenching at my intestines.

I scooped up the bag and started back for the house. I heard the voices just before I crossed through the woods back into our yard.

Male voices.

Two white vans stood in our driveway; both said TALBOT ENTER-PRISES in bold red letters on the doors. Three men stood near our front door.

The Plymouth Duster was gone.

Mother and Mrs. Carter had left with Mr. Smith. I was sure of this. I was alone.

84

Porter

Day 2 • 5:31 p.m.

314 West Belmont had a glass front, and although most of the windows were sealed behind plywood, the large glass turnstile door was not. Porter gave it an exploratory push, expecting it to be locked, but the revolving door moved, spinning on its axis. With one last glance back at Marcus, he stepped inside and followed it around. The sounds and smells of the city quickly evaporated, replaced by utter silence and the powdery scent of drywall dust. He stepped out of the revolving door into the lobby of the building.

Porter's first thought was that there was no way in hell this place would be open by spring. All the walls were exposed concrete with steel two-by-four framing scattered randomly. He imagined they would eventually be closed in and form walls and rooms, but right now the space housed nothing more than calculated chaos. The floor was littered with dozens of footprints heading off in all directions. Light from the street lamps shined in from the large windows at his back, illuminating the room, but visibility was quickly fading with the waning sun.

Porter knelt down and studied the prints. He flicked on the flashlight and swept the beam over the floor with the slow steadiness of a lighthouse waxing across a bay. The footprints all appeared to be work boots, every set but one. He stood and walked over, leaning down for a better look. Men's dress shoes. Beside them he found a trail in the dust, as if something had been dragged.

He followed the pattern to the back west corner of what would become the lobby and found himself standing at a bank of elevators, six in all, lining the back wall. He pushed the Call button, but nothing happened. He didn't expect them to work. The power appeared to be off. The steel doors were sealed shut with red safety tape around a note that read: DANGER — NO CARS.

The trail through the dust continued past the elevators and down the hall to the left. As he turned the corner, he came upon a door — the emergency stairs, he presumed. Scrawled across the faded green paint in bright red were the words SEE NO EVIL. On the floor at his feet were two human eyeballs. They stared up at him with an unsettling calm.

85

Clair

Day 2 • 5:31 p.m.

"Miranda, is he still in the house?" Nash asked again, more firmly.

The housekeeper's eyes were crusted with dried tears. She whimpered softly, shook her head, shrugged, then nodded quickly. "I don't know," the woman replied. "I didn't see where he went."

"How long since you last saw him?"

She appeared confused by the question. Her eyes dilated slightly. "I . . . I don't know."

"Did he drug you?"

Staring at him, she seemed to contemplate this. "I don't know. I think so. I don't remember him tying me up. Everything's hazy."

"Is anyone else in the house?" Nash asked.

The housekeeper took a deep breath and glanced at the staircase. "Ms. Patricia and Mr. Talbot are in their room." Her eyes grew wider still. "He went up there. I remember him heading toward the stairs."

Nash followed her gaze to the staircase, barely visible in the waning light. "What about Carnegie?"

"I'm not sure if she's home. I haven't seen her since this morning. She might be in her room."

Clair knelt down beside the woman, her eyes and weapon still trained on the hallway.

"Miranda, right?"

She nodded.

"I'm going to untie you. When I do, I want you to get outside. You'll see my car, a green Honda. It's not locked. Climb inside and wait for the police to get here. Stay low, and keep yourself hidden until they arrive," Clair said. "Do you think you can do that?"

Miranda nodded.

Clair made quick work of the cord around the woman's feet while Nash untied her hands. When the housekeeper tried to stand, she wobbled, almost collapsing. Nash caught her and helped her find her balance. "Whatever he used could take a little while to work completely out of your system, so try to move slowly."

"I think I'm going to be sick," Miranda said, her face ashen. She steadied herself on the end table.

"Take it slow," Clair told her. "Help will be here soon."

They watched the woman follow the wall until she reached the front door and stepped outside into the darkening night. When she disappeared from sight, they both turned back and faced the staircase, weapons at the ready.

86

Porter

Day 2 • 5:32 p.m.

Porter ran his finger over the paint. It was still wet.

The eyes were blue.

He wanted to shout out Emory's name but knew it would do little good other than give away his position. He also knew he should bag the eyes, but he didn't have any bags. Porter knelt down. Bishop plucked them out whole, optic nerve and all. This wasn't easy to do. Eyes popped rather easily, and it took a skilled hand with the correct tools to properly get behind them and remove them from the socket without damage. They appeared fresh. The blood had only begun to congeal and dry.

Porter reached into his pocket and pulled out the cell phone. "Kloz? I'm inside. I found Emory's eyes outside the emergency stairs on the first floor. Did you call for an ambulance too?"

He heard nothing and glanced at the phone—NO SIGNAL.

"Shit."

He placed the phone back into his pocket.

His grip on the bat tightened as he stepped over the eyes and gently pushed on the door release, swung it open, and stepped into the stairwell. The beam of his flashlight rolled across dust and debris that hung in the air like a dry fog, and he had to fight the urge to cough. It was impossible to follow the trail through here. So many footprints converged on that first step, Porter couldn't be sure how many people had traipsed through, but it could easily be dozens.

Porter directed the beam straight up.

How tall did Kloz say this building was? Had he even said? It appeared to be at least fifty stories from the outside. Porter wasn't sure he could do that on his best day, let alone with a fresh stab wound in his thigh. He pulled the hospital greens down and got a better look at the wound. Although it was bleeding slightly earlier, it had stopped. His leg still throbbed, though. Damn near hurt more now than when the knife went in. From what he could see around the bandage and tape, the surrounding flesh was purple and black.

Porter pulled the box cutter from his pocket and used it to cut a length of cloth from his shirt. He wrapped it around the existing bandage, securing it in place. He cut another piece and tied it tight just above the wound—not as restrictive as a tourniquet, but enough to slow the blood flow. Hopefully it would be enough to hold him together, at least for a little while.

Porter started up the steps.

87

Clair

Day 2 • 5:33 p.m.

Nash took the lead and crossed the hallway in one fluid motion. Clair followed close at his back. The setting sun had not only pitched the house into darkness, but a fall chill had found its way into the air. The hair on the back of her neck and arms stood on end, and she told herself that was because of the cold too, but the pounding of her heart within her chest told a different story.

The first step creaked under Nash's weight, and she heard him swear softly. Clair squeezed his shoulder with her free hand. She heard the floorboards creak under her weight too and considered taking off her shoes, then figured it would probably be of little use in a house like this. Structures of this age tended to have wooden floors that groaned underfoot.

They ascended slowly in an attempt to minimize the noise, feeling their way up the steps. When Clair's fingers trailed into something moist on the banister, she stopped and brought her fingertips to her nose. There was no mistaking the coppery scent of blood. She had smelled it more times than she could recall, but that didn't make it any easier.

Nash stopped too and looked back at her, his face shrouded in shadows.

Clair held up her fingers.

"Blood," she whispered, the word escaping on a single breath.

Nash looked down at his own hand. Clair watched as he wiped the blood on his pants before continuing up the stairs.

Her palms began to sweat, and the Glock grew heavy in her grip.

At the top of the steps they found a landing with a hallway branching off in either direction. There was a bathroom directly in front of them. Nash entered low with his gun out front, confirming that the room was empty.

Clair stood with her back to the wall, her own weapon pointing in from the hallway, until he returned to the landing.

A small row of LED lights built into the baseboard illuminated the hallway, and they could see three closed doors down the left and a pair of double doors at the end of the hallway on the right. The walls were lined with family photos of various shapes and sizes. Clair assumed the double doors led to the master bedroom while the others belonged to guest spaces and Carnegie's room.

"Which way?" she asked in a whisper.

"Master," he replied, already moving down the hall.

88

Porter

Day 2 • 5:33 p.m.

Porter stopped just short of the third-floor landing. The small six-foot-by-four-foot space was littered with dust and discarded fast food wrappers. The walls were painted lime green.

He heard a voice.

With the bat in hand, he climbed the last few steps, swinging the beam of his flashlight back and forth against the thickening darkness.

"Are you getting tired yet, Sam?"

The voice was followed by a quick crackle, static, then silence.

"Where are you, Bishop?" Porter said, his own voice sounding higher than he had hoped as the words echoed across the concrete.

"I know you're out of shape, but come on now, I've seen old ladies with walkers climb a flight of stairs faster than you."

"Fuck you."

"Maybe the exercise will do you some good, burn some of that gut away." *Crackle.*

Porter spotted the radio as he ascended and made the landing. A small black Motorola with a rubber antenna stood against the riser at the beginning of the next flight of stairs.

When Bishop spoke again, a small red LED pulsed with his voice. "How about a little rhyme to pass the time? You up for that, Sam?"

Sam picked up the radio. Bishop's singsong voice crackled back.

"*Goose Goosey Gander, whither shall I wander? Upstairs and downstairs and in my Lady's chamber. There I met an old man who wouldn't say his prayers, so I took him by his left leg and threw him down the stairs.* Have you ever wondered what that nursery rhyme was about, Sam? I mean, it's a little dark for kids, but tell it to kids we do. My mother used to love to tell me that one whenever we went up or down a flight of stairs."

Porter pressed the button on the radio and held the mike close to his lips. "I'm coming for you, you crazy fuck."

"Sam!" Bishop's voice came back. "You finally made it. I was getting worried about you."

"Where are you, Bishop?"

"I'm close, Sam. I wanted to wait for you. I knew you'd puzzle it out. You're the sharp one in your little band of misfits. It took some coaxing, but you got it. I'm so proud of you."

"I found the eyes. Is Emory still alive?"

Bishop sighed. "I am so sorry I didn't have time to wrap them for you. I was half-afraid a rat might stumble upon them before you got here and walk away with a tidy snack in its jaws. Not much I could do about that, but I'm glad you got here first."

Porter realized he should have covered them with something. He hadn't thought about rats. "Where are you?"

Bishop chuckled. "Oh, you've got a ways to go, I'm afraid. The climb can't be easy with that wound. I'm really sorry about that. I hope I didn't hurt you too bad, but I had to improvise. You and your friends really put me on the spot." He dropped off for a second, then: "You best pick up the pace, Sam. We don't have a lot of time left. Wound or not, you've got a lot of stairs in your future."

Porter started climbing the steps again. Standing still, even for such a short amount of time, had caused his leg to tighten up. He forced the muscles to respond and gritted his teeth when the pain came. With each step it felt as if the knife were back in his thigh, slicing through the muscle and fat. "Let me talk to her. You owe me that much. Let me know she's still alive."

He was answered by a moment's static, then Bishop's voice echoed through the tiny speaker. "I'm afraid Emory is not available right now."

Porter rounded the corner of the fourth floor and kept going, his lungs burning.

"So, did you finish it?" Bishop asked.

"Finish what?"

"You know what."

"Your little diary?"

"Don't mock me, Sam. Don't you ever mock me. Mocking is an evil all its own, and one I'm not very fond of."

Sam wiped his forehead on the shoulder of his scrubs. "Your mother mocked you at the end. How did you like that?"

"So you did finish."

"Yeah, I finished."

"My mother was an evil witch of a woman who deserved whatever happened to her," Bishop said.

"Sounds like your mother was one hell of a lay. She had everyone wrapped around her finger. The hot ones are always crazy."

"I see what you're trying to do, and it's not going to work, so put an end to the jabs right now," Bishop shot back.

"So they never came back? They just left you there?"

A clicking noise came from the radio. It sounded like Bishop was pushing the Talk button repeatedly at a rapid pace, like a nervous tic. "Remember the matches? I burnt the house to the ground with Talbot's people roasting inside. Figured I'd follow through on the gasoline Mr. Stranger and Smith spread around. The fire department called child services, and they took me to something called a residential treatment center. I spent two weeks there before I was placed with my first foster family. Nobody had a clue I'd set the fire. If Mother ever came back for me, I wasn't aware of it."

"Sounds like she rode off into the sunset with that Carter woman and didn't want her brat of a son tagging along on her Thelma and Louise fantasy. They never intended to bring you."

"I was better off without them."

"In foster care? I guess you're right. If half of what you wrote actually happened, you grew up in one fucked-up household."

"Language, Sam, language."

"Right. Speak no evil. Sorry about that. I'd hate to violate one of your blessed father's rules."

Fifth floor.

"Your mother wanted your father to die that day, planned for it. She was done with him. Who was banging the blond guy? Your mother or Carter? Both of them? Hell, I bet that guy was tagging both of them while you played with your pecker in the corner."

"Language, Sam."

"Fuck you, Bishop. *Hell* is not a bad word."

Bishop took a breath. "Cursing of any kind is a sign of a weak mind, and I know you are anything but weak-minded. I bet you've already worked out a plan to get even with the guy who shot your wife. What was his name? Campbell? You walked away all calm and forgiving, but I could see the anger burning behind your eyes, the hatred."

"We're not all out for revenge."

Bishop chuckled. "If I were to lock you in a room with him and you were assured there would be no repercussions for whatever you did, you wouldn't hurt him? You wouldn't put a bullet between his eyes? You wouldn't take a knife and gut him from neck to groin and watch him bleed out? Don't kid yourself, Sam. We all have it in us."

"We don't act on it, though."

"Some do, and the world is a better place for it."

Porter snickered. "Maybe if you weren't such a sniveling little twat of a boy, she wouldn't have run off without you. Maybe the three of them would have included you in their little plan. You could have made a life with your new daddy and two mommies, and whatever the fuck they were hoarding in those safe-deposit boxes."

Bishop let out a soft laugh. "I bet your friends at the Fifty-First plan to leave Campbell's cell door open tonight. Let you in through the back so you can have a little private chat with him. If they found him hanging from the rafters in the morning, would anyone really care? Nobody sheds a tear over the loss of someone like that. You deserve that, right? For what he did?"

"What was his real name? The blond guy."

At first Bishop didn't answer, but then his voice came back with a crackle from the speaker. "Franklin Kirby."

"Your mother and Mrs. Carter planned to run off with Franklin Kirby all along."

"Yes."

"Your father wasn't part of that plan."

Bishop said nothing.

"How did your mother and Mrs. Carter even know Kirby?" Porter was making small talk now. He didn't give a shit about Kirby or the Carters or Bishop's parents, but he knew as long as he kept Bishop talking, Bishop wasn't hurting Emory further. He needed him to not be hurting Emory.

Bishop clicked at the microphone again—five times, a dozen times. "Kirby worked with Simon Carter at the accounting firm in the operations department. I believe he was responsible for moving the money out. Most likely, the two of them planned to split the funds and keep the documents as collateral to ensure nobody came after them."

"Nobody's going to chase after a few million dollars and risk information leaking that could take down their entire operation."

"Correct."

"But Kirby somehow double-crossed him, with your mother's help," Porter said. "His partner too. Just killed him like that."

"Simon Carter abused his wife. She saw a way out and took it. I think Mother agreed to help her, and the other man was collateral damage."

Porter felt a trickle of warmth on his leg and looked down; his stitches were bleeding again. He pressed his hand against his thigh and continued to climb. "You saw Talbot's name on the vans, so you made the connection?"

The line went silent.

"Bishop?"

"Father taught me to approach every situation with a well-thought-out plan. By sixteen I had multiple fake IDs. It's easy to get your hands on them when you're in the foster care system. I met my share of criminals in training from the moment I set foot in my first group home. I stayed clean though; I avoided the fights and the drugs. I focused on one thing—I eventually got a job working for Talbot. I was patient. Started as an intern and worked my way up. I was always good with computers, a gift I guess. It didn't take me long to work my way into the IT department. I traced Simon Carter's steps. He made it easy. All the files he stole? He backed up copies on their own servers. Left it right under their noses under the names of bogus clients. Within two years, I had everything he had put together and more. Mr. Carter had amassed information on dozens of criminals throughout the city, dating back nearly twenty years. Not only did he have detailed records of their crimes, but he also had accounting records for nearly every dollar exchanging hands. These were bad people, Sam. Everything from gambling to sex slavery. All of them connected, all of them working together, this underground of evil breathing like a living being. I spent my days working for Talbot and my nights piecing all of this together."

"You were living on your own at sixteen?"

"I lived in a vacant tenement on the West Side. I shared the apartment with five other kids I had gotten to know in the foster system. Anything was better than the group homes. Don't interrupt me, Sam. It's rude."

"Sorry."

Bishop continued. "All of those criminals tied together like a spider web, every one, and there was one man at the center, one man with his hand in all of it."

"Talbot."

"Kirby's partner may have pulled the trigger on my father, but all of those people were standing behind that gun," Bishop said solemnly. "Talbot most of all."

"How many have you killed?" Porter asked, nearly out of breath as he rounded the corner on the ninth floor.

"I'm not so pure anymore, Sam. But I did what needed to be done."

"You killed innocents."

"Nobody is innocent."

"Let me talk to Emory," Porter asked again.

Tenth floor.

"Hey, you want to hear something funny?"

"Sure."

A scream erupted from both above and the tiny speaker in Porter's hand—a bloodcurdling scream of pain so jagged, he felt the ache under his own skin.

"Better hurry, Sam. Chop chop."

89

Clair

Day 2 • 5:34 p.m.

The door was locked.

Nash twisted the knob again as if expecting a different result, then turned in frustration.

Clair pressed her ear against the door.

Nothing.

Nash motioned for her to step back and leaned in, holding up three fingers.

Clair understood.

She knelt down and pointed her gun toward the door, elbows locked.

Nash lowered one finger, then the other. On three, he slammed the weight of his body into the door and nearly tumbled into the room as the frame gave way with a defiant crack.

Still crouched, Clair swept the space, gun at the ready.

A large four-poster bed stood at the back of the room, positioned under an elaborate tray ceiling. To the left she spotted a small sitting area with book-lined shelves and a desk with a large couch separating the space from the rest of the room. A fireplace sputtered in the corner of the sitting area. On the far end of the master, another hallway led around a corner.

Nash moved cautiously and Clair followed.

A woman lay on the floor beside the couch, bound and gagged like the housekeeper downstairs.

Nash went straight for the walk-in closet on the far right, swatting clothes, making sure it was empty. Clair went on and turned the corner. She found herself standing in a large bathroom of white marble. The elaborate space offered no place to hide; the shower was encased in glass and clearly empty. A linen closet stood on the left, lined with thick towels and enough bottles of shampoo, conditioner, and cleaning supplies to stock a small hotel. Nobody hid in there.

She returned to the bedroom to find Nash checking beneath the bed.

Clair knelt down beside the woman and removed her gag. "Is he still here?"

"I . . . I don't think so," the woman said, her voice shaky. "Oh God, I think he took Arty!" She thrashed frantically now, trying to force her body into a sitting position. Nash helped her up, untied her, and eased her into an overstuffed chair beside the bed.

"What about your daughter?" Nash said.

"Carnegie won't be home until . . ." She craned her neck back toward the fireplace in the far corner where a small mantel clock ticked away the minutes. "What time is it? It's dark. I can't make it out."

"About five thirty."

"After five?"

A siren cried out in the distance.

Clair stepped over to the large window beside the bed and pulled back the curtain. She couldn't see anything. "Ma'am, how long ago did he leave?"

Nash had untied her hands, and she rubbed at her temples. "Arty came home at a little after two to change for a meeting. He got here right after that. Ten minutes later at the most."

"What happened?"

"I don't know exactly—it all happened so fast. I was over there on the couch reading, and someone knocked at the bedroom door. I figured it was Miranda. Arty said he'd get it. I heard a loud bang a second later, and when I stood to figure out what was going on, this man came rushing in. He barreled into me and shoved me down onto the couch. I think I hit my head because I blacked out for a second. When I came to, my hands were tied and he was working at my feet. I screamed and he just smiled at me. He actually apologized for intruding on my afternoon, said that he simply must have a word or two with my husband. Then he tied the gag over my mouth. I saw Arty lying right over there"—she gestured toward the hallway—"he was moving but not very fast. I think he was trying to stand up. The man went back to him and stuck him with a needle in the neck, some kind of narcotic, because Arty was out after that. Then he came back to me, apologized again, and jabbed a needle in my arm. I blacked out again, and when I woke, most of the fire had burned down, so I must have been out for a while. Then the two of you got here."

Clair loaded a photo of Bishop onto her phone and held it out to the woman. "Is this him?"

She nodded. "Is he going to hurt Arty?"

Nash located the light switch and flicked it on. He wished he hadn't.

Scrawled across the bedroom wall in blood were the words DO NO EVIL.

90

Porter

Day 2 • 5:40 p.m.

When Porter reached the eleventh floor, he tasted a sinking rot in his gullet. Scrawled across the door in fresh blood dripping down the faded green paint were the words SPEAK NO EVIL. Discarded in the dust at his feet were a human tongue and a pair of bloody pliers.

This was his floor.

He dropped the radio into his pocket, switched off the flashlight, and tightened his grip on the baseball bat before pushing through the heavy metal door. He entered the space swift and low, ignoring the throb in his leg.

A hallway lit by candles.

Small white candles about an inch wide and two inches tall lined the left wall. They followed the corridor nearly thirty feet before disappearing around a corner.

Porter pulled the cell phone from his pocket and hit the Home button; still no signal. He put the phone away and rolled the bat between his hands.

Guns N' Roses began to howl through the air midsong—

Welcome to the jungle
We take it day by day

Porter nearly dropped the bat while attempting to cover his ears. He pressed both palms against the sides of his head, holding the bat with his fingertips. He had never heard music so loud. It was like standing in the first row of a concert. He didn't see any speakers, but the music was clearly coming from up ahead, up ahead and around the corner.

He started down the corridor.

It didn't seem possible, but the music grew louder. Porter swore the flames were dancing to the bass.

When he reached the end of the corridor, when he was ready to turn the corner, he had no choice but to lower his palms from his ears and grip the bat with both hands. He did just that, rushing around the corner with the tiny barrel of the weapon leading the way and his bleeding leg lagging behind. He found himself in a lobby of sorts, one littered with the remains of whatever business once occupied the space.

An old desk stood at the center of the room surrounded by candles on the floor. On the desk stood a battered boom box the likes of which Porter hadn't seen in twenty years. The black plastic housing was covered in dust and paint, one of the two cassette doors was missing, and the glass meant to protect the tuner made the station numbers nearly unreadable beneath a spiderweb of cracks. LED lights flickered and danced across the display in time with the music, a sea of red, green, yellow, and blue. A wire protruded from the top, snaked over the desk, and terminated in four large loudspeakers stacked beside one of three open elevator shafts. A sign taped to the front of the boom box read: CHANGE THE CHANNEL FROM 97.9 AND I'LL TOSS YOU FROM THE ROOF. SIGNED, YOUR FRIENDS AT LOCAL 49. Below that, someone had scribbled: CLASSIC ROCK 4-EVR.

All of the hardware was plugged in to a red Briggs & Stratton generator, which huffed at Porter's right. He reached down and flicked the kill switch. The generator sputtered and went dead, cutting off the music.

"You don't like GNR?" Bishop's voice cracked from the tiny radio in his pocket.

Porter yanked out the radio and jammed down the Talk button. "Where the fuck are you?"

"I forgot to tell you who Mrs. Carter became in her new life."

"What?"

"Lisa Carter died the same day as my father, but she was born anew, a brand-new identity to go with her new life. Want to know her new name? I think you may recognize it."

Porter heard Bishop's voice crackling not only from the radio but from somewhere else too, his real voice, somewhere close, like an echo. He couldn't pinpoint the source, though. His ears were still ringing.

There were four open doorways surrounding the elevators, two on either side. The candles surrounding the desk made it impossible to see into the gloom beyond. He could feel Bishop's eyes on him.

"Don't you want to know who Mrs. Carter became after that day at our house?"

Porter started toward the first open doorway, the bat held high, ready to swing.

"Don't."

Porter froze.

The shadow across the room moved as Anson Bishop emerged from the gloom, pushing Arthur Talbot on a rolling office chair. The man was duct-taped to the frame, his hands, feet, and torso bound. A crude bandage covered his eyes, and blood dripped from his mouth.

Anson Bishop stood behind him with a knife pressed to Talbot's throat. "Hi, Sam."

Porter approached with caution, his eyes scanning the otherwise empty space. "Where is she?"

"Do you have a gun, Sam? If you do, I'll need you to leave it over there in the hallway."

"Just this." He held up the bat.

"You can hold on to that if it makes you feel better. Stop there, though. No need to come any closer."

Talbot let out a watery moan from the chair, his head lolling to one side.

Porter heard sirens in the distance. "Let me get him to a hospital. He doesn't have to die."

"We're all dying, Sam. Some are just better at it than others. Isn't that right, Arty?" He pressed the knife against Talbot's throat, and a thin trickle of blood appeared. Talbot didn't react; he must have been in shock. Bishop glanced back up and frowned. "You should get that leg checked out. All those stairs might not have been a good idea."

Porter looked down and realized his entire pant leg was soaked in blood; the stitches must have opened up completely now. He pressed his hand against the wound, and blood seeped through his fingers. He was growing lightheaded. The bat slipped from his left hand and fell to the floor. "I'm fine."

"You're a good detective, Sam. You should know that. I knew you'd puzzle it out. And putting others before yourself? That is admirable. It's not something you see much of these days, not anymore."

Porter drew in a deep breath and forced himself to stand up straight, ignoring the white flecks dancing around his vision. The sirens were getting close. "They'll be here soon. You still have time to do the right thing. Tell me where Emory is, and let Talbot go. Just walk away. I can't chase you, not like this."

Bishop eased the wheeled chair toward the first open elevator shaft, a grin at his lips. "Let him go?"

"No! Don't!" Porter started toward him.

Bishop held up the hand with the knife and pointed it at him. "Stop! No closer."

Porter fell still.

Talbot's blood dripped from the tip of the blade and landed on his arm. The chair was no more than five feet from an eleven-story drop plus the subbasements. Porter tried to do the math, but his thoughts were fuzzy. One hundred feet? One twenty? He wasn't sure. It didn't really matter. It was far enough.

"Emory I understand, but why do you want to protect this scumbag? You'll see the files soon enough, Sam. I'm sure Clair and the boys have found them by now. This man has had his hand in every dirty deal passing through this city for thirty years. All the murder and corruption you live to prevent, he lives to create. How many people died because of him? How many more will die so he can line his pockets?"

Outside, the steady *chomp chomp* of helicopter blades approached, the copter landing on the roof. Bishop heard it too; his eyes flashed quickly to the ceiling, then back to Porter. "Sounds like your friends have arrived."

"They're coming from the top, and SWAT is probably already on the stairs. You're out of time, Bishop. It's over." Porter's vision clouded for a second, and his legs felt wobbly. He forced himself to steady. "Step away from Talbot and get on your knees."

Bishop spun the chair in a slow circle. "This world will be a better place without him, don't you think? That's what Father would have wanted."

"Kirby's partner, how was he connected?" Porter said, a distraction at best. "The man who shot your father."

"What?"

"Kirby planned to run off with your mother and the Carter woman, but what about the other man, the one you called Mr. Stranger?" Porter was having trouble standing up. His entire body was heavy. He wanted to sleep. He had to keep Bishop talking, though, long enough for backup to arrive. Long enough—

"His name was Felton Briggs. He worked for our friend here," Bishop said, giving Talbot another spin. "I believe he was some kind of security specialist. I asked Arty about him, but he wouldn't answer me, just kept babbling on about his eyes—'Can't see! Can't see!' Blah, blah blah. I finally had to shut him up. You should have seen it."

"Was he involved?"

"Until he pulled the trigger on Father, he was probably the only innocent man standing in the house that day. Just doing his job. He had no idea Kirby was involved, and he surely didn't know that Kirby planned to kill him."

Talbot's body jerked in the chair, his head snapping back. His fingers stretched out in an odd array as every muscle in his body began to convulse.

"He's going into shock. You need to let me get him to a hospital."

Bishop smiled. "Your friends will be here soon enough. I'm worried about you, though. Are you okay? You look awfully pale, Sam."

Porter wasn't okay. He saw two Bishops standing in the corner instead of one, and his arms were numb. He wanted to reach down, pick up the baseball bat, and charge across the room to beat this man senseless, pound his head into a pile of bloody pulp, but he had to concentrate on standing right now. He needed to focus on *not* passing out. "What was Mrs. Carter's new name?"

Bishop's face brightened. "Ah, yes! In all the excitement, I nearly forgot. Thank you, Sam, for reminding me."

Talbot had fallen still. Porter couldn't tell if he was breathing.

Bishop continued. "Mother changed her name to Emily Gerard. Took me a few years to learn that. Sadly, I think that identity died right there or she figured out how to live off-grid. I tried to track her down, but the name never popped up. No credit records, land sales, nothing. I don't think she ever used it. Mrs. Carter, though, she *did* use her new identity. She didn't even attempt to hide. I think it's a name you may be familiar with too, one you've picked up in the last handful of days. Mrs. Carter changed her name to Catrina Connors."

Porter's brain was fuzzy. The thoughts were there, but they were moving slowly, molasses. He recognized the name, knew it, but couldn't place it. Then —

"Emory's mother?"

A grin spread across Bishop's face, and he spun Talbot around like a top. "You asked me to gather information on her back at the war room, and I wanted desperately to tell you what I already knew, but there would have been no fun in that."

"But how?"

"Simon Carter had moved over fourteen million dollars into offshore accounts, and I know she and Mother lived off that money for a while. But they also bought property, a lot of property. Property she knew Talbot would one day want. When he finally approached her about a particular stretch of warehouses along the waterfront, she seduced him. Emory was the result. On Emory's first birthday, she moved all the property into their daughter's name, then told Talbot who she really was. She also told him she had all the documents her husband had stolen years earlier and would release them to the press unless Talbot agreed to transfer all his legitimate holdings to Emory at the time of his death. He changed his will shortly thereafter."

"How did you learn all of this? You said you didn't know where your mother or Mrs. Carter disappeared to."

"Gunther Herbert was very forthcoming," Bishop replied. "We had a wonderful chat about a week back."

"Talbot's CFO?"

"Yes."

"So if Talbot dies—"

"Emory inherits billions and all criminal activity he's attached to will crumble."

Porter looked down at Talbot. He was moving again. His head bobbed from side to side, and a deep, guttural moan rose in his throat. "You can't kill him."

"No?" Bishop replied, shoving the chair.

Talbot skidded across the floor toward the open elevator shaft on the far left, and Porter dove for the rolling chair, forcing every ounce of strength he had into his legs. He landed hard on the concrete and slid, his hands reaching out, fingers brushing the cold steel, grabbing at one of the wheels as it rolled over the edge. He held on for the briefest of seconds before it tugged away and disappeared into the black.

He heard Talbot crash far below, followed by a scream. A girl's muffled, weak scream from the next elevator shaft over, the one in the center of the room, only a few feet to his right.

Emory.

From the corner of his hazy vision, he spied Bishop as he walked calmly to the third elevator shaft and stood with his back to the door's edge. Porter watched as the man gave him a final wave and said, "Good-bye, Sam. It's been fun," before stepping backward through the opening and disappearing into the dark chasm.

All went dark then as Porter finally passed out.

91

Porter

Day 2 • 5:58 p.m.

"Sam? Can you hear me? I think he's coming around—"

It was Clair.

Clair-bear.

Five little bears heard a loud roar, one ran away, then there were four.

Where had Bishop gone?

"Please step back, ma'am."

Bright light.

The brightest of all possible lights.

"Detective?"

The light disappeared with a click, and Porter blinked. His head was pounding. "Where?"

Clair pushed the medic aside. "Ground floor, just outside the building. We brought you down with the chopper basket. Carrying your fat ass down all those stairs was not an option."

"Bishop killed Talbot."

Clair brushed a strand of hair from his eyes. "We know. Hey, look—"

Porter followed her finger.

Nash pushed through the glass door beside the revolving turnstile and held the door open as two paramedics wheeled out a stretcher containing a young girl. An IV bag hung above her. Her head and wrist were wrapped in white bandages.

"Is she . . . ?"

"She's going to be okay," Clair said. "Bishop had her handcuffed to a gurney at the bottom of the elevator shaft. She's severely dehydrated, and the cuffs did a number on her wrist, but I don't think she'll lose the hand. Other than the ear, he didn't touch her. Just left her down there. Construction crews have been in and out of the building this entire time, but nobody had a clue she was down there. They've been working on the upper floors."

Porter licked at his lips. His throat felt really dry. "Bishop jumped down the other elevator shaft. Is he dead?"

Clair took in a deep breath and let it back out. "He didn't jump; he *rappelled*. He had a rope and harness rig set up on a service platform just inside the elevator shaft; he took it to the bottom. When we got down there, we found a hole in the wall leading to another one of those underground tunnels, like the one we found in the Mulifax Building. He's gone, Sam. We've got patrol officers checking every tunnel entrance and exit on record with the city, but I don't think we're going to find him. While half the force was in that building trying to get to your floor from the top and the bottom, he dropped down right past us and disappeared somewhere under the city."

"Ma'am?" a paramedic interrupted. "We need to get him to the hospital. He's lost a lot of blood."

Clair shot the paramedic a dirty look, then smiled down at Porter. "You done good, Sam. You found Emory, and we've got an ID on 4MK. He'll slip up and we'll find him. By tonight, the world will know his face. He won't have anyplace to hide."

Porter squeezed Clair's hand and watched as they loaded Emory into an ambulance at his right. Then he closed his eyes. He just wanted to sleep.

92

Porter

Day 3 • 8:24 a.m.

When Porter opened his eyes again, he found himself in a hospital room. It looked like the same hospital room he was in before . . . What time was it? He searched for a clock or his phone but saw neither. Sunlight streamed in from the window and warmed the blanket on his bed. Had he really slept through the night?

"Where's the damn nurse Call button?" He fumbled through the sheets looking for it but only managed to twist his IV line around his head.

"I can't leave you alone for a minute," Nash said, coming in from the hall carrying a cup of vending machine coffee and a pack of Twizzlers. "I can see the headline: DETECTIVE ESCAPES SERIAL KILLER ONLY TO STRANGLE HIMSELF IN HOSPITAL BED."

"I didn't escape. He never intended to kill me." Porter's voice was hoarse.

Nash reached for a paper cup on the nightstand and handed it to him. "Here, try these. The nurse brought them in a few minutes ago."

"What is it?"

"Ice chips."

Porter took the cup and tipped it at his lips, spilling cold water down his chin and chest.

"Okay, maybe it's been more than a few minutes. I guess they melted."

Nash reached beneath the bed and came up with the Call button. He clicked it once. "I'll get her to bring some more."

Porter lifted the sheet and surveyed his freshly bandaged leg. He had some new scrapes and bruises on his arms. He told Nash what happened with Talbot.

"Maybe Watson or Bishop or whatever the hell his name is did us a favor."

Porter raised his eyebrows but said nothing.

"We found a file box at Bishop's apartment with enough information to implicate twenty-three separate criminals acting in and around the Chicago area. And you know what they all had in common?"

"Talbot?"

"Talbot."

"Bishop told me."

Nash let out a snort. "If you had asked me about him a week ago, I would have thought the guy had a shot at becoming our next mayor."

"He just might have, if this hadn't happened."

"Something is still bugging me, though. How did Bishop bankroll all of this? He sent three hundred grand to Kittner for stepping in front of that bus. Where did he get that kind of money?" Nash asked.

"Maybe he found it under the cat."

"What cat?" Nash frowned.

"You need to read the diary."

Nash sipped at his coffee. "I think I'll wait for the movie."

Porter eyed the Twizzlers. "Can I have one of those?"

Clair Norton poked her head into the door. "I'll be damned, you got the same room?"

"Hey, Clair-bear."

She walked over and wrapped her arms around him. "You crazy bastard. I've got half a mind to handcuff you to that bed so you don't run off again."

Nash perked up. "I'm up for that if he's not."

Clair picked up the empty ice cup and tossed it at him. "Pervert."

"I'm a proud card-carrying member."

She turned back to Porter. "Are you ready for a visitor?"

He shrugged. "If I can handle the two of you, I think I'm up for just about anything."

Clair straightened out his sheets and smiled. "Don't go anywhere. I'll be right back." She disappeared out the door and returned a few seconds later pushing a teenage girl in a wheelchair. Her head and wrist were bandaged and her skin was deathly pale, but there was still no mistaking her.

"Hello, Emory," Porter said softly.

"Hi."

Porter turned to the others. "Can you give us a minute?"

Clair grabbed Nash's hand and tugged him toward the door. "We'll go find some breakfast."

Nash smiled back at Emory and Porter. "I think she likes me."

When the door closed behind them, Porter returned his gaze to Emory. All things considered, she looked good. From the few images he had seen of her, she'd clearly lost weight. Her face was thin and contained a few lines that normally wouldn't find their way into a girl's skin for another ten years or so. He knew this was most likely from dehydration and would fade with time. Her eyes betrayed her, though. They weren't the eyes of a fifteen-year-old girl; they were the eyes of someone much older, someone who had seen things she should never have seen. "So," he said.

"So."

He gestured at the nightstand. "I'd offer you something, but I don't even have ice chips anymore. As hospital rooms go, this one is poorly stocked."

Emory pointed up at the IV bag attached to her wheelchair. "I brought my own snacks. Thank you, though."

Porter pulled himself up into sitting position. The room seemed to swim. "Whoa."

"Painkillers?"

He licked at his chapped lips. "I think they gave me the good stuff this go-around."

Emory held up her wrist. "They gave me some good ones for this, the ear too. I asked them to hold off on the dose this morning so I could come and see you."

Porter turned to the floor. "I'm sorry I didn't find you sooner, Emory. I—"

But she was shaking her head and placed a hand on his arm. "Don't do that to yourself. You *did* find me. Detective Norton told me everything you did for me over the past few days, and I don't know where to begin to thank you."

Emory followed his eyes to her bandaged wrist. "They operated on it last night. There's some nerve damage and I broke the scaphoid —that's the little bone beneath the thumb—but for the most part, it should be fine. I'll lose some feeling, but all my fingers still work the way they're supposed to, and the doctor says I'll have full range of motion." She wiggled her fingers to demonstrate, then cringed as the pain washed over her.

"What about the ear?" Porter wasn't sure why he asked. Normally he would never ask about something like that unless she offered first. He blamed the drugs.

"I think they're going to grow me a new one."

"What?"

"I met with a doctor this morning who told me he can grow a replacement ear on my arm using cartilage from my ribs," Emory explained. "It's going to take about three months, but he said it should be indistinguishable from the original."

Porter fell back against his pillows. "They definitely gave me the good stuff. I thought you just said they were going to grow an ear on your arm."

Emory giggled. It was good to hear.

Porter gazed at her, at those eyes that held experiences they should not hold, at the girl behind them, and he knew she was going to be okay. "Why don't we talk about your mother? I've heard a lot about her recently. We can compare notes."

Emory smiled. "I'd like that."

Epilogue

Two Days Later

"Shit." Nash lifted his foot and stared at the dog crap stuck to his shoe.

"I should have warned you to watch out for that," Porter said, fishing for his keys. "It's kind of a thing around here. The place probably wouldn't feel like home without dog poop on the stoop."

Night had taken hold and the city was alive with lights. A chill had crept up with the falling sun, and Porter welcomed it, the brisk air reminding him what it was to be alive.

They were standing outside his apartment building. The doctors had held him in the hospital for two days to make sure the stitches took before they would allow him to leave. Apparently he had lost a little trust when he walked out on his own and chased a serial killer up ten flights of stairs shortly after surgery. They were worried about infection, but the concern had passed and he was mending nicely.

"You didn't need to bring me home. I could have managed."

Nash waved him off. "I'd never hear the end of it from Clair."

"You don't trust me."

"That too." Nash walked over to the edge of the sidewalk and scraped the waste away on the corner of the concrete.

Shortly before leaving the hospital, Porter had received a phone call from Detective Baumhardt at the Fifty-First Precinct. Harnell

Campbell, the man who killed Heather, had somehow managed to make bail.

"How could that shit knocker come up with half a million dollars?" Nash asked.

"If he used a bail bondsman, he'd only need ten percent," Porter pointed out.

"If he's robbing convenience stores, he doesn't have that kind of money, either."

"Probably has a buddy who's dealing or owed him a favor. Doesn't matter. Baumhardt thinks they've got a strong case. He's going down, just not today."

Nash shrugged. "As long has he decides to show up at the trial."

"You're not helping."

"Sorry."

They entered the lobby and Porter opened his mailbox. It was stuffed full.

"How long since you last checked that?"

"A few days." He picked through the mess, grabbed next week's *TV Guide,* then squeezed the remaining letters back inside before closing the tiny door. He started for the stairs, but Nash grabbed his shoulder and pointed him at the elevator. "Not a chance—you can work on your figure next week. No exercise, definitely no stairs—doctor's orders."

"I'm going to have to move to a place on the first floor. Bishop ruined stairs and elevators for me," said Porter.

Nash pressed the Call button. The elevator doors opened and they stepped inside.

"Any luck trying to find him?" Porter had been banned from the war room and ordered to stay away from the investigation until his doctor cleared him, but he couldn't help himself. Knowing Bishop was still out there just ate at him.

"We've fielded more than a thousand tips over the past few days but nothing solid. He's been spotted as close as the Hard Rock down by the lake and as far away as Paris. The one in France, not Illinois. CSI combed his apartment, and it doesn't look like he ever actually lived there, just staged the place for us to find. Who knows where he actually called home."

"What about his childhood home? The one from the diary. Any luck locating it?"

"Kloz is searching nationwide for houses that burnt down near a pond or small lake within the past twenty years but hasn't turned up anything yet. CPAs and accountants are registered, so he searched for anyone named Simon Carter with a financial license, but that came up blank too. He also put together a list of all Plymouth Dusters registered in the country, found more than four thousand of them, and I've got no clue what we're going to do with a list like that. It's probably a dead end. We subpoenaed employment records from Talbot's various companies but didn't find anyone named Carter, Felton Briggs, or Franklin Kirby. Part of me thinks the entire diary was bullshit, just another distraction. The feds arrived yesterday, four of them in dark suits and darker egos. They wanted to take over the war room, but I put them in the room across the hall instead."

Porter frowned. "The room with the weird smell?"

"Yeah. They're feds. Maybe they can figure out where it's coming from."

The elevator doors opened on the fourth floor, and they walked down the hall to Porter's door.

Porter slipped his key into the lock. "I think that diary is the only real thing he allowed us to see of himself. He wanted us to know where he came from."

"Well, I only care about where he's heading."

They stepped inside and Porter flicked on the lights. His eyes went to the spot on the floor where he had fallen after Bishop stabbed him. "Who cleaned up?"

"Clair came by yesterday. We didn't want you coming home to that, and she drew the short straw. Probably for the best. I would have just put a rug or a plant on top of it. Bloodstains give a place character. You should see my apartment."

Porter could only imagine.

"Thank her for me when you see her."

Nash shuffled his feet. "So, how long before you come back?"

"Probably a week, maybe two." He reached into the refrigerator and pulled out a beer. "Want one?"

"I can't. I'm still on the clock." He turned back toward the door. "I'll stop by tomorrow, okay?"

"You don't have to check in on me. I'll be all right."

Nash smiled and nodded. "I know you will. Good night, Sam."

"Good night, Brian."

Porter locked the door behind him and twisted the cap off his beer. There was something about an ice-cold beer that just made everything seem better.

Heather's picture watched him from the end table. He walked over and slipped his finger across her cheek. "I miss you, Button." He reached for his new cell phone, began dialing her voice mail, then set it back down. "Sleep tight, beautiful."

He finished the beer and left the bottle on the table before heading into the bedroom.

At first he didn't see the small white box sitting on the side of the bed, and when he did, he half thought he was imagining it, but there it was—a small white box with a black string around it, next to Heather's note. His hand instinctively went for his gun, and he realized he still didn't have it.

Porter rounded the bed and picked up the box, trying to steady his shaking hand. He knew he should put on gloves, but he simply didn't care. He tugged at the string and pulled it away, letting it drop to the floor. He removed the top and looked inside.

A human ear rested upon a bed of cotton. The flesh was riddled with piercings, six diamonds and four small hoops. It had been cut off smoothly, with surgical precision. The cotton was stained with brown flecks of dried blood.

Along the outer edge of the lobe, the word FILTER was tattooed in black letters.

He recognized it immediately. Tareq had pointed out the tattoo back at the Fifty-First.

Taped to the inside of the box top, in Anson Bishop's scratchy script, was a note:

Sam,

 A little something from me to you . . .
 I'm sorry you didn't get to hear him scream.
 How about a return on the favor?
 A little tit for tat between friends.
 Help me find my mother.
 I think it's time she and I talked.
 B

Acknowledgments

First and foremost, I would like to point out I grew up in a happy home in South Florida; we didn't even have a basement. None of the poor parenting decisions made by little 4MK's mom and dad were based on real life, at least not my real life. This story was born of "what if" and an imagination that lost its governor some time ago, nothing more.

My thanks to the wonderful team at Houghton Mifflin Harcourt: Tim Mudie for seeing something in this story and helping me bring it to light, Michaela Sullivan for a wonderful jacket, Katrina Kruse in marketing, Stephanie Kim in publicity . . . there are so many of you, if I left out your name, please forgive me but know you have my gratitude and I can't wait to work with you again!

Special thanks to my agent, Kristin Nelson, for finding this book a good home and helping me navigate the waters of today's publishing world.

I would also like to thank my first readers: Summer Schrader, Jenny Milchman, Erin Kwiatkowski, Darlene Begovich, and Mary Hegemann. Without your suggestions and input, this would have been a very different story, and I'm quite fond of the one we told. As always, thanks to Jennifer Henkes for pointing out all the things that can go wrong when you sleep through English class.

Finally, my favorite person, my wife, Dayna. I may never understand why you put up with me, but I'm grateful that you do. I can't imagine taking this journey with anyone but you.

J. D.

A little something from me to you . . .

Be on the lookout for the next 4MK Thriller

The
Fifth to Die

By J. D. Barker

Coming Summer 2018!

Can't wait for the next 4MK thriller to hit shelves in the summer of 2018? Visit www.whois4mk.com. We've hidden a lost chapter. Can you puzzle it out?

Good luck!